BATTLE OF WILLS

"I shall not tolerate blatant disrespect of my authority," Damien said through clenched teeth. "You, Miss Elliott, must learn to curb your unruly tongue."

Kate rose, her head held high. "I shall pack my trunks and be gone by the time you return." She sank into an over-elaborate curtsey, then started purposefully toward the door.

"Miss Elliott . . ."

She spun, a picture of outraged dignity. "Must you always have the last word? Once, just once, Mr. Ashcroft, you might concede to me the victory of a dignified exit!"

His sudden bark of laughter was as unexpected as it was appealing. "I should have known," he said. "Kate the shrew."

He reached her in a few strides. This, he realized as he bent his head to hers, was what he had wanted to do for a long time. His mouth covered hers with ruthless disregard of her startled gasp, and the sweetness of her lips drove rational thought from his mind.

Kate's senses reeled, then full mental powers returned with startling clarity. She, Kate Elliott, respectable duenna, was locked in Damien Ashcroft's arms! And—perish the thought!—she was enjoying every moment of his embrace. . . .

DISCOVER THE MAGIC
OF ZEBRA'S REGENCY ROMANCES!

THE DUCHESS AND THE DEVIL   (2264, $2.95)
by Sydney Ann Clary

Though forced to wed Deveril St. John, the notorious "Devil Duke," lovely Byrony Balmaine swore never to be mastered by the irrepressible libertine. But she was soon to discover that the human heart — and Satan — move in very mysterious ways!

AN OFFICER'S ALLIANCE   (2239, $3.95)
by Violet Hamilton

Virginal Ariel Frazier's only comfort in marrying Captain Ian Montague was that it put her in a superb position to spy for the British. But the rakish officer was a proven master at melting a woman's reserve and breaking down her every defense!

BLUESTOCKING BRIDE   (2215, $2.95)
by Elizabeth Thornton

In the Marquis of Rutherson's narrow view, a woman's only place was in a man's bed. Well, beautiful Catherine Harland may have been just a sheltered country girl, but the astonished Marquis was about to discover that she was the equal of any man — and could give as good as she got!

BELOVED AVENGER   (2192, $3.95)
by Mary Brendan

Sir Clifford Moore could never forget what Emily's family had done to him. How ironic that the family that had stolen his inheritance now offered him the perfect means to exact his vengeance — by stealing the heart of their beloved daughter!

A NOBLE MISTRESS   (2169, $3.95)
by Janis Laden

When her father lost the family estate in a game of piquet, practical Moriah Lanson did not hesitate to pay a visit to the winner, the notorious Viscount Roane. Struck by her beauty, Roane suggested a scandalous way for Moriah to pay off her father's debt — by becoming the Viscount's mistress!

Available wherever paperbacks are sold, or order direct from the Publisher. Send cover price plus 50¢ per copy for mailing and handling to Zebra Books, Dept. 2691, 475 Park Avenue South, New York, N.Y. 10016. Residents of New York, New Jersey and Pennsylvania must include sales tax. DO NOT SEND CASH.

An Improper Companion

KARLA HOCKER

ZEBRA BOOKS
KENSINGTON PUBLISHING CORP.

ZEBRA BOOKS

are published by

Kensington Publishing. Corp.
475 Park Avenue South
New York, NY 10016

First printing: June, 1989

Printed in the United States of America

To Käte, my mother

Chapter One

"Kate, I could not bear it!" the dowager Lady Elliott protested.

Smoothing the gray poplin of her gown, severely cut and unadorned as befitting a senior mistress at one of Bath's renowned academies for young ladies, Kate stifled a sigh. She had known it would be no easy feat to convince her mother and had arrived at the small Queen's Square flat armed with a good deal of resolution and patience.

"It would be for a short while only, Mama," said Kate for perhaps the sixth or seventh time that afternoon. "Only until I find a new position."

Lady Elliott's faded blue eyes filled with tears. Two or three clung to her lashes, while another coursed down her delicately powdered and rouged cheek. Crying was an art she had mastered in her salad days, and it had never failed her yet. "But why must I go to Elliott Chase?"

Leaning closer to the daybed where her mother reclined against a multitude of silk cushions, Kate clasped the frail hand held out to her in a beseeching gesture. "If we write now," she said coaxingly, "Richard can get the dower house ready for you. Then you need—"

"The dower house!" Tears forgotten, Lady Elliott snatched away her hand. "You may as well put me up in the stables. At least they'd be less drafty."

"—not stay at the house nor need you see Marga-

7

ret and the children unless you wished to," Kate finished, but without hope that it would induce her parent to regard a brief stay with her son and daughter-in-law in a more favorable light.

"The dear children." Pressing a lace-edged bit of snowy lawn against her eyes, the dowager moaned softly. "I am the fondest of grandmothers, as you well know, Kate. Sweet Harriett . . . so high-spirited! And little Dickie. What a darling, mischievous boy!"

Kate suppressed a smile. When sweet Harriett and darling Dickie had visited Bath for an afternoon the previous summer, their fond grandmama had apostrophized them "ill-mannered harum-scarum children."

Peering over her handkerchief, Lady Elliott noted the telltale twitch of Kate's mouth. She tucked the frothy bit of lawn into her sleeve. "I'm afraid Dr. Thistlethwaite would categorically forbid a move to Elliott Chase. Especially at this time of year."

"We've had such a mild winter, Mama. I shouldn't wonder if the bluebells in the spinney were to start blooming in a week or two."

"The view from the dower house is lovely," the dowager admitted grudgingly. "But I must take the waters every day. How, pray tell, could I do that some forty-odd miles removed from Bath?"

"Just for a week or two you might drink bottled water."

"It's impossible, Kate." Lady Elliott wilted into the cushions. A hand went to her brow. "Only this morning Dr. Thistlethwaite warned me . . . my palpitations, you know."

Automatically, Kate reached for one of the phials arrayed on a table within easy reach of her mother's couch. "No, not that one," Lady Elliott said feebly. "The green bottle, Kate. Oh, if only Miss Peevey were here! She'd know what to do for me."

"Your nurse needed a breath of fresh air."

Kate poured a small glass of the tonic and handed it to her mother. While Lady Elliott sipped and indulged in a bout of self-pity, Kate rose to stand at the window overlooking Queen's Square. It was not that Kate was unfeeling or doubted her mother's claim to ill health. After giving birth to a stout son, Richard, seven subsequent miscarriages, and, at a rather advanced age, the birthing of a daughter, Kate, Lady Elliott was, indeed, in delicate health. But nowhere near death's door.

Kate considered explaining once more just how difficult their situation would be if she did not find a new post immediately, but she dismissed the notion. There was little hope that her mother would attend to anything she might say. Lady Elliott had chosen to forget that her small jointure covered only the rent of her rooms and the purchase of daily necessities, and she would not thank her daughter for bringing a painful subject to her attention. It was Kate's salary at Miss Venable's Seminary for Young Ladies that paid Dr. Thistlethwaite and Nurse Peevey—expenditures that had not allowed her to gather a nest egg. And now Miss Venable was dead. The school would be closed within a fortnight.

"So inconsiderate of Miss Venable," Lady Elliott said querulously, just as though she had at least in part followed her daughter's thoughts. "She should have known it takes time to find a new position!"

"Miss Venable could hardly help it," Kate said dryly.

"Kate! How can you speak so—so callously! And," Lady Elliott added in the tone of one neatly clinching the matter, "Miss Venable's death is no excuse to close the school. Miss Graintree—or you, Kate—could run the seminary quite efficiently if you would but try."

Abandoning the sight of gray, drizzling March skies, wet cobbles, and an occasional sedan chair,

9

Kate returned to her mother's side. "Miss Venable's heirs are not interested in the school, Mama. They have already sold the house."

A new thought struck Lady Elliott. "Kate! Where will you—surely you're not planning to stay at Elliott Chase until you find another position?"

Under Kate's clear, steady gaze, Lady Elliott began to fidget with the tartan rug covering her legs. "No. How silly of me," she murmured. "Not after what Richard . . . And yet . . . Kate, I believe your brother would forgive you if only you would make some conciliatory gesture."

"I'd do *anything*," Kate said passionately, "anything at all rather than creep back to Elliott Chase and ask Richard to take me in!"

"If only I had another chamber. It would have been rather jolly," Lady Elliott said with a noticeable lack of conviction, "to have you stay with me awhile. Where will you go, Kate?"

Kate might have replied that without her salary to pay for the nurse, Miss Peevey's room would stand empty. But she only said, "I'll find something. Don't fret, Mama."

Hearing Miss Peevey's firm tread on the landing of the tiny flat, Kate gathered her reticule and her cape. "I must be getting back. It's almost tea time." She kissed her mother's scented cheek, then quit the room before Lady Elliott could point out that Miss Graintree, the headmistress at the school, was perfectly capable of supervising the girls' tea.

As fast as the leather soles of her walking shoes would allow her to move on the rain-slick cobbles, Kate hurried toward Lansdown Mews, where Miss Venable's Seminary for Young Ladies had served daughters of the nobility and gentry for over three decades and where Kate had lived for eleven years— briefly as a pupil, then as a teacher.

Mayhap she should have taken a chair, but Kate

relished the cool moisture on her face. An hour's visit in her mother's sitting room, where a fire was laid and carefully nurtured from morn till night until well into the summer, always gave Kate a headache. Besides, Bath chairmen were not renowned for respectful silence, and she would be inundated with offers to carry her to the Pump Room, to the fashionable shops in Milsom Street, and to one or several of Bath's lending libraries. In short, all the places Kate had avoided since her disgrace.

As she approached Bennett Street, a gentleman beneath a huge umbrella turned the corner into The Circus at great speed. Kate sidestepped to avoid a collision, and her left foot slid out from under her. With an exclamation of annoyance, she clutched the gentleman's arm.

It seemed at first that he would shake her off as one would the unwelcome clawing of a kitten, but he thought better of it and grasped her arm with his free hand, steadying her. Kate was aware of a pair of cold, dark eyes looking at and through her as though she were not really there. She had a brief glimpse of a swarthy countenance and harsh features dominated by a patrician nose before she was put aside like a piece of baggage.

"Beg pardon," he muttered in a deep voice that might have been appealing had it not conveyed total indifference to the mishap he had caused.

"And so you should, sir! I came perilously close to a nasty fall."

One black brow rose, and before Kate could guess his intent, he pressed a coin into her palm—a shilling by the size of it.

"No doubt this will appeal to you more than mere words, my girl." He turned on his heel and strode off in as great a hurry as he had approached, his speed and the proud bearing of his carriage not a bit impeded by a slight dragging of his left leg.

11

"Insolent oaf!" Kate said wrathfully when she regained her speech, but the large black umbrella and his broad back were annoyingly unresponsive. It was his startled oath as the silver piece hit his neck just below the crisp, dark hair that erased the scowl on her face.

Having vented her spleen and thereby reduced the throbbing in her temples, Kate sped along, even hummed a catchy little tune she had picked up from her pupils. She had covered about half the distance to Miss Venable's school and had mentally reviewed the fairly long list of girls' academies in Bath where she might apply for a teaching post, when a carriage-and-four rumbled past her, drenching the skirt of her gown with a spray of mud and filthy water.

Tare an' 'ounds! As though she hadn't borne enough this afternoon. Kate glared after the carriage. She could have sworn that behind the coach window, she had seen the harsh profile of an arrogant, dark-haired gentleman. The same gentleman who had almost knocked her down in The Circus.

She looked at her skirt. Threadbare and faded as it was, it had been fresh that morning. Another washing might strain its worn seams past mending. And a new gown . . . well, it was not to be thought of.

The last stretch of Lansdown Street seemed longer and steeper than it ever had before, but finally Kate turned into the mews and opened the high creaking iron gate to Miss Venable's Seminary for Young Ladies. A graveled path led to the front entrance. Long before Kate had reached the three-storied building of weathered Bath stone, the door was flung open by a diminutive young lady.

"Miss Elliott! Oh, Miss Elliott, I've been waiting for you this age!"

"So I perceive." Trying to look stern, Kate stepped into the foyer. "Liza, hadn't you better tidy your hair and go into the dining room?" she said with a glance

12

at the girl's guinea-golden curls tumbling and bouncing in wild disarray around a charming little face. "Twice already your name has appeared in the conduct book. Miss Graintree—"

"Oh, pooh! So much for the stupid book," said Liza, snapping her fingers. "In less than a week, all the school's books will most likely be burned. And besides, Miss Graintree said I may watch for you."

Kate had looked forward to a few moments of quiet before she resumed her duties, but Liza's heated countenance, the glitter in the girl's deep blue eyes, put any such notion from her mind. "Come," she said, leading the way to the top floor. "You may tell me all about it while I change."

"My father is home!" Liza burst out before the door to Kate's narrow little chamber had closed behind them. "He arrived from Rome last night! Isn't it exciting? I wonder what he brought me."

Kate flung her damp cape over a chair and started to unbutton her gown. "I hope," she muttered under her breath, "he brought time for you." To Liza, she said, "That is good news, indeed. I know you've been counting the days. Did your father receive the solicitor's letter about the closing of the school?"

"I don't know and, to tell the truth, I don't give a straw whether he did or not. He's coming tonight to take me to Dearworth, and I'm never going back to school!" Liza executed a pirouette that sent the skirt of her sprigged muslin gown flying.

"I shall be Papa's hostess," she said breathlessly. "I shall be going to balls and parties! I'll attend the theater and concerts!"

"Whoa, there," said Kate, slipping a fresh gray poplin gown over her head. "You're not quite seventeen yet. Your papa may consider you too young." In fact, thought Kate, it was a guinea to a gooseberry that Mr. Ashcroft would remove his daughter from Miss Venable's seminar, only to deposit her as soon as possible in a similar institution.

"Too young!" Liza ceased her whirling. She stared, horrified that her dear Miss Elliott should entertain such a Gothic notion. But then, Miss Elliott was quite old. She must be all of eight-and-twenty. "My mama," Liza said with dignity, "was married when she was seventeen."

Kate responded with a suitably apologetic smile. She knew that Liza's mother was dead and could not pass to her daughter any bits of wisdom she might have required during her early come-out and marriage. Kate knew even better that Liza, like all the older pupils at the seminary, was eagerly looking forward to her debut. Most of the young ladies had already been fetched in their parents' stately traveling chaises and conveyed to London to enjoy their first season; but Liza, Kate believed, was too immature to be cast into the sophisticated world of the London *ton*. Surely, Liza's father was aware of that.

"Papa will take me everywhere," said Liza, bouncing on the edge of the bed and watching Kate as she repinned her hair. "He's so handsome, all the ladies will turn green with envy because he is my escort and not theirs."

"My dear, it is more likely that you will attend the assemblies in the company of an aunt or a cousin."

Liza shook her head decisively. "Grandmama Ashcroft was my only relative, and she died years ago."

Kate said nothing, but her face must have reflected some of the misgivings she felt, for Liza sat very still for a moment.

"I daresay I ought to have a chaperon," the girl said quietly. Her troubled eyes met Kate's in the mirror. "How does one go about engaging a chaperon, Miss Elliott? I never needed one before, you see, but I was only a child then."

"Why don't you let your papa worry about engag-

14

ing a suitable companion for you?" Kate jammed a last hairpin in place, then turned to smile at Liza. "For all you know, he may have done so already."

"Oh, no! I shouldn't wonder, in fact, if Papa were quite opposed to installing a lady in our house. Papa, you see, is a misogynist."

"What!"

"It means—"

"My dear child, I know what it means. But whatever gave you such a silly notion?"

"I heard the vicar say it to Sir Shafto. Sir Shafto is the squire and our closest neighbor, and *he* said that Papa has far too many—"

"Indeed!" Kate said sternly when Liza broke off, blushing. "I am disappointed in you, Liza. You promised not to eavesdrop again." Yet, she couldn't help but wonder what the dickens the squire had said. Too many . . . *affaires* to be a misogynist?

"I didn't, Miss Elliott! I heard it *before* you said I mustn't. I swear I haven't eavesdropped." Liza rose, hung her head, and added softly, "Except, perhaps, when I couldn't help it."

"Liza Ashcroft, you're an outrageous little baggage!" Kate shook her head, her dancing eyes at odds with her prim mouth. "And I shan't listen to any more of your nonsense. Misogynist, indeed! Let me tell you, my forward young lady, that a companion would no more interfere in your father's life than your maids would. You do have maids at Dearworth, I presume?"

"Yes, but they don't live in. Papa won't have females living at Dearworth."

"Then," said Kate, taken aback, "who looks after you while you stay there?"

"Mrs. Boughey does."

"Is she not a female?"

Liza looked startled, then succumbed to a fit of the giggles from which it took her a moment to

15

recover. "Mrs. Boughey is a martinet," she finally managed to say. "She was Papa's nurse, but now she is our housekeeper. Papa wouldn't dare suggest that she find lodgings elsewhere. Besides, if Mrs. Boughey left, we'd also lose our butler. They're married, don't you see?"

"I think I do," Kate said faintly. Not for anything would she admit that she didn't understand at all. The more she heard about Damien Ashcroft, the less she believed him a suitable guardian for a young girl about to take her place in society. "You had better make yourself tidy before you come downstairs for the readings," Kate said absently. She picked up a volume of Miss Austen's *Sense and Sensibility* and started for the door. "I'll make your excuses to the other young ladies."

With a shrug, Liza followed Kate into the corridor. "We'll never finish the novel now. So what does it matter whether or not we read tonight?"

"You can always finish it at home."

"I don't like to read by myself. And," Liza added with a toss of her saucy curls, "I daresay I'll be too busy!"

Yet, when Kate reached the half landing of the wide oaken stairwell, Liza's voice drifted down to her—quite wistful now. "Much as I'm looking forward to leaving this dreary old school, I wish I didn't also have to leave you. I wish you could come to Dearworth, Miss Elliott!"

Touched and disturbed, Kate stopped in her tracks. If Liza but knew it, her words conveyed so much more than the child realized. Despite her ecstasy over her father's arrival, Liza obviously knew she'd be neglected once she was installed at Dearworth.

Kate turned, half tempted to go back to Liza; but when she looked up, the girl had gone. And it was probably just as well. The way Kate felt, she might

16

have said a word or two about Liza's father that would be quite unsuitable for a daughter's ears.

Kate had never met Damien Ashcroft. It had always been Miss Venable or Miss Graintree who had received the widower when he arrived dutifully every summer to accompany Liza to Dearworth, his estate several miles south of Bath. After a few weeks, Liza would return to school, while Mr. Ashcroft went haring off again to the Mediterranean or the East in his pursuit of ancient cultures. Liza was always tearful and brittle-tempered after her visits to Dearworth, and during the five years that the girl had spent at the seminary, Kate had formed a less-than-favorable opinion of the scholar. Undoubtedly, he cared more for shards of ancient pottery than for his young daughter, and how Liza could adore such a man was beyond Kate's understanding. But love and worship him she did, as was evident from her artless prattle.

Slowly, Kate resumed her descent to the students' parlor, where the older girls would be waiting impatiently to read another chapter of Miss Austen's novel. Kate tried to shake off her troubled thoughts about Liza's future. She had no need to add more worries to her already cumbersome load. Her day had not been an auspicious one, starting with the receipt of Dr. Thistlethwaite's account for services rendered to her mama during the winter months. Kate had caught her breath at the sight of the staggering sum.

And why she had ever thought she could persuade Mama to live at the dower house when she knew that the widow would not go anywhere near Elliott Chase and be subjected to her daughter-in-law's barbed remarks about malingerers and hypochondriacs, Kate did not now recall. Whatever her reason had been, it was undoubtedly an extremely foolish one. Just as foolish as hoping that her brother Richard would contribute toward Mama's medical bills until Kate found a new teaching post. Richard had said he would not pay a penny as long as the dowager persisted in shunning the new Lady Elliott's company, and he would doggedly stand by his word. Margaret would see to that.

And on top of all her troubles, she must needs encounter the most odious, most arrogant coxcomb, who not only knocked her down—well, almost knocked her down—but added insult to injury by offering her a shilling. He was also, unless her eyesight was less keen than she believed it to be, responsible for the ruin of her gown.

It was perhaps not surprising that Kate, when she arrived in the students' parlor and opened Miss Austen's novel to the thirty-first chapter, did not feel as she ought about poor Marianne's misery. Her own problems were daunting, her heart ached for poor little Liza, and besides, Marianne's misery was one that would soon dwindle. The mere symptoms of a passionate attachment—fluttering pulse, blushes, increased heart rate—Marianne might be able to vaguely recall, even years later. Not, however, a clear image of the gentleman who had once inspired that passion. Kate knew.

Miss Graintree, preceded by a dry cough and the rustle of stiff skirts, entered the parlor. "Miss Elliott! A word with you, please."

Thus firmly brought back to present circumstances, Kate nodded to one of the girls to take over the reading, then followed the headmistress out into the dim corridor. "Liza is leaving now," Miss Graintree said without preamble. "You may join her in Miss Venable's study if you wish to tell her good-bye. Mr. Ashcroft has kindly consented to wait."

"Generous, I'm sure."

If Miss Graintree noticed Kate's sarcasm, she chose to ignore it. "I'll supervise the reading. And,

18

Miss Elliott"—the headmistress gave Kate one of her rare smiles—"I heard this afternoon from the Swithin's Academy. I've been accepted."

"That is wonderful," Kate said warmly. The closing of the school had possibly been hardest on the headmistress, who had taught at the institution since the day Miss Venable opened its doors in 1785. Now, well past fifty years of age, Miss Graintree had not held high hopes of finding a new position. "Swithin's Academy is to be congratulated."

Kate mentally crossed the academy off her list of prospective employment as she followed the long hallway to the dark little room tucked beneath the staircase—Miss Venable's study. It had been there, in the study, that Kate had found Miss Venable slumped across her desk in the throes of a seizure from which the elderly lady had not recovered. In the study, the solicitor had informed Miss Venable's staff that the school would be closing by the end of March. Was it surprising, thought Kate as she approached the narrow door, that she felt as though some new calamity were awaiting her?

After a perfunctory knock, Kate entered.

"Oh, there you are, Miss Elliott!" Blushing guiltily, Liza hopped off the edge of Miss Venable's desk. She grasped Kate's hand. "Come, I want you to meet my papa."

But Kate stood transfixed, staring at the gentleman lounging in the comfortable visitor's chair in front of the desk. The coxcomb who had almost knocked her over! The *arrogant* coxcomb who had pressed a shilling into her hand!

Chapter Two

He turned, and Kate saw a gleam enter his dark
eyes, a gleam quickly hidden by drooping lids and
outrageously long lashes. She could not be certain
that he had recognized her but thought it very likely,
for his expression was harsh and no smile softened
the tight-lipped mouth beneath the patrician nose
when he addressed her.

"So," he drawled, "you're Miss Elliott." He rose in
a leisurely fashion, raking her from head to toe with
cold eyes. If the look was calculated to put her in her
place, it achieved just the opposite. Memory of their
earlier encounters still rankled, and Kate advanced
regally.

"Mr. Ashcroft, how do you do? Liza has spoken
of nothing this past sennight but your impending
return. I am pleased you did not disappoint her."

He lifted one dark brow and cast a somewhat
quizzical look at his daughter. Liza said nothing. She
stood, her shoulders tensed and her eyes darting
from her father to Kate and back to Damien
Ashcroft, as though she feared either or both would
do something quite outrageous.

"Pray be seated, Miss Elliott."

Damien Ashcroft offered the armchair he had occupied. Kate elected to sit on one of the straight-
backed chairs reserved for pupils and staff. It was
her turn to raise a brow, and she did so very

eloquently.

Liza, who had taken up a position beside her father's chair, held her breath. Just so did Miss Elliott look when she was about to administer a trimming. It was certainly not the look of the gentle, timid lady she had described to her papa.

"The closing of the school came as no small surprise," her father was saying, and he sounded quite mellow, as though he didn't mind Miss Elliott's quelling stare. Liza relaxed, but tensed again when her beloved teacher responded in acerbic tones.

"Sir, not only to you," said Kate, noting with some satisfaction that once again a flicker of emotion lit Mr. Ashcroft's cold eyes.

It could have been surprise, might have been annoyance. Kate had no time to speculate, for Liza flew to her side and, draping an arm around her shoulders, whispered, "Oh, pray don't set up Papa's back, Miss Elliott. I'll explain it all to you later, but for now, please, please, humor him. *Everything* depends upon it!"

"If you're quite done with your impertinence, Liza," said Damien Ashcroft, "perhaps I may be permitted to speak?"

"Yes, Papa."

Liza melted into the background, and Kate was left to face the man whom she had come to regard as a most uncaring father. The sarcasm he employed toward Liza did nothing to endear him to her. She would relish giving him a piece of her mind, but if, as Liza seemed to think, the girl's happiness depended upon it, Kate could play the meek and biddable female as well as anyone. She only wished she knew exactly what Liza was up to.

"You were saying, sir?" Kate murmured, her gaze demurely lowered to her folded hands.

There was a brief silence, during which Mr. Ashcroft's eyes lingered most penetratingly on her.

Finally, he said, "I expected Liza to be settled here for another year at least. Since that is obviously out of the question, and my daughter appears to have made up her mind that she is too old to move to another school, I find myself in somewhat of a bind."

Under different circumstances, Kate would have admired that deep, well-modulated voice. It flowed like rich music, striking a chord somewhere deep within her. But he was saying just what she had expected, that Liza would be very much in his way. Well, if he thought to get sympathy from her, he would soon learn his mistake.

"Mr. Ashcroft, Liza will be seventeen next month. At that age, a young lady can usually expect to be prepared for her debut."

"So my daughter informed me before I had time to remove my greatcoat. Seventeen is such an advanced age, Liza assured me, that she would find herself on the shelf were I to postpone her come-out another year."

Kate risked a peek at him. The tone of his voice had implied a smile, but no such redeeming feature lightened his sternness. "Quite," she said. *Heavens!* Couldn't he see the humor of that childish pronouncement? Then, fearing he'd take her reply literally, she directed a frown at him. "I hope you're not planning to take the child to London for the season."

"Miss Elliott!" Liza squealed in indignation. "I am not a—" A look from her father silenced her.

Having effectively quelled his daughter's protests, Damien Ashcroft turned that same look on the lady whom Liza had begged him to employ as her companion. That same young lady who had first jostled him, then, when he had apologized for *her* carelessness, had snapped at him.

"Miss Elliott," he said coldly. "Miss Graintree assured me that you are a lady of sense, superior understanding, and excellent qualifications. Without wishing to doubt her judgment, I must ask what gave you the harebrained notion I'd take a child Liza's age to London."

"I beg your pardon." Kate hastily looked down at her hands. "What *do* you intend to do with Liza?"

"There's little a father can do for a grown-up daughter."

He narrowed his eyes as he once again took stock of Miss Elliott. It was hard to believe that this young lady, who scarcely raised her head, could have flung a coin at him—the silver piece meant to smooth her ruffled feathers. He might have imagined the episode, as he must have imagined the sarcasm in her soft voice a moment ago.

Yes, Miss Elliott was meek enough to suit him. Rather drab and colorless, but that was only in her favor. He might be able to tolerate the presence of a female in his house if that female were no more noticeable than a piece of furnishing.

But what really made it tempting to offer her the post was the fact that she seemed to think Liza too young to participate in the social whirl. Miss Elliott, he judged, would be easily persuaded to fall in with his own schemes for Liza's future.

"I believe," he said quite kindly, "that you are looking for a position, Miss Elliott? Perhaps you would consider coming to Dearworth with Liza."

Her eyes widened, but before he could make up his mind whether Miss Elliott's eyes were blue or gray, she lowered her gaze. "Surely Liza is too old for a governess," she murmured.

"Of course she is," he said curtly as forbearance gave way to irritation. "I'm offering you the post of companion."

So that was Liza's scheme. Kate stared at the man who was Liza's father and wondered how he could have produced such a sunny, lovable—not to forget mischievous!—child. His person exuded harshness, arrogance, and conceit. And already he looked as though he regretted having offered her the post. If she were to follow her inclination, she'd measure him with her haughtiest look and sweep from the room, leaving him openmouthed and goggle-eyed.

But he offered a position near Bath, which was a prerequisite for her acceptance of any kind of post. If she didn't stay close enough to keep an eye on Mama and her penchant for extravagances . . .

"Miss Elliott, don't you want to be my companion?" Liza asked wistfully. "I thought you'd be thrilled."

Before Kate had time to formulate a soothing remark, Damien Ashcroft said, "Your salary, Miss Elliott, will be one hundred guineas."

Kate swallowed. She hardly heard his rider that she would be entitled to one free afternoon a week and a full day once a fortnight. A hundred guineas! Kate's annual salary as a teacher was sixty pounds. Another school would hardly pay more.

On the other hand, a teaching position offered the protection of anonymity. As Liza's companion, she'd be bound to meet some Bath resident or other whose memory reached back eleven years. . . .

"Please, dear Miss Elliott?"

Kate could feel Liza's pleading look on her. Poor motherless girl, craving fun, excitement, and love. How would she fare without female guidance? So easily could a young lady stumble and fall into one or more of society's pitfalls.

As had Kate so long ago.

"Very well, Mr. Ashcroft." Kate looked up and met his cool, dark gaze. "When do you wish me to come to Dearworth?"

Damien Ashcroft stood at the open window of his

24

first-floor study and watched his daughter and Miss Elliott approach from the direction of the Bluebell Woods. His eyes softened as they lingered on Liza. So dainty and graceful. So beautiful . . .

His hand on the window frame tightened. Liza was as beautiful as her mother Elizabeth had been at that age. The Incomparable, Elizabeth had been hailed by some; a pocket Venus by others. And Liza was her mirror image.

There was no doubt that one glimpse of Liza's adorable smile, the impishly dancing eyes, would stoke memories of Elizabeth in the hearts and minds of Bath residents. Tongues would start wagging, and before Liza had enjoyed so much as one dance in the Assembly Rooms, talk of Elizabeth and the lurid scandal she had caused would spread and blight Liza's life.

No, dammit! Damien's fist crashed onto the windowsill. He had protected his daughter for nigh on seventeen years. He'd fight to spare her forever, but he knew that not much longer would a father's love suffice to keep Liza content at Dearworth. Damien was too much a man of the world not to recognize the portent of a dreamy abstraction and of speculative looks directed at even the most unprepossessing youths on the strut in Bath's fashionable districts. Damien knew when a young lady was dreaming of love. And he knew even better that such a young lady would do all that lay within her power to make her dream come true.

There was no time to be lost. Liza must speedily be introduced to a man who would not only catch her fancy—for that, no doubt, would pass in the twinkling of an eye—but who would capture her heart. A dashing gentleman, surrounded by an air of melancholy that would pique a romantic young lady's interest.

Damien knew just such a gentleman: Lord

Nicholas Adair, with whom he had spent many a companionable hour exploring the mysteries of ancient Egypt and the architectural splendors of Greece and Italy. If Nicholas were to come to Dearworth, there would be no need to take Liza to Bath or London to meet eligible gentlemen . . .

Damien was about to turn from the window when he realized that the ladies had crossed the lawn and stood directly below. "Papa! Oh, pray don't go away," called Liza, waving a bouquet of the tiny flowers that gave their name to the wooded acreage west of the house. "Miss Elliott wishes to speak with you most urgently."

Damien's gaze slid to his daughter's companion. He raised a brow, and it was not because she looked anything but eager to speak with him. Since Miss Elliott had arrived at Dearworth three days earlier, he had never seen her other than meticulously groomed—if he had noticed her at all. Now, several strands of her hair had come unpinned. It was very long hair, straight but full and glossy, and tucked behind one ear was a spray of bluebells. The deep blue against the rich dark brown of her hair looked decidedly improper, he noted with displeasure.

A gentle March wind and the sun peeking now and again through the chasing clouds had brought color into Miss Elliott's face. Under his stern regard, the pink glow deepened. She put a hand up, as though to remove the offending blooms, but checked herself and merely touched a finger to the delicate blossoms.

"A definitive sign that spring is here to stay," she said, and for the first time, Damien noticed the firm set of her jaw—mulish, he'd call it—and the militant spark in her eyes.

They stared at each other until Liza started to giggle and broke the tension. Damien sketched a bow. "I am at your service, Miss Elliott. Liza will show you to my study if you don't know your way yet."

He turned abruptly and stalked to his desk, where he snatched up a sheet of vellum. He stabbed his pen into the inkwell. With firm strokes, he started his letter to Lord Nicholas Adair, thus dismissing the untidy companion from his mind. She'd need at least half an hour to make herself presentable.

Alas, not three minutes had passed when the study door opened after the briefest of knocks. Miss Elliott entered unbidden and trod across the rug spread between the door and his desk, a bit of torn hem trailing on the soft pile. She had removed the flowers from her hair, though, and pinned up the loose strands.

"Thank you for seeing me so promptly, Mr. Ashcroft."

He nodded and waved her into a chair. Kate sat down, feeling very much at a disadvantage. She had, indeed, wanted to speak with Liza's father but could have cheerfully wrung the girl's neck for demanding the interview at such an inauspicious moment. However, there was no help for it now.

"Mr. Ashcroft," she began firmly. "Liza must have a new wardrobe. She has outgrown her gowns, and now that she no longer attends school, a slightly more mature style of dress would be quite in order."

"Very well. Send for the dressmaker and order whatever Liza requires."

"Liza would like to have her gowns made in Bath, Mr. Ashcroft. If you'll order the carriage out, we can leave early tomor—"

"No."

He had not raised his voice, but the one syllable had been pronounced with such implacability that Kate blinked in astonishment. "No?"

"I trust you are not hard of hearing, Miss Elliott? I do not at all care to have to repeat my orders."

Kate held her breath, then slowly expelled it. "Mr. Ashcroft," she said stiffly. "I shall be the first to obey a reasonable order, even anticipate it. But, in this case, it is Liza's request that is reasonable. A Bath modiste will have the latest fashion plates. No village seamstress—"

Again he cut in. "I did not say you should ask the village seamstress, Miss Elliott. You have my permission to send for any or all of the Bath dressmakers, or a London couturiere if you prefer. And while we are discussing gowns," he added bitingly, "please remember to make use of your dress allowance."

Under his cool stare, Kate was painfully reminded that she had not taken the time to change her gown in her haste to show him she was not easily intimidated. "My . . . dress allowance?"

"My mother's ear trumpet should be around somewhere," he said with a wolfish curl of his mouth. "I'll ask Boughey to search the attics."

Kate drew herself up. "Much obliged, sir," she said with ironic gratitude. "It seems I am indeed hard of hearing. I certainly missed the mention of a dress allowance when you offered me this position."

"I didn't offer it then," he said impatiently. "But I daresay you'll require a few gowns for those occasions when you accompany Liza to the squire's or the vicar's." Picking up his pen, he nodded dismissal.

Kate rose. Wondering whether the emotions roused in her breast denoted gratitude for his generosity or wrath at his high-handedness, she started toward the door. His next words checked her.

"Don't forget to order riding habits, Miss Elliott. I've bought two mares. They should arrive before the end of the week. You do ride, I presume?"

She whirled and flashed him a smile. "Indeed, Mr. Ashcroft. I was known to be no mean horsewoman."

Her step held a bounce as she left the study, and

the door closed behind her with an exulted snap. Damien frowned. While she sat across the desk from him, her eyes had been gray. But a glow of excitement and that brilliant smile had turned them as blue as the flowers she had worn in her hair. He could have sworn to it.

He started to read his interrupted letter to Lord Nicholas when it occurred to him that Miss Elliott was rather aggressive for a meek and biddable companion, and that some of her drabness had peeled off when he mentioned the mares. In fact, the faded look about her had begun to vanish along with the meticulous propriety of her appearance.

Like a butterfly emerging from its chrysalis.

Damien gave a derisive snort and directed his attention where it belonged—to his daughter's future husband.

By the time Kate reached the next floor, where she had been assigned rooms adjacent to Liza's luxurious suite, she did not feel quite as elated as she had upon leaving the study. She might have proven herself unflustered by Mr. Ashcroft's arrogance, but she had failed miserably in her mission. After all, it was not as important to Liza to have her gowns fashioned by the hand of a Bath dressmaker as was the visit itself to the city where the girl hoped to make her come-out this spring.

Kate had been at Dearworth three days, long enough to see that Liza was chomping at the bit to assume her new status as young lady of fashion. But for some reason or other, Damien Ashcroft had shown himself deaf whenever his daughter had broached the subject of a drive into the city.

And I, thought Kate, *should not have given in so easily.*

Feeling craven and a traitor, Kate tiptoed past the

29

half-open door of Liza's sitting room and into her own. As on her first day at Dearworth, the thickness of the rugs, the quiet elegance of a satin-covered loveseat and several Queen Anne chairs, the velvety crimson and gold of draperies, had a soothing effect on Kate. Kicking off her slippers, she flopped onto the loveseat.

There was nothing quite like having a sitting room of one's own, she thought gratefully as she stretched and snuggled against silken cushions. The last time she had enjoyed such luxury had been at Elliott Chase, before Papa's death. Before Mama decided to move to Bath, with Kate in attendance.

Kate's gratification did not last long, however. Just when she guiltily remembered her failure to win permission for the visit to Bath, she became aware that she was no longer alone. She had not heard the door open, but there stood Liza, regarding her rather whimsically.

"Papa's bark is worse than his bite," said the young girl as she sat down on the foot end of the loveseat. "Did he rake you over the coals, Miss Elliott? You look quite crushed."

"He did not, but neither did he agree to order the carriage for us. I'm afraid you must be content to have the dressmaker visit here."

Liza's face fell. "Did you tell him how important it is to me? Did you stress that I absolutely *must* go to Bath? How can I expect to be asked to dance at the assemblies if no one knows about me? We must take out subscriptions at the libraries. Must see the masters of ceremonies at the Upper and the Lower Rooms!"

"There's time yet to do all that and more, child. Give your papa a week or two to get used to the notion that his daughter is a grown-up young lady."

"He has had two weeks already, before you arrived," Liza said tearfully. She rose, her face flushed.

"There is *no* time to be lost, Miss Elliott. Why, in another month or so, everyone will have left. *No one*," she declared dramatically, "stays in Bath during the summer!"

"You exaggerate. We have at least two months." Kate was aware that by the end of June most of Bath's elegant visitors would desert the city in favor of country seats and seaside resorts, and she admitted to herself that only her reluctance to venture into the crowded, fashionable districts had prevented her from protesting Mr. Ashcroft's verdict more vigorously. But she had accepted the post of companion and thereby taken on certain duties, a part of which was to see to her charge's introduction into society.

"I will speak to your father once more, Liza. This time, pray allow me to choose the right moment for an interview."

"Dearest Miss Elliott! I knew I could depend on you." Liza, her face radiant, threw her arms around Kate. "Meanwhile, do let us look at the latest fashions. I've just received a copy of *La Belle Assemblée*."

As Liza danced off to fetch the periodical, Kate reflected that in all probability she was making too much of her reentry into fashionable Bath circles. No one could possibly recognize in her the giddy seventeen-year-old who had made a byword of herself.

Eleven years ago, she had worn her hair down, coaxing it into long, bouncing curls by forcing it on curl papers every night. Now her dark brown tresses were brushed back and pinned in a sleek knot at the nape of her neck. In the spring of 1808, she had worn high-waisted muslin gowns in white and palest pastels that floated around a boyishly slim figure. Now she wore gray poplin, and although far from plump, she had filled out in certain places.

And the young ladies and gentlemen with whom

she had associated that long-ago spring would by now be married and spending their time raising children or hosting lavish dinners in London . . .

Fleetingly, an image passed through her mind of a golden-haired young man whose avowals of love had stirred her blood and tempted her to indiscretion. But the image was vague, as though each of the past years had flung a veil across the features she had once believed unforgettable.

Kate slid her feet off the loveseat and sat up primly. How foolish to resurrect memories that were best forgotten, or to allow hurt and anger to surface. Besides, she hadn't given him a thought in years. And a good thing, too! Mr. Ashcroft, no doubt, would speedily send her packing if he suspected his daughter's companion might nourish a silly dream of romance.

She suddenly burst into a peal of laughter. Words of dismissal were the last she wanted to hear from his tight-lipped mouth. Indeed, she was looking forward to many a battle royal over Liza's future.

Chapter Three

Kate's opportunity to confront her employer came sooner than she expected. When she went downstairs early that afternoon to fetch Miss Austen's novel from the morning room, she saw a footman drag a heavy portmanteau out the front door, which Boughey, the round-faced, ever cheerful butler, obligingly held open. Mr. Ashcroft, attired in a driving coat with several shoulder capes, a hat set at a jaunty angle atop his crisp, dark hair, crossed the vast expanse of tiled hall with a purposeful stride.

"Mr. Ashcroft!"

At Kate's peremptory call, he came to a halt just this side of the threshold. He pulled on his driving gloves, then turned, his face registering annoyance and impatience. "Yes, Miss Elliott?"

Kate advanced unhurriedly. Not until she stood directly before him did she speak again. "Mr. Ashcroft, if you intend to be gone awhile, perhaps you would care to leave instructions?"

His mouth tightened as though he were swallowing a blistering retort. He could not have been successful, for the reply he delivered after a brief pause was still biting. "I have a steward, a housekeeper, and a butler who do not require instructions regarding the running of my estate. Are you saying that you, whom I engaged as a capable, efficient companion to my daughter, require my guidance for Liza's entertainment?"

Kate did not flinch under his stare, although she

33

did feel warmth creep into her face. "Since your notions about what Liza may and may not do appear to differ from mine, I believe — "

"You know what is proper and suitable for a young girl," he interrupted curtly. "Just don't take her into Bath until we've had a talk." He saluted her by touching two fingers to the curled brim of his hat, then swept past the interested Boughey, whose ears beneath the halo of wispy white hair had literally pricked up.

Kate followed Damien Ashcroft out, her eyes boring into his back as he descended the wide, semicircular steps into the courtyard. His limp was slightly more pronounced than when he strode across even ground, but still too negligible to be an impediment to a speedy departure.

"I shall be looking forward to that talk, Mr. Ashcroft!"

Without a check, he continued toward the waiting curricle. Kate stiffened. She might be a lowly companion in Mr. Ashcroft's eyes, but that did not excuse his arrogance. How dare he ignore her as though she were . . . one of the pillars gracing the front of his house.

"Is there a message you'd like to leave for your daughter?" she called after him, resenting his treatment of her even more when the March wind bit through the thin fabric of her gown.

He climbed into the waiting curricle. His portmanteau had been securely strapped behind, and as he took up the reins, the groom let go of the leaders' heads and hurriedly clambered onto the box beside his master. But if Damien Ashcroft had been in a rush before, he appeared now to be in no hurry to leave. Holding the restless team in check with a firm hand, he looked at Kate.

"Miss Elliott," he said, and the caustic tone of his voice hit her like a slap in the face. "I admit to a certain degree of admiration for your temerity, but I must warn you not to let that knowledge go to your head. Your rashness might carry you a step too far."

The reins dropped, and he was gone in a clatter of hooves and a cloud of dust and flying gravel.

Needless to say, it did not endear him to Kate when she learned later on from Liza that he had personally informed his daughter of the proposed journey while Kate was engaged in penning a letter to her mother.

"Papa wrote to one of his friends," said Liza, whom Kate had found stretched out full length on a soft rug in front of the library fireplace with her nose buried in one of Mrs. Radcliffe's bloodcurdling tales. "But then he decided to see him in person. So he's gone up to London. Two or three days only, he said."

"But why didn't you tell me?" asked Kate. Seated in a worn but comfortably soft armchair, she warmed her toes at the fire. Her slippers had been no protection against the cold stone of the front steps, and well over an hour after Mr. Ashcroft's departure they still felt cold. "After all your cries of no time to be lost! Didn't you realize that your father's absence would delay your visit to Bath?"

"Oh, no!" Liza scrambled into a sitting position. "How can you say so, Miss Elliott? Surely, since you agree with me, we can go into Bath tomorrow. You are responsible for me. Papa would expect you to make the decisions about my welfare during his absence."

"You know your father well," said Kate, her eyes narrowing. She should have known that Liza would regard Mr. Ashcroft's departure as an excuse to do just as she liked. "Those might have been his own words."

Liza clapped her hands. "Then we'll go?"

"Unfortunately for your schemes, you little imp, I

caught your father on his way out the door, and he expressly forbade me to take you into Bath."

"Oh." Liza was crestfallen. But not for long. With a sidelong look at Kate, she said, "I daresay your mama misses you dreadfully by now. Papa could have no objection if we paid her a visit. Just a very short one."

"Your papa could and—make no mistake about it—*would* object," Kate said wryly. "And let me point out, my dear, you have never yet done well when you decided to scheme behind my back."

"It was worth a try," said Liza defensively. "If you hadn't chanced upon Papa when he left, you would have taken me. You know you would, Miss Elliott, for you never can bear an injustice."

Liza's reasoning was all too sound, but Kate felt duty-bound to depress her young charge's flights of impropriety. "Liza," she began in her most school-masterly voice, but was instantly cut short.

"I know, I know!" Liza said cheerfully. "Next time I shan't go behind your back. I'll take you into my confidence. Then *you* may try to outwit Papa."

This last pronouncement came so close to Kate's intention that she deemed it best to pretend a sudden deafness. Rising, she said, "I shall pay a visit to Mrs. Boughey. She might know of a good seamstress who wouldn't be averse to working here at Dearworth."

"The only dressmaker I'd entrust with an order is Mrs. Moppit in Bath." Liza stretched out in front of the hearth again. With her chin propped into her hand, she mumbled, "Belinda and Susannah said—"

"Very well," Kate interrupted. "I'll write to Mrs. Moppit." She did not have to be told what those two damsels, Liza's closest friends at Miss Venable's school, had said. Lady Belinda Undersham and Miss Susannah Abbots had left no one in doubt about their preferences and opinions.

Kate had not quite reached the first floor when the

rapid tattoo of the door knocker against the brass plate reached her ears. She heard the front door open and Edward, the first footman, inform the visitor in haughty accents that she should use the back door.

"The nerve!" The woman's voice, high-pitched and raised in vexation, drowned the footman's next words. "I am Mrs. Moppit, young man! I don't use the Earl of Lansdown's back door, and I certainly shan't use Mr. Ashcroft's."

Kate flew down the stairs. "It's all right, Edward. I believe Mrs. Moppit is here to sew for Miss Liza."

Smiling, she turned to the matron, whose girth all but hid four mousy young women laden with bandboxes and bulging parcels. "My dear Mrs. Moppit, how on earth, since I have not yet written, could you know about Miss Ashcroft's needs?"

With much rustling of gray silk skirts, the dressmaker stepped inside. She gave Kate a sharp look. "Mr. Ashcroft engaged my services. Stopped on his way to London, I believe, 'to save Miss Elliott the trouble of writing,' he said to tell the young lady. You, I take it, are Miss Elliott?"

While Kate fought against a surge of indignation, for she had no doubt that Mr. Ashcroft had presented his message heavy with irony, Mrs. Moppit turned to address the footman. "Young man, be careful when you unload the trunks! Don't stand them on end. I don't want my silks and satins crushed."

It seemed, thought Kate when Mrs. Moppit and her seamstresses had been installed in rooms on the third floor, that the formidable dressmaker had carried her entire staff and stock of fabrics to Dearworth. Kate watched Liza flit from figured muslins to bolts of silk and lace in the delicate colors suitable for a very young lady, and she remembered herself as a seventeen-year-old.

37

That younger Kate had been bubbling and glowing with excitement and pure *joie de vivre*, which could not be dimmed even by her mama's plaintive requests not to dawdle over a choice of gowns, or by last-minute disappointments when, instead of chaperoning Kate to the Assembly Rooms, Lady Elliott retired to her couch. That young Kate was outgoing, exuberant. She quickly made friends with other young ladies, and her mama raised no objections nor asked questions when Kate's friends invited her to outings.

Kate was abruptly torn from the past by Liza's exclamation. "What a heavenly blue! Miss Elliott, look! The silk perfectly matches my eyes."

"Yes, indeed. You may have a length and embroider it for a shawl."

Liza's delicate features settled in the mulish look Kate knew well. "I should like a dinner gown made of the material, with a full skirt embroidered in silver thread."

"Yes," murmured Kate, tilting her head a little and subjecting girl and royal-blue silk to a close inspection, as though she were considering Liza's suggestion. "It may serve our purpose admirably. Surely, if you look seven-and-twenty rather than seventeen, your papa can have no objection to your entry into the social whirl."

Liza was startled. "You're bamming, Miss Elliott, aren't you?"

Mrs. Moppit, tape measure in hand, desired Liza to step onto a footstool. "Miss Elliott is quite right," she said in a no-nonsense voice. "The deeper shades are suitable only for her."

"I wear gray, Mrs. Moppit," Kate said absently. "You may take my measurements for a dinner gown of gray silk." Her eyes strayed to a bolt of satin, the shade of red lilacs. "Although a bit of trim couldn't hurt. Colored trim."

The dressmaker directed another of her sharp

glances at Kate. "The deeper shades are for you," she reiterated. "I chose them with particular care after asking Mr. Ashcroft about your coloring. And you, Miss Ashcroft—bend your arm a little, if you please—you'll wear white mostly, and primrose, the way your lady mother did. You have her looks, you do. Gave me quite a start when you first came in."

"Oh, do I really look like Mama? Did you make her gowns, Mrs. Moppit?"

"Indeed I did. Now turn around, miss. I need to measure your shoulders."

"Did Mama have many gowns? What was her favorite color? How did she wear her hair?" Liza asked excitedly.

Mrs. Moppit, however, had said as much about Liza's mother as she intended. Pursing her mouth, she said sternly, "Mr. Ashcroft is not paying my fee for talking, miss. And please stand still. You'll not thank me if your gowns don't fit properly. Besides, we must get on if I'm to take Miss Elliott's measurements before the day's over."

Liza said no more, but Kate could feel her disappointment. Except for a small likeness, which Liza kept on her bedside table, Kate had seen no portrait of the late Mrs. Elliott in the lofty rooms of Dearworth. To hear about her mother from one who must have known her well would seem like a golden opportunity to Liza.

"Mrs. Moppit," said Kate, "surely you can answer a few questions while you work."

The dressmaker shook her head, a guarded look on her face. "Talking pays no toll," she muttered, then subjected Liza and Kate to such a barrage of commands and proddings and pokings that they were quite happy to be dismissed when, finally, Mrs. Moppit rolled up her tape measure.

Shutting the door to the temporary sewing room, Kate let out a sigh of relief. "I'm going for a walk.

Care to join me, Liza?"

"But it's almost dark!"

Kate raised a brow. "Did that deter you when you sneaked out to meet Lady Belinda's brother in the Sydney Gardens?"

A dimple appeared in Liza's cheek. "If I could be certain that a young man is waiting for me outside," she said with a saucy smile. "Oh, all right. I'll get my wrap. I wouldn't want you to get lost."

A few moments later, the two ladies crossed the gently sloping south lawn toward the heavily timbered rise that was the game preserve. "Not that there is much game," said Liza, buttoning her pelisse to the throat. "Mr. Ramsden, our gamekeeper, allows Hubert and Algernon to shoot here when Sir Shafto's woods are exhausted."

"We'll have nothing to fear, then. The hunting season is over." Kate chose the widest of two paths leading into the woods. A bridle path—if only the two mares would arrive. "Tell me about Hubert and Algernon. Are they prospective beaux?"

Liza giggled. "They're our neighbors' sons. The oldest of several. Last time I counted, there were six boys in Sir Shafto and Lady Usborne's family, and Emily—you remember Emily Usborne, don't you, Miss Elliott? She was at the seminary last year."

"I remember. You and Emily never could pass up an opportunity to quarrel."

"I shan't quarrel with her now that I am out," Liza said with dignity. "I daresay you'll meet Lady Usborne soon. She called on us just after Papa brought me home but didn't even stay long enough that I could order refreshments. By now she'll have heard, though, that I have a companion. She and Emily will call to inspect you."

"The mere thought makes me quake in my shoes."

"Oh, no, it doesn't." Liza hurried to keep up with Kate's longer stride. "You're never afraid of anything. And if Lady Usborne is too curious, you'll simply give her one of your quelling looks."

"Gracious, child! Am I so formidable that I can intimidate a determined matron?" Kate made her voice sound light, but Liza's words filled her with dismay. A crotchety, stern old spinster, that was what Kate Elliott had become—and seemingly overnight. When she was with Liza, Kate often felt as though it were only yesterday that she, too, had been a young girl. But eleven years would not be denied.

Liza, at least, did not make the attempt to deny anything. "I wish they'd call on us tomorrow," she said. "I want to start being a hostess. I'll ask Pierre to bake some pastries and a cake, and Edward must polish the silver tea set."

"Hush, child. Listen." Kate placed a restraining hand on Liza's arm and drew her to a halt. "Did you hear?"

Liza cocked her head and listened to the rustling and crackling sounds of the woods. "A hare probably," she said with a shrug.

But Kate had grown up in surroundings quite similar to those of the Dearworth estate and had heard the unmistakable crunch of human feet. "The game-keeper?"

Again Liza shrugged. "Mr. Ramsden?" she called hesitantly.

There was an instant breathless silence. Then a volley of suppressed snickers and the thud of running feet marked the progress of two or more persons through the undergrowth on the left-hand side of the winding path. Kate let go of Liza's arm. When she judged the noisy intruders to be parallel to her position, she darted into the thicket of ferns and hazelnut bushes. Before Liza could so much as blink an eye, Kate returned, having collared two scruffy boys and propelling them before her.

"There!" said Kate when she had them on the wide

path where the trees overhead did not quite meet and allowed the fading light to penetrate. "Let's have a look at you."

The boys, no more than ten or twelve years of age, shuffled their feet and hung their heads. Even so, it was plain to see that they were as two peas in a pod: identical freckled features, identical snub noses, identical mischievously curved mouths. They were barefoot. Their jackets and breeches showed many a patch and did not convey the prosperity one might expect of Mr. Ashcroft's neighbors, but, Kate reasoned, the boys might have discarded their shoes and their mama might have admitted the futility of providing her sons with new clothes.

"Two of Sir Shafto's brood?" she asked with a questioning glance at Liza.

"I don't believe the Usbornes ever had twins," Liza said doubtfully. Then, recalling her duty as mistress of Dearworth, she addressed the boys sternly. "Who are you? And what are you doing here?"

"I'm Walter, miss." One of the boys looked up, his brown eyes wide and innocent. "And this be Peter. Me brother," he added rather superfluously.

"Are you from the village?" Liza shot him a dark look. "You're not allowed on the estate. What were you doing?"

"And you need not bother to lie." Releasing their collars, Kate snatched slingshots from the boys' pockets. "We caught a pair of poachers, Liza."

"Aw, now, miss!" Peter finally looked up. He scratched his mop of pale blond hair and screwed up his face in an effort to think of a believable excuse. "Walter an' me, we ain't never poached anything. May have found a rabbit or two that Mr. Hubert or Mr. Algernon shot an' forgot to bag. But that ain't no crime, ain't it now?"

"We couldn't hit a tree at two paces," Walter corroborated. An engaging grin spread over his freckled face. "An' if we gets deported, what would our poor ma be doin' without us? We's the providers of our large family, ma'am."

Kate suppressed a smile, but Liza asked suspiciously, "How many are there in your family?"

"Twelve, miss. An' our pa dead these past seven years."

"You are the oldest?" asked Kate.

Walter hesitated, but Peter saw no trap in the question. "Aye, ma' am. That we are."

"Well," Kate said with admirable calm, "I can see how important you must be to your family. We can't have you get lost. So we'll just escort you to Mr. Ramsden's house, and he can drive you home."

"Ain't necessary!" they shouted simultaneously and, even before they finished, took to their heels and raced down the path, away from Dearworth.

"Your slingshots!" Kate called after them, but they neither heard nor cared.

"And we don't even know their full names or where they live." Liza stamped a foot in vexation. "Mr. Ramsden may wish to take them up before the magistrate."

Kate stuffed the slingshots into her cape pocket and slowly started back toward the manor. "They are only mischievous children. Surely your father wouldn't want them sentenced for poaching. That boy—now which one was it? Anyway, he was right about deportation, you know."

"It does seem monstrously unfair," Liza agreed after a moment's thought. "But they shouldn't trespass. If I knew where they live, I could send some provisions to their mother."

"Lady Bountiful?" Kate said, smiling. "You shouldn't have any difficulty finding out about them. They strike me as a pair impossible to forget or to ignore."

"Indeed. I wouldn't be at all surprised to learn

43

that Mr. Ramsden has already made their acquaintance." Liza seemed abstracted, and for a few moments they proceeded in silence. With every step, Liza increased her pace, and it was Kate now who had trouble keeping up. There was nothing ladylike about the way the young girl rushed down the sloping path, her skirts hitched almost to her knees, her hair tumbling wildly, and her breath loud and rasping.

"Liza, slow down!" Kate grew warm. She unbuttoned her cape and let it slide off her shoulders. "Do you want us to take a fall?"

But Liza did not stop until she burst through the last rows of trees and stood on the open expanse of clipped lawn. "I'm sorry," she said breathlessly when Kate caught up with her. "There's something about the game preserve at dusk—oh, I don't know what!" She gave a shaky laugh, then spoke more calmly. "I suppose it's because I suffer a nightmare now and again. For years and years I've dreamed about Papa stumbling out of these woods, and always he's bleeding dreadfully."

"How horrid. Perhaps, as a child, you saw your father hurt?"

Liza shook her head. "I don't think I did. I told Papa about my dreams. He laughed and said I have a lurid imagination."

Kate looked back at the woods. They were dark and silent, but certainly not the sinister kind of forest that would inspire gory dreams.

She gave Liza's arm a comforting squeeze. "Let's have a glass of sherry before dinner. If you wish to be a good hostess, you must learn to hold your wine."

"Oh, famous!" Liza gave Kate a quick little smile. "I've never tasted anything more potent than ratafia. Shall I like sherry?" She did not wait for a reply but dashed ahead. "Race you to the rose border!"

Kate watched her fly across the grass—seemingly happy and carefree. In her mind, Kate chalked up several marks against Damien Ashcroft. If he were caring, he would not laugh at a child's nightmares. If he were loving, he would share his memories of Liza's mother—even if it reopened wounds her early death must have caused him—and Liza need not be pathetically eager to listen to casual remarks dropped by a dressmaker. If he were . . .

A determined gleam lit Kate's eyes. Damien Ashcroft might believe he could ignore his daughter's companion—or threaten her if she proved mettlesome—but he would soon learn that Kate Elliott did not shy at her fences.

And if a race would take Liza's mind off her troublesome dream, then a race she should have. Picking up her skirts, Kate set off in hot pursuit—and the devil fly away with propriety.

By the time they reached the bare thorny stalks that would in summer be a sweet-smelling, colorful bank of rose bushes, it was impossible to tell whether it was the companion, clad in demure gray poplin and a serviceable black cape, or her young charge, gowned in finest wool and fur-trimmed pelisse, who had won the race. They were both glowing with a heady sense of victory.

Chapter Four

That feeling of exhilaration stayed with Kate for the next two days. It sustained her through pin pricks suffered in the sewing room, through days of sleet and rain as the April weather belatedly conformed to its reputation and Liza complained that there was nothing to do. Kate's mood began to change, however, when several gowns and two riding habits were completed by the nimble fingers of Mrs. Moppit's seamstresses and neither Mr. Ashcroft nor the promised mares made an appearance.

The return of bright, sunny skies did nothing to lift Kate's increasing listlessness. It was too bad! She had made up her mind to fight for Liza's happiness, and her adversary, as though sensing his imminent defeat, stayed away. Cavorting in London.

Kate suppressed a sigh as she and Liza shared luncheon in the breakfast parlor, a cheerful room with silken Chinese wall hangings, a small round table and chairs with gracefully curving legs. So much more suitable for two young ladies than the dining room with all its splendor of dark, polished oak, and yet it only served as a reminder of Damien Ashcroft's continued absence.

"What shall we do after luncheon?" Liza asked petulantly, poking at a bite of Dover sole, which the French chef had lovingly prepared in the hopes of tempting her appetite.

Kate counted to ten before answering this oft-repeated question. "Let's play a game of backgammon."

"No, thank you."

"Pick more bluebells?"

"No."

"We could finish the last two chapters of *Sense and Sensibility*."

Liza sent her chair crashing to the floor in her haste to rise from the table. Two bright red spots flamed high on her cheekbones, and her eyes glittered ominously. "Walking and reading! That's all we ever do. I might as well have been sent to another school!" Angrily brushing at a tear with the back of her hand, she turned and flounced to the window overlooking the gardens.

In silence, Kate watched as the footman righted Liza's chair. "Thank you, Edward. That will be all," she said quietly when he started to remove Liza's plate. "Please ask Mrs. Boughey to send coffee to the morning room in half an hour."

Only when the dining room door had shut behind Edward did Kate speak to Liza. "I remember the tantrums you displayed at school. Quite impressive, but sending you to your room without dinner or tea snapped you out of the sullens. Perhaps I should resign my post as companion and be your governess instead, so I might apply those remedies again."

Liza flung herself around, her eyes still flashing angrily and her hands clenched at her sides. Kate met that stormy look with a quizzing half smile and knew the satisfaction of seeing the rebellious flame wither and die.

"I'm sorry, Miss Elliott." Sighing, Liza came back to the table. She did not sit down but stood behind her chair. "Why is it so difficult to be happy?"

"Because you have expectations, my dear, but have not yet acquired the patience to wait for fulfillment."

"And if I don't learn to be patient? What will

47

happen to me, Miss Elliott? I don't want to be thought a troublesome child or a shrew!"

Kate's head felt curiously light. She knew what disastrous results impatience could have. She rose and stepped around the table to stand beside Liza. "I'll help you. And I'll also see that your patience will be rewarded, so that you'll neither turn into a shrew nor — horrid alternative! — become a resigned old maid."

"That, never!" Even as she uttered the fierce vow, Liza's eyes widened. Kate could almost hear her question: *Is that what happened to you?* But the words remained unspoken. Instead, Liza exclaimed, "How different you look, Miss Elliott! Somehow . . . younger, prettier. Oh, I'm sorry! I daresay that was impertinent of me."

Kate had started to lead the way to the morning room, but at Liza's words she checked and looked over her shoulder with a wry smile. "Pray don't apologize for your compliment. Or do you want to crush the last vestige of my self-confidence?"

"Oh, no! It's just that I never saw you look so modish before. Fine as fivepence, as Mrs. Boughey would say."

"Mrs. Boughey," murmured Kate, proceeding down the hall, "has gone out of her way to avoid me. Does your housekeeper not approve of my employment?"

Giggling, Liza pushed past Kate into the sunny morning room. "You mustn't take Mrs. Boughey's behavior personally, Miss Elliott. She told Papa that it was unseemly for a young lady to live in a gentleman's establishment without a chaperon. And Papa said, 'The devil, Mrs. Boughey! The young lady *is* the chaperon.' "

Kate could easily imagine Damien Ashcroft, his voice dripping icy sarcasm, as he confronted his housekeeper. But Mrs. Boughey had been his nurse.

Perhaps he didn't dare be arrogant with her.

Plopping into one of the brocade-covered armchairs, Liza drew up her legs and tucked her feet beneath the skirt of her gown. "And then, as a clincher, Papa ordered Mrs. Boughey to chaperon you. So now she's on her high ropes — at least until she's watched you for a while and made up her mind about you. You'll see, she'll come around shortly. She always does, for Papa can wind her around his little finger."

Kate did not doubt it. "But in the meantime," she said dryly, "Mrs. Boughey will amuse herself by heartily disapproving of my new gowns. As, in fact, I do myself. I feel like a peahen who suddenly sprouted her mate's feathers." She gave the folds of her gown a playful twitch before sitting down on a chaise longue. "It's still poplin, but there all similarity to my former garb ends. I don't know what Mrs. Moppit could have been thinking of when she selected colors for me. A deep rose morning gown and lace trim for a companion!"

"I think it's perfect," said Liza, snuggling deeper into her chair. "No one will take you for my companion now. Oh, I know! We'll pretend that you are my cousin. And when we go to the assemblies, we'll find you a beau."

"An earl," said Kate, entering into the spirit of make-believe. "Or mayhap a duke. A young, handsome, and rich duke. I'll marry him and live happily ever after."

"He'll sweep you off your feet and carry you away in his chariot," said Liza, her eyes wide and dreamy.

Kate's smile froze. Make-believe games never did last long. "In his carriage-and-four," she said very softly.

Liza gave her a sidelong glance. Blushing a little, she asked, "Why did you not get married, Miss Elliott?"

"Perhaps because no one asked me."

"I cannot believe that," Liza protested, but Kate heard the note of uncertainty in her voice.

"You might say I spoilt my chances of marriage through impatience," said Kate, meaning to drive home what she had stressed earlier. But she was not displeased when the butler entered, thereby precluding more questions from Liza and the need to elaborate on a statement that had undoubtedly sounded cryptic and intriguing to a young girl.

Boughey placed a silver coffeepot, sugar, cream, and cups on a table near Kate. "Miss Elliott," he said, bowing respectfully. "There's Master Hubert and Master Algernon, Sir Shafto's sons, asking to have a word with Miss Liza."

Before Kate could invite the two gentlemen in, Liza cried, "And you let them kick their heels in the hall! Shame on you, Boughey! When you know how moped I've been."

The butler gave Liza an indulgent look but addressed himself once more to Kate. "Shall I show them in, Miss Elliott?"

"I fear you must," said Kate, her eyes dancing. "Unless you want us both to end up in Miss Liza's black books. Please send up two more cups, Mr. Boughey."

The butler's cheerful expression changed to one of doubt. "Yes, Miss Elliott. But if you don't mind my saying so, I believe the young gentlemen would prefer ale."

"Very well. Ale it is."

Bowing, the butler withdrew, and moments later Master Hubert and Master Algernon made an entrance only slightly less exuberant than Liza's reception of them.

Kate's presence was forgotten or ignored in the flurry of questions and answers the young people shot at each other, and she had ample time to study

50

the two gentlemen. In fact, she thought, they were hardly more than boys, with all the lankiness and noisy awkwardness that beset many of the male sex from that first shave until the time of total acceptance into the world of manly arts and diversions. Hardly the material to turn a girl's head—yet.

The arrival of two foaming tankards of ale and Liza's impetuous demand to be told why Lady Usborne and Emily had not seen fit to visit Dearworth finally reminded the older Usborne son of the reason for their visit.

With a sheepish grin, Master Hubert turned to Kate. "I beg your pardon, ma'am. My mother sends her apologies for not calling personally, but she's kept awfully busy. Charles—he's her favorite cousin, ma'am—arrived out of the blue, and she's planning a dinner to introduce him to the neighbors."

"A dinner!" Liza tugged at Hubert's sleeve. "Is that why you're here? To invite me? Why didn't you say so at once, stoopid?"

"Because you don't let a fellow get a word in edgewise," he retorted with friendly candor. "You're as much a prattlebox as ever, Liza."

"Oh, come now, Hubert!" Painfully shy once he was no longer trying to outshout his brother or trump Liza in exuberance, Master Algernon nudged Hubert's arm and stammered something about minding one's manners and the presence of ladies.

"I didn't say anything to make a lady blush!" Hubert defended himself instantly and heatedly. "Stop tugging on my coat, you lunkhead. It's my newest, from Weston! What's that you're mumbling?"

"Message from our sire," muttered Algernon. "*You* know. About the horses."

"Thanks, Algy. I plumb forgot." Again Hubert turned to Kate. "Father wants to know, ma'am, if he should send the mares over, or if you'd rather wait until Mr. Ashcroft's back."

"Now!" squealed Liza, pommeling Hubert's arm in her excitement. "Immediately!"

Kate did not reprimand her. Did she not feel an equal impatience, even exasperation that she had not known where Damien Ashcroft had bought the mares? She'd have sent a note to Sir Shafto the moment Mr. Ashcroft's curricle passed through the gates of Dearworth. However, Kate was aware of three pairs of watchful eyes on her, and she remained very much on her dignity.

"Pray be seated," she said, waving Liza to her previous place and indicating chairs for the brothers. "We may as well partake of refreshments while we discuss the particulars of your messages, gentlemen."

Liza giggled at the awed expressions on her friends' faces at being thus addressed, but a look from Kate soon put a stop to that. After agreeing that the mares should, indeed, be sent to Dearworth that very afternoon, Kate asked such pertinent questions as the date of the dinner, whether it was to be a formal affair, and whether Lady Usborne was aware when she issued her invitation to Liza that Mr. Ashcroft was from home.

"Lud, yes!" Hubert said carelessly. After fortifying himself with a draft of ale, he added, "Mother said that there wouldn't be any danger of Liza flying into a pelter if her father didn't return in time to bring her, since she has a companion now to take her about."

Liza protested that she *never* flew into a pelter, but Kate gathered from Lady Usborne's words that Mr. Ashcroft had more than once failed to take Liza to join her friends in some activity or other. Her mouth tightened, but seeing Liza's anxious look, she summoned a smile. "Of course we'll go, Liza. You may assure your mother, Mr. Usborne, that Liza and I are looking forward to tomorrow night."

"Famous! But, won't you call me Hubert, ma'-

am?"

Kate was sorely tempted to stipulate that he cease calling her ma'am, but she merely nodded assent. Sitting as chaperon with these . . . children made her feel as though she were an octogenarian at least.

Shortly afterward, the young Usbornes asked to have their horses brought from the stables. "We'll have to hurry if you want to ride this afternoon," said Hubert when Kate and Liza accompanied the brothers into the courtyard. "It still gets dark early."

"If you're back within the hour, I may let you ride with us," said Liza, pertly tossing her curls.

Hubert grinned. "Done. Wouldn't want to miss her first tumble, would we, Algy?"

Algernon, forgetting Miss Elliott's awesome presence, shot Liza a look brimful of mischief. "Want to have another go at Lord Severeign's wall?"

Liza drew herself up to promise rashly that she'd have a go at any wall or fence *he* would jump, but Kate forestalled her. "It would be unfair to rider and horse if we were to attempt such feats the first time out," she said quietly but with authority ringing in her voice. "Today we'll take the path through the game preserve. I've long wondered where it leads."

"Yes, of course! Didn't mean—" Blushing furiously, Algernon bit his lip. He bowed, turned abruptly, and hurried toward the groom who was leading two horses across the yard.

Kate felt a twinge of remorse but also pity for the young man. She was so accustomed to her brother's thick-skinned carelessness that she hadn't taken Algernon's sensitivity into account.

As Algernon rode off, she said to Hubert, "Please tell your brother not to mind my sharp tongue. Tell him I hope he'll still ride with us, and that Liza and I would be delighted to take him up on his dare some other time."

"Lud, ma'am!" Hubert mounted, grinning down

53

at Kate with cheerful unconcern. "Algy's all right. He just don't like anyone to see him blush like a girl. He'll be back." And with this assurance, he set off after his brother.

"Will he?" Kate asked as she and Liza returned to the house.

"Oh, yes. Algy wouldn't want to miss anything. You see," Liza said without looking at Kate, "I often take a toss—whether I jump or not."

"Why?"

"I suppose I'm just not a good horsewoman. Papa says I have the worst seat in the county."

Kate closed the front door with great care. "Did your papa teach you to ride?"

"Yes." Liza darted across the foyer. "Race you upstairs, Miss Elliott! See who is changed first!"

But Kate could not be tempted. Slowly, she mounted the stairs while trying to control her equally mounting temper. Everything, absolutely everything that a father should do for his daughter Damien Ashcroft had bungled. But no more! Kate vowed.

She changed hurriedly, so as not to keep Liza waiting, but when she looked for her charge a little later, she found her still seated in front of her mirror.

"Oh, Miss Elliott, shall I wear my hat with the feather dipping over my ear or down the back?"

Kate stepped behind Liza and adjusted the saucy little hat. "Like this, I think. The feather may tickle your cheek a bit, but when you ride it'll blow toward the back."

"I look dashing!" Liza regarded her image with awe, and Kate, looking at the charming little face framed by gleaming golden curls beneath the pale blue velvet hat, agreed silently. Mrs. Moppit had done Liza's beauty justice with the severely cut blue velvet habit and a shirt of sheerest lawn. Snowy ruffles of lace frothed at the girl's neck and on her

54

wrists, making her look elegant and utterly adorable.

"And you look stunning, Miss Elliott. Let's go down." Liza gathered her gloves and riding crop. "They may be early, and we don't want to keep the horses standing."

But the courtyard was empty when Liza burst through the front door. "Slowtops!" she muttered, perching herself on the top step and staring hopefully in the direction of the Bluebell Woods. "They'll cut across the fields and through the woods," she said, reassuring herself. "Surely they will!"

"You know best, I'm sure." Kate was looking toward the gate, where the drive joined the road to Bath. A little farther down a side lane branched off, leading to Sir Shafto's home. "But I see several horses—four, I think—approaching on the Bath road. Oh! It's a carriage-and-four."

"Papa!" Liza shot up and dashed down the stairs long before the driver of the sporting carriage could be recognized.

Kate remained standing just within the portico that ran the full length of the house. The vehicle approached at breakneck speed, and within the blink of an eye, Kate could see that it was a curricle. The driver, one moment no more than a vague shape in a voluminous gray coat, was fast taking on familiar features: straight, broad shoulders, a dark head held at an arrogantly proud angle.

Damien Ashcroft drew his sweating team to a halt well before he reached Liza, tossed the reins to the groom beside him, and jumped down. Kate saw him reel when his feet hit the ground. She took an involuntary step toward him, but he recovered quickly and caught his daughter in a mighty hug! "Liza, you little bubblehead! Did I not forbid you to step into the drive when a carriage approaches?"

His words delivered a scold, but his voice, deep and warm, robbed them of their sting. The dark eyes, which Kate had seen cold and disdainful only, glowed with warmth. His mouth was no longer harsh but curved in a proud, appreciative grin as he held his daughter at arm's length and studied her glowing face. "You look gorgeous, Princess. I take it, Sir Shafto sent the mares over?"

"Hubert and Algy are fetching them. Oh, Papa!" Liza bounced with joy and excitement. Pulling her father close again, she threw her arms around his neck and gave him a resounding kiss. "Will you ride with us, Papa? Please?"

A shadow passed over his face. "I'm sorry, Princess. It was a long drive from London. Tomorrow?"

"All right. I'll be patient if I must. Did you bring me a present?"

He laughed and turned Liza toward the house. Keeping a hand on his daughter's elbow, he came toward the stairs. Slowly, he mounted the first two steps, then halted. Kate saw his eyes come to rest on her. He raised a brow—politely inquisitive, as though he didn't know her. Surely he could not have forgotten that he engaged her!

Just when his look changed, just when that disturbing gleam had appeared, Kate could not say. But suddenly she found it hard to breathe, and her knees were curiously wobbly. She put out a hand, steadying herself on one of the slender columns supporting the upper story.

"Devil a bit!" he said, letting his eyes move from her high-crowned hat with its tiny veil and long satin streamers to her black riding habit, frogged and braided with gold trim à *la hussar*. She started to feel warm under that roaming gaze, as though he were using his hands to trace each curve of her body. But that was utter folly!

Kate raised her chin and took a step toward her employer. "Mr. Ashcroft. Welcome back."

He came up the last steps alone, for Liza had

56

pulled free of his grasp and was running across the courtyard to join Hubert and Algernon, who had stopped at the stables and were showing off two sleek mares to the Dearworth grooms.

"Mrs. Moppit has done her work, I see," Damien said when he stood on a level with her. He was looking down at her now, and although his eyes still held a certain gleam, it had subtly changed. It was a cold gleam, and his mouth was harsh, one corner twitching up as though he barely suppressed a sneer.

Kate braced herself for a disparaging remark about her appearance. Although there should be nothing objectionable about a black riding habit and a very plain high-necked shirt without frills or ruffles, the gold braid and the way the soft woolen cloth molded itself to her body could be described in no other way than flamboyant. Mrs. Moppit had refused to spoil her creation by removing the gold trim. If Miss Elliott wished to look a fright, the dressmaker had said huffily, she must perform the desecrating deed herself. But Kate hadn't had time yet to undo the countless tiny stitches.

Now she might never do it. After all, Damien Ashcroft himself had sent the dressmaker to Dearworth.

"Why are you scowling, Miss Elliott? Surely I cannot have offended you during my absence."

Kate blinked, caught off guard. But not for long. "It's not my place to say so, Mr. Ashcroft, but would anyone dare scowl at you?"

"I recall several instances when you dared. Since I'm not aware of any misdeeds, however, I assume Liza has been quite a handful. What has the little minx been up to?"

"Why, absolutely nothing, Mr. Ashcroft. And that is the trouble. Liza is moped to tears. She would have been better entertained had you placed her at another school."

"Then what have *you* been doing, Miss Elliott? I engaged you to keep Liza entertained. Why the deuce don't you do it?"

"You engaged me as Liza's chaperon, sir," said Kate, matching the frigidity of his tone. "But there's no activity here at Dearworth that she could not in all propriety enjoy, accompanied only by a groom or a maid. Liza, however, doesn't even have a maid!"

"And if you're thinking of asking me to employ one, put such notion out of your mind!"

"Every young lady needs a maid," Kate said stubbornly. "And she needs to get her feet wet by mixing with Bath society before you take her to London next—"

"Liza does not go to London," he cut in sharply. "And now, if you don't mind, Miss Elliott, I should like to enter my house so that I may remove the dust of a day's travel."

"Don't let me detain you." Kate swept up the short train of her riding habit. Without a backward glance, she marched down the steps and across the courtyard.

Chapter Five

Shutting his front door with unnecessary force, Damien stalked into the house. His gaze fell on the junior of his two footmen, who approached bearing a wide brass receptacle filled with daffodils, bluebells, and twigs of silvery hazel catkin.

"Put that down, Ben! And bring up my bath water."

"Right away, sir." The young footman hastened to the polished oak table upon which Boughey generally placed the hats and gloves of gentlemen callers, and he set the vase beside the salver holding calling cards.

"What is this foolishness, Ben? We've never had flowers in the hall! Has Mrs. Boughey entered on a new kick of fashion?"

"No, sir. Miss Elliott picked 'em this morning. I meant to bring 'em up earlier, but—" Observing his master's deepening scowl, Ben prudently shut his mouth and hurried toward the kitchens. He'd rather lug water for ten baths than be in Miss Elliott's shoes when she next encountered Mr. Ashcroft.

With a look of loathing at the lovingly arranged harbingers of spring, Damien strode across the foyer. On the stairs, he was obliged to proceed more slowly. "Damn!" he muttered. "Damn this blasted leg. And the devil fly away with Miss Elliott!"

The door to his bed chamber shut behind him with as loud a slam as had the front door. Marston, his valet of many years, took one look at the drawn face, the deep lines etched along the corners of the tight-lipped mouth, and stepped to the tallboy to pour a generous measure of cognac. Without a word, he handed the glass to Damien.

"Well, Marston? I'm waiting for your 'I told you so.' " Watching his valet over the rim of his glass, Damien downed half of its contents. "I really can look after myself, you know. It's only that I was a damn fool, driving back in one day."

"Yes, sir," Marston said woodenly, and was rewarded with a glint of amusement in the dark eyes. Deftly, he shook out the heavy driving coat and hung it over a chair. "And Hinkson not even trying to talk some sense into you, I've no doubt. Now, if you'll let me remove those boots, sir, you'll feel more the thing in no time."

"Stop feuding with Hinkson. He's the best groom I ever had." Damien sank into a chair. "Knows when to keep mum, unlike some others I could name," he muttered darkly

His words might have been meant for Marston, but Damien was thinking of a certain female with flashing blue-gray eyes and a cutting tongue who had briefly rendered him speechless. He hadn't even recognized her for a moment or two. How could he, when the donning of a riding habit had transformed the drab Miss Elliott into a diamond of the first water?

Damien stretched out his left leg. A sigh of relief escaped through his clenched teeth as the valet eased the boot off. "Thank you, Marston. That's better. Gad, how I hate being crippled!"

"It'd be easier on you if you wouldn't try so hard to hide your limp, sir."

"Damn your impudence," Damien said without heat. "I want none of your pity. Now go and see if that's Ben with my bath water I hear making such a racket."

"I am well aware when pity is wasted, sir." Marston bowed stiffly and disappeared in the dressing room.

Leaning against the winged back of his chair, Damien sipped his drink. He should be feeling elated, as he had driving down from London, for Nicholas Adair had agreed to pay an extended visit to Dearworth. Granted, when he had first learned that Liza, newly emerged from the schoolroom, would be in residence, he had declined the invitation with unflattering promptness. Lord Nicholas cared no more for female companionship than did Damien. However, Nicholas had not been immune to Damien's appeal for assistance with the sifting of new information on the Emperor Vespasian, which Damien had unearthed during his latest stay in Rome. And when Damien casually mentioned that Liza would be kept busy by her very strict and efficient companion, Nicholas had been completely won over.

Envisioning the first encounter between his friend and his daughter, Damien grinned wryly. Nicholas might believe himself immune to female charm and beauty, but once he set eyes on Liza, he'd be bowled over—as had been Damien when he saw Elizabeth nineteen years ago.

Damien's grin vanished abruptly. Instead of Elizabeth's pink and golden beauty, he saw Miss Elliott's countenance, set in lines of strong disapproval. Not in any way could his daughter's companion compare to Liza's and Elizabeth's perfection. The tilt of her chin was too stubborn, her nose too long, her expression too forceful. . . .

"Your bath, sir."

Damien rose, handing his glass to Marston. "Bring me another." Another became two and three more, while Damien sat in the steaming water into which Marston had, undoubtedly, poured a quantity of

Epsom salt.

Whether it was the salt or the warmth of the water, when Damien stepped out of the large copper tub, he felt as he had that morning at dawn when he had left Nicholas Adair's London townhouse — relaxed, content, and as full of vigor and energy as Nicholas, almost ten years his junior.

That his resolve to once and for all put Miss Elliott in her place had anything to do with his feeling of well-being, Damien denied absolutely. His daughter's companion was no concern of his. And if she hadn't deceived him at Miss Venable's school, he wouldn't be thinking of her at all. But she had led him to believe she was meek and timid — and drab. He'd show Miss Elliott that no one crossed swords with Damien Ashcroft and did not come to regret it.

Planning to divert his mind until shortly before dinner, the earliest he could summon Miss Elliott since she and Liza would undoubtedly be trying out the mares, Damien withdrew to his study. Here he kept his books, his records, and references necessary to the *New History of Roman England* he was writing. Here he kept another bottle of finest mellow old cognac. Here he was sure to be undisturbed.

He was soon engrossed in his reading, a glass at his elbow, a pencil in one hand, and a cheroot in the other. Some time later, Liza's voice drifted down the hallway and broke his concentration.

"How right you were, Miss Elliott. They *are* poachers, the rascals!" she said excitely. "Wait till I tell Papa."

Damien could not make out Miss Elliott's reply, but Liza's "At least we know that they live in Combe Down" was again clearly audible.

Then all was quiet — they must have reached the second floor — and Damien, after a glance at his watch, again settled down to his reading. He'd give Miss Elliott one hour to change, then ring for her.

That would allow him ample time before dinner to administer the trimming she so richly deserved.

A scarce half hour later, a firm, quick tread in the corridor warned him of Miss Elliott's approach. He did not question why he felt certain that it was the companion and not Liza or Mrs. Boughey, but he did acknowledge a measure of respect that she had not waited for his summons.

As on an earlier occasion, Miss Elliott, dressed once again in gray, entered after the briefest of knocks. A quick glance at her set face convinced Damien that his initial plan to remain seated, thereby placing her firmly in the category of servant, would not do the trick. She appeared single-mindedly purposeful; she would not notice if he sat atop his desk. He rose, according her the curtest of bows and indicating a chair just in time to forestall her seating herself without invitation.

She instantly went into attack. "I have come about Liza. When you left for London, you promised—"

"I never promise, Miss Elliott."

She was unflustered. Inclining her head, she said, "Very well. You *stated* we'd have a talk about Liza."

His respect grew, but now he acknowledged it with reluctance. He had no intention of allowing her to get the upper hand. "Miss Elliott, before I inform you of my plans for my daughter, let me point out one or two rules that apply when I am closeted in my study."

"Yes, Mr. Ashcroft."

Her demurely folded hands, her lowered gaze, recalled that other time at the school when she had tried to bamboozle him with her posture of meekness. And why the devil was she wearing that drab old gown? Granted, it was silk; but it was dull with age, and in some spots the material had frayed.

His eyes narrowed as he took a puff on his cheroot. "Come now, Miss Elliott. Do you take me for a

63

flat? Surely you have realized that you need not pretend timidity for my sake."

She looked up, the hint of a smile curving her mouth. "Indeed. In that case, I suggest that you acquaint me with your rules, and then, for goodness sake, let's talk about Liza. I must warn you, sir. I, too, have quite a few things to point out."

"Proceed. What I wanted to say can wait."

"Liza needs a maid."

"I told you I won't have females cluttering up my house."

"That is not a good enough reason. But then"— she shrugged her shoulders, a gesture that more than words showed her intolerance of his judgment— "why should that weigh with you? *You* don't have to do without the services of a valet because of your prejudice against female servants."

He bit down on the cigar, then, with an exclamation of disgust, tossed it into the hearth. "Point taken. I'll speak to Mrs. Boughey about a possible candidate for the position. What else?"

She acknowledged her victory with a cool nod. "Are you aware that Liza is afraid in the game preserve? She has nightmares about it."

"What! I believed she had overcome those fancies years ago. Why didn't she tell me?"

"You laughed at her when she told you of her dreams. A child will not invite ridicule a second time."

"The devil you say!" He sat up. "I never ridiculed Liza in my life. That one time when she told me of her dream, I tried to alleviate her fears."

She glared back at him. "Liza described her nightmares, but when I asked her if she had ever seen you hurt, she denied it."

His anger fled. Taking up his glass, he slumped against the back of his chair. "I obviously bungled. Liza did see me hurt. Shortly before her mother . . .

ah . . . died—" He broke off, cursing his tongue that still, after all these years, stumbled over the word.

"Liza was twenty months old," he said. "A lively, precocious child. She could never bear being cooped up indoors, always wanted to play outside, where she could run. Liza and her nurse were on the south lawn when I came out of the game preserve. A poacher, mistaking me for a rabbit, no doubt, had peppered my leg with shot. Have you seen a shotgun injury, Miss Elliott?"

She paled. "No, Mr. Ashcroft. But I have no doubt that it bled profusely."

"It did. Liza, unfortunately, saw me before I saw her and could retreat."

"And she remembers the blood and the game preserve in her dreams."

"But the nightmares didn't start until she was eleven," he said with a frown. "It was just after her grandmother died, I remember."

"At eleven, a child understands that death is irrevocable. Undoubtedly, her grandmother's demise filled Liza with dread of losing you, too, Mr. Ashcroft. I feel certain that she has forgotten about your old injury and believes she is dreaming about some future happening. Liza should be told immediately what she witnessed as a child."

"Miss Elliott! You must be living with your head in the clouds. There's no way Liza could have forgotten that old accident. My limp serves as a constant reminder."

"Limp?" She opened her eyes wide. "Oh, *that*," she said dismissively. "Your limp is so insignificant as to be unnoticeable. And now, if you don't mind, I'd like to discuss your refusal to let Liza go into Bath."

Damn! How she jumped around. Or, mayhap, he'd had a glass too many and was getting sluggish. So his limp was not noticeable, was it?

"Why, Mr. Ashcroft? Why cannot Liza enjoy the season in Bath?"

Her low musical voice was too dashed persistent to permit careful consideration of a reply. "Suffice it to say, Miss Elliott, that I have a very good reason to keep my daughter away from the Bath quizzes."

She shot him a look that would have made a lesser man flinch, but he continued undismayed. "Liza has no need to suffer through the boredom of assemblies and all that nonsense merely to attract a gentleman who will someday be her husband. In a sennight — ten days at the most — a friend of mine is coming down from London. He'll make the perfect husband for her."

"A friend of yours? Do you believe Liza is interested in meeting older gentlemen? She is dreaming of romance, of love, not of a father figure."

His mouth curled. *"Older* men, Miss Elliott, have more experience in fulfilling such dreams."

Momentarily disconcerted, she did not quite know how to reply.

"Or do you have reason to disagree with me, Miss Elliott?" he asked, a glint in his eyes.

"It is immaterial whether or not I agree with your views on elderly gentlemen, Mr. Ashcroft." He winced a little at *elderly*, she noted. "I am, however, more qualified than you to recognize a young girl's aspirations."

Kate rose, unable to sit still while her emotions seesawed and her temper alternately flared and cooled. "You, Mr. Ashcroft, have shown nothing but poor judgment in your dealings with Liza!"

He muttered something under his breath. It sounded very much like, "Not as poor as the day I engaged your services." But her startled look was met by one of polite inquiry.

She must have misheard, she decided, which was not surprising with all that rustling of her skirts as she paced. She stopped, facing him. "Lady Usborne issued an invitation to dinner. Tomorrow night. I accepted for Liza and myself."

One of his brows rose in that supercilious manner she was quickly coming to detest. "Am I excluded from the invitation?"

"Of course not." Again she felt the heat of temper warm her face. "But it seems that more than once *you* declined or forgot to take Liza. And perhaps," she added facetiously, "you do not wish Liza to meet the guest of honor, Lady Usborne's cousin? At least until your friend has had time to fix his interest with her?"

"Have you met Lady Usborne?" He rose and came around the desk. "No? I thought not."

Again she was aware of his powerful presence as he stood looking at her with an unreadable expression in his dark eyes. She wished she hadn't given in to impulse but had remained seated, for then the solid barrier of the desk would still be between them.

"She's a very worthy lady," he said with a faint smile. "But an utter bore. Rest assured, Miss Elliott, that Liza will be in no danger of having her head turned by any relation of Lady Usborne."

"If you say so, Mr. Ashcroft."

She gave him a sidelong look. During their ride, Hubert and Algernon had described their cousin as a Corinthian, a go amongst goers. In their eyes, Major Charles Dashwood was a Byronic hero who, by sheer daring and bravery, had single-handedly won the battle of Waterloo. And Liza was agog to meet the dashing officer.

"Is there anything else you wish to discuss, Miss Elliott?"

She was not deceived by the casual tone of his voice; she wouldn't press her luck by issuing more demands. "Some other time, Mr. Ashcroft. But, I believe, you had something to say to me."

He turned to pick up his glass. "Some other time."

She walked to the door, very much aware of his gaze following her.

"Miss Elliott," he said softly.

She stopped, her hand on the doorknob, and looked at him over her shoulder. Instead of the usual mocking curl of his mouth, she caught an expression on his face that was strongly reminiscent of Liza in her more mischievous moods.

"You still have half an hour to change for dinner, Miss Elliott. Or do you mean to fling your dress allowance at me the way you flung the silver piece?"

She stifled a laugh. "I would, Mr. Ashcroft, could I but have the satisfaction that it would smart as much."

Kate heard his chuckle even after the door had shut behind her, following her along the hallway until she reached the stairs. A new dinner gown of royal-blue silk hung temptingly in her armoire on the floor above, but with barely a check and an unconscious upward tilt of her nose, she descended to the ground floor where she had agreed to meet Liza in the morning room. He should not think that he could tease her into complaisance.

If Damien Ashcroft felt provoked by Kate's show of opposition, he concealed it well. He was affable, even charming, when he came downstairs just in time to offer an arm to each of the ladies and lead them with due ceremony into the dining room. He talked about his visit to London, sending Liza into alt with the promise that soon she'd be able to play hostess.

"To one of my *oldest* friends," he added with a glance at Kate. She met his look with limpid innocence and turned to the butler with a request for the vegetable platter.

Liza assured her father gravely that the visitor might be as old as Methuselah, and she'd welcome him so long as he promised to stay for a long, long time. She then chattered about the mares and various other matters until Kate rose, signaling that it was time for the ladies to withdraw.

"Oh, but we never observe such starchy formalities when we dine *en famille!*" cried Liza. "And I have yet to tell Papa about—"

"Best get into the habit of formality now, Princess," her father interrupted. "Besides, I have work to do. I'll be taking my port in the study, and I don't wish to be disturbed."

"Oh, very well. Good night, Papa." Liza's shoulders drooped as she left the room. She headed straight for the stairs, saying to Kate, "We may as well retire. When Papa says he does not wish to be disturbed, he often stays in his study for days at a time."

"I believe he plans to attend Lady Usborne's dinner tomorrow night," Kate said consolingly.

Liza brightened. "And he promised to ride with us in the morning."

Kate gave a small groan. "Must we? I'm not at all certain I'll be able to rise from my bed in the morning, let alone mount a horse. Do you realize that this afternoon was my first time in the saddle in . . . oh, in a decade!"

"That settles it. We'll ride before breakfast." Pushing open the door to her bedchamber, Liza gave Kate a mischievous look. "If you don't, you'll be so stiff tomorrow night that you'll creak like Mrs. Boughey's corsets."

"Forward girl!" Kate said with mock severity. Liza's words, however, came back to haunt her when she donned her black riding habit on the following morning, and when she bent to pull on boots, she was sure that her groans could be heard all along the upper floor.

It was to be hoped that Mr. Ashcroft had forgotten his vague promise to Liza. Perhaps he had spent all night in his study and only now retired to snatch a few hours of sleep. The comforting thought sustained Kate during her slow descent, and she gave a sigh of relief when she saw the foyer empty. However, her relief was short-lived.

Munching on a muffin, Liza burst through the baize curtain that hid the back stairs from view. "I was afraid you overslept, Miss Elliott! Please hurry. Papa is waiting for us in the stables."

Kate managed a smile and followed Liza across the yard. "You might have remembered *my* stomach," she said. "How can you be so utterly selfish? And where on earth did the chef find blueberries?"

"In Lady Usborne's succession houses. And I did remember you. Here!" Liza delved in the pocket of her riding coat and extracted a second napkin-wrapped muffin, which she offered to Kate.

It was thus that Damien Ashcroft, emerging from the stables with his mount, caught Miss Elliott with a blueberry smudge at precisely the spot where her luscious lower lip started to curve upward. As on the day when she wore flowers in her hair, the sight unsettled, even angered him. Yet he had no explanation for the sudden swing of his mood.

As though his stare had alerted her, Miss Elliott checked in her stride. Damien caught a glimpse of the tip of her tongue. The smudge disappeared, and instantly Miss Elliott was once again the meticulously groomed lady companion. A very dashing companion in her riding outfit.

Damien flung the reins to Hinkson, his head groom, who was leading the ladies' mares. Effortlessly, he swung Liza into the saddle, but when he turned to Miss Elliott, he found that she had made use of the mounting block and was watching him with a look that he could only interpret as triumphantly mocking. So she did not want his help, did she? But, dammit, he would have enjoyed spanning that slim waist and tossing her up into the saddle.

They rode toward the Bluebell Woods but did not enter the shelter of the trees. "It's about time I checked Lord Severeign's wall," said Damien. "Ramsden was telling me that part of it is crumbling."

Kate was content to let Liza and her father take the lead and to listen to their discussion of the eccentric neighbor who had walled and fenced his property like a fortress. Viscount Severeign stubbornly refused, even though he was in desperate need of funds, to sell as much as the arrow-shaped wedge of his land that intruded into the Dearworth acreage between the Bluebell Woods and the game preserve.

When they rounded the tip of the arrow, the bridle path widened so that they could ride three abreast. "If we jumped the wall here," said Liza, "we could visit Lord Severeign's Norman chapel. May we, Papa? I feel sure Miss Elliott would like to see it. Wouldn't you, Miss Elliott?"

"The little I learned about the viscount makes me extremely doubtful that he would welcome our intrusion," Kate said wryly.

Damien gave her a curiously twisted smile. "Your intuition is remarkable. Severeign would as soon pepper us with shot as encourage a visit to his Norman chapel."

His words about his long-ago accident echoed in her mind. He had said it had been a poacher, but . . .

Kate dismissed her suspicion. How melodramatic and imaginative she was becoming in her old age. There could be no reason for the viscount to shoot Mr. Ashcroft.

"But he's always in London," protested Liza. "You said yourself Lord Severeign can't bear being away from the gaming tables, Papa."

"Nevertheless, I forbid you to cross the boundary. And," Damien added with a smile that robbed his words of their sting, "I forbid you to jump and break your neck before our visitor arrives."

I'm not *that* cow-handed, Papa!"

Before Liza could protest further, Kate reined in. "Isn't this the spot where yesterday Hubert almost rode down our pesky twins?" she asked, pointing to the path exiting the game preserve on their left.

Successfully diverted, Liza said, "Yes, indeed. And when I wanted to tell Papa about it last night, you wouldn't let me." Turning her horse, she explained to her father, "Miss Elliott and I believe that the boys are poaching. First we caught them with slingshots, and yesterday they carried a shovel. I think they're digging traps!"

Damien nodded. "Ramsden was telling me about a pair of twins from Combe Down. As far as he knows, they've never yet caught anything."

"Couldn't hit a tree at two paces," murmured Kate, earning herself a puzzled look from Liza's father. "That's what Walter-Peter said about their ability with the slingshot."

His mouth twitched. "A pair of young hellions, I gather. Perhaps we should pay Walter-Peter a visit."

"Do you know them, Papa?"

"So far, only by hearsay."

A high-pitched scream pierced the quiet of the woods. Startled, Kate's mare whinnied and reared. Damien's hand shot out, bringing the animal under control with an iron grip on the reins.

Kate's eyes flashed. "I can handle her! I promise you, Mr. Ashcroft, when I can no longer control my mount, I shall give up riding altogether."

He dropped the rein. "We can argue the merits of my interference some other time, Miss Elliott." Setting his horse in motion, he tossed over his shoulder, "Right now, if I'm not mistaken, your pesky twins are in need of assistance."

With Liza and Kate following, Damien urged his

mount along the steadily climbing bridle path. After a short while, he slowed to a walk, motioning to his companions to do the same. He strained his ears for any slight sound, but it was not until he reached the top of the rise, the farthest point of his own property, that he heard muffled sobs and a young voice raised in argument.

"But I promise I'll be right back, Peter!" a youngster said. "I'll just fetch Ma. Surely you ain't afeared?"

A mumbling and some doleful sniffs were the only reply.

Quickly, Damien dismounted. "Tether the horses, Liza."

Without waiting for a reply, he forged through the heavy undergrowth bordering the bridle path. He didn't have far to go before he found the twins, one stretched out on the ground beside a gaping hole and the other standing protectively beside his brother.

"We've done nothin' wrong!" Damien was greeted belligerently by the upright twin.

"You don't say." Damien swept the pit and the shovel in the boy's hand with a speaking look. "You're Walter, I assume? What's wrong with your brother? Shovel fell on his toe while you were trapping?"

Peter screwed up his face in an effort to stifle his sobs, but Walter said indignantly, "We don't trap! We's excavatin'! We—" He broke off as Kate and Liza squeezed through the shrubs and joined them in the small clearing. He bowed to Kate with quaint dignity. "I say, ma'am! Me brother, he broke his leg or somethin'. Would you take a look at him?"

"Of course I will." Kate knelt beside Peter. She gave him an encouraging smile and, before examining his leg, brushed her hand across his tousled blond hair. It did not take her long to diagnose that Peter's ankle, though scratched, swollen, and already showing signs of bruising, was only sprained.

While she wrapped his foot and lower leg with strips ripped off her petticoat — and she did not miss her employer's amused look — Damien questioned Walter about their "excavating."

"Well, sir, we found the dirt caved in." He gestured. "Right here, sir. And when we was pokin' around, we found a coin like they have in the museum in Bath, and we thought if we just keep diggin', maybe we could find a treasure, don't you see?"

"I do indeed. And how did Peter sprain his ankle?"

"More dirt caved in, sir. See how big the hole is now?"

Damien squatted. With narrowed eyes, he followed the contours of the crater, then lowered himself into it. For the most part, the sunken area was no more than knee-deep, and only at the south edge did he disappear up to his waist.

"That's where it caved, and Peter fell in," said Walter.

Kate, tying the last knot of her makeshift bandage, caught an intent look on Damien's face. His hand brushed at the soft dirt on the side of the pit, then stilled and lingered as though feeling a pulse beat.

"By Jupiter!" he said reverently. "I'll eat my manuscript if this isn't part of a Roman wall."

Chapter Six

Drawn by the note of excitement in his voice, Kate approached the sunken area. She would have liked to join Damien in his exploration, but he looked up and, as though he read her mind, said, "Let us see the boys home first."

With Peter in the saddle before Damien, and Walter riding pillion behind Kate, they soon reached the small village of Combe Down—just in time to prevent a search party setting out. The boys had slipped away before their mother had risen, and when they did not return for breakfast, Rose Grimes had become worried enough to alert her neighbors. She now swooped down upon her sons, scolding and asking questions all in one breath.

When the mishap and the boy's rescue had been explained to Mrs. Grimes's satisfaction, she would not rest until the party from Dearworth stepped into her parlor and sat down to drink a dish of tea, while Walter marched off to see if he could catch the doctor before he set out on his rounds.

Mrs. Grimes entertained her company with tales of sorrow about the difficulty of raising two energetic youngsters without the help of a father's strong hand. Kate murmured a few words of commiseration, then, with a look at Peter, who promptly turned beet-red, added, "You must count yourself lucky, Mrs. Grimes, that you do not have a dozen young 'uns to raise."

75

During the exchange, Damien Ashcroft sat with an expression of intense concentration on his countenance. Not for one moment did Kate believe he was interested in the widow Grimes's tales of woe. In fact, her own thoughts strayed more than once to that fascinating glimpse of masonry she had caught in the shallow dirt cavity on the estate.

The noisy return of Walter with Dr. Bullen in tow finally provided an excuse for departure without hurting the widow's feelings. Damien briefly shook hands with Arthur Bullen, a youngish man with sandy hair and a pair of whiskers that made him look more dashing than his quiet, unassuming manner indicated.

"We'll leave you to your patient, Arthur. There will be time aplenty to get acquainted with my daughter and Miss Elliott when we see you tonight," said Damien, already shepherding his ladies out the door.

Liza cast a wistful look over her shoulder. "Dr. Bullen is quite handsome, don't you think, Miss Elliott? But," she added, after her papa had tossed her into the saddle, "I have a feeling Major Dashwood will be even more handsome."

"We shall see," said Kate, flustered because Damien Ashcroft did not cup his hands in the usual manner of assisting a lady into the saddle, but he encircled her waist and lifted her bodily as he had Liza. Warmth flushed Kate's cheeks. "Handsome is as handsome does," she muttered obscurely as she bent to adjust the skirt of her riding habit.

She need not have worried that her blush had been observed. Her employer galloped off without a backward glance, and when she and Liza caught up with him on the Dearworth estate, he handed his horse's reins to his daughter and bade her lead him home.

"Ask Hinkson and two of the stable lads to come out here with shovels and brooms," he said, a note of excitement in his voice. "And don't delay lunch-

76

eon on my account. I'll probably be here most of the day."

"May we help?" Kate blurted out.

Briefly, his eyes rested on her with approval, but he shook his head. "I must first ascertain that it's safe. Some other time, Miss Elliott."

With that, Kate had to be content. She did not see him again until evening, when the carriage was pulling up at the front door to convey them to Sir Shafto's home, and his startlingly elegant appearance drove all thought of the ruin from her mind. She was alone in the foyer. Liza, searching through her trinket box for a suitable necklace to wear with her gown of white organdy over a pale blue satin slip, had sent Kate off with instructions to forestall her papa's irritation with her tardiness.

"Won't you please go downstairs, Miss Elliott? Tell Papa I'll be ready to leave in the twinkling of a bedpost."

From her vantage point in the foyer, Kate first saw a pair of long, muscular legs encased in black pantaloons descending the stairs in a leisurely fashion; then Damien Ashcroft's slim waist came into view, and broad shoulders shown to advantage in an evening coat of dark cloth. Liza had once described her papa as "a mix of a Roman god and a Castilian nobleman." It was a very apt description of his darkly noble countenance and proud bearing.

"Miss Elliott, you frighten me. Is my coat wrinkled? My cravat askew?"

The deep voice with its inflection of mockery roused Kate from her contemplation of his sartorial elegance. "On the contrary, Mr. Ashcroft," she said with some asperity. "I was just thinking that it would require two stout men and the aid of a shoehorn to coax you into a coat that fits like a second skin."

He closed the distance between them. "And my pantaloons?"

"A lady, Mr. Ashcroft, does not consider a gentleman's nether garment."

"In that case, Miss Elliott, you are not a lady."

"And you are no gentleman."

"I never claimed to be."

In vain, Kate tried to summon <u>indignity</u>. "If your intent is to put me to the blush, you're wasting your efforts."

"Am I?"

"I doubt I ever suffered from that malady. There's nothing like a blunt brother to cure a girl of missishness." She noted the wicked gleam in his eyes with wariness. "Besides, I am well past the age of maidenly blushes."

The glint deepened. "I must have mistaken your age, Miss Elliott. I thought you no older than nine-and-twenty."

"Eight-and-twenty!"

"Just so. You were, in fact, sewing your samplers when I was sowing wild oats. But you must have realized that. You already pointed out to me just how elderly I am."

"That rankled, did it?" she said with a little smile. Kate removed the short fur cape that her mama, in an unprecedented show of affection, had bestowed on her on the occasion of her departure to Dearworth, and laid it on the hall table. Nudging one of the catkin stalks in the copper vase an infinitesimal degree to the right, Kate gave Damien Ashcroft a sidelong look. "But then, you engaged me to look after Liza's interest, not to pay you compliments."

His eyes were riveted to her new dinner gown, and for a moment he said nothing at all. Finally, he transferred his gaze to her face. "Miss Elliott," he said in a tight voice, "how can I possibly introduce you as Liza's companion?"

"I beg your pardon?"

78

"You look too young and beautiful in that gown to be anyone's chaperon." He frowned. "Sir Shafto, for one, will instantly suspect me of having evil designs on your virtue."

Kate believed he was teasing her and she said, on a chortle of laughter, "What a reputation you must have! I am surprised you dare show your face at all."

"The devil you say!" He took an impatient step toward her, tipped up her chin with a careless finger, and scrutinized her face. "I believe you to be many things, Miss Elliott, but not naive. You should know better than to go about flaunting your charms while living under the roof of a wicked rake."

A flash of anger darkened her eyes. She tossed her head, twisting her chin away from his finger. "You may be a rake, Mr. Ashcroft, but you cannot accuse me of impropriety."

"Oh?" he said silkily. "Can I not? And what about your gown, Miss Elliott?"

"My gown is perfectly appropriate for a small country dinner. Had it been left to my discretion, I admit I should have chosen a gray silk. But *you* sent the dressmaker posthaste, giving me no opportunity to inform her of my preference."

"I do not object to the color, Miss Elliott. That deep blue is eminently suitable. Even makes your eyes look blue. It's the style of the gown. I'd call it dashed provocative!"

His gaze roamed over the front of her new dinner gown, cunningly pleated in the shoulder and draped across her bosom and upper arms to reveal delectable curves and a tiny waist before falling in softly clinging folds to her ankles. A goodly bit of creamy smooth arm was visible above her long gloves, a fact he noted with strong disapprobation. And he had none to blame but himself and the damned impulse that had made him want to see her other than a drab little gray mouse.

Permitting himself one more glance at her décolletage, he noted that it wasn't as deep as he had at first feared. But what little he could see of her neck and bosom was well worth a second look. She should wear a necklace to hide some of that lustrous skin.

As he watched, the tone of her flesh deepened. "So!" he said. "You do blush after all."

"If my color is high, it is due to anger. You, sir, are insolent. Ogling me as though I were a piece of Haymarket ware!"

"Surely I am *ogling,* as you put it, my daughter's respectable companion. Surely, Miss Elliott, if you *are* appropriately gowned, you cannot read insolence into my scrutiny."

She returned stare for icy stare. "If my apparel is so highly improper, I am surprised you don't turn me off."

"So am I, Miss Elliott. Turn you off without a reference I undoubtedly should—"

"No, Papa!" Liza came tripping down the stairs. She hurtled across the tiled hall and into her father's arms. "Please don't let Miss Elliott go! What should I do without her?"

His eyes didn't leave Kate as he disengaged Liza's hands from his lapels. "Alas for my principles," he said. "My daughter appears to set great store in your companionship."

Turning to Liza, who still clung to his sleeve, he put her gently aside. "Princess, you look charming. But I must tell you that a proper young lady has no business eavesdropping. Am I not right, Miss Elliott?" he added, his voice cutting.

"Oh, undoubtedly, Mr. Ashcroft. I suspect, however, that Liza—or anyone else in this household—would have to be deaf not to overhear your words."

Sweeping aside her skirts, Kate brushed past him. She snatched up her cape, then took Liza's elbow and shepherded the girl toward the front door. "I heard the carriage when I came down, which must have been at least ten minutes ago. I am sure your papa would not want us to keep the horses standing, nor would he want to appear rag-mannered by arriving late."

Silence followed Kate's words, and silence reigned for the better part of the half-hour drive to Sir Shafto's estate. Kate sat stiffly in her corner of the carriage, Liza beside her, and Damien Ashcroft on the forward seat. Liza made one valiant attempt to engage her two companions in a discussion of Walter and Peter and their predilection for the Dearworth estate. Her father restricted his replies to monosyllables, and Miss Elliott was so obviously inattentive that she murmured assent when Liza repeated Hubert Usborne's threat to see the young varmints delivered to the gallows.

Liza's bottom lip trembled. Her very first grown-up dinner party—and it was doomed to failure due to the horrid behavior of the two people most dear to her heart. She might as well not have gone. Reading Miss Austen's novel in the seclusion of her bedchamber would have afforded more pleasure than she could expect from *this* experience. And she had so looked forward to the dinner!

These morbid reflections were dispelled when, upon arrival at the sprawling ivy-covered manor house, Hubert and Algernon pounced upon her. The brothers barely gave her time to remove her cloak before pulling her into the drawing room. A bevy of giggling, chortling, and chattering young people had gathered in the bow of one of the large windows, a strategically advantageous position that afforded a clear view of all new arrivals.

They greeted Liza with pleasure—and goggle-eyed adoration on the part of the young gentlemen—but it was obvious from impatient exclamations dropped now and again that Liza had not been the object of their keen vigilance. It was Lady Usborne's cousin they awaited with impatience and eagerness. A new face must always be welcome in their restricted circle. And if that newcomer was a hero of Waterloo, a battle five years past but still held in awe by every self-respecting Englishman and Englishwoman, they were prepared to admire and revere him—even if he should turn out closer in age to Lady Usborne than Hubert and Algy had led them to believe.

In the excitement of greeting her special friends Emily Usborne, Patience and Chloe Charteris, the vicar's offspring, and Susannah Abbots, her dear friend at Miss Venable's, Liza was the only young lady who did not cast longing glances toward the drawing room door and therefore missed the exact moment of Major Charles Dashwood's entrance. Susannah's gusty sigh and wide-eyed stare finally drew Liza's attention to the door.

She forgot what she was about to say to Patience. Her lips parted, curving in a dreamy smile. Admiration held her gaze spellbound on the splendid figure pausing just inside the room. What shoulders! What bearing! Here, indeed, stood a *man*.

The sudden change of Liza's expression was not lost on Kate. Conscious of her duties as chaperon, she had kept the girl under observation even when Lady Osborne led her clear across the spacious room to introduce her to the Reverend and Mrs. Godfrey Charteris.

"Just look at those girls, Miss Elliott," said Mrs. Charteris, breaking off in the midst of assuring Kate that her two daughters would gladly walk the distance of three or four miles from Monkton Combe to visit Liza at Dearworth. "Moonstruck! Every single one of them."

In one accord, the two ladies deserted the Reverend Charteris and started to maneuver closer to their respective charges. Following the direction of Liza's rapt gaze, Kate said wryly, "Major Dashwood, it seems, is as great a proponent of strategy as is the Duke of Wellington."

The major stood just to the left of the door, where the light of a dozen candles in a branched wall sconce danced on his chestnut hair and could not fail to show off the gold lacing on his scarlet coat. Kate judged him to be about her own age, perhaps a year or two older, and quite as tall and powerful as Damien Ashcroft. But there any likeness to her cold, haughty employer ended. The proud set of the major's head, the thrust of his shoulders, evinced discipline rather than the arrogance of Mr. Ashcroft's bearing. Major Dashwood's handsome countenance appealed, while Damien Ashcroft's saturnine features fascinated.

Kate stopped, looking toward the fireplace some distance behind her, where she had last seen Damien with Sir Shafto and Dr. Bullen. The three gentlemen had been joined by the vicar and were engaged in what appeared a most lively debate. As though she had called out to him, Damien Ashcroft turned his head. His eyes met hers across several ladies and gentlemen seated in Lady Usborne's elegant if uncomfortable "Egyptian" chairs. She expected to see him still irritated, but his expression was oddly speculative.

"A magnificent figure of a man, don't you think so, Miss Elliott?"

For one crazy instant, Kate believed Mrs. Charteris was referring to Damien Ashcroft. In the nick of time, she saw that the vicar's wife fluttered her fan toward Major Dashwood, who suddenly found himself surrounded by his young cousins and their equally youthful friends.

Firmly turning her back on her employer, Kate subjected the officer to a second judicious scrutiny. It was utterly ridiculous to use Liza's aggravating father as a measuring stick for manly attractions—and it was disturbing to find the other man wanting. A sudden chill made Kate shiver, and yet the room was warm. Coal fires lit at either end of the long chamber dispelled any draft that might creep through doors or windows, and a great number of candles in sconces and chandeliers gave off additional warmth.

"The major looks quite splendid," she said, realizing that Mrs. Charteris might misconstrue her long silence. "But then, I've heard say that a uniform can transform the plainest of men."

Mrs. Charteris laughed. "I see you're not about to be bowled over by a handsome face and the tales of unsurpassed bravery that preceded the major. I could tell at a glance that you're a young lady of sense, Miss Elliott. A bit too young, perhaps, to be in charge of a little quicksilver like Liza."

"Looks can be deceptive, can they not?" a deep voice murmured very softly in Kate's ear. Then Damien Ashcroft bowed gracefully over Mrs. Charteris's hand, leaving Kate to wonder just what he meant to imply. Not that she was old; more likely he believed her a woman of *no* sense.

"My dear Phoebe," he said, giving Mrs. Charteris one of his rare warm smiles. "How do you do? Godfrey told me you were one of the unfortunates recently struck down by influenza. I expected to see you look pulled, and here you are as lovely as ever."

"I am quite recovered, thank you, Damien." The vicar's wife was not immune to flattery. She was pink with pleasure, but she had known Damien Ashcroft too long to be overwhelmed by his charm. Her plump, good-natured features settled into severity, and a note of coolness crept into her voice. "It's good to see Liza home. Finally."

"And I see you already made Miss Elliott's acquaintance," he retorted, a hint of mockery back in his voice and eyes. "What do you think, Phoebe? Will she do—despite her youth?"

"You're outrageous, Damien!" Mrs. Charteris turned to Kate with an apologetic smile. "He always was, and I doubt he'll change. But you do not seem upset, Miss Elliott. You've lived at Dearworth how long? A week? Ten days? I must say you've become accustomed to his manner in a very short time."

"I have." Not for anything would Kate admit that she was indeed *very* annoyed. "But you forget, Mrs. Charteris—or perhaps you did not know—I taught school in Bath for several years. One of the first lessons a teacher must learn is not to be easily provoked."

"Bravo, Miss Elliott!" Mrs. Charteris beamed with approval. "That's what I call giving him his own."

Damien's mouth curled. "Phoebe, my dear, you never cease to amaze me. Your friendship and loyalty are surpassed only by your goodwill toward me." He bowed to Mrs. Charteris, then turned his attention to Kate.

She was not a small woman, but when Damien Ashcroft bent his gaze on her, Kate was aware that he had to look down. His lids drooped and his lashes—she still thought them outrageously long—hid the expression in his dark eyes.

"Laudable sentiments, Miss Elliott. It is to be hoped that one day I shall have the privilege of observing the results of those lessons in self-restraint. Shall we go and see if we can pry Liza away from the dashing major?"

It was very hard, but she exercised that restraint now. With a murmured excuse to Mrs. Charteris, Kate placed her hand on Mr. Ashcroft's proffered arm. Under the cloth of his sleeve, his muscles contracted, and as on that day in The Circus when she clutched at him for support, she could not help but think that he would like to shake her off.

85

He whisked her around a chaise longue occupied by gossiping matrons. "Just look at Liza!" he said, not bothering to disguise his annoyance. "She's all but hugging the coxcomb. You're supposed to keep an eye on my daughter, not stand by and watch her make a cake of herself."

"I am not standing by. If you walk much faster," she pointed out as he charged on at a pace more suited to the open fields than a drawing room, "it will be you who is making a cake of himself. Do you want the company to think you're loping off with me?"

"And Phoebe thought *me* outrageous." He frowned at her but slowed to a casual amble.

"Thank you, Mr. Ashcroft," she said in a tone heavy with irony. "Why the rush? Liza will come to no harm with the major. I distinctly remember what you said to me on the subject."

"I had not counted on his uniform, Miss Elliott. I believed he had sold out."

They had almost reached the major, still holding court near the doorway. Kate could see signs of dissipation on Major Dashwood's handsome countenance—puffiness around the eyes, a heaviness of jowls and chin. Yet his appeal was undiminished. His head was bent attentively to Liza's golden one, and it was painfully obvious that the girl was enthralled by every word he uttered.

"You believe," Kate said musingly, "he would appear less splendid without the scarlet coat?"

"So you find him splendid. How like a woman! Let me speak plainly, Miss Elliott. I—"

"Do you ever speak otherwise?" she murmured, her attention on Liza and the major. "Oh!"

He had stopped so suddenly and swung around to face her that only by flinging out a hand and pushing against his chest did she avert full-tilt collision. "What the dickens!"

Her startled look changed to one of dismay at the sight of his face. His dark skin could not hide the fact that he had paled. The set of his jaw made her wish she were an ant and might disappear in a crack between the oaken floorboards. This time, she had truly gone too far—betrayed by her unruly tongue.

She raised a brow in what she hoped was a fair imitation of his "haughty" look and squared up to his ire, but still he said nothing. In the charged silence between them, the buzz of conversation in the drawing room swelled until she was forcefully reminded of a raging ocean pounding a rocky shore.

His fingers closed around her elbow like a vise. Before she could gather her wits, he propelled her past Major Dashwood and his admiring acolytes, past a goggling footman in the foyer, and into another chamber. A candelabrum set atop the mantel shelf shed sufficient light to disclose a desk, several armchairs, and well-stocked bookcases along two of the walls. Though deep and lofty, the room seemed far too small to hold both her and her captor, whose grip on her arm bespoke tightly controlled fury soon to be unleashed.

Kate heard the door shut. Her arm was abruptly freed. She might have run, yet all she could do was sink into the nearest chair. She would have appreciated a glass of wine or even water, but Damien Ashcroft did not ask her wants.

Chapter Seven

He towered above her, intent only on venting the stormy emotions that had started to build in him since he saw her with bluebells in her hair. Since he discovered that she had entered his home under false colors. He was in such a passion that he did not ask himself why it should have been her ogling the major that snapped the tight control he had kept on his feelings for so long.

"From the outset, you were determined to pull caps with me," he said, forcing the words through gritted teeth lest he shout to raise the rooftop. "Were you not, Miss Elliott?"

I—"

"You were determined to oppose me!"

"Mr. Ashcr—"

"You do not like the way I deal with Liza. You disapprove of every one of my decisions regarding my daughter."

She could not deny that charge.

"You flaunt my authority! You're waspish and argumentative."

She considered rising, but he stood too close. "Mr. Ashcroft, permit me to point—"

"You interrupt. You're too assertive. You invade my study and take me to task as though you were mistress of my house."

"I daresay I broke your stupid rules." Her eyes flashed. "But if you want—"

"You did!" he cut in savagely. "And what I want to know is why the devil you accepted this post if everything about me antagonizes you?"

"I am fond of Liza."

"Ha!" His finger jabbed at her. "And so you schemed and deceived. And I was fool enough to swallow the picture of meekness you presented."

Her temper flared. "Yes, Mr. Ashcroft. You were."

A jerk went through his body. His hand clenched.

Kate remembered her brother's rare but wild rages. She raised an arm instinctively, as though prepared to ward off a blow.

A dunking in arctic waters could not have doused Damien's anger more effectively. His fist dropped. He felt drained, even ashamed. But what the devil had *he* done to feel ashamed? It was she who had committed outrageous deceit. If Liza had aided and abetted her in the scheme . . . well, Liza was a child and knew no better.

He regarded his daughter's companion with coldness. "You need not cower, Miss Elliott. I shall not hit you."

She returned his stare without a blink, and only a quickly suppressed tremor of her mouth betrayed her distress. Steeling himself against the unconscious appeal to his chivalry, he said curtly, "I shall not, however, tolerate blatant disrespect of my authority. You, Miss Elliott, must learn to curb your unruly tongue."

She rose, her head held high. "I shall pack my trunks and be gone by the time you return to Dearworth."

"And how will you get to Dearworth, Miss Elliott?"

"I'll walk if I must." Her smile mocked. She sank into an over-elaborate curtsy, then started purposefully toward the door.

89

Dammit! But she had backbone. He admired spunk in a woman. Never could stand a mealy-mouthed toadeater. So why the deuce did her behavior aggravate him?

Two more steps would take her out of his life. And out of Liza's.

"Miss Elliott . . ."

She spun, a picture of outraged dignity. "Must you always have the last word? Once, just once, Mr. Ashcroft, you might concede to me the victory of a dignified exit!"

His sudden bark of laughter was as unexpected as it was appealing. "I should have known," he said. "Kate the shrew."

He reached her in a few strides. One arm encircled her waist, the other cupped her face. This, he realized as he bent his head to hers, was what he had wanted to do for a long time. Miss Elliott's contrariness might arouse his ire, but it was all of her provocative self that played havoc with his carefully banked desires. His mouth covered hers with ruthless disregard of her startled gasp, and the sweetness of her lips drove rational thought from his mind.

The sudden passionate assault robbed Kate of breath and reason. Feeling as though she were caught in a whirlwind, she clutched at the cloth of his coat. Her senses reeled; she did not know if she were floating on air or sinking to the depth of a bottomless pool. It was a heady sensation. Glorious.

Full mental powers returned with startling clarity. Kate Elliott, respectable duenna, stood with both feet firmly on the floor of Sir Shafto's dimly lit study—locked in Damien Ashcroft's arms! And—perish the thought!—she was enjoying every moment of his embrace. Even more so did she relish his highly improper kiss.

Kate placed her hands against the hard chest that was such unexpectedly comfortable support. She gave a tentative push and to her disappointment found herself instantly released. For a moment they stared at each other—he inscrutable, she with an expression of bafflement on her face.

Why had he kissed her—and with every appearance of satisfaction? "I believed you a misogynist!"

Again he burst out laughing, as he had done before his assault. Kate could not help but notice how such a seemingly irrelevant act transformed his face. He looked almost handsome. Definitely younger. She had judged him to be about five-and-forty. Now she doubted he had seen his fortieth anniversary.

"Whatever will you say next, Miss Elliott? And whatever gave you that notion?"

"Is it not on your order that the maids leave the house just as soon as they've finished dusting and polishing? Did you not refuse Mrs. Boughey the help of a scullery maid even though the boot boy breaks more dishes than he washes? Did you not, initially, refuse Liza the services of a maid?"

He held up a hand. "Say no more! I know when I am bested. But did you not know, Miss Elliott," he asked, smiling wickedly, "that even a misogynist must now and again submit to the lure of woman?"

Kate took a step backward. "I daresay. Pray remember, though! This is hardly the time to discuss such matters. I was on the point of leaving when you so rudely manhandled me."

At once, he turned serious. "The carriage is at your disposal should you still wish to leave. But I'd appreciate it, Miss Elliott, if you would reconsider."

She widened her eyes at him. "Are you, by chance, apologizing?"

"Not for the kiss. I will, though, for losing my temper."

She looked at him expectantly, but he said no more. To him, apparently, a declaration of intent was paramount to an actual apology. "And you're asking me to stay on as Liza's companion?"

"Until she's safely betrothed or married."

"In spite of my waspish, shrewish temperament, Mr. Ashcroft?"

"If you will overlook an occasional outburst of rudeness on my part," he said, his expression wry, "I'll ignore your prickliness."

"Humph." True, she'd like to accept his offer. In her temper, she had not given a thought to Liza. The girl would need her companionship and support more than ever when Mr. Ashcroft's mysterious friend arrived—a man old enough to be Liza's father.

But then there was Damien Ashcroft—obviously not too old to kiss his daughter's companion.

"Fainthearted, Miss Elliott?" Damien asked softly.

"On the contrary. I find it a challenging proposition."

He held out his hand to seal the bargain, a gesture that both touched and disquieted her. A handshake was as binding as a written promise.

She clasped his outstretched hand. Did she imagine it, or was there a gleam of triumph in his dark eyes?

"Reservations, Miss Elliott?"

She thought his expression smug and withdrew her hand. "Let there be no misunderstanding. If I remain—for Liza's sake—there must be no repeat of your most improper conduct. I neither invited nor, let me assure you, shall I suffer your unwelcome advances without retribution should you be so unwise as to repeat them."

"I promise you," he replied, his solemn voice oddly at variance with a devilish look in his eyes, "I shall not subject you to any uninvited embraces."

She raised a brow. "Your promise, sir, leaves much to be desired. But, very well. I shall stay with Liza, at least until she is betrothed."

"Let us rejoin the company, then," he said briskly. "But first, permit me to secure one or two of the pins in your hair."

"Much obliged. I'm sure I can—" As he made a move to follow up on his offer, she retreated another step and pushed the pins firmly in place. The last thing she needed now was his touch on her hair, a reminder of how the pins had loosened in the first place.

When they emerged from the study, Sir Shafto and Lady Usborne were leading their guests through the foyer into the "baronial dining hall," as Lady Usborne fondly referred to the vast chamber with its high vaulted ceiling, its life-size murals depicting hunting scenes, and its overpowering gilt and crimson decor.

Kate saw Mrs. Charteris and one or two of the other ladies give her curious looks, and she hurriedly made her way to Liza's side.

"Oh, Miss Elliott! I've been looking for you. I want you to meet Major Dashwood." Blushing, Liza raised her glowing face to the officer who, to the very obvious envy of the Misses Emily, Patience, Chloe, and Susannah, had singled out the young lady from Dearworth.

Shaking hands with the major, Kate found herself looking into a pair of green eyes that regarded her with wariness and speculation. She could not like that look, nor his smile—practiced and suave but lacking in warmth. Her impression of a dissipated ladies' man was strongly enforced when he held her hand longer than necessary and said, "I am charmed, Miss Elliott. Miss Ashcroft has sung your praises until I was prepared to wager that such a paragon of virtue and loveliness could not possibly exist. I admit to being totally and utterly in the wrong."

"And I was prepared to take Hubert and Algernon

to task for bragging." With barely concealed distaste, Kate disengaged her hand. "But they're young; no judges of character as yet. A few more years in their dish and, I daresay, they will realize that your social skills equal, if not surpass, your prowess on the battlefield."

His mouth tightened, but he did not allow his anger to show for long. Summoning an easy, charming smile, he turned to Liza, who had been listening to the exchange with a puzzled look on her face. "A compliment from your Miss Elliott," he said with a chuckle. "I daresay that is high praise indeed."

"If it *was* a compliment." A tiny frown marred the smoothness of Liza's forehead, but before she could question Kate, footmen ushered them to their seats at the long dining table. Major Dashwood, the guest of honor, took his place beside the hostess, Liza was shown to a chair between Algernon and Dr. Bullen, and Kate, to her astonishment, was seated to Sir Shafto's right.

"Knew your father," the squire greeted her in his booming voice.

Her breath caught, rendering her incapable of making a reply. But her confusion went unnoticed, for Sir Shafto spoke up again. "A capital rider to hounds was Sir Hugo. Saw him every year at Melton-Mowbray and, of course, at Ascot and Newmarket. Do you hunt, Miss Elliott?"

"I don't. My favorite event has always been the steeplechase." Kate's breathing returned to normal. "Papa and I used to be bitter rivals," she said, smiling a little. It had been a long time since anyone had talked to her of her papa. The dowager only sighed and reached for her cordial when her late husband's name was mentioned, and Richard still came close to an apoplexy, for all he remembered were the sums of money his father had spent on horses and at the races—money lost to Richard.

While she listened to Sir Shafto's glowing accounts of various exciting hunts, Kate glanced from face to face. No one looked at her askance. None of the ladies seemed to mind that Liza's companion—baronet's daughter or not—was placed above her. Phoebe Charteris caught her look and smiled, as did stern-faced Mrs. Abbots, Susannah's mother. Kate's eyes met Damien Ashcroft's and again, as in the drawing room, she noted that he watched her with an oddly speculative look.

Resolutely, Kate turned away and directed her attention back to Sir Shafto.

Damien laid down his shovel and stretched. He had been out since the first light of day, steadily scraping and digging until only a thin layer of dirt remained on the length of wall he and the stable lads had traced the previous day. Now the sun stood overhead, warming his neck and shoulders. He would dig no more until he had made a close study of the site.

Using a brush and his fingertips, Damien started to bare the ancient masonry. It was slow, painstaking labor, and the thought occurred to him that Miss Elliott, with her long, slender fingers, might be of assistance. His mouth curled. She had asked if she might help, but the offer had no doubt been made in a spurt of curiosity—curiosity that would wane as quickly as her submission to his embrace.

"Helloo!"

Recognizing the voice, Damien bit down an exclamation of annoyance. Good-natured and jovial as Sir Shafto was, he was also long-winded and nosy. *Mayhap I shouldn't have cleared the brush from the bridle path to the excavation site,* Damien thought wryly as the squire guided his powerful, raw-boned gelding through the trees.

"So you really believe you may have found some

old ruin?" Dismounting, Sir Shafto eyed the patch of masonry Damien had cleaned. "Think it might be a Roman villa? Like those found at Witcombe last year?"

Damien climbed out of the trench. "It's early days yet to say what this might be, Sir Shafto, save that it's part of a Roman structure. Bits of colored stone I found while we dug indicate there might be a mosaic beneath all this rubble. If there is, then I'll know it to be a building of some significance."

"Well, I wish you luck, Ashcroft. M'wife was saying only this morning how good it'd be to have you home for more than a few weeks at a time. Nothing better than a Roman villa to keep you here, eh?"

"Even without the lure of discovery I shall remain at least until Liza is settled."

"Hmm. Thinking of launching your gal, are you? A bit young, your Liza. But, I daresay, with Miss Elliott to show her the ropes, she'll come to no harm."

Absorbed in wiping his hands on a piece of toweling, Damien did not look at Sir Shafto. "You are acquainted with the Elliott family, I take it?"

"Knew Sir Hugo," the squire said cheerfully. "A capital fellow. She has the looks of him, your Miss Kate."

"There is a brother, I believe."

"Hmm, yes. Richard Elliott." Sir Shafto gave a grunt when the gelding's forehead pushed none too gently against his shoulder. He patted the sleek neck, then released a bit of rein to allow the horse exploration of the young greens sprouting on the forest floor.

"His father called him a dull stick and worse," he said. "Married the oldest Astley girl. A whey-faced, sharp-tongued harridan if ever I saw one." The squire chuckled. "No wonder Sir Hugo cocked up his toes shortly after his son's nuptials. And no wonder

Miss Elliott prefers governessing to sharing a roof with her sister-in-law."

Damien tossed the towel aside. The white cloth caught on a hazelnut bush, dangling for a moment like a limp flag. *A flag of truce. A handshake with Miss Elliott.*

The towel dropped. Absently, Damien nudged it aside with his foot. Miss Elliott's position at the school, her clothing, had all pointed to an impoverished if genteel background. Then, last night at the dinner, Sir Shafto had disclosed that she was the daughter of a baronet. Listening to the squire now as he reminisced about Sir Hugo Elliott's feats, the splendid hunters he had ridden, his race horses and beautifully matched carriage horses, it became increasingly difficult to reconcile his image of Miss Elliott as he had first seen her with that of a daughter of the sporting-mad Sir Hugo.

"But, of course, all that was years ago," said Sir Shafto, catching Damien's full attention. "Come to think of it, Sir Hugo has been underground for a dozen years or more."

"No doubt, then, the family has fallen on hard times."

"That I wouldn't know. Never met Sir Richard — he doesn't hold with hunting or racing — and never laid eyes on Elliott Chase, their estate somewhere near Ilchester if I recollect rightly."

Sir Shafto received another, even more forceful nudge from his horse, but he ignored it. He gave Damien a hard stare. "Seems to me, you should know more about the gal than I. After all, 'twas you who hired her. Didn't you ask about her background?"

Damien didn't relish being found out in a neglect. "What was there to ask? The headmistress recommended her, my Liza wanted her, and she seemed suitable for my purposes."

The squire's rumbling laughter exploding in the stillness startled the gelding and some birds nesting in the high beech trees. With cries of alarm and much flapping of wings, the feathered homebuilders took flight.

"Your purposes, eh? I can imagine what they were." Wheezing, Sir Shafto pushed the horse's nose toward a tuft of tender grass. "And now I've thrust a spoke in your wheel by telling you she's quality!"

"You quite mistake the matter," Damien said coldly, but the older man didn't listen.

"Never thought to see you blunder, Ashcroft. Even my boys, green as they are, knew she was quality the moment Liza introduced them to her. And Phoebe Charteris and the wife . . . well, you should have heard Louisa! Couldn't say enough about Miss Elliott's elegance and refinement. If Hubert were a few years older, Louisa'd be planning a match between him and Miss Elliott. As it is, she'll no doubt try to throw Dashwood in her way."

"Excellent." A vein throbbed in Damien's temple. "Lady Usborne could not have chosen a better mate for the major. Miss Elliott perfectly matches him in flamboyance and arrogance."

"Flamboyant?" Sir Shafto puffed his cheeks as he pondered. "Now, if you had called her attractive, even striking, I would have agreed. She has poise, your Miss Elliott. And not once did she show that I'm a foolish old man who bored her with tales of his wilder days. She's what I call a lady."

The squire mussed his horses's clubbed mane. "Come along, old fellow. We have invitations to deliver." Hefting himself into the saddle, he grinned down at Damien. "A picknick! Would you believe it? The prospect of matchmaking must have turned Louisa's head. I'll eat my saddle if we don't have snow again."

Through narrowed eyes, Damien looked after Sir

Shafto as he guided his gelding back to the bridle path. He gave no sign of having heard when, just before passing out of sight, the older man called over his shoulder, "You're invited, too. It's on Saturday."

"A lady," Damien muttered. He had never doubted that Miss Elliott was a lady. A not-yet-acknowledged desire to seduce that same lady was firmly banished.

His booted foot nudged the piece of toweling, kicking and tossing it until it rested atop a block of sandstone he had dug out earlier. An attractive lady, Miss Elliott. Yes, and more. Had no one but he noticed? Her eyes, her smile, her figure provoked. Appealed to a man's senses.

Fool!

The clop-clop of many hooves on the bridle path and the sound of voices carrying through the unseasonably warm air put a halt to thoughts that could lead nowhere. Damien stepped into the trench and picked up his brush. Yet he did not resume his labor; he listened. The hoofbeats ceased, but the voices, after a moment, came closer. The riders must have tethered the horses. He could hear Sir Shafto again, Liza, and Miss Elliott. And a second male voice. Warm and suave. Liza's tinkling laughter. Miss Elliott's tones, dry, quelling. Caustic? Louisa Usborne would not have an easy victory if she planned a match between her precious cousin and Liza's companion.

And then they were upon him. Major Dashwood, handsome and bold in his regimentals, a striking contrast to Damien's dirt-streaked leather breeches and rolled-up shirtsleeves. Miss Elliott . . . But his eyes passed over her quickly, fastening on his daughter instead.

"Papa! Papa!" As always when she was excited, Liza could not stand still. "Miss Elliott wanted to come out here to help you, but Major Dashwood

99

invited us to ride with him. Please say you don't need us. You never like help with your work, do you, Papa? Pray tell Miss Elliott so."

Even though he stood in the crater dug by the stable lads, his eyes were still level with Liza's. Never had his daughter looked more beautiful to him. She was radiant, no longer a girl but a young woman. He looked at the major and felt the stirring of anger in his breast. The man's air of complacence, his smugness, left no doubt that he knew what he was about and considered Liza's enthusiasm as his due.

Devil a bit! He should have insisted that Nicholas come to Dearworth immediately. Nicholas should have been the man to awaken Liza to womanhood, not some perishing half-pay officer.

Propping his left foot against the slanting side of the trench, Damien flicked the soft brush against his daughter's chin. "You're wrong, Princess. But a moment ago I was yearning for help. Your and Miss Elliott's nimble fingers would be very much appreciated, I assure you."

Liza wavered. Papa had never before requested her help, but never before had she been asked to ride out with a dashing officer. A real man, not a mere boy.

"We'll plan a riding party for tomorrow," suggested Kate, and was rewarded with an approving nod from her employer. "Hubert and Algy may wish to come, and perhaps Emily and Susannah?"

Liza clapped her hands. "What fun! And if Sir Shafto"— she swung around with a coaxing smile for the squire who had stayed in the background— "will provide mounts, I'm sure Patience and Chloe will be glad to join us. Mayhap we could ride as far as Wells. We could eat luncheon there and look at the cathedral and, oh, all kinds of things!"

It seemed as though matters would be settled to everyone's satisfaction, but then Major Dashwood said softly, "Cruel fates! What have I done, Miss

Ashcroft, that you wish to punish me?"

The sun reflected in his eyes, making them glow like emeralds. Liza's heart skipped a beat. He wanted to be with her. Now. He did not want to wait until tomorrow. And neither did she wish to wait. She heard her father's derisive snort and knew a setdown for Major Dashwood was forthcoming. *Oh, please . . .*

The squire's voice boomed out. "Perhaps Miss Elliott could stay to help excavate, and I'll chaperon our little Miss Liza until we've found Emily and my boys. There can be no harm in the chit's riding with her oldest friends and their cousin."

With a squeal of joy, Liza hugged the squire. Surely Sir Shafto's clever suggestion had come in answer to her silent prayer. Spinning on her heel, she rushed off but turned back to grab Sir Shafto's arm and drag him with her. "If we dawdle, the boys may take it into their heads to ride off to a cock fight or some bloody mill."

"There are no fights or mills this morning, missy." The squire huffed and puffed but nevertheless moved as fast as his stout form permitted.

Liza looked over her shoulder. "Hurry, Major Dashwood!"

Charles Dashwood locked eyes with the impatient young lady's father. "Well, Ashcroft," he said with a curl of his fleshy mouth. "Do you wish to call your daughter back?"

"I wish you joy," Damien said acidly. "Few men would choose to accompany a nursery party on an outing."

The major bowed and stalked off. Damien scowled at the three retreating backs. He had seen the gleam of deviltry in Sir Shafto's eyes when he made the outrageous suggestion. Certainly there was no harm in Liza's riding out with Emily Usborne and accompanied by several gentlemen, two of whom had known her from the cradle. But, by George, he didn't like it!

And Miss Elliott would be alone with him.

He looked at his daughter's companion and caught her poised to run after Liza, but with her eyes longingly on the bit of exposed Roman wall. He felt a grin tugging at the corners of his mouth. This was a rare moment of indecision for the decisive Miss Elliott, and she wouldn't thank him if she knew that he had noticed.

Yet her interest in his excavation was genuine, no mere curiosity. The knowledge lightened his mood.

"The devil fly away with Sir Shafto and his notions," he said cheerfully. He held out his hand to help her into the trench. "I must admit, though, I have never had such a charming assistant."

whom had two or her Jane, thoughts of Tun. In
George, he didn't have Gas in future pas.
And Miss Elliot should not have met him.

Chapter Eight

Raising the skirt of her riding habit, Kate stepped
down into the trench. "You should not have given
permission," she said, firmly shutting the door on
further compliments her unpredictable employer
might be inclined to bestow on her. She had not
lain awake half the night, torn by conflicting emotions over his kiss, only to have her hard-won decision overset by further intimacies. She had vowed to
dismiss the incident from her mind. To forget it
totally.

She arched a brow. "You should have supported
my suggestion to wait until tomorrow. The presence
of several young ladies would have made it extremely difficult for the major to monopolize and
charm Liza."

"My daughter is a romantic young fool. Had I
forbidden her to go with Dashwood today, she
would have immediately scented star-crossed love."

"You might have refused my help here." Kate
looked about her. "What *am* I to do? I haven't the
faintest notion how to go about archaeological digging."

Damien handed her a brush and a small knife.
"Just clean the masonry without destroying inscrip-
tions or drawings if there are any." Then, in the
same matter-of-fact tone, he added, "I had no intention of refusing your assistance. I've been wanting to talk with you."

Kate subjected the Roman wall to an experimental scrape. "Oh? Have I been insubordinate again?"

"On the contrary. I find that you've been too reticent. Where is your home, Miss Elliott?"

There was a sinking feeling in her stomach. "Are you asking where was I born? Surely Miss Graintree at the school did not keep that a secret from you?"

"You mentioned a brother to me. A brother who would not stand for missishness. Is he Sir Richard Elliott of Elliott Chase?"

He knew! Sir Shafto must have remembered. And he had informed Damien Ashcroft of her humiliation, her disgrace.

"You look stricken, Miss Elliott."

He stood close. His presence enveloped her, making it difficult to formulate a reply.

"Why is it that you do not wish to be reminded of your brother?"

"We are not on speaking terms." She stooped, scraping away at the masonry with a will. "This pit is too small for both of us. If I'm to do neat work, you will have to find someplace else to stand."

"Very well, Miss Elliott."

Her eyes never left the bit of wall she was cleaning while he moved to higher ground. Yet she was certain that if she looked at him, she'd see his face alight with cynical amusement. He was the sort of man who would know why she wanted him at a distance.

"I'll sift through the rubble we dug up yesterday," he said. "After all, Walter-Peter found a bronze coin. There may be more, or shards of ceramic."

For a while they worked, their silence covered by the stirring and rustling of the woods and the rasping of their tools. Kate thought about the past years of her life. Eleven years, which she had spent at Miss Venable's Seminary for Young Ladies. Like a nun secluded in a convent. She had made friends of the other teachers, had occasionally been asked to join their families for a holiday, but outside the school she had seen only Lady Elliott and her two attendants, Nurse Peevey and Dr. Thistlethwaite. When Margaret and the children came to visit the dowager, Richard would write to Kate, forbidding her to go to Queen's Square during that time. Kate had considered ignoring his order but decided in the end to let it go. There was no point in spilling the bitterness into the children's lives as well.

And there was much bitterness. Resentment of Richard and his treatment of her welled anew. She could not forgive that he had made public her humiliation, then cast her off, locking her away at school.

By the time she had reached her majority and was at liberty to go her own way, she was an established school mistress. She had realized that she did not wish to exchange her post at the seminary for a life with Richard and Margaret, or in her mother's hothouse rooms.

The school had meant independence; it had also left her vulnerable, as her quick surrender to Damien Ashcroft's arms had proven.

An image flashed through her mind of a slight, golden-haired young man with adoring eyes the color of the sapphire he had planned to buy for her ring. Planned. Promised. They had not been allowed to exchange vows.

What a fool she was, stirring the ashes of memories best forgotten. What a fool, believing that anyone who remembered her family would also remember the scandal.

A foolish spinster, who found it impossible to forget a single meaningless kiss.

The knife slipped from her fingers. Her hand

shook. Carefully, she wiped it on the skirt of her riding habit.

"I suggest that next time you plan to help, you wear one of your old gowns," Damien said dryly.

Startled, she spun to face him where he worked not far from her—one knee on the ground, a small trowel in his hand, a mound of dirt to one side of him and another mound that he had already examined on the other.

"Next time," she said, blinking. "Oh, yes. Next time I surely will."

Damien laid down the trowel. "You look as though you've seen a ghost." He swung his legs over the edge of the trench and sat, staring at her. "Is it because I spoke of your brother? If you dislike it so much, I shan't ask any more questions. After all, most families count a black sheep or two among their number."

"Even your family?"

She had spoken to keep the conversation turned from her and her brother. She had not expected to see pain shadow his face. "I beg your pardon," she murmured. "I did not mean to—"

"It does not matter," he interrupted. "Your comment evoked a stray thought. That is all." He rose, paced for a moment as though his leg needed limbering, then briskly set about his task of sifting through the rubble.

Picking up the knife and brush, Kate, too, concentrated on her work. A stray thought. No more. That was all her own memory had been. And as for the rest, she had known she might have to face recognition when she accepted the post as Liza's companion. She must accustom herself to being asked about her family, must learn not to jump every time she was questioned.

"I shall have to go into Bath next week," she said,

106

"to see my mother."

"Send word to the stables when you wish to go. Hinkson or Henry will drive you."

"Thank you. I thought to invite Liza to join me. Mrs. Moppit recommended a haberdasher in Gate Street who has all the silk and velvet ribbons a young lady might require."

In the silence that followed her words, the scraping of her knife against stone was unnervingly loud. She switched to the brush.

Suddenly Damien gave a bark of laughter. "You don't trust me to keep her away from the dashing major, do you? Very well. Take her to see your mother. But take the maid as well. There's no need for you to cut your visit short merely to chaperon my daughter while she buys a ribbon."

Slowly, Kate turned. "Liza's maid!"

A corner of his mouth curled. "Liza's maid!" he mimicked. "Your faith in my word unmans me. Didn't I say I'd arrange it?"

"Yes. But—"

"Doubting Kate! Rest easy. One of Mrs. Boughey's London nieces will be arriving by the weekend."

Kate did not mind his mocking. It was the victory that counted. Two victories, although she would not consider the Bath visit a total success until Liza made an appearance in the Pump Room and the theater and . . .

"Liza will be thrilled," she said. "And if Mama is not having one of her spells, we'll take tea at the Assembly Rooms."

"No."

The flat refusal left no room for argument. Yet Kate tried. "It's not as though I were planning to attend a ball with Liza. There's nothing more sedate and decorous than tea at the Assembly Rooms."

"I do not wish to see my daughter in the Assembly Rooms or in the Pump Room. Not even in one of the lending libraries. There are copies of all the latest novels here at Dearworth, and if I overlooked a publication, you have only to inform me of it."

Kate's withering reply was never uttered, for Damien's gamekeeper came striding toward them. In one hand Mr. Ramsden carried his fowling piece; the other propelled a boy by the scruff of his skinny neck. A towheaded, barefooted boy who stared at Damien with a mixture of apprehension and excitement.

"One of Rose Grimes's twin brats," said Mr. Ramsden with a little shake to the boy's neck.

"I'm Walter! And ye needn't hold me collared as though I was gonna hare off! I was plannin' to come here anyways an' have a word with Mr. Ashcroft."

The wiry gamekeeper paid no heed. "Caught him just as he was coming over Lord Severeign's wall, Mr. Ashcroft. If I've warned him and his brother off your property once, I've warned them off a dozen times. To no avail. I turn my back, and there they are again."

"His brother won't be out for a day or two." Damien rose, towering above Walter. "And if you'd take a lesson from his book, my boy, you wouldn't be climbing that wall. It's crumbling. You could end up in worse shape than Peter if it collapsed."

Walter tore his fascinated gaze away from the pieces of shard Damien had found. "No coins, sir? Can I help? I know 'xactly what to look for."

Damien's face registered impatience and annoyance. Sensing a brusque denial, Kate forestalled him. "Mr. Ramsden, please let go of Walter. I really don't think he'll run off."

And when the boy rubbed at the smarting impressions left by the gamekeeper's callused fingers, she gave him an encouraging wink. "How is Peter's ankle? Was my diagnosis correct?"

"Aye. It's sprained, ma'am. But not badly." Walter's freckled face split in a mischievous grin. "Dr. Bullen told Ma to stop fretting about him bein' quiet an' all. By tomorrow — or latest the next day — Peter will be hisself again. A menace to the neighborhood."

"I suspect," said Damien, "that *you* are the instigator of any deviltry, with Peter following your lead."

Walter accepted this as tribute. "How about it, sir? Can I help? And Peter, too, when he's better?"

Looking at the boy's eager face, Kate held her breath.

"I doubt you'd take no for an answer," Damien said wryly. "You may be my assistant tomorrow when Miss Elliott will be otherwise engaged. But — " He held up his hand, cutting short Walter's shout of pleasure. His face was set in the cold, forbidding lines Kate remembered well from her early encounters with him, and his voice held an edge of sharpness that must be intimidating to the most daring eleven-year-old.

"If I catch you or your brother here at the site when I've not specifically requested your company," he said, "you'll have a taste of my crop. Excavating is no child's play. We don't know what lies below ground, or if there'll be another cave-in. Do you understand?"

Walter stood ramrod straight. "Aye, sir. We'll come only when we're bidden." His dignity vanished, and he added breathlessly, "Besides, ye wouldn't want me an' Peter to be the ones to find the treasure. You'll want to be here yerself."

Damien chuckled. "I doubt you'd know the treasure if it slapped your face."

"I'd know, Mr. Ashcroft! I've heard all about the bronze an' silver an' gold treasures found by men who excavated on the downs. I'd know! Believe me."

"They're spoilers, Walter. Greedy artifact hunters, digging, shoveling carelessly and destroying more than they gain with their finds."

Walter looked at him uncomprehendingly, and Damien rubbed his forearm across his brow as though the gesture could erase the image of the history spoilers.

"Go on home now, Walter," he said with one of his rare, open smiles. "Tomorrow is soon enough to introduce you to the art of archaeological study."

"And mind you don't use the stone wall as an entryway, Kate reminded the boy as he started to walk away.

"Yes, ma'am."

Mr. Ramsden, following Walter, threatened, "You heed Mr. Ashcroft and Miss Elliott, you little gallows bait. Else you'll find yourself at the receiving end of my fowling piece!"

Noting the frown Kate sent after the boy and the gamekeeper, Damien said, "He wouldn't, you know. Ramsden is all bark and no bite."

Kate got busy with her knife and brush. Of course it was a relief to know that Mr. Ramsden wouldn't shoot at Walter and Peter, but worry about the twins was not what had made her frown. She had been wishing she could trade places with Walter. She began to wonder if she could persuade Liza to give up the notion of a ride to Wells—an undertaking that would occupy all day. Perhaps Liza could be coaxed into helping her father instead.

When the young lady finally returned from her ride, however, and burst into Kate's room less than an hour before dinner, Kate had changed her mind. A preference of old ruins to Liza's needs was what she had held against Damien Ashcroft. Kate would not be guilty of that same selfish neglect. That she had second thoughts about spending time in Damien's company she dismissed as a reason too cowardly to be considered.

Kate looked at Liza and felt a stab of apprehension. The girl was aglow and bubbling with excitement over the past ride and the entertainment planned for the morrow. Mrs. Charteris, Liza explained, had not given permission for Patience and Chloe to ride to Wells. It was too much exertion for Chloe, who was not strong. The weather worried Mrs. Charteris. It was too warm for early April. A quick, drastic change was sure to come about, and the riders might find themselves battered by hail or icy rain. Instead, the reverend's good lady had suggested they show Major Dashwood over those parts of the immediate neighborhood that he had not yet visited and then come to the vicarage, where she would serve tea and cakes in the pavilion Reverend Charteris had built in the vast garden.

After these disclosures, Liza's conversation deteriorated to a rapturous account of what Major Dashwood had said and done, what he had praised and what he disparaged, until Kate sent her charge off to her room to change for dinner.

Kate sat at her dressing table, comb in hand and eyes on the gilt-framed mirror. She did not see herself, her tumbling hair that must be combed and twisted and pinned. She saw Liza's sparkling blue eyes, Liza's mouth curved in a dreamy smile, the blush of excitement in Liza's cheeks.

Liza was falling in love: A natural occurrence in the life of a sixteen-almost-seventeen-year-old. It could be a glorious experience for a young lady—if

111

the recipient of her stormy emotions were any other than the dashing major. There was an air about Charles Dashwood, an aura of dissipation and ruthlessness, which Kate instinctively distrusted.

A man of honor would not have used his rakish charm to sway a young girl against her father's wishes. Although Kate understood why Damien had not put his foot down, she wished, for Liza's sake, that he had. Or that he would withdraw his refusal to allow Liza's attendance at Bath functions. A diversion for Liza, any diversion, would be a godsend. Kate almost looked forward to the arrival of Damien Ashcroft's mysterious friend.

Meanwhile, the arrival of a maid on Saturday and a visit to Kate's mama on the following Tuesday would have to serve as a distraction. And Kate's vigilance must serve to diffuse the major's advances to the susceptible Liza.

The ride on the following day and tea in the vicar's pavilion passed without mishap. In fact, Kate found she could relax her vigilance and enjoy herself. Charles Dashwood had quickly noticed that Liza, though intrepid and untiring, was anything but proficient in the saddle. While they were on horseback, he made no attempt to monopolize or distract the girl with fulsome compliments.

In the vicarage garden in Monkton Combe, he offered his arm to Liza and led her into the wood-framed octagon that was more a gazebo than a pavilion, except that a miniature onion-shaped dome sat atop each of the eight corner posts and a larger one graced the tip of the pointed roof. Inside, cushioned wicker chairs provided comfort; laden trays beckoned with scones and cakes, butter and thick cream, as well as a variety of jams and jellies; Bohea and Darjeeling steamed in thick earthenware teapots.

Hubert and Algernon fell upon the feast as though their mama had kept them on bread and water for days. Not a word did they utter that had not to do with passing food or drink. Major Dashwood, refusing all but a cup of tea, turned to Liza with a winning smile. He prepared to make the most of his cousins' rare silence and Liza's proximity.

He had reckoned without the Misses Patience and Chloe, and without Emily and Susannah. These young ladies had mastered the art of chattering and questioning without neglecting the cakes.

Kate watched with interest as the four girls cornered the major with the skill of seasoned matrons. Beads of perspiration appeared on Charles Dashwood's high brow, and he began to look rather like a hunted hare. No, not a hare. A fox, waiting for his moment of triumph when he'd outwit the hunters. He had not a chance on this day. Not with Mrs. Charteris adding her chaperonage to Kate's.

As though she had read Kate's thoughts, the vicar's plump lady said, with a covert glance at the major, "I vow I could almost feel sorry for him."

"Could you, ma'am? I cannot help but feel that he's hoist with his own petard. And I cannot help feeling glad."

Phoebe Charteris suppressed a chuckle, but she could not hide the twinkle in her brown eyes. "Miss Elliott, I can't tell you how wonderfully invigorating it is to have someone other than Louisa Usborne to talk to," she said, and proceeded happily to expand on all manner of topics, from her grandmother's recipe for Bath buns and the mixing of potpourri, to the names and relationships of the leading families living in and around the villages of Combe Down and Monkton Combe.

"And, of course, Damien is our most illustrious

113

resident," she said proudly. "He is a member of the Society of Antiquaries. Has, in fact, written many essays for their publication. Godfrey is a subscriber, and he says that Damien is by far the most knowledgeable contributor. He even wrote a book, you know. On ancient Egypt."

"And now he's writing a *New History of Roman England.*"

"Oh. You knew that already." Phoebe's mood changed. "Damien is also," she added with an unusual display of hesitancy, "the most gossiped-about resident here."

"Why?"

Phoebe shrugged. Giving Kate a sidelong look, she said wryly, "Did I say I like your frankness? How rash of me."

Kate met and held Mrs. Charteris's gaze. "If you hadn't wanted me to follow up, you wouldn't have mentioned it. In fact, I cannot help but think you meant it as a warning, ma'am."

"You're quite right, my dear." Phoebe frowned, an exercise that gave her pretty rounded face a pouting look. Kate was certain, however, that pouting was not a pastime in which the vicar's wife indulged.

A noisy squabble broke out in the window embrasure, where the young people, after eating their fill of cakes and cream, had dragged the major to show him the vista of the budding garden.

Instead of shushing them, Mrs. Charteris leaned toward Kate and said, under cover of the five young ladies' squeals and squawks, "Pray don't misunderstand, Miss Elliott! It's only that you're so young. Hardly more than a girl yourself."

"I am eight-and-twenty," Kate said a trifle stiffly.

"A girl compared to my forty years," Phoebe said firmly. "And I have known Damien since he was old enough to spend the summers with his uncle at Dearworth."

Kate was surprised to hear that Dearworth had not always been her employer's home, but Mrs. Charteris's next words were even more astounding.

"I know Damien can be charming. Devastatingly so. But, my dear Miss Elliott, you must know that he will never marry again."

Kate blinked at Phoebe Charteris. She had not heard right. Could not have heard right.

"I know I made a mull of it. Pray don't misunderstand me, Miss Elliott. I only wanted you to be prepared . . . to know that matters may not be quite as they seem."

With a harassed look at the youngsters who were still squabbling and had started to call for arbitration, Phoebe patted Kate's hand. "We'll talk again. But not now. What on earth can they be arguing about?" She rose, clapping her hands together in a way Kate had often employed when confronting an unruly class, and addressed her two daughters sternly.

Kate's thoughts tumbled. She *had* heard correctly. Phoebe Charteris *had* stressed that Damien Ashcroft would never marry again.

But why make a point of it to Kate?

The question still loomed in her mind during the ride back to Dearworth. It preoccupied her to such an extent that she refrained from correcting Liza's seat in the saddle. It was amazing that a young girl, so light and graceful on solid ground, could be so awkward on horseback. Kate had long ago begged silent pardon for accusing Damien of slipshod teaching.

Damien Ashcroft . . . who was harsh and cold and overbearing. But who had laughed at her, had drawn her into his arms and kissed her with a

115

warmth that was hard to forget.

Damien Ashcroft might be a misogynist, but he was not averse to a bit of philandering. And that was the reason Phoebe Charteris had issued her warning. Kate was sure of it.

That evening and the following day when she helped out at the site, Kate watched Damien with new eyes. But if he was a rake, it was not obvious in his manner. His find, his hopes of proving that an Imperial estate had once been situated where Dearworth now sprawled, filled his conversation to the detriment of more mundane topics. When Liza mentioned the upcoming picknick on Saturday noon, Damien only pointed to the heavy coat of clouds hiding the sun and said that the wind had shifted, was blowing in from the coast and, no doubt, would bring with it squalls of rain.

His prediction proved all too true, but Lady Usborne, not to be outwitted, moved her picknick into the succession houses. Tables groaning with food and drink stood among the flowers and strawberries she raised in abundance; cushions, rugs, and chairs for those of her guests who did not care for informality were scattered in the large orangery.

Chaperoning Liza in the sprawling glass buildings that led from one into the other, four-deep, would not be as easy as it had been in the Charteris pavilion. Ever watchful, Kate traipsed after Liza and Major Dashwood while Emily Usborne tried to impress her officer cousin with her knowledge of oranges.

"These are the bitter ones we use for making the marmalade you like so much, Cousin Charles. And those"—she pointed to the farthest corner of the structure—"are the sweet oranges we'll serve as dessert."

"Let's try some now." Adroitly, Charles Dash-

116

wood guided Liza away from Emily, who had stopped to speak to a young gentleman, a latecomer and obviously embarrassed about it if his blushes and stammers were an indicator of his feelings.

Determined not to let the major out of hearing distance, Kate followed him and Liza as they walked away from the laughter and chatter of the main party. The air was heavy with the sweet perfume of orange blossoms and the more pungent scent of the ripening fruit. Intrigued by this miracle of nature that produced blossom and fruit in various stages of ripening on the same tree, Kate slowed her steps. She was reaching for one of the white blooms when a familiar deep voice spoke up directly behind her, making her jump.

"Perfect for a bridal wreath."

Kate's hand dropped—empty. Irritation flared at his silent approach, at the mockery she heard in his words. But she would not show how he could unsettle her. She turned and met Damien's look with cool poise.

"Perfect, indeed. Liza will make a beautiful bride. And now, if you'll excuse me, Mr. Ashcroft—"

"Stay a moment. Please."

"If you detain me much longer, you may have to substitute Major Dashwood for your intended groom."

"Would I dare detain you?"

The gleam in his eyes told her clearly that he was thinking of the time he had held her captive in Sir Shafto's study. Indeed, he was a rake. *But, dash it!* When he had that devilish look, he was more appealing than when he stared at her with icy disdain.

"Pardon me," she murmured, turning away. "Duty calls."

"Fustian! There's light and glass everywhere.

117

They can be seen no matter where they go."

"Ah!" she said, advancing on Liza and the major. "But they cannot be heard."

He followed her. "My dear Miss Elliott! It's not words we need to fear from the dashing major."

"But I fear them for Liza," she shot back. "Lud! She's not seventeen yet. Do you believe him fool enough to scare her off with passionate embraces?"

She heard his soft, deep laughter. His breath fanned her ear and stirred wisps of hair that had escaped her chignon. She hastened her steps.

"Tell me, clever Kate. Would a lady of eight-and-twenty be frightened by a passionate embrace?"

Warmth flooded her cheeks, but her impetuous rush had taken her too close to Liza and the major to tell him what she thought of his devious ways. She could only give him a speaking look and watch as he and Charles Dashwood exchanged frigid bows.

Liza, unaware of tension, smiled impartially at her father and at Kate. "Isn't it lovely?" she cried. "We can pick oranges and strawberries, and Emily said there are grapes in the third house. Oh, this is the most wonderful picknick ever!"

Damien offered his arm. "May I have the honor, Princess?"

Major Dashwood, per force, offered his arm to Kate. He walked slowly, making certain that Damien and Liza were out of earshot before he spoke.

"There was no need for you to come charging after us, Miss Elliott," he said, making no effort to hide his scorn. "I promise I shan't devour your little lamb."

"Strange. Mr. Ashcroft said something to the same effect."

The major's green eyes narrowed. After a moment, he said, "There! You see! Surely you, too,

118

can give Liza a bit of space to allow her to spread her wings."

"Just enough for that, Major. But I'll be close enough to make certain she doesn't singe her feathers."

"My intentions are honorable!" he protested.

Kate looked at him. He was serious. And he was handsome, she admitted. The lines of dissipation etched in his face were lines that would lure many a young lady into believing she could soothe them away. Kate was not one of the young ladies so tempted. But Liza might be.

Kate swore to keep an even closer vigilance, and she was not surprised when, during the course of the afternoon, Damien remained at her side as she pursued Liza and the major on their various strolls through the succession houses.

He was no fool after all. He knew he must guard his daughter until his friend arrived.

Chapter Nine

"Where on earth could Liza be?" asked Kate, exasperation in her voice.

She stood at her mother's drawing room window and scanned the square below. Not that she could blame the girl for drawing out her visit at the haberdasher's. The Queen's Square apartment with its cloying odor of camphor and lavender water was no inducement for a quick return. The fire burning in the hearth should have been enticing since the weather had changed back to showers and cooler temperatures, but in Lady Elliott's small apartments the glowing coals created a stifling atmosphere, reminding Kate of the Hot Baths she had visited as a child and escaped, screaming that she suffocated in the steamy vapors.

Wishing she might open the window, Kate used her handkerchief as a fan. "Where could she be?" she said again as worry began to override her irritation with Liza's delinquency. "She's been gone for the better part of two hours."

"Oh, leave the child be. No doubt she's amusing herself," Lady Elliott said wearily. She shot a look of reproach at her daughter's back. "You haven't listened to a word I said! Kate, I tell you I am not at all happy with your employment now that I have learned of Mr. Ashcroft's rakish reputation."

"I should never have given her permission to walk back from Gate Street," said Kate, still inattentive to her mother's woes. "Henry could just as well have driven her."

She turned from the window and poured a cup of tea she did not want. "Only now that she has Mary, it seemed pettish not to allow her that bit of freedom."

"Kate, will you listen! Mrs. Wroxton just returned from a six months stay in Rome. She saw him when he was there, flaunting a different woman every night. And he was keeping a mistress besides!"

Kate allowed herself to be sidetracked. "He did? Was she fiery and dark? An Italian opera dancer?"

"Kate! Don't be vulgar."

But Kate's thoughts had returned to Liza. "She should be safe with her maid, but then I'm not at all certain of Mary's dependability. She may be Mrs. Boughey's niece, but she's a London girl. She may be pert and forward. I don't know her well enough to judge."

"From what you've told me, I'd say it's your Liza who is forward." Lady Elliott waved a hand, impatiently, dismissively. "Ashcroft . . . I wish I could remember."

She refilled her teacup and, for good measure, poured a glass of her cordial. A memory stirred, vague, disturbing. About Damien Ashcroft and some woman. Mistress? Wife? She could not remember. It had been so long ago, during Hugo's last illness. Before she moved to Bath.

After a careful inspection of the cake platter, the dowager selected a thin sliver of saffron cake. "And what's that I hear about the treasure your employer is looking for? Family silver buried during Cromwell's time?"

Kate burst out laughing. "Trust the country gossips! Still, I wonder how the news traveled so fast."

"Then there is a treasure? I felt sure it must have

been an exaggeration."

"The *treasure,* Mama, is a Roman ruin Mr. Ashcroft found on his property. By the by, who is spreading this rumor of buried silver?"

"No one's spreading any rumors," Lady Elliott said huffily. "I heard it from Mrs. Wroxton, who had it from her abigail, who heard it from the groom. The groom, I believe, is chummy with one of the ostlers at the White Hart, who is brother to the baker's wife at Combe Down."

"The twins!" said Kate. "I should have known they'd blab about a treasure to all and sundry in Combe Down." She set her cup on the table and strolled to the window for another peek. "I'll tweak their noses, the little—" She broke off, leaning closer to the glass pane.

Not wanting to believe what she saw in the square three floors below, Kate blinked. But the sight of Major Dashwood strolling across the cobbles with Liza, her hand drawn intimately into the crook of his arm, was not a figment of her imagination.

She saw them stop a few yards short of the building. Liza's cloak flapped around her legs and the ribbons on her hat fluttered in the wind. Laughing, Liza put up a hand to keep the streamers off her face. The major bent his head to Liza's. Under Kate's incensed gase, he said something into the young girl's ear, then clasped her hand and brought it to his lips for a lingering kiss.

Mary, the young London maid, had been walking some distance behind the couple. When she caught up, Major Dashwood released Liza's hand, bowed, and strode off in the direction of The Circus.

Kate whacked the flat of her hand against the windowsill. The audacity of the man! The gall! With her forehead pressed against the glass, she glared after the scarlet coat.

"Kate! Kate, what is it? Are you unwell?"

Kate swung away from the window. Taking a deep breath, she said, "It's nothing, Mama. Merely relief to see Liza returning."

"Didn't I tell you not to worry about the chit?" Lady Elliott drew herself up amidst the bank of cushions surrounding her on the chaise longue. "Now, Kate. Quickly, before she comes upstairs. Promise me to resign your position!"

"What!" said Kate, incredulous. "Leave my post because of a bit of gossip? Such trifling stuff at that! Mama, you must be joking. Now, if he were married and flaunted a different ladybird every night—"

"If he were married, I wouldn't have to suffer the agonies I suffer now, knowing that you're living in his house."

"I told you that Damien Ashcroft is a widower."

"I didn't know his reputation then! I imagined someone elderly, respectable."

"He's not a green boy," said Kate, remembering how he had flinched when she called him elderly. "But he's respectable enough for Sir Shafto and Lady Usborne."

"That's neither here nor there," Lady Elliott said tartly. "They do not live under his roof."

Kate was silent, recalling Phoebe Charteris's warning.

The dowager snatched up her vinaigrette. Releasing the pungent odors under her nose, she gasped, "Kate, you cannot afford another scandal. You must resign!"

"Mama, I gave my word to stay with Liza until she marries."

"Kate—" Lady Elliott moaned but could say no more when she heard Liza's skipping steps in the corridor.

The drawing room door opened, and Liza whirled inside. "Oh, did I miss tea? I am so very sorry, Miss Elliott."

Kate took in the starry eyes, the glowing cheeks, and the sweetly smiling mouth. "What kept you, Liza?" she asked. "Surely you didn't get lost on your way back from Gate Street."

The color in Liza's cheeks deepened. Her fingers, covered in soft kid, worried the folds of her cloak. "Oh, you know! So many ribbons and trims," she said airily. "It took ages to look at them all. And then I saw how late it was, and I chose none!"

Raising her brows, Kate gave the girl a long, level stare.

Liza giggled. "Not a one! Can you believe it?"

"That is too bad." Kate picked up her reticule. "Well, I'm glad you kept your cloak on. It's going on five o'clock, and we must be on our way." A rumbling noise in the street drew her to the window. "Yes, there's Henry with the carriage now."

"Kate," Lady Elliott said feebly. "You must—"

"I am sorry, Mama," Kate cut in. She bent to kiss her mother's scented cheek. "You cannot persuade me to break my promise. And besides, you're worrying quite needlessly."

As the coach made its lumbering way through the cobbled streets, Kate could not help but wonder whether her mother's fretting was indeed as needless as she'd like to believe. After all, when Damien Ashcroft had kissed her, she had neither swooned nor boxed his ears as a proper lady should have done.

She thrust the thought aside, debating instead whether to challenge Liza immediately, in the presence of her maid, or to wait until they reached Dearworth. It was not until they clattered across the bridge spanning the river Avon south of Bath that

124

Kate made up her mind. Liza had started to chatter about the many delightful items she had seen at the haberdasher's. She insisted that she really must go into Bath again soon to take her pick and quite obviously intended to keep her meeting with Charles Dashwood a secret.

Firmly, Kate interrupted the flow of Liza's chatter. "Where did you meet the major? Surely not at the haberdasher's."

Drawing in her breath with a gasp, Liza darted a look at her maid before turning to Kate. "You spied on me. Fie, Miss Elliott!"

"Did you meet him by chance? Or did you have an assignation?"

Liza looked mutinous, and it seemed as though she would not reply. Suddenly she laughed, her eyes alight with impish joy. "Oh, Miss Elliott! 'Twas an assignation! And it was the most exciting thing. We walked in the Sydney Gardens and we talked. Charles—Major Dashwood—is the most fascinating man I ever met. He has done so much, seen so much!"

The girl lapsed into silence, her expression dreamy, and Kate did not know what to say. It was clear that in Liza's mind it had all been fun. A harmless lark.

But secret trysts spelled disaster.

Kate looked at Mary, huddled in a corner of the forward seat. She was a lass no older than Liza. Her eyes shone as brightly as her mistress's, and her rounded cheeks glowed rosily with suppressed excitement.

With a sigh of irritation, Kate acknowledged that no help would be forthcoming from that quarter. The maid had been at Dearworth but a few days, and already she saw herself in the role of Liza's champion. If Liza were forbidden to see Charles

Dashwood again, Mary would undoubtedly smuggle notes from the handsome major to her young mistress.

"Liza," Kate said after a moment of indecision, "I admit that your afternoon must have been vastly more intriguing and entertaining than mine. One cannot help but wonder, though, why a gentleman would endanger a young lady's reputation by asking her to meet him secretly."

"Stuff and nonsense!" Liza, who had been gazing out the carriage window, sat up and gave Kate a look of mischief mingled with defiance. "First of all, I had my maid along. So my reputation was quite safe. And secondly, 'twas I who suggested the meeting, not Charles."

Kate noted this second use of the major's first name but decided to ignore it for now. "Why the secrecy? You have not been forbidden to see Major Dashwood. In fact, as long as he's staying with the Usbornes, it'll be impossible *not* to see him."

"Only in company! And even then you and Papa made quite certain that I wouldn't have a private moment with Charles, didn't you?"

"A young lady does not spend time alone with *any* gentleman. You know that as well as I do. For goodness sake, Liza! Why did you do such a corkbrained thing just when your Papa was beginning to relent? Couldn't you be satisfied that he allowed you to go into Bath?"

Liza gripped Kate's hand, squeezing it tightly. "Oh, Miss Elliott," she breathed. "Don't you see? I think I'm falling in love!"

What a child Liza was. In a sudden rush of tenderness, Kate drew the girl into her arms. "My dear, you would have surprised me more if you did not believe yourself to be falling in love. After all, it is springtime. In less than two weeks you will be

126

seventeen. And the major is a very handsome gentleman."

"Oh!" Liza pushed Kate away. "You think I'm merely mooning over Charles like Patience and Chloe. Even Emily makes sheep's eyes at him. And Charles is her cousin."

"Major Dashwood is Lady Usborne's cousin. And, no, I do not believe you're merely mooning. But only time will tell what you truly feel for Charles Dashwood. So, please, Liza! For your own sake, be patient."

Liza vouchsafed no reply. The bumping and jolting of the coach seemed not to affect her as she sat rigidly beside Kate. After a moment, Kate said quietly, "True love cannot flourish in secrecy."

With a disparaging sniff, Liza turned her back on Kate and sat staring out the window for the rest of the journey. When the coachman pulled the horses to a halt before the house, she jumped up and flung herself from the carriage before the steps had been let down.

"Hurry, Mary!" she called out impatiently. "I have a headache. I want you to bring some tea to my room. And make sure that I am not disturbed!"

"Well now," muttered Kate. "If that wasn't a snub." Despite the rain, she approached the welcoming front door slowly. In the foyer, she stripped off her gloves and removed her hat and cloak, handing them to the butler. "I assume Mr. Ashcroft did not go out to the site today?"

Boughey said cheerfully, "Oh, he did venture out, Miss Elliott. But he returned two hours ago, soaked to the skin. He's in the library now."

Kate squared her shoulders and started toward the large book-lined chamber next to the morning room. Might as well get it over with. He'd be furious; probably rake her over the coals for not keeping an eye on Liza, but at least she had no need to "invade" his study as he had accused her of doing.

Strangely, the encouraging thought did not make her task easier. She knew that Damien must be apprised of Liza's meeting with the major, yet she felt like a traitress. Perhaps she was overanxious. Perhaps, if left alone, Liza would come to see reason.

Even as she hesitated at the library door, it swung open to reveal her employer. "Miss Elliott!" he said in a tone of voice that indicated he had expected someone other than his daughter's companion. His next words, however, were delivered in quite his usual mocking manner. "You've come to complain about my carriage, I see. Don't tell me! The roof has a leak."

Automatically, her hands went to her hair. The strands framing her face were wet. So much for the protection of a hat. She ignored his taunt, saying, "Mr. Ashcroft, about Bath. I'm afraid—"

"And I am afraid you'll catch cold standing in this drafty hallway," he said, giving her one of his charming smiles. "Whatever it is that you feel you must confess to me, wouldn't you be more comfortable near the fire?"

"Confess!" She raised her chin, looking at him indignantly, but was met with such a teasing twinkle in his eyes that she blinked in confusion.

"I also recommend a glass of brandy, Miss Elliott."

"No brandy, thank you." Kate stepped past him, walking to one of the armchairs by the fireplace. "I shan't take up much of your time. Unless," she added, cocking an eyebrow and giving him a sidelong look, "you'll insist on starting an argument."

"I? Miss Elliott, you wrong me. I never argue."

His grin was infectious; she barely managed to

swallow a chuckle. There was a change in him. He was relaxed and at the same time vibrating with an air of expectancy so palpable that it made her spine tingle.

She accepted the glass he handed her, saying, "No, of course you don't argue. You merely insist until your victim feels utterly browbeaten."

"Just so, Miss Elliott." He sat down on the upholstered arm of the chair opposite hers, stretching his long, muscular legs toward the fire. After sampling his own drink, he set it on the floor beside his feet and leaned back with his arms crossed over his chest.

"What worries you?" he asked. "Did you find your mother in ill health?"

"No," she said, wishing she need not tell him, wishing she need not bring news that would harden his mouth to a narrow line of disapproval and douse the warmth in his dark eyes. "No, I'm afraid it's Liza."

"I should have known." His brow creased, but the forbidding frown did not last. "She gave you the slip, I assume?"

"Pray remember that you did give her permission to shop for ribbons and that she was with her maid at all times."

He narrowed his eyes. "Now why, I wonder, do you think it necessary to remind me of the obvious? Out with it! What has Liza been up to?"

"She met with Major Dashwood."

During the ensuing silence, Kate took recourse to the brandy he had given her. His face was inscrutable, as was his gaze that remained fixed on her for a disturbingly long time. Faintly, she heard Boughey's voice in the foyer. The sound, slight though it was, interrupted whatever it was that Damien had been thinking.

"The minx!" he said, but he did not sound half as angry as Kate had expected him to be.

She approached the next hurdle. "And the worst part is that I do not think we should try to discourage her from seeing him again."

Footsteps could be heard in the hallway. A man's firm tread. Damien rose unhurriedly, looking toward the door. His mouth stretched in a smile, the smile of a hunter whose prey is walking straight toward his trap.

"Don't fret," he said as the door opened. "You need have no more fears for Liza and our dashing major. Allow me to present my friend Lord Nicholas Adair."

Nicholas! Only a lance could have impaled Kate more firmly to her chair than that name. But not more painfully.

She stared transfixed at the slender golden-haired gentleman who greeted Damien with a slight smile, his narrow face so achingly familiar and yet so strange, with its faint lines of maturity and the golden tan that had not been there eleven years ago.

Why? she thought as the walls of her secure little world crashed around her. *Why has he come back into my life now?*

Then Nicholas's blue eyes came to rest on her. She saw them widen in sudden recognition, saw his leaping joy, his quick, impetuous move toward her. "Kate!"

She held up a hand as though wanting to ward him off, but not a word left her mouth, neither in greeting nor in denial.

"I see that you two know each other," said Damien.

It might have been the tone of Damien's voice, dry and sarcastic, that halted Nicholas's approach and snuffed the light of pleasure in his eyes, or it might have been the look on Kate's face. For her, there had been no moment of joy. Only shock, dismay, and then resignation. Her past had caught up with her.

Nicholas turned to Damien. "Had I known you were planning a house party, I would not have imposed on your hospitality."

Kate heard the touch of ice in Nicholas's voice. He finally realized that meeting her again could only embarrass him.

"It's not a house party. What the devil made you think so?" Damien still stood beside the chair on which he had perched so carelessly but a moment ago. Gone was his air of anticipation. Gone was his smile. He looked from Kate to Nicholas in tight lipped silence. Watchful. Leery. "You are my only guest."

The reassurance had no noticeable effect on Nicholas. His posture was rigid, the cloth of his coat drawn taut across his straight back. With his arms held stiffly at his sides, he faced Kate. His bow could not be faulted in execution; neither could it be surpassed in formality.

"Kate. How very nice to see you again," he said in accents that gave his words the lie. "Will I have the added pleasure of meeting your husband?"

Chapter Ten

"My *husband?*" Kate shot to her feet.

"*Husband!*" Damien echoed as though the word were poison in his mouth.

Kate did not have so much as a glance to spare for him; she could concentrate on one man only. On Nicholas, who long ago had won her heart with sweet and tender words and gentle kisses. Who had vowed eternal devotion, then fled before his father's wrath, leaving her alone to face Lord Adair's contempt and Richard's vile accusations.

"Nicholas, how dare you mock me! I am not married."

She saw uncertainty in his look, a moment of doubt. "I beg your pardon," he said stiffly. "You can hardly blame a fellow for jumping to a conclusion after you refused to see him. It was painfully obvious to me that you had changed your mind."

"I *never* refused to see you," Kate said hotly.

Common sense demanded that she speak calmly and show the proper reserve as befitting a lady of her age, but the hurt she had felt as a young girl and the subsequent anger were resurfacing. Nicholas spoke as though she had betrayed him, while it had been he who meekly accepted his father's verdict that the Elliotts were ineligible to form a marriage connection with the illustrious Adairs.

"But you did change your mind?" Nicholas asked.

"You are a fine one to talk about changing one's mind!" Her heart pumped wildly, threatening to leave her breathless. "Where were you during those first days when Mama insisted that I go about as though nothing untoward had happened? Where were you when the wagging tongues grew vicious, and Richard locked me away, first at Elliott Chase, then in a boarding school?"

"And may I ask what the devil is going on?" questioned Damien, his voice silky. "If I may be permitted, I'd like to point out that you two are carrying on like novice actors in a very bad play."

Kate rounded on him. "Will you *kindly* stay out of this!"

"Kate, forgive me," said Nicholas, looking distraught. "I totally forgot Damien's presence."

"Never mind my presence. Simply speak in terms that will enlighten me."

Nicholas inserted two fingers behind his cravat and tugged as though it had become too tight. "I shouldn't have said anything at all while you were in the room. Please leave us, Damien."

"Not on my account." Kate started for the door. "Nicholas, I have nothing to say to you."

"Kate!" No longer cold and formal, Nicholas grabbed her arm, pulling her to a stop. There was a haunted look in his eyes. "If you did *not* refuse to see me — Kate, don't you realize what that means?"

She shook her head. "No, I—"

"You owe me at least a hearing," Nicholas interrupted. "Damien, I must insist that you leave us alone. A lady's honor is at stake."

"Don't talk fustian." Damien crossed his arms over his chest. "The lady is under my protection. I'll stay until *she* tells me to leave."

133

"What!" shouted Nicholas, advancing on Damien. "What the deuce do you mean *under your protection?*"

"Not what you so obviously believe it means." Kate glared at him. "How dare you!"

Nicholas was instantly contrite. "Kate, I beg your pardon. Coming face to face with you so unexpectedly . . . I think it addled my brains. But what *are* you doing here?"

She darted a look at Damien. He, however, was totally absorbed in the removal of a speck of invisible lint from the sleeve of his elegant dark coat.

"I am in Mr. Ashcroft's employ," she said. "His daughter's companion."

Resuming her seat on the chair she had so abruptly vacated, Kate added, "I daresay that entitles him to some kind of explanation after the stir you caused."

"Yes," said Nicholas, albeit doubtfully. "I suppose so. But surely it would be best if we talked first?"

"*Best?* No, Nicholas. It would have been by far the best had you never come to Dearworth."

From the corner of her eye, Kate saw Damien turn away and cross to an elaborately carved and embellished Louis XIV desk standing at a right angle to the fireplace. Only when he perched on a corner of the desk, separated from her by half the room's width, did Kate realize how strongly she had felt the tension emanating from him. A tension that puzzled and disturbed her.

"It seems, Miss Elliott," he said, "that Nicholas wishes to spare your blushes."

Frowning, she met his dark look. She'd give almost anything in exchange for an unblemished past, but not once did she consider hiding the

134

truth now that Nicholas had reappeared. "Maybe so. But perhaps his protective instinct awakens a little too late."

"Kate!" Nicholas protested.

She silenced him, saying, "I'd rather Mr. Ashcroft learn the true story from us than from some long-memoried gossipmonger who wishes to enlighten him."

It took courage to meet Damien's eyes again. Her throat too tight for speech, but speak she did. "Eleven years ago, Nicholas and I eloped to be married. We were headed for the Scottish border when his father caught up with us just this side of Cheltenham."

"Oh, my poor Miss Elliott!" The cry drew three pairs of eyes toward the doorway. None of the occupants of the library had heard Liza's approach or knew how long she had been standing in the open door. "How perfectly awful for you!"

A look of disgust crossed Damien's face. "In fact," he said, "it's a perfect Cheltenham tragedy. A bungled elopement. Pshaw! Nicholas, my friend, I expected better of you."

Nicholas stiffened. "And you, *my friend,* are forgetting your manners." Turning his back on Damien, he bowed to Liza with courtly grace. "Miss Ashcroft, I assume?"

Kate dug her fingers into the arms of her chair. Why the devil should she feel hurt? If she had expected anything other than blighting scorn from Damien, well, then she was a bigger gaby than she had been when she eloped with Nicholas. And surely she couldn't have expected Nicholas to call Damien out or do something equally violent. Nicholas had ever been conciliatory—and a stickler for punctilio.

While Liza smiled and showed her dimples and invited Nicholas to call her by her first name — "Otherwise I might forget to answer, Lord Nicholas. I'm still quite new at being a hostess, you know!" — and Nicholas murmured suitable replies, Kate picked up the glass of brandy Damien had poured for her. Like a blaze of fire, the liquor burned down her throat, then hit her stomach, but she didn't stop until the glass was empty. Gasping, her eyes streaming with brandy-induced tears, she groped for the table to set her glass down. Someone removed it from her clutching fingers and replaced it with a square of soft linen.

"Don't you know better than to toss down a double measure of brandy in a gulp?" Damien asked gruffly while she dried her eyes and blew her nose.

"No, I don't." Wadding the soggy handkerchief in a ball, she tucked it away under a cushion. "I'm afraid I have no previous experience with brandy."

"It appears your experiences are limited."

She shot him a suspicious look, but if he meant to be insulting, he hid it well. He was watching her from hooded eyes and with a brooding expression on his dark face.

"I'll take Liza to the drawing room," he said brusquely. "You and Nicholas will want to discuss the sordid details of your elopement. As Liza's chaperon, you'll no doubt agree that those are not for her tender ears."

"She has already heard the worst," Kate pointed out with icy dignity.

He raised a skeptical brow but did not challenge her statement. "I don't mind admitting that it goes against my grain to leave you and Nicholas alone," he said. "But if I send Liza away she'll only sneak back and listen at the keyhole."

Her eyes flashed. "And just what do you think I'll do with Nicholas? Seduce him into a second elopement?"

As on various other occasions, he noted that emotion changed the color of her eyes. But he must not let himself be diverted from his anger. Miss Elliott and Nicholas. It must not be.

"Nicholas is such a damned romantic fool," he said with a dismissive shrug, then added, "He is also quite a matrimonial catch."

She pokered up, as he had known she would, but she turned to look at Nicholas and Liza, both fair and blue-eyed and with an air of delicate beauty that would always draw attention.

Liza, a golden sprite in a dinner gown of primrose silk, was gazing at Nicholas. "Even close up you don't look old," she blurted. "Not as old as Papa."

Damien saw Kate's eyes widen, and he said, "So you do remember my plans for Nicholas and Liza. They make a stunning couple, don't they?"

"Yes," she said tonelessly. How could she have forgotten! No wonder Damien was tense and irascible after learning that she and Nicholas were more than casual acquaintances.

"I'll lay you odds they'll be married before the end of the summer," he said.

Stung, Kate retorted, "And what, pray tell, makes you so certain?"

"I know Nicholas—and I know you. Shrewish Kate," he added with a devilish grin.

Before she could formulate a blistering reply, he walked away. "Come, Liza," he said in a voice that brooked no opposition. "Let's give these two starcrossed lovers a few moments of privacy. Nicholas,

I'll have dinner set back. You and Miss Elliott may join us in the drawing room at your convenience."

He clasped his daughter's elbow and ushered her firmly from the room. Kate saw the door close, heard Nicholas's urgent "Kate!" But she did not move. She was still thinking of Liza and Nicholas. Surely that was not pique churning in her breast?

"Kate!" Nicholas's voice was low and husky. He sank down on one knee before her. "Dear Kate, I believe there is much that we must discuss. I—"

"Nicholas," she interrupted. "Please get up. I agree that we have much to talk about. At the least, you owe me an explanation, but you'll be more at ease sitting on a chair."

He gave her a whimsical look but did not move from his kneeling position. "And here I thought it was you who must do the explaining. First, though, shall we start over greeting each other?" Capturing her hands in his, he brought them to rest against his heart. "Kate, I never gave up looking for you."

Where was the warm flutter his touch used to cause in breast? A lock of hair had tumbled onto his forehead. She used to smooth it back that long time ago. Now, she had no such desire. In fact, she was hard pressed not to repeat Damien's references to theatricals and Cheltenham tragedies.

"Is that what you did in Italy and Egypt?" she asked dryly. "Search for me?"

A coppery glow suffused his golden skin. "Kate, you're not being fair. You must know from Damien that I spend but a small part of my time looking for antiquities."

Firmly, she freed her hands. Flicking a fingertip across his forehead, she said, "The sunshine agrees with you. I remember you used to be very pale."

"And you used to be less caustic. Less—"

"Less shrewish?" she supplied.

Nicholas shook his head. "You could never be shrewish!" he said fiercely.

Had her aggravating employer still been in the room, he would have speedily contradicted Nicholas. Kate was about to give thanks for small mercies, when it occurred to her that Damien's leaving was quite inexplicable considering the wager he had tossed at her. What devious scheme was he weaving now?

"Kate, what happened?"

It took her a moment to understand Nicholas's question. "Eleven years of Miss Venable's Seminary for Young Ladies happened to me."

Nicholas groaned. "I am sorry."

"Oh, don't misunderstand. Once I got used to it, I was perfectly content. Especially when I became a teacher. And what about you? I assume you did not go to the Continent right away. After all, there was a war going on."

He looked at her as though he did not comprehend the question. "Father shipped me off to New Orleans. But you know that! I wrote to you."

She caught her breath. "I received no letter."

"My valet personally delivered it in Queen's Square. I do not think he would have lied to me."

"Mama must have taken it." Her face hardened. "Or Richard. He was there at the time."

"Then you thought I had deserted you?"

"What does it matter now?" Giving Nicholas a wry little smile, she said, "So you were in New Orleans. You did once mention relations there, but it was a possibility I didn't take into consideration. I did not think that your father would let you out of his sight."

"He personally conveyed me to Bristol the very next morning."

"And I walked past Adair House those first days, picturing you inside, thinking that you were hiding behind its solid walls and dark windows." Trying to suppress painful old memories, she said, "I do wish you'd get up!"

Nicholas recaptured her hands. "I was so certain you had received my letter explaining it all, my promise to come for you as soon as I was of age."

Silence lay heavy between them. Briefly, Kate allowed her thoughts to dwell on what might have happened had Nicholas's letter not gone astray. Probably nothing would be changed, she acknowledged. With or without a letter, the fact remained that Nicholas had not claimed her as his bride after he returned from New Orleans.

Curious, she asked, "When did you leave New Orleans?"

"A little over six months after I arrived. As you know, my birthday is in November. And that," he said with a deprecating halfsmile, "is not a time when shippers like to send their vessels across the Atlantic. I finally got passage on a moth-eaten frigate whose Irish captain was eager for a glimpse of the Emerald Isles. The crossing took two months. I came straight to Bath. To Queen's Square."

This, she had not expected. "You did?" Her voice sounded hollow. "My mother didn't tell you where I was staying?"

"She wouldn't see me. I drove out to Elliott Chase to call on your brother, but he was away from home. Lady Elliott, your sister-in-law, was there."

"And?" prompted Kate when Nicholas fell silent.

"Didn't Margaret give you my direction?"

Nicholas abruptly let go of her hands. He rose, taking a step away from her. "I can see now that I went about it the wrong way. I was tired and disgruntled by then."

He started to pace, running his fingers through his hair the way he always did when he was upset. He swung around to face her again. "Kate, I was a fool! Over the butler's protest, I stormed into your sister-in-law's drawing room. I demanded to see you. When she said it was impossible, I believed she was shielding you, that you didn't want to see me."

She was glad to know that he had not deserted her, but she felt none of the bubbling happiness she might have been expected to feel. "So that's how you jumped to your famous conclusion that I got married."

"Yes. It sounds foolish, doesn't it? Telling you about it now, I cannot understand how I could have been such a dunce. But then! Kate, then it seemed so logical! You were—you are so beautiful. I knew some other man must have married you while I was gone."

"Didn't you realize that our escapade cost me dearly? I lost my reputation. I cannot possibly receive a proposal, save an improper one."

"I don't understand. My father vowed he'd see to it that there would be no scandal!"

"It was Richard who talked to some of his cronies. Within days, it was known all over Bath that I had run away with you."

"He must have been in his cups."

"Is that a justification?" asked Kate.

She felt drained and exhausted. Somewhere in the house a clock struck eight times. She rose. "I must change for dinner. It will hardly endear us to your host and my employer if we overset his orderly household."

"I can deal with Damien." Nicholas stepped into her path. "Kate, you know the saying about spilt milk. So let's not think about the might-have-been. Let us think about now, about our future."

She searched his face. Nicholas couldn't possibly wish to marry her now, after all these years. And didn't he know the future Damien Ashcroft had planned for him? She shook her head at Nicholas and would have left had he not placed his hands on her upper arms.

He looked deeply into her eyes. "You're wrong if you believe I'll let you walk away without settling matters between us," he said huskily. "Kate, now as then, I want to marry you."

Kate stood motionless. Despite his apparent desertion, she had hoped and prayed every day, every night during those first painful months for Nicholas's return and his proposal. Even when he did not come for her after reaching his majority, she had clung to the forlorn hope that, perhaps, he was waiting for Richard's guardianship to lapse. But her twenty-first birthday had come and gone without a word from Nicholas, and finally that tiny flame of hope had died. Over the years, she had barely given him a thought.

And now, it was too late for them. Or was it?

She started to ward off his embrace, then changed her mind. Let him place his arms around her just once. She'd know if that old magic still sparked between them.

His arms encircled her waist—and nothing happened. She might have been a gate post, so stiff and unresponsive did she feel. Or was she merely numbed by the shock of his sudden appearance?

"Nicholas," she murmured into his shoulder. "This is not the time for a decision. We are both shaken; we are not thinking straight. Leave it be for now."

"Kate, look at me!"

Ah, well.

Kate raised her face. His mouth covered hers in a soft and gentle caress. For a moment or two, she clung to him, trying to recapture the bliss they had shared in the past. It was a futile effort.

Firmly, Kate pushed against his chest. But Nicholas did not let go. He might be slender, he might be no more than an inch or two taller than she, but there was muscle beneath the cloth of his sleeves. His arms tightened, and his kiss grew more demanding, more passionate.

Frantic now, she struggled harder as his hands roamed over her back, up her sides, and came to rest against her breasts.

Kate recalled another kiss: Damien Ashcroft's in the squire's study. But Damien's hands, his mouth and tongue, had made her senses reel until she wanted nothing more than to cling to him in abandon.

Truly frightened—whether by Nicholas's passion or by her adverse reaction to his embrace, she did not know—Kate kicked the heel of her half boots against his instep. With a shout of pain, Nicholas released her.

"What the devil!" Crimson flooded his face. "I beg your pardon! Kate, I apologize. I did not mean to frighten you."

Kate instantly denied any such cowardly emotion. "Frighten me? You forget I am no innocent! I have experienced my share of kissing. Remember, Nicholas?"

"I remember very well," he said quietly. "And I am convinced that nothing has changed since then. If anyone dares question your innocence, he'll have me to answer to."

"So I am *not* a fallen woman," she said with a shrug. "But it is futile to make believe that we can pick up where we left off. Too many years have passed." *Another man has kissed me since.* "We have changed, Nicholas."

"Only for the better. I am a man now, knowing my own mind and answerable to no one but myself. Kate, I want you."

"Nicholas—"

His fingers sealed her lips, cutting off her protest before she could fully formulate her thoughts. "Say nothing, Kate. I shan't press you for an answer now. I merely want you to understand how I feel."

"How can you know what you feel, Nicholas? Aren't you at all confused? You must have tried to forget me at one time If you believed me married."

"How could I ever forget you? Kate, I look upon this meeting as a miracle," he said in a voice that was deep and compelling. "The fates have granted me a second chance to claim you as my wife, and I intend to fight for my happiness. For *our* happiness."

Kate's thoughts spun so fast, she could make no sense of them. Marriage to Nicholas had once been her heart's desire. Surely it must still be her wish. But if her love for him was still alive, it was not the wild, stormy feeling that set her aflame the way it had eleven years ago. Whenever she was near him then, she had been unable to refrain from touching him. And now?

And how important was love in marriage?

"Thank you," she murmured. "I am aware of the great honor you're doing me." *Dear God!* she thought. *I am as nervous as a debutante.* "But I'm also grateful that you're giving me time to consider. Nicholas, I shall take you at your word, for I don't know how I feel about us."

A shadow of sadness crossed his face. "I understand. Just remember that I have all the patience in the world now that I have found you again."

Kate nodded. Half turning away, she said, "I'll join you in the drawing room, Nicholas. Can you find your own way?"

"Kate, I love you.

She gave him a tremulous smile, then walked quickly from the room.

Chapter Eleven

Damien threw a covert glance at his riding companion, but he need not have bothered to hide his interest. Nicholas showed no awareness of him or of their surroundings. Lush meadows, fields bright with the new green of wheat and rye, all passed unnoticed as Nicholas rode on, his eyes fixed on a point between his gelding's ears.

"Last night you fobbed me off with excuses," said Damien, breaking the silence that had accompanied them since they left the stables half an hour ago. "Remember, my friend, Miss Elliott lives under my roof—"

"Under your protection?" Nicholas cut in, urging his mount to a faster pace.

"Precisely. I must, therefore, ask your intentions toward her."

Nicholas gave a dry little laugh. "*My* intentions are most honorable. I wonder about you, though. Whenever I saw you near a beautiful lady before, your intentions were decidedly dishonorable."

"Miss Elliott is my daughter's companion," Damien said repressively. "I have no interest in her but to keep her name unsullied." If his color deepened a little, it was nothing to be wondered at, for he was leaning over his mount's neck to open a gate with the leather handle of his riding crop. "Or am I too late to worry about her good name?"

Nicholas's mouth tightened in anger, and Damien

said hastily, "Come now, my friend. There's no need to fly into a pelter. After all, she did consent to elope with you."

"She was seventeen, Damien! And I implored her, begged her on my knees to come away with me. It is I who should have known better! I should have been wise for both of us. Kate, the poor darling, had none to guide or advise her."

Damien raised a skeptical brow. "She lived with her mother then."

"Lady Elliott spent her days on a couch surrounded by smelling salts and tonics. The only two people she'd rouse herself to pay attention to were her nurse and her physician."

Damien's mouth curled cynically. "In fact, the perfect chaperon for an enterprising damsel."

Nicholas reined his horse in. "You have been a good friend," he said, a note of warning in his voice and a look of ice in his eyes. "But I will not allow you to cast aspersions on the character of my future wife."

Damien's hands tightened on the reins as his chestnut stallion showed signs of wanting to charge past his companion. "Then I may congratulate you?"

"Eventually, yes." Nicholas moved on, fixing his gaze once more on the point between his mount's ears. "Right at present you are premature with your congratulations."

"Don't tell me she refused you."

"She did not refuse me. Kate needs time to consider my suit."

A burst of satisfaction made Damien's blood pump faster. He paid the astonishing emotion no heed but said dryly, "Very commendable, I'm sure."

They had left the fields and meadows behind,

147

and Damien led the way up an incline to the top of a hill where he intended to check on reports of damaged timber. For a while, only the sound of hooves could be heard and the horses' short, raspy breaths as they picked their careful way up the narrow, rock-strewn path.

When the terrain leveled, Damien gave his friend a sharp look. "Do you still love her?"

"Of course I do!" Nicholas drew the gelding to a halt. Dismounting, he looped the reins across an overhanging branch. "How could I not love her? Kate is beautiful, sweet, and gentle. She is . . . everything a man could wish in a woman."

Sweet and gentle. Lud! Damien came close to a fall as he slid off his mount. Where the devil had she hidden those qualities when she came to live at Dearworth? He did, though, agree with the last part of Nicholas's proclamation. Kate was indeed everything a man could wish in a woman. She was strong, proud, stubborn, and feisty.

"You haven't seen her in—what? Eleven years? Nicholas, a person can change drastically in half that time. How do you know you still love her? How do you know it's not mere guilt or pity that made you propose to her again?"

"I couldn't be mistaken! I have always loved her. I love her still."

But there had been just enough hesitation before Nicholas's protest to convince Damien that his friend had rushed his fences. "And Kate?" he asked. "Why does she not snatch at the opportunity to become Lady Nicholas?"

"Damn you!" Without waiting to see if Damien followed, Nicholas strode off into the pines that covered the upper third of the hill. "You make her sound like a mercenary husband hunter."

"If she were that," said Damien, catching up with some difficulty, "she would have sent a notice to the *Gazette* by express courier. No, I'm beginning to think that Kate has more sense than you. She knows that you fell in love with a young girl whose romantic dreams matched your own, that perhaps you never stopped searching for that girl, but that the woman you found is someone completely different."

"Then I'll just have to convince her that she's wrong."

Damien did not try any longer to keep up with his friend. In time, Nicholas would see that he was right.

As Damien strode across the hill, his eyes scanning the trunks and branches of the tall pines for signs of disease, he concentrated on his strategy toward Kate. He must stay away from her, give her no opportunity to pick a quarrel with him the way she was wont to do whenever they spent more than a few minutes in each other's company. It would be no hardship to spend the days at the excavation site and teach those curious twins about Roman England while Nicholas did his courting and would, inevitably, fall victim to Kate's sharp tongue. Let her do her quarreling with Nicholas. That, better than anything else, would teach the misguided fellow that Kate was too headstrong for him.

And there was a way to teach Miss Elliott to cross swords with him and to spoil his plans. A way that would, moreover, convince the maddening lady that Nicholas was not the man for her.

A gleam lit Damien's eyes as he leaned against a tree to rest his leg. He remembered how Kate had fitted into his arms, how she had melted against him and had returned his kiss with ardor until her sense of decorum had nudged her and she had pulled away.

Yes, he wouldn't mind at all repeating the experience. Slowly, kiss by kiss, he'd chisel away at her resistance until she dropped that cloak of straight-laced respectability into which ladies wrapped themselves.

But, damn it! Was that how she had passed the time with Nicholas until Lord Adair had caught up with them? What other favors had she bestowed on Nicholas?

Damien started walking again. As he strove for the top of the hill, it was not difficult to ignore the stabs of pain in his leg. His mind was preoccupied with the lessons he would teach Kate—lessons about the ways of man and woman.

Only later, much later, when from his study window he observed Nicholas, Liza, and Kate during a game of croquet, did Damien remember that his scheming, as it separated Kate and Nicholas, would naturally serve his daughter.

During the days following Nicholas's proposal, Kate asked herself more than once why she had not jumped at his offer. She must be mad to entertain even the slightest doubt that they would suit. That her feelings for him had cooled was only natural, a sign of maturity and a result of their long separation. Nicholas had told her he loved her, and that should be enough. Unfortunately, it wasn't. Nicholas's avowal did not help her sort the conflicting emotions raging in her breast.

To the inhabitants of Dearworth and the neighboring countryside, Kate presented a calm face and a cheerful disposition. No one could accuse her of wearing her heart on her sleeve, but the nights she spent tossing and turning or pacing her bedchamber began to take their toll. Dark shadows circled her eyes, her cheeks lost the bloom previously brought out by long walks and rides over the estate, and her lovely new gowns began to look as though they had been borrowed from the wardrobe of the vicar's plump wife.

In fact, it was Phoebe Charteris who first commented on Kate's appearance while they were chaperoning the young people at yet another tea party in the vicarage garden. They were alone in the pavilion for a spell. Liza and Emily Usborne had been lured away by Chloe and Patience to try their hands at brass rubbing in the old Monkton Combe church. Hubert and Algy had followed the young ladies, while Major Dashwood and Lord Nicholas had stepped into the garden to blow a cloud.

"Is Damien starving you?" Phoebe asked bluntly. "Here, try some of the clotted cream on your scone."

Kate accepted the cream. "I took the gown in this morning," she said with a rueful look at the seams. "But it still shows, doesn't it, that I lost a little weight?"

"Definitely. You look as though you haven't eaten or slept for several weeks. Although," Phoebe added shrewdly, "I think your strange malady started only about a sennight ago. More or less at the same time that the charming Lord Nicholas came to stay."

Two bright flecks of color burned on Kate's drawn face. The vicar's lady was too perspicacious by far.

Busying herself with her cup, Kate stirred sugar that had dissolved long ago. She was of two minds

151

to confide in Mrs. Charteris. On one side of the argument was her common sense that told her to hold her own counsel. On the other hand, she felt desperately in need of a confidante. The more she thought about Nicholas's proposal, the more confused she became—when an answer should have been so easy to give.

"People always start out with the assurance that they do not wish to pry," Phoebe said cheerfully, "and then they fire off one question after another. I shan't make the same mistake. I'll ask but one, and I hope you know it is only my regard for you that makes me step beyond the bounds of polite intercourse."

The older woman's gaze rested on her with warm concern, and Kate nodded reluctantly. "You may ask me anything you want, and I promise I shan't take it amiss."

"You see, I couldn't help but notice how very attentive Lord Nicholas is toward you. How very concerned for your comfort. Miss Elliott, is there an understanding between you and Lord Nicholas?"

While Kate blushed even more fiercely than before and cast about in her mind for an appropriate reply, Nicholas and Major Dashwood could be heard outside the pavilion. Moments later, the voices faded as the gentlemen moved on. In a flash of irritation, Kate asked herself what right Nicholas had to become so chummy with Charles Dashwood. Didn't he see how the major fawned on Liza, how he annoyed Kate?

Drawing a ragged breath, she turned to Mrs. Charteris. Without hesitation or reservation, she recounted her and Nicholas's story. Kate did not try to justify her behavior, nor did she indulge in self-recrimination. She told of the love that had

152

blossomed between her and Nicholas, of Lord Adair's refusal to acknowledge their pledge and his direct order that they were not to see each other again.

She told of the moment of rebellion when Nicholas had procured a chaise-and-four while Kate bought such necessities as combs and toothbrushes; how they met at Pultenay Bridge and set out for Scotland when the dowager Lady Elliott and Lord Adair believed them to be with their respective parties at the theater and the subscription ball. Three hours later, when Nicholas should have returned from the theater, Lord Adair had set out in hot pursuit.

Phoebe Charteris listened attentively until Kate concluded her tale with Nicholas's renewed proposal of marriage. Then a beaming smile lit her face. "Allow me to wish you happy, Miss Elliott. Oh, this is above anything great! The most romantic story, and a most satisfactory ending."

"I have not accepted, ma'am," Kate said quietly.

Phoebe's eyes widened in disbelief. "You refused?"

"No." Kate hesitated. Aside from her own doubts, there was also Damien's scheme for Liza and Nicholas to be considered. But it did no good fretting about it; Liza had eyes only for Major Dashwood, and Nicholas . . . well, as Phoebe had noted, he devoted himself to Kate.

"You see," Kate explained, "I asked Nicholas to give me time to consider."

"I always said you were a girl with uncommonly good sense," Phoebe said, but she looked as though she found it a trifle hard to believe in her own words. She leaned across the tea table to give Kate's hand a pat. "Understandably, you are put

153

out by his long absence. You don't want him to think you're snatching at his offer. That's it, isn't it?"

Kate couldn't help but smile a little. "You feel, no doubt, that I should take him up the aisle as soon as possible, before he realizes that I've been considered on the shelf these three or four years past."

"Rubbish!"

"Well, ma'am, I am not playing coy with Nicholas. I truly don't know if I love him sufficiently to make him a good wife."

"Love comes with marriage. My mother and grandmother told me so, and I've seen it come true often enough."

"A marriage of convenience," Kate said.

While Phoebe tried to gather ammunition against that shot, Kate rose to look through one of the arched window openings into the garden, where male and female voices mingled pleasantly as the returning brass rubbing party met up with Charles Dashwood and Lord Nicholas.

"Would you wish it — a marriage of convenience — if one of your daughters were concerned?" Kate asked.

"No, I shouldn't like it," Phoebe admitted, albeit reluctantly. "But if Chloe and Patience do not meet the men with whom they can share the deep love Godfrey and I have found, and if they should receive advantageous offers, I'd feel it my duty to encourage them to accept."

Kate cast a speaking look over her shoulder. "To escape the awful fate of spinsterhood."

"Yes. And you cannot deny, Miss Elliott, that a match with the son of the Marquis of Adair and grandson of the Duke of Welby would be more desirable than a post as companion."

"I do not deny it." Kate watched as Major Dashwood possessed himself of Liza's hand to lead her down a path overgrown with budding hawthorn. Then Nicholas joined them.

Kate turned away from the window and sat down. "No," she said as if confirming it to herself, "I do not deny Nicholas's eligibility. And marriage would certainly eliminate the necessity of looking for another post once Liza is settled."

Phoebe nodded. "It is good of you not to contemplate an immediate wedding," she said just as though Kate had indeed set a date. "Liza has had a hard enough time so far, but perhaps something can be arranged for her that will suit her as well as staying at Dearworth and playing at being her father's hostess."

Again Kate could not help but think of Damien's plans for Liza.

"However," Phoebe continued, suddenly switching to the role of devil's advocate, "material comfort is not the most important ingredient in a marriage. I remember Damien and Elizabeth. They had everything: youth, looks, more money and friends than they'd ever need. Yet their life was a total disaster."

Kate frowned. This was not the way she had pictured Damien Ashcroft's short marriage. Not that he had ever said anything. Yet somehow, despite the absence of a portrait of the late Mrs. Ashcroft or, perhaps, because of it, for her likeness must always be a painful reminder, Kate had formed the notion that his had been a happy union. Or, perhaps, it was because he had not remarried.

"It is quite possible," she said, trying to imagine

a very young Damien, "that their youth was to blame for any differences they may have had. With increasing maturity of the couple, their marriage might have taken a turn for the better."

"Who can tell? Elizabeth was seventeen—Liza's age—when they married. Damien was three-and-twenty," said Phoebe, then abruptly changed the subject. "Besides chaperoning Liza, how are you filling your time, Miss Elliott?"

"Well, I—"

"Moping about and pacing your room, I doubt not. What you need is a distraction to take your mind off Lord Nicholas's proposal. You must give him time to court you and yourself the opportunity to enjoy his attentions."

"Chaperoning Liza is distraction enough," Kate protested. "She is bent on seeing Major Dashwood daily, and I must confess I do not like it."

Phoebe waved away the argument. "Lord Nicholas, I believe, spends quite a bit of time at Damien's excavation site. Why don't you join him there? I know you're fascinated with Damien's ruin, and Liza's outings always include Emily and my daughters. Louisa Usborne and I can easily share the duties of chaperon, except when the girls go riding. Neither Louisa nor I care to be seen careening across the fields."

"You are very generous, ma'am, but I could not possibly agree to the scheme. Mr. Ashcroft is paying me a very steep salary to look after Liza."

"I'll deal with Damien."

Kate remembered that a week ago Nicholas had used almost those very same words. Was she the only one who could not "deal" with Damien Ashcroft? He had been very distant since learning of her connection with Nicholas, having exchanged nothing but common courtesies with her. Once or twice, she had caught him watching her, and the look of speculation in his eyes had made her spine tingle.

As Liza and her friends started to swarm into the pavilion to take their leave of Mrs. Charteris, Kate busied her hands by stacking cups and plates on a tray, but her mind stayed occupied with thoughts of Damien.

Irritating man! Undoubtedly, he'd like to dismiss her on the spot, but he feared that Nicholas would leave Dearworth the moment she did. Well, he was too much in the habit of expecting to get his own way, and he must learn that there were some people he could not bend to his will and some emotions — like love — he could not manipulate.

With that thought in mind, and totally forgetting that it was Nicholas she was supposed to concentrate on, Kate found the prospect of spending time at the excavation site much more desirable. She missed her spats with Damien. More so, she told herself, than she missed the rare moments of being utterly won over by his smile.

Her chance to go out came the following morning when Liza decided to write letters to Lady Belinda Undersham, who had already spent a glorious four weeks in London, and to Miss Susannah Abbots, who had departed for the metropolis five days ago. With Damien's words in mind that a riding habit was not the correct apparel for an excavation, Kate donned one of her old gray poplin gowns, pulled on a pair of stout walking boots, and set out on foot.

The air was still and balmy, as though it were late June rather than the third day of May. As she entered the woods, Kate was immediately aware of the sweet yet pungent scent that had not been there a week ago. Lilies-of-the-valley. Unlike the bluebells, these delicate white flowers had not allowed themselves to be teased into early bloom by spring-like winter months.

Lilies-of-the-valley always marked the celebration of her birthday, Liza had told Kate. Her seventeenth birthday on the eighth of May would signify the young girl's official entry into the circle of adults. Something must be arranged, some small surprise for Liza.

Kate stepped along briskly, anticipating the ensuing discussion with Damien Ashcroft about his daughter's birthday. He would find it very difficult to restrict his responses to monosyllables or common courtesies.

As she turned from the bridle path into the tunnellike walk that had been cut through the dense shrubbery, she heard Damien's shout, urgent and at the same time irritated. As though wanting to prove to her that he was very well able to produce more than monosyllables, he released a string of expletives — in various languages — that made Kate blink in astonishment.

"Hurry with those boards!" he shouted when, apparently, he had run out of invectives. "Damn it, Nicholas! Hurry! The side's caving in!"

Picking up her skirts, Kate ran, bursting into the clearing that marked the excavation site just as Nicholas pushed planks of wood down into the trench where Damien was visible only from his neck up.

"By the great Jehoshaphat!" Nicholas panted. "If you had listened to me and not dug so deep, you wouldn't be in danger of getting yourself buried alive. But do you ever listen to advice?"

158

"I'm not afraid of a bit of dirt. It's the mosaic I don't want buried again." Damien dashed a grimy hand across his damp forehead, leaving a wide dirt smear on his swarthy skin. Catching sight of Kate, he called out, "Miss Elliott! Lend me a hand, will you?"

"Dash it, Damien!" shouted Nicholas. "You cannot ask her down there. It's not safe."

But Kate had already scrambled down the rough ladder and started to shovel sandy soil and limestone sediment into a large wicker basket while Damien pounded planks against the crumbling side of the trench.

"I did not realize you had progressed so far this past week," Kate said with a look at the large expanse of Roman wall that had been laid bare. "You did not even tell me that you had discovered a floor. A mosaic floor?"

"Well," he said, giving her a sidelong look, "there was another matter that kept me preoccupied whenever I set eyes on you."

"Kate!" Nicholas called. "Please come up. That is no place for a lady."

"Rubbish, Nicholas. Are you suggesting it would be more suitable if I lugged those heavy planks in your stead? They must be close to six feet long."

"And we need a half dozen more," said Damien.

Nicholas gave a grunt of exasperation, but he went off to fetch more boards from the stack of lumber piled up at the edge of the clearing.

"And now, Mr. Ashcroft?" asked Kate, stabbing her shovel purposefully at a large mound of dirt.

"And now, *what?* Ouch! Dammit, Kate! Will you watch where you dig! That was my foot."

"Sorry. *Now* you're no longer preoccupied with that other matter?"

159

His look at her was unreadable. "Even more so. But since I forgot myself so far as to hail you with joy when you arrived, I daresay it would be churlish to ignore you now."

"It was churlish even before now," she pointed out. "I can hardly help it that Nicholas and I know each other. And since you did not bother to give me the name of your friend, I could not very well alert you to the fact."

Damien pounded another board in place. "It is not your knowing Nicholas that I object to. It is *how* you know each other. The ex-lover of Liza's future husband is hardly the proper companion for my daughter."

Kate heard her blood roar in her ears. She dropped the shovel. Quick as lightning, her hand shot up, aimed to land a stinging blow to his cheek.

But Damien was faster. He caught her wrist in a bruising grip, forcing her hand down. His other hand grasped her shoulder and dragged her roughly against his hard body. Through the thin lawn of his shirt, she felt the play of his muscles and the drumbeat of his heart.

"Don't," he said with silky menace. "Don't ever raise your hand against me unless you're prepared to take the punishment."

Staring into his glittering dark eyes, Kate felt her legs grow weak. Surely she wasn't afraid of him. She couldn't be, not when a part of her wanted to explore the punishment he threatened.

"Helloo there! What's the matter?" Nicholas set three boards down with a crash. He peered anxiously into the trench. "Kate, did you get hurt?"

"No . . . I am quite all right."

Damien released her. "Of course she didn't get

160

hurt. She merely endangered my project with her carelessness, and I set her straight. Did I not, Kate?"

She was too concerned about hiding her shaking hands and trembling knees to bother with a reply.

"I told you it's no place for a lady down there," said Nicholas. "Give me your hand, Kate. I'll help you up."

Kate shook her head. "Not now."

"Kate, I'm asking you to come up. I couldn't bear to see you get hurt."

"I'll be careful," she said with growing impatience. In fact, she felt so shaken by her encounter with Damien that it was more likely she'd get hurt tumbling off the ladder than by falling debris. "Now that I'm down here, I want to clear the floor and see the mosaic for myself."

Damien muttered for her ears alone, "Shouldn't you be running from me?"

"Dash it, Kate," said Nicholas, "if you aren't as bad as Damien!"

"You mean to say, of course, that she is courageous," Damien retorted, but added under his breath, "Or foolhardy."

Kate threw him a fulminating glance, which he quite missed, since he was looking toward the bridle path, his head cocked to listen. And then Kate heard it, too, the sound of hooves and the soft whinny of a horse.

"Nicholas," she said. "If that is Liza, would you please keep her distracted while I discuss a matter of some urgency with Mr. Ashcroft? You see, it's Liza's birthday on the eighth."

"We must hold a ball," said Nicholas.

Damien frowned. "You have windmills in your head, my friend. I haven't held a ball at Dearworth

161

in years."

"Then it is high time you did." Kate waved Nicholas on. "Go! Keep her away from here."

But it was too late. Liza rode up to them, saying, "I changed my mind, Miss Elliott. I don't want to write letters after all. It is such a bore. Belinda brags about balls and routs and Almack's, and I have nothing to report but tea parties in the vicar's pavilion."

Kate raised a brow. "Nothing else?"

Liza blushed and turned to Nicholas. "I thought you might be bored, too. After all, you didn't come to Dearworth to dig in the dirt, did you?"

"Well—" Nicholas looked startled. He cast a helpless look at Damien, but *he* appeared to be totally absorbed in shoring up the side of the trench and offered no support whatever.

"He certainly did not," said Kate.

"No." Rising magnificently to the occasion, Nicholas told Liza, "I came to enjoy a little riding and to be entertained by two lovely young ladies. But since one of the ladies appears to prefer digging to entertaining, I shall inflict my poor company on you. Will you take pity on me?"

Liza's peal of laughter rose into the air. "I'd be delighted to take you up on my horse, Nicholas."

He mounted behind her. "Only back to the stables to get my own mount," he said, reaching around her to take the reins. "A lady's saddle doesn't leave a fellow much room to sit."

Kate barely waited until horse and riders were out of sight and earshot before saying severely, "Mr. Ashcroft! You may stop pretending that you're busy. They're gone. Just as you intended, didn't you?"

Damien grinned. Dusting off his hands, he said,

162

"Let's sit in the shade. The dig is safe enough for now, and I have a feeling that our discussion will be heated."

"Why?" Kate scowled at him. "Do you mean to deny Liza a birthday ball?"

"No. But that, I fear, will not be the only topic under discussion."

Chapter Twelve

Spreading his coat, Damien invited Kate to sit against the tall beech tree whose bright green roof already shaded a covered hamper. He scrubbed his face, neck, and hands with a damp towel, but when he stretched out on the ground beside Kate, she saw that he had missed the streak on his forehead.

"Where are the twins?" she asked, little by little easing her body away from his.

Her cautious maneuver brought a gleam to his eyes, but he answered her question civilly enough. "I daresay they're nursing their grievances. Yesterday they actually brought along a score of sightseers. I raked them down in thundering style—the twins, that is—and made them give back the pennies they had collected as guides to the site."

He took a bottle of wine and two glasses from the hamper. "There's chicken, ham sandwiches, a meat pie, and a jam tart. Care to join me in a bite of luncheon?"

"I'm not hungry." Again and again, her eyes were drawn to that smear of dirt on his forehead. He didn't look so formidable now but rather endearing. It was wonderful what transformation one small flaw could bring about.

"I will drink a glass of wine, though, to bolster my courage," she said, the hint of a smile curving her mouth.

He gave a grunt that might have been an indication of his doubts in her lack of courage, or his satisfaction in the successful removal of the cork.

"It is to be hoped that a drop of wine will put some color in your cheeks," he said. "Conscience been robbing you of your beauty sleep, Kate?"

"I should prefer it if you continued to call me Miss Elliott."

"*You* may prefer it, but I don't. It's easier to pull caps with Kate than with Miss Elliott."

Her brows drew together in a puzzled frown.

"Miss Elliott, on her dignity," he said, "might walk out on me, while Kate will fight back."

"Have you changed your mind, then, about meek ladies?"

He only grinned in reply, and when they were both supplied with a glass of sparkling hock, he said, "You are staring, Kate. Are you trying to put a spell on me?"

Her face grew warm, but perhaps the sun shone just a little stronger than before. Fanning herself with her hand, she said, "I must be a better witch than I supposed. You have a mark on your forehead."

"Then you had best take it off."

There was a challenge in his voice and in the look he gave her, and Kate responded instinctively. Picking up the damp towel, she knelt at his side. "The dirt has caked. Hold still," she commanded. "I don't want to get any in your eyes."

She dabbed gently at first, then scrubbed harder. And all the while, her heartbeat increased and her breathing became more labored as her nostrils and mind filled with the musky scent of his skin and the smell of the sandalwood soap he used. Without quite knowing how it happened, her ministrations

165

to his forehead turned into caresses.

"Witches burned at the stake not long ago," he said.

Her hand moved slowly across his brow. "And what happens to witches today?"

"You'll find out. Tell me, Kate. Shall you marry Nicholas?"

She sat back on her heels. The towel slipped from her fingers when she saw his look of speculation. So he thought she would confide in him, did he now?

"Yes, of course I shall," she said promptly.

A spark ignited in the depth of his eyes. "No, you won't. And I'll show you why."

He gave her no time, no chance of escape. He was up on his knees, his arms locked around her waist, and his mouth claimed hers as he pulled her against his chest.

But Kate had no thought of fighting him. Like molten fire, her blood burned in her veins, heightening her sensitivity to his touch.

Somehow, her fingers found their way to his hair, burying themselves in the thickness and richness of it. She heard him give a groan deep in his throat. His mouth moved more demandingly against hers, and his hands slid up her sides to cup her breasts. Her body glowed under his hands, yearning to be held closer yet, wanting to be singed by the flame of passion that heated his flesh.

Like pliant wax, Kate molded herself against him, and still it wasn't close enough to appease the hunger he had awakened in her. Dimly, she recalled Phoebe Charteris's advice to her: You need opportunity to enjoy his attentions. Wise Phoebe! Kate had never enjoyed anything so much as Damien's attentions.

But Phoebe was referring to Nicholas!

Blind panic doused the yearning of her flesh. Her lips that had, but an instant ago, parted so willingly under his stiffened with denial. But before Kate could push Damien away, he released her.

Unmindful of decorum or dignity, Kate scrambled away from him until the solid trunk of the beech tree put a halt to her flight. Weakly, she leaned her back against the rough bark and smoothed her mussed skirt over her legs. What was happening to her that she forgot herself so?

She risked a peek at Damien. He was breathing hard, and his face was flushed. But even as she thought that he was just as startled as she by the consuming fire of their embrace, the strange glitter in his eyes died.

"You see, Kate," he said as though he were explaining a simple fact of life. "I kept my promise. There was no need for me to make *un*welcome advances. You wanted this as much as I did."

Her face flamed. She was breathless and shaken. Only too well did she remember. Rashly, as she now knew, she had told him in Sir Shafto's library that she would not again suffer his unwelcome advances without retribution. But not only had she *not* boxed his ears as any lady of breeding and sober years should, she had actually *invited* his embrace.

He stretched out on the ground in his former casual pose. "How can you possibly marry Nicholas," he drawled, "when you go about kissing me?"

Her shame was forgotten in a sudden flare of anger that made her sit up on her knees. "Why, you scheming, calculating wretch!" She glared at him. Surely, if it didn't involve moving closer, she'd reach out and strangle the cad. "And to think that

167

you call Nicholas friend!"

Unmoved by her fury and scorn, he poured more wine. "Do you believe Nicholas could arouse you to the heights of passion as I did?"

"Let me assure you, Mr. Ashcroft, that I have grown too old and wise to be taken in by mere physical desire. The experience we shared will not have a repeat. Ever. Good day!"

And on these pungent words, Kate rose, hoping her legs would carry her out of his sight before buckling under her.

"Tell me, Kate," he said, looking up at her through half-closed eyes. "Were you and Nicholas lovers?"

"You'll never know," she said scathingly. "Will you?"

"But you know the punishment for witches now and for impudent ladies who dare raise a hand against me. Heed my words, Kate. I want Nicholas for Liza."

Afterwards, she could not recall how she had found the way from the clearing without stumbling or falling. Her body and mind seemed unconnected, for she could see only Damien's half-closed eyes, his mocking smile; could still hear his taunting words.

How dare he use her thus! Kissing her, mauling her, merely to show that he could awaken desires no lady should know save in the arms of her lawfully wedded husband. Even at the height of her infatuation with Nicholas, she had not felt such abandoned, brazen desire as she experienced in Damien's arms.

What was happening to her? she wondered yet again. Was she a wanton, or a love-starved old maid? A horrid thought. Quickly, she shunted it aside.

How dare he threaten her! She might not marry Nicholas because her love for him had waned, but never would she *not* marry because Damien willed it so.

Engrossed in her dark thoughts, Kate stormed along the bridle path. An elderly gentleman rounding the bend from the direction of Dearworth gave her a rather startled look as she shot past him, then called out to her.

"Ma'am! Pardon me, ma'am. I wonder if you can help me?"

She stopped, turning to look at him with such an air of distraction that he regretted having accosted her. But he had come with a purpose in mind, and the sooner he found his quarry, the sooner . . .

He doffed his hat, a shabby affair with a dented crown and drooping brim. "I am looking for Mr. Ashcroft, ma'am. Damien Ashcroft."

His voice, low and cultured, finally captured Kate's full attention. Oxford, she thought. But would a respectable gentleman show himself abroad in a wrinkled coat and a shirt and waistcoat that bore witness to the meals he had consumed? Kate thought not. Prudence demanded she turn her back on the stranger and get away as fast as possible.

"What is your business with Mr. Ashcroft?" she asked. The elderly man did not look as though he could do her physical harm, if that were his intention. At least a head shorter than she and of sparse build, he'd have a difficult time overpowering even one of the twins.

He pulled a pair of wire-framed spectacles from a bulging coat pocket and, perching them onto the bridge of his nose, peered shortsightedly at her.

"Are you Mrs. Ashcroft, then?"

An innocent question, yet it took her breath away. Striving for control, Kate said haughtily, "I am Miss Elliott. And you still haven't told me your business with Mr. Ashcroft."

"Perhaps because it's none of your concern," he replied testily. "What's the matter with folks around here? I inquire at the house and get nothing but faradiddles about Mr. Ashcroft not receiving. I don't want to be received!" Waving bony arms and fists for emphasis, he said, "I want a look at the ruin he's supposed to have found."

"Ah!" A spark lit in Kate's eyes. She spoke quickly, before common sense could tell her nay. "Mr. Ashcroft is working at the excavation site now. I daresay he'll be happy to show you around."

"Well, how far is it?"

"Just follow this path awhile, then watch for an opening in the shrubbery on your left. You can't miss it. It's wide enough for a horse and cart, and it'll lead you straight to Mr. Ashcroft."

Having stowed away his spectacles, he doffed his hat again, displaying long, untidy gray hair. "Much obliged to you, Miss Elliott."

"And don't feel shy about asking questions. Mr. Ashcroft enjoys showing off the ruin."

He gave her a strange look, but nodded and walked off with a surprisingly spritely bounce to his step.

Kate watched until the next bend in the path took him out of sight, then set out briskly toward Dearworth. She wished she could see Damien's face when the funny little man presented himself. Another curious sightseer to provoke him, but Kate, unlike Walter and Peter, had not asked a penny for providing the directions to the site. *Her* reward was of a less tangible nature: satisfaction at having scored against Damien.

But when Damien returned late that afternoon, he seemed less aggravated than resigned. Kate was going downstairs to join Nicholas and Liza on the lilac-bordered terrace that could be reached through the morning room or the library, when she saw him in the foyer in conference with Boughey.

Her breath caught in her throat, and she came to a dead stop on the stairs. He was still in his rolled-up shirtsleeves and carried his coat slung across his shoulder like a field laborer. But it wasn't his lack of dignity that worried her; it was the sight of his tanned, sinewy arms that had held her a willing captive but a few hours ago, the sight of his bare head that she had cradled and caressed, and now served as a reminder of her wanton behavior.

Her hand stole to the banister, clutching it tightly. She could not face him now.

"I've already spoken with Ramsden and Hinkson," Damien said to the butler. "There is to be an hourly patrol of the site, and if Edward or Ben are needed to relieve the stable lads, Hinkson will send you word."

Kate saw Boughey's cheerful face crumble into lines of woe. "It'll make us very shorthanded in the house, sir," the butler said dolefully as she turned and started to tiptoe back upstairs. "Very shorthanded indeed. Especially with company present."

"Dammit, you're right. We'll have to think of something else."

Kate peeked over her shoulder just as Damien crossed the entrance hall with long, impatient strides. His gaze alighted on her, and he stopped, looking up at her from the foot of the stairs. It was as though he were reaching out across the distance to touch her, lightly, tenderly. Then he spoke.

"Ah, Miss Elliott," he said with a sarcastic edge to his voice. "No doubt *you* will know what to do."

"Yes, indeed." Never let him see that for an instant she was fooled by his dark eyes. Raising her chin, she descended to the foyer.

She gave the butler a reassuring smile. "We'll simply ask Mrs. Boughey to make arrangements with the maids. They can stay until dusk and, I daresay, one or two of them would be quite willing to live in. That'll give the footmen sufficient time to go on patrol."

Boughey's countenance resumed its cherubic aspects. "Yes, Miss Elliott. That will work out splendidly."

He trundled off toward the baize curtain that hid the access to the nether regions behind the staircase. Halfway there, he stopped and, giving his employer an inquiring look, said politely, "If it is all right with you, sir?"

Without removing his gaze from Kate's face, Damien motioned the butler away. "Miss Elliott, a word with you please."

"If you dislike my suggestion regarding the maids, you need only call Boughey back."

"The maids? No, no." Clasping her elbow as though he sensed her reluctance to be with him, he started to walk toward the library. "Mrs. Boughey has been asking for some time to have the arrangements changed. It's another matter entirely that I wish to discuss. Where is Liza?"

"With Nicholas." Kate wondered if Damien could hear the beat of her heart. With a simple gesture such as touching her arm, he could reduce her to

172

the state of a girl just entering puberty. "On the terrace."

He came to an abrupt halt. "You had best come to my study, then. Liza is entirely too fond of eavesdropping."

Kate followed him upstairs, glad that he had released her arm and allowed her to regain her composure. Without speaking, they traversed the first-floor corridor, and still without saying a word, he opened the door to the corner room where they had fought two previous battles.

Kate preceded him into the study. Someone had drawn the drapes against the oncoming dusk and lit a lamp atop the mantel shelf, giving the room a cozy, intimate atmosphere. Choosing a chair at some distance from the desk, she gave him a questioning look. "If it is about that strange little man I sent to the site—"

The corners of his mouth twitched. "Oh, was it you?" he asked blandly. "Much obliged. That was Professor Crabb, an eminent antiquary. We've had a long-standing acquaintance via the publications of the Society of Antiquaries but never met personally until today."

"Well!" said Kate, feeling cheated. "Why didn't he introduce himself to me?"

Damien was busy with the decanter and glasses set out on his desk. "Had you known, would you not have sent him?"

"Of course I should have. It's only—"

"It's only that you wanted to annoy me, and now you fear that I may be pleased." He offered her a glass of brandy and when she shook her head, he said commandingly, "Take it! Haven't you learned yet that inexperience only puts you at a disadvantage when you tangle with me?"

173

She gave him a startled look. He was not merely referring to her lack of familiarity with brandy. A world of meaning lay behind his words. But if he had read inexperience in her kiss, surely he need not have asked if she and Nicholas had been lovers.

Warmth stole into her face. She accepted the glass Damien still held out to her but set it down on a small lamp table. "Why, then, the patrols?" she asked to cover her confusion.

"Because Crabb's visit did annoy me. And because the site is too dangerous to leave unguarded."

Watching her, he sipped from his own glass. There was puzzlement in the look he gave her. "You are an unusual woman, Kate. So wise when it comes to your dealings with Liza, and then you perpetrate a prank worthy of Walter-Peter."

She wanted to lash out at him with angry words, but none came to mind. He was right. A lady of her advanced years should not have engaged in a schoolroom prank. But when dealing with Damien, her age was of no benefit at all. She felt as uncertain and confused as though she were no older than Liza.

"I apologize," she said stiffly. "I allowed myself to be carried away by anger."

She could read nothing in his face, but he nodded as though satisfied with her response. Pulling up a chair, he sat down close to her. It was not what she had intended when she chose a seat away from the desk. She had wished to put a safe distance between them.

"If that is all, then?" She started to rise, but Damien motioned her to remain seated. This time, his expression was easy to read: the cynical curl of his mouth, the mocking gleam in his eyes.

"No, Kate. This was not why I wanted to speak with you. In fact, I was perfectly willing to ignore your little jest. It was *you* who felt the need to explain and apologize for your wayward conduct."

"The devil you say!" Finally, the anger she had earlier summoned in vain surged up. "How dare you speak to me of wayward conduct. You, who are as wayward as they come!"

"Tsk, tsk. What strong language for a lady. I recommend a sip of brandy. It is very soothing."

"And I suggest you get on with what you want to say to me. I must go to Liza and Nicholas. They'll wonder what has become of me."

"Ah, yes. Let us talk about you and Nicholas. And Liza."

Her spine stiffened. "Mr. Ashcroft, we've said all there is to say about Nicholas and me. I do not intend to discuss the matter further. And quite frankly, I don't understand why you wish Liza to marry a man who obviously loves another."

"He *believes* he does. At the moment," he interposed smoothly. So smoothly that it could have been the voice of Kate's own doubts.

But she'd never admit her doubts to Damien. "If you force the issue, only disaster can result from their union."

A brooding look came into his eyes. "I'll not force Liza. Nor Nicholas. But they're made for each other. He'll adore her capriciousness, her naivete; she'll love him for the care and attention he'll lavish on her."

As though Nicholas would not lavish that same care on *her!* Kate swallowed a stinging reply and only pointed out, "Liza believes herself in love with Major Dashwood."

"Dashwood is a gazetted fortune hunter," Damien said savagely. "Is that the kind of man you'd wish for Liza? Pshaw! And you said you love my daughter!"

"You are wrong." She rose, her face pale. "I would not wish the major on *any* woman. But I do wish, Mr. Ashcroft, you'd have the decency to let me make my own decision regarding Nicholas instead of trying to browbeat me!"

"Indeed? Are you so keen, then, on getting leg-shackled that you'll decide in Nicholas's favor whether you love him or not?"

Too late, she realized that rising had been an error. As a gentleman, Damien could not remain seated while she stood. His height and the width of his shoulders threatened her, yet, like the lodestone attracted metal, his strength and power attracted her.

But she must not show him how he affected her.

With as much disdain as she could muster, she said, "And just why, I wonder, are you so keen on marrying Liza to the man of *your* choice? Knowing you, I can only suspect a very ulterior motive."

Damien thought of the pain he wished to spare Liza, and he grimaced wryly. But, of course, Kate didn't know of the scandal Elizabeth had caused. She didn't know that once Liza's resemblance to her mother was noted, the *ton* would shake its collective head and speculate with vicious pleasure that undoubtedly Liza's character as well as her looks resembled that of her mother. And Liza's chances of marriage—except to a bounder like the major—would go to the devil. Nicholas knew, and some day, when she was less irritated, he'd tell Kate.

But it was not the reason he'd give her now.

"This time it is you who are quite wrong," he

176

said, taking a step toward her. "You see, mainly I want to prevent your marriage to Nicholas."

"Well!" Kate bristled. "And why, pray tell?"

"Because, dear Kate, Nicholas is not the man for you. Do you remember how he fussed when you were working in the trench? You'd never put up with that for long."

"Nicholas loves me. There is no question of *putting up* with anything."

His black brows knitted as he stared at her in growing vexation. "Nicholas fell in love with a seventeen-year-old. He is still in love with that child. He doesn't know *you* at all."

Unwilling to admit the truth, or at least partial truth, of what he said, Kate retorted, "We'll get to know each other."

Her words echoed in his mind. He heard himself, a twenty-three-year-old utterly confident in his judgment and his love for Elizabeth, hurl that very same argument at his mother when she pointed out that he could not possibly know Elizabeth's character after his brief, tumultuous courtship of her.

His mother had been correct, but she had not been able to stop her headstrong son. Blindly, he had entered into a marriage that had been doomed from the beginning.

Shaking his head as though he could with that motion shake off unwelcome memories, he started for the door.

Kate stared after him, wondering if he had forgotten her presence, but as he turned the knob, he looked back at her.

"And besides," he said, the words seemingly torn from him against his will, "I have different plans for you."

Chapter Thirteen

Damien's footsteps faded away in the corridor when Kate finally roused herself from the stupor into which his words had sunk her. *Different plans.* And just what did he mean by that? Two possibilities sprang to mind with alacrity, as though they had long been hovering, waiting only for the opportunity to pounce.

He intended to wed her himself — or make her a proposal of the other kind.

While her legs and body started to move, slowly and with the subconscious sureness of a sleepwalker, her thoughts tumbled as though they were so many rings tossed into the air by a juggler. She had barely caught one when another thought popped up, forcing her to abandon the first.

Surely she must have been affected by the sun to even consider that marriage might be a part of his plans for her. An irrational thought indeed when they had been at daggers drawn since the day he engaged her services, and when she knew that his kisses were meant as a form of punishment rather than an expression of affection. Besides, Phoebe Charteris had emphasized that Damien had no intention of ever marrying again. And Phoebe should know. Hadn't she been acquainted with Damien since childhood?

And the other possibility . . . well, it was just as ridiculous. Damien might be a rake and not above kissing his daughter's companion, but he'd hardly proposition her while she was chaperoning Liza and living under his roof. Even the most dissolute philanderer would strive to preserve the sanctity of his house.

But what if he were only waiting for Liza to marry and leave his home? He had sounded reluctant, as though he hadn't planned to say as much as he did.

And why did she even bother with Damien's plans for her? *She* was in charge of her life, had been since Richard's guardianship lapsed seven years ago. *She* would make her own plans, and Damien Ashcroft had no part in them.

But he had already insinuated himself into her life. He had given her a small taste of the pleasures he could give a woman.

Kate came to an abrupt halt at the top of the wide stairs. The by-now familiar feeling of breathlessness that she associated with thoughts of Damien or with being near him gripped her. She still remembered the feel of his hands upon her body, the taste of his mouth, the smell of his skin. She came alive in Damien's arms, became a woman of flesh and blood, of feelings and yearnings she had never known before.

Panic washed over her, leaving her weak and trembling when she realized just how vulnerable she was. If she hadn't promised to stay with Liza, if she hadn't given her hand on it . . .

But no, Kate Elliott had never yet run from difficulties. She had faced Lord Adair's wrath. She had defied Richard when, just before her twenty-first birthday, he had given her the ultimatum either to marry their lecherous seventy-year-old neighbor or live at Elliott Chase and play nursemaid to his children and companion to Margaret. She had faced problems then; she would face and deal with her weakness for Damien's embraces — if he should dare approach her again.

And now, the sooner she joined Nicholas and Liza, the sooner she'd be able to banish Damien Ashcroft from her mind. Purpose lending swiftness to her step, she descended the stairs and swept into the library whence a pair of French doors opened onto the terrace. Her exit was blocked, however, by the bustling entrance of Mrs. Abbots, Susannah's stern-faced mama.

Stepping aside to avoid a collision with Mrs. Abbots, Kate said, "This is a surprise, ma'am. I hope it wasn't sickness that brought you back from London so soon?"

"No, it wasn't, Miss Elliott. Susannah will spend a few weeks with her aunt and cousins before I rejoin her toward the end of the season."

Mrs. Abbots looked sterner than ever as she measured Kate from head to foot with cold gray eyes. "Miss Elliott, I deem it only fair to warn you that I plan to seek an interview with Mr. Ashcroft, and that I also feel it my duty to drop a word of warning in Phoebe Charteris's and Louisa Usborne's ears."

Kate swallowed. There was no need for Mrs. Abbots to say more. Kate knew there was one more matter she would have to face and deal with.

She met Mrs. Abbots's cold look. "You may save yourself the trouble of speaking with Mr. Ashcroft and Mrs. Charteris. I have already told them about Lord Nicholas."

"You did?" Mrs. Abbots looked taken aback, but only for an instant. She gave a disdainful sniff. "I wonder how truthful you were, Miss Elliott. I doubt Mr. Ashcroft would keep you on if he knew just how disgraceful your behavior was. He is not one to tolerate a scandal of any kind."

"And I wonder that you waited so long to come forward," Kate said coldly.

"Indeed!" Mrs. Abbots drew herself up to stare down her long nose at Kate. "I should have done so sooner," she said righteously, "had I realized why your name was familiar. But it was my sister in London who immediately remembered the scandal. Your face meant nothing to me when I met you at the squire's dinner, because I had never laid eyes on you before. Susannah was stricken with the measles at the time you eloped with Lord Nicholas, and so I only learned of it secondhand."

"You know my story through gossip, and yet you feel qualified to disclose the *truth* about me to your neighbors."

Mrs. Abbots's color deepened. "You often chaperon Louisa's and Phoebe's daughters. *Somebody* must warn them about your true character, especially now that I've learned Lord Nicholas is staying at Dearworth."

"I shan't take up any more of your time, then. I daresay you'll need it all to make the rounds. Good day, Mrs. Abbots." Sweeping aside her skirts, Kate stepped past the older woman.

Only when she stood on the terrace and breathed deeply of the clear spring air did the protective mantle of insouciance slip. She *did* care. She did *not* want to have to face cold stares, backs turned pointedly as she approached, or sly remarks made in her presence—indignities that she had borne eleven years ago before Richard had whisked her out of Bath and thereby had tacitly confirmed even the vilest rumors.

And now the scandalbroth was to be reheated; gossip and innuendoes would fly again.

Kate thought of Mrs. Abbots's remark that Damien was not the man to tolerate scandal of any kind. A strange observation, considering that he had been surrounded by gossip when he dallied with opera dancers and sported a mistress in Rome. But, of course, here he had Liza to consider, not just himself.

The crunch of gravel alerted her that someone was approaching on one of the meticulously raked walks behind the lilac hedge. A few moments later, Nicholas turned the corner. A deep frown marred his high forehead, and he was obviously lost in thought, for he did not see Kate until he ascended the shallow steps that led to the highest level of the terrace where she stood.

His step faltered, and she thought he was not particularly pleased to see her. But then he smiled. Tossing aside the cheroot he had been smoking, he hurried to her side.

"Kate! Well met. I was just thinking about you."

"Oh? I hoped it was someone else who had brought that dark look to your face."

His sensitive skin flushed. For a moment, he looked like a little boy caught in an untruth. Quite unlike Damien, who would have shown her his devilish grin and said something sarcastic.

"If I seemed troubled," Nicholas assured her, "it was because of an unpleasant encounter I had ten or fifteen minutes ago."

"Mrs. Abbots."

His embarrassment deepened, but a hint of anger contributed to his high color. "She dared accost you, too? A vile-mouthed creature with talons and the sharp eye of a hawk. Kate, she is one of those harpies who will not rest until she has torn your character to shreds."

"*My* character? What about yours, Nicholas? Are you to get off scot-free?"

"It is the way of the world that a man is given more license than a woman."

Kate knew Nicholas well enough to realize that he did not mean to hurt her, but he sounded so insufferably smug that only with difficulty did she keep her temper in check.

"Where is Liza?" she asked. "If that woman upset her—"

"Don't fret, Kate. I am glad to say that Mrs. Abbots spoke to Liza only of London and her daughter's success at Almack's. She waited until Liza left to read Miss Susannah's letter in the privacy of her room before—"

"Before what?" Kate said impatiently when he didn't complete the sentence.

Nicholas gestured to a cushioned bench that stood among the lilacs. "Let us sit down for a moment and discuss our situation."

She gazed from the open French doors and windows of the house to the seclusion of the bench. Without ado, she accepted his invitation. Whatever they had to say to each other was best said in privacy.

He sat down beside her. Rather close, she thought, but his proximity, unlike that of Damien Ashcroft, did not make her feel threatened. Nicholas's presence was like that of an old and well-known friend; it soothed. Damien's stirred her blood.

Nicholas's words, however, were anything but soothing. "Kate," he said urgently, "you've had over a week to consider my proposal of marriage. I

183

honor your feelings. Indeed, I understand your doubts, but under the circumstances, I can only urge you to accept my offer with all speed."

So he understood her doubts, did he? Perhaps he experienced some of his own?

"That wouldn't stop the gossip, Nicholas."

"Perhaps not, but I'd have the right to stand up for you. As it is, Mrs. Abbots wants your instant dismissal without reference."

"Only Mr. Ashcroft can dismiss me," Kate pointed out.

Nicholas gave her an intent look. "Do you have reason to believe that he would not do so?"

"No, of course not!"

Her denial must have been too hasty or too emphatic, for Nicholas did not believe her.

"Kate," he said, "what is it between you and Damien? There are times when I can feel the tension between you as though I'd put my hand on a brick wall."

"A fitting metaphor," said Kate, trying to keep her voice light. "I often feel as though I'm knocking my head against a wall when I argue with him about Liza. He keeps her far too secluded, don't you agree? She should be trying out her wings in Bath, visit the theater, the Pump Room, even attend a ball or two."

"There are reasons—" Nicholas broke off. He took Kate's hand, pressing it gently. "I am sorry, Kate. If Damien has not told you why he keeps Liza here, among his friends, I would be betraying his confidence if I explained it to you. And besides," he added with a slight smile, "you were only trying to change the subject, were you not?"

She should withdraw her hand, but she did not wish to hurt him. And after all, his touch did not diminish her capacity for clear thought the way Damien's did.

"Is Liza not a subject that concerns us both?" she asked. She watched the color deepen in his narrow face and wished that he weren't quite so sensitive. She'd rather hear him tell her to mind her own business than see him blush.

"I have begun to suspect that Damien wants me to marry Liza. Do you know this for a fact, then?"

"Are you asking *me* to betray a confidence?"

"Forget that I asked." After a slight hesitation, Nicholas added, "I daresay that is his *only* reason to oppose our marriage?"

"Yes," Kate said firmly. "He believes that you and Liza are well suited. If you had not met me again, would you think so, too?"

Nicholas stared at the tips of his highly glossed Hessians. Had he not heard her question?

"Liza is a child," he said finally. He moved a little on the bench to face her more fully. Brushing the back of her hand with his lips, he gazed at Kate with affection and concern. "Will you marry me?"

Gently, she withdrew her hand. "No, Nicholas. We would never suit."

She read regret in the look he gave her, but also a hint of relief.

"Kate, may I be your friend? You see, I'm asking, not assuming," he said ruefully. "I've learned quite a bit about you these past days, and I have taken particular note of your pride in your independence."

She smiled. "Are you sure you don't mean my 'cursed mule-headedness'? That's what Richard calls it, you see."

"To the devil with Richard!" said Nicholas.

"But," he added on a note of warning. "An inde
pendent lady can easily be misunderstood. Espe
cially by someone of the opposite sex."

"If you're warning me about Damien," she said
gruffly, "there is no need to do so, I assure you
Mrs. Charteris already told me that his marriage
was an unhappy one and that he has no intention
of marrying again."

"But you do not deny that you're attracted to
him? Are you"—he cleared his throat—"are you in
love with him?"

"Lud, Nicholas!" Kate jumped to her feet with
such undignified haste that she ripped the flounce
of her skirt.

"Now see what you made me do," she scolded
"How can you talk such fustian? In love with Da
mien Ashcroft! Ha! What woman in her right
mind would fall in love with an overbearing, deceit
ful, and totally despicable rake?"

And on these words, Kate snatched up her trail
ing skirt, turned on her heel, and marched pur
posefully toward the house.

Shaking his head, Nicholas remained standing by
the bench. "The lady does protest too much, me
thinks," he quoted softly.

He withdrew a cigar case from his pocket and
carefully selected a cheroot. When it was lit to his
satisfaction, he resumed his seat on the bench to
smoke his cigar and to ponder several amazing rev
elations.

For eleven years, he had believed himself and
Kate to be star-crossed lovers. He had met many a
beautiful woman during his travels, but never one
like Kate. And then he had found Kate again
There had been no doubt in his mind that the
meeting was destined by the fates. He and Kate

were meant for each other. They would marry and live happily ever after in the manner of a fairy tale prince and princess.

But Kate had refused him. He should feel devastated, and yet he felt only a vague sadness, as though he were waking up from a dream that he knew had been exceptionally wonderful and special, but that he could not remember clearly.

Blowing smoke rings, he watched them spiral higher and higher, then dissolve. Perhaps Damien had been right. He had loved the dreamy-eyed seventeen-year-old Kate who adored him and looked up to him as though he were a semi-god. When he got to know the woman Kate had grown into, his love had proven as insubstantial as the smoke rings he blew.

Kate was strong now, a woman of will. Even if she denied it, she admired Damien, whose willpower matched her own and probably surpassed it. But if Kate were falling in love with Damien . . .

Nicholas's mouth tightened. It had been years since Damien had spoken of Elizabeth. In the spring of 1810 it had been, while Congress was making a gay time of it in Vienna. He had known some of the awful things Elizabeth had done, but not all, and Damien had told him the worst part only because they had both been invited to Vienna by the Count and Countess von Oberndorf. Nicholas could never forget how bitter Damien had been, how scathingly he had spoken of marriage. And he did not think that Damien's views had changed.

Poor Kate.

Light dancing footsteps drew his gaze toward the terrace. Nicholas dropped his cigar. He rose, smiling, his blue eyes filling with warmth and tenderness.

"May I join you, Nicholas?" Liza tilted her head and fluttered her long lashes at him.

"I'd be devastated if you didn't." What an adorable little flirt she was. Too bad she couldn't go to London. She'd be the toast of the town, and no doubt about it.

Carefully, Nicholas plumped the cushions on the bench, then, with a bow and an inviting sweep of his hand, asked Liza to sit down.

Chapter Fourteen

Since Mary, Mrs. Boughey's niece, had taken up her post as Liza's personal maid, the housekeeper had mellowed toward Kate, as though she knew that it was Miss Liza's companion who was responsible for Mary's employment. And when the village girls who helped keep the large house dusted and polished were hired as full-time maids, Mrs. Boughey showed her approval of Kate by conferring with her on household matters that she would formerly not have dreamed of broaching to a mere companion.

Kate's days, therefore, were filled with preparations for Liza's birthday ball. She was too busy to waste a single thought on questions that did not pertain to Liza's gown, to the floral arrangements for the ballroom, the dinner menu and refreshments, or the choosing of rooms for those guests who would spend the night at Dearworth rather than brave the hazards of dark, rutted roads after the ball. Yet, once in a while, none of the innumerable chores she had offered to perform could stop Nicholas's question from popping into her mind.

Are you in love with Damien?

Then an angry flush would mount in her cheeks, and she would push aside the place cards she was penning in her best copperplate, or she'd snap at Liza, who complained that she had wished for a ball gown of spangled tulle, not one of white silk. She'd snatch up a shawl and go outside to walk off her irritation in the still-bare rose garden. Here, screened from the house by tall, sculpted yew hedges, she was the least likely to be observed while she cooled her cheeks and her temper, and she could mutter aloud and grumble about the sheer idiocy of Nicholas's question.

She might be attracted to Damien—much as a nubile chambermaid was attracted to a stalwart footman—but those stirrings of the blood were passing fancies. She'd be over this attack of madness before long, and it had nothing, absolutely nothing to do with love. She was a lady of great common sense. Hadn't Phoebe Charteris confirmed this more than once? Well, a sensible woman did not fall in love with a man of so few redeeming qualities as Damien Ashcroft had to offer.

Kate freely admitted that she had wronged him when she thought him uncaring of Liza, but he was still the insufferable, overbearing, arrogant coxcomb who had bumped into her in The Circus, then tried to soothe her with a shilling piece. And he'd never change. He would always pursue his course, would forge ahead regardless of obstacles.

Recollection of their first and subsequent encounters generally restored her to good spirits and she could return to whatever chore she had abandoned. If, briefly, on the way back into the house, she remembered her passion for steeplechases and how she used to urge her mount to jump hedges, ditches, and walls, she quickly suppressed the memories. To acknowledge her own drive to soar above obstacles would be to acknowledge sympathy with Damien, and that she was not prepared to do.

She found herself watching him, though, when

he joined Liza, Nicholas, and her for dinner, the only meal he shared with them, since he left for the excavation site before breakfast and did not return until dusk forced him to lay aside his tools. She waited for him to make some comment about her and Nicholas. Surely by now he knew that they had decided they would not suit. But he spoke only of his excavation and of the twins' eagerness and their aptitude for the work.

"Peter found three lead seals," Damien reported the night before the ball, when he had returned especially late and sat down to dinner just as the two footmen carried in dessert. "The seals all bear the emblem of a sheep, which leads me to believe that they came off bales of wool."

"Another small piece in the puzzle about Roman times," said Nicholas. He raised his wineglass in a salute. "Here's to your success, Damien. May Lady Luck remain favorable to you and your quest to prove that an important Imperial estate was once located right here on Dearworth."

"I wish I had been there," said Kate. "How much of the mosaic floor have you uncovered?"

"About eight square feet." Damien refused the soup Boughey offered him, but he accepted a slice of veal and some artichoke bottoms. He gave Kate a long look across the table. "Too bad you were in such a hurry to leave the other day. You never did get a glimpse of the floor, did you?"

She would *not* blush. "I shall come on a tour of inspection after the ball," she replied with dignity.

"And what does the ball have to do with your visit, pray tell?"

"Don't you know," Liza chimed in, "that Miss Elliott is making all the preparations for my ball? Mrs. Boughey says she wouldn't know what to do without Miss Elliott's help."

Damien laid down his knife and fork. "And who," he asked with awful calm, "is chaperoning you when you make sheep's eyes at the major?"

"Papa!" The shrillness of Liza's voice and the ominous glitter in her blue eyes presaged stormy recriminations.

Smoothly, Nicholas intervened, saying in his quiet way, "Since Kate was overburdened these past days, and since you, my friend, see nought but the dirt at your feet and ancient shards of mosaic, I asked Kate if she would entrust Liza to me."

"And a stricter chaperon you'd hardly find," said Liza with a moue of discontent. "He accompanies me everywhere. You'd think Nicholas is my suitor instead—instead of Major Dashwood," she finished defiantly.

Kate caught her breath. She reminded herself that young ladies were prone to exaggeration. Surely, in just a few days, matters between Liza and the major could not have progressed so far that he had declared himself, especially in Nicholas's presence.

She noted Damien's raised brows, but he made no comment on his daughter's startling disclosure. Instead, he stared intently at Nicholas, then transferred his probing look to her.

"I wonder," he said. "Do I really not see what transpires right in front of my nose?"

Kate returned his look steadily. He was not referring to Liza and the major, she knew. But if Nicholas had not told Damien that she had turned down his proposal, she certainly would not do so either.

"I don't know what you can or cannot see, Mr. Ashcroft," she said crisply. "But you ought to take

192

a look at the list of wines for tomorrow. Boughey placed it on your desk three days ago."

"Boughey knows my preferences. I trust his selections."

"Thank you, sir." The butler filled Damien's Burgundy goblet, then served him with a generous portion of saddle of lamb and green beans. "I'm certain I chose the Madeira and port to your liking. But as to the champagnes and dinner wines—"

"All right, Boughey. I'll look at your list after dinner."

Kate withdrew a piece of neatly folded paper from her evening bag. "I have a copy right here. You might look it over while you eat."

Damien's mouth tightened. He waved away an apricot tart offered by the butler. "Pass me the mint sauce, Boughey. Then you may leave us."

"Very well, sir."

Kate braced herself for scathing remarks on her interfering ways, but when the dining room door had closed behind the butler and the footmen, Damien turned to his daughter.

"And now, Princess," he said sternly, "I think it is time you enlightened me about this suitor of yours."

Liza pushed away her dessert plate piled high with her favorite meringue and luscious strawberries. She looked, despite the sophisticated style in which Mary had looped and curled her hair atop her head, like a little girl who wishes nothing more than to be excused from the table.

"Mr. Ashcroft," said Kate, a strawberry halfway to her mouth, "may I suggest you contain your curiosity until after the ball?"

Liza nudged Kate's wine list closer to her father. "Papa, shouldn't you be studying this?"

193

"Later." Damien pocketed the slip of paper. He leaned back in his chair, his arms folded across his chest. "How is it, Liza, that I am the last to hear about this suitor? Shouldn't Major Dashwood have approached me *before* speaking to you?"

Liza's eyes opened wide. "How Gothic!"

Damien's face darkened. Nicholas, Kate noted, barely suppressed a smile. He was absentmindedly twirling the stem of his wineglass, but there was nothing absentminded about his gaze, which roamed from Damien to Liza, then to her.

"Gothic, indeed," said Kate, forestalling any biting comment Damien might have wished to make. And it would be just like him to set up Liza's back by forbidding her to dance with the major at her ball. "Considering, however, that you are barely seventeen, your father does have a point."

"Thank you, Miss Elliott," Damien said dryly.

With a toss of her curls, Liza raised her chin. The look she gave her father and the tone of her voice were as haughty as a queen's. "Charles told me that he would seek an interview with you tomorrow, during the ball."

"Excellent," Damien said with cold emphasis. "I know exactly what I will tell him."

"Papa! If you—" Liza broke off, stifling a sob and a cry of pain, for beneath the table Kate had kicked her smartly on the shin.

"Liza, show Nicholas the rose garden," said Kate, her fierce look daring her three companions to point out that there was nothing to show in the rose garden for at least another month.

From the corner of her eye, she saw Damien's compressed mouth, the twitch of a tiny muscle in his lean cheek that warned of his growing annoyance. Would he countermand her order?

But Nicholas had already risen. Sweeping up his own and Liza's glass, he said to the young girl who still hesitated, "Let us enjoy our wine under starlight. Have I told you about the stars I saw when I was in Greece? They seemed so near, I felt I had only to reach out to touch one of them."

Intrigued, Liza shook her head and allowed him to usher her to the door. Before she left the room, she turned back once more. "Miss Elliott," she said urgently. "Do you remember your promise when we talked about the fulfillment of my dreams, my expectations?"

Kate frowned, trying to recall the conversation. "I believe that was when you were pining for some excitement in your life. I said that if you learned to be patient—"

"No, no!" Liza tapped a foot impatiently. "*After* you talked about patience. You promised you'd help me!"

"Yes, I remember. But, I believe," Kate said with a smile, "that my promises have already come true."

She was aware of Damien's suddenly intent look. In fact, he looked downright suspicious. But of what?

"Most of them have come true, but not all," Liza said insistently. "You must speak to Papa about Charles. You promised that you won't let me become an old maid!"

Kate was about to point out that at seventeen Liza was in no danger at all, but the words stuck in her throat when she heard Damien's comment.

"Like Miss Elliott?" he said icily.

Damien saw Nicholas, his face thunderous, take a threatening step toward him, then saw him stop when Kate shook her head. But most of all, Damien was aware of the sudden look of hurt in Kate's eyes. It only made him angrier. She deserved that barb, the deceitful little wretch. Promising Liza her help with Dashwood while assuring him that she wouldn't wish the major on any woman, least of all his daughter. He knew that all females were deceitful by nature, yet, somehow, he had expected better from Kate.

"Liza," he said curtly. "If you wish to escape, I suggest you do so immediately. Whatever Miss Elliott may have taught you about patience, *mine* is running out."

"You promised, Miss Elliott!" Liza cried. Picking up her skirts, she fled from the room, with Nicholas following at a more leisurely pace and closing the door behind him.

"Well, Miss Elliott," Damien said in that silky smooth tone of voice Kate had come to dread. "You've played your trump—but too soon, I'm afraid, for I still hold my ace."

"I'm no card player," Kate said irritably. "I don't know what you're talking about."

"Your clever maneuver to get Liza and Dashwood together."

Kate gasped. She had been about to point out how fascinated Liza was with Nicholas and his tales. That Nicholas, in his undeniably charming manner, would more certainly cure Liza of her infatuation with the major than Damien could with a blunt paternal veto. But now, all she could think of was the totally unjust accusation he had hurled at her.

"You are mad!" she cried.

"Are you so uncertain of Nicholas that you must scheme to get Liza safely shackled and out of his way?"

196

"How dare you judge me by your own base standards!"

He thrust back his chair, and Kate wondered if he would leap at her to wring her neck or do something equally violent. When he only stretched out his long legs and crossed them at the ankles, she realized that her fear was born of her own violent wish to throttle him.

Drawing a deep breath, she said, "You, sir, are despicable! If you truly cared for Liza, and if you truly believed that I would stoop so low, you would dismiss me on the spot. But you fear that Nicholas will leave with me, and all that really bothers you is the realization that your precious schemes may come to nought. And that's why you insult me and berate me instead of giving me notice."

She stopped to draw another breath and to adjust the cadence of her voice, which had risen steadily during her verbal assault. "But I warn you, Mr. Ashcroft. I do not cringe and cower, and neither do I resign. I, indeed, promised Liza my help and support, and she shall have it for as long as I am at Dearworth."

As Damien watched her expressive face, which showed such a mixture of fury and hurt, and her blue-gray eyes, which threatened all kinds of retribution, he asked himself how he could possibly have suspected her of deliberate and purposeful neglect of her duties to Liza so that the major could pursue his nefarious schemes. She had, apparently, not objected when Nicholas offered to take her place—a mark in her favor, and one that he should have thought of sooner.

He remembered when Elizabeth had schemed to deceive him and he confronted her with her duplicity. She had shown only glittering triumph and satisfaction. Never hurt or anger. Kate was either a consummate actress—after all, she had deceived him before with her act of Miss Meek-and-Mild—or he had wronged her. He knew he wished it to be the latter, even if it meant he must apologize.

Drained of his anger, he felt only fatigue and weariness from the long days he had spent at the excavation site. A twinge of pain in his leg made him shift uncomfortably. He wanted to get up and walk off the soreness, but he'd be damned if he'd show his weakness.

Silence hung thick and heavy between them. They were glaring at each other as though they were bitter enemies, when all he wanted to do was pull her into his arms and . . .

When Damien reached this point in his ruminations, he did get up. He rose so abruptly that his chair toppled backward. He strode around the table to stare down at Kate. One of these days he'd find out if she and Nicholas had been lovers. If they had been, he could finally silence that bothersome conscience of his. He could set her up in a nice little house in Bath. . . .

Kate's voice dispelled the rosy dream that was just beginning to form in his mind. "Have you run out of insults?" she asked. "Or are you for once considering an apology to me?"

"I might be," he said. "Tell me, Kate. Why the devil did you promise Liza you'd help her with Dashwood?"

Still angry, she said cuttingly, "I never did. And neither did Liza say that."

"You're quibbling over words. So you promised her she wouldn't end up an old maid. Isn't that the same as promising she could have Dashwood?"

"No."

Baffled, he asked, "Why then were you at such pains to stop me from making it clear that I'd never consent to a marriage with the bounder?"

"Because it is her birthday tomorrow." She gave him a scornful look. "There is to be a ball, if you remember. A ball which Major Dashwood will most certainly attend."

"I'll send him off with a flea in his ear!"

"Indeed! And what do you suppose Liza will do? You might as well thrust her into his arms."

He started pacing. "If he weren't Louisa's cousin, I'd whip him!"

Against her will, she felt herself softening toward him. He did not see that Liza's infatuation would pass once the blinders of awe and pride in her conquest of a man—not a mere boy—had come off her eyes.

Kate was half tempted to tell him that Nicholas was free and well on his way to paying quiet court to Liza. But Damien's accusations had cut too deeply, so she merely said, "Mr. Ashcroft, I advise you to put your trust in Liza's good sense. In another week or two, she will have recognized the major for the fortune hunter that he is."

Damien grimaced wryly. So far, Liza had shown precious little sense. As much as he loved her, there were times when he feared she was as flighty as her mother.

"No," he said, sharper than he intended. "I cannot wait. Liza must learn to bow to my judgment."

"Of course," said Kate. "You must have it *your* way, mustn't you? You might consider, however, that Liza is just as pigheaded as you are."

He gave her a black look, but undaunted, she continued. "Opposition at this point will only make her more stubborn. As long as she's meeting the major openly—"

"Openly?" he cut in. "What about the meeting in Bath?"

"She has not repeated her folly, but if you forbid her to see Dashwood again, she most certainly will."

He stepped closer. She read anger and some emotion she could not define in his eyes.

"You would know, wouldn't you?" he said in a voice so low that his words were barely audible.

Slowly, Kate rose. Her throat constricted as stupidly, foolishly, tears started to burn in her eyes. But she measured him coldly from head to foot.

"Yes, Mr. Ashcroft. I know from bitter experience."

She turned and walked away from him.

"Kate!" he said imperiously, but she did not look back. He must not see that she was close to losing her composure, mustn't see the moisture that welled up in her eyes.

"Dammit! I *should* dismiss you!" he shouted.

She kept walking, and as she left the dining room where the sudden chink of glass against glass told her that he was pouring wine with an unsteady hand, her mood lightened. She started to feel almost light-headed.

He would no more dismiss her than she would consider resigning her post. They were like fencers, testing each other, seeking the other's weaknesses and strengths. They were committed to battle.

Chapter Fifteen

Damien tossed off his wine and was about to pour a second glass when a battery of electrifying and most unwelcome thoughts assaulted him. Abruptly, he set the bottle down and left the dining room. Despite the painful protest in his left leg, he took the stairs two steps at a time, stormed into his study, and slammed the door.

Solitude was a must when memories of Elizabeth flooded him with bitterness, which they still did after a decade and a half. And during the past seven or eight weeks, such memories had been forced upon him more often than during all of the previous years.

He did not wonder that Liza, when he had arrived from Rome to take her out of the school, should have awakened memories of Elizabeth. When he had seen his daughter the previous summer, she had still worn her hair in braids. The resemblance to her mother had been there, of course, but it had not prepared him to face an exact duplicate of Elizabeth in the spring.

Liza had not noticed his perturbation. *Thank God!* Children were quick at jumping to conclusions, and she might have believed that it was *she* who had given him such a shock rather than his sudden realization that her appearance in Bath or London would revive old scandal and would, most assuredly, cause her grievous hurt.

Damien sat down, his feet propped on the shiny surface of his desk and his fingers laced behind his head. Might as well be comfortable while he sorted his thoughts and, possibly, arrived at answers to some very disturbing questions.

Most disturbing of all was that it should be his daughter's companion who, more than once, stirred up memories of Elizabeth. And why, when dealing with Kate, did he lose his head and say things he would not say in a saner mood?

Only Elizabeth had been able to rouse him to such fiery rages — when he still believed he loved her and was ridden by the demon jealousy.

Elizabeth had made certain he was well acquainted with that "green-eyed monster," that "jaundice of the soul." As soon as the knot was tied and she was assured of his wealth and the protection of his name, she had shown her true nature, that of a shallow, vain, greedy woman. She had flirted with and ogled every male in sight, from the serious-minded vicar to the dissolute Lord Severeign, down to the most bashful stable lad.

At first, Elizabeth was content with harmless dalliance, but after Liza was born, she had changed. Elizabeth was furious that the baby was a girl. She wanted a boy so that she might be done with childbearing once and forever. She wanted nothing more to do with disfiguring pregnancies, with the seclusion forced on a woman during the last months, or the pain of birthing.

That was not to say Elizabeth did not want a man in her bed. She was insatiable when it came to bedsport. She even accepted Damien, whom she hated by then, for he had the right — were he inclined to exercise it — to force more pregnancies on her until he had the desired male heir.

But Elizabeth made certain that there would be no heir. She made no secret of her visits to Mrs. Peggy Dribble, a retired Covent Garden abbess who lived as a "respectable merchant's widow" in the then fairly recent addition of Laura Place in Bath. Mrs. Dribble kept a supply of love potions for ladies whose husbands went astray and, for the more sophisticated and knowing ladies of the *ton,* the latest contraptions that were said to prevent unwanted pregnancies.

Neither had Elizabeth made a secret of the fact that Damien was not the only man sharing her bed. It was then that the last shreds of his love had withered. He had stopped caring and had locked his door against her. Elizabeth had lost the power to hurt him—or make him jealous. Nor had any other woman been able to rouse that destructive and, in the end, utterly wasted emotion in him.

Until he began to fear that Kate would marry Nicholas.

Damien's feet hit the floor with a crash. He winced at the pain shooting from his ankle to his thigh and started to reach for the cognac, then changed his mind. He needed a clear head.

Why the devil should he be jealous? Nicholas was not Kate's lover now, and whatever they had been to each other eleven years ago did not matter one whit. It should not matter. After all, he planned to install Kate as his mistress, not as his wife. A rational man did not feel jealous of his mistress's former lover.

Mistress-to-be, he corrected himself. He had yet to convince Kate that he was better suited to her temperament than Nicholas. And he'd never do that by losing his head and hurling insults and accusations, which, moreover, he knew to be unjustified. Despite her fall from grace when she was no older than Liza, Kate was a lady of strong principles. She would not do or condone anything that would harm Liza.

A knock on the door brought his ruminations to a halt. *Who the devil?* . . . Boughey knew better than to disturb him in the study.

Kate.

But it was Nicholas who strolled into the room. With a knowing look at Damien, he said, "Didn't expect me, did you, old boy? Well, you should have."

He poured two glasses of cognac, pushed one closer to Damien, and settled with the other in a chair that he pulled up to the desk.

"Come to rake me over the coals, have you?" asked Damien. He raised his glass and drank. A clear head did not matter as much as the need to hide his thoughts from his friend. He didn't think Nicholas would approve of his plans for Kate Elliott.

"I should plant you a facer," said Nicholas. "As I would have done earlier had Kate and Liza not been present."

"You could have *tried*." Damien sent Nicholas a challenging look. "No one would have called Kate an old maid with impunity had our roles been reversed. It would have been pistols at dawn, my friend."

Nicholas responded with a grin and a shrug. "You always were more hotheaded than I. But I would have tried to knock you down, except Kate shook her head at me."

"And you always listen to Kate."

"Look here," said Nicholas, the grin wiped off his face. "*You* may not think twice about going

204

against a lady's wishes, but even had Kate not told me nay, it would have gone against the grain to hit you in the presence of your daughter."

Damien gave Nicholas a thoughtful look. "No," he said slowly. "The lady's head shake would not have deterred me, and neither would a daughter's presence stop me from defending the lady I plan to make my wife." *Or mistress.*

Nicholas muttered an oath as he realized that Damien still believed him to be Kate's suitor. His face grew hot. He should have made it clear to Damien several days ago that Kate had turned him down. Instead, he had assumed Kate would tell her employer. He should have known better.

"Kate and I—" Embarrassed, Nicholas cleared his throat.

"Yes?" Damien drawled lazily. "What about Kate and you?" But the suddenly intent look in his eyes and the tension in the long fingers that held the cognac glass were not lost on Nicholas.

The deuce! Only deep personal interest could betray Damien into showing his tension. But what was his interest in Kate? She was not a merry widow or a married woman set on escaping the boredom of her marriage. Kate was an innocent who knew nothing of the rules that governed brief, passionate affairs.

Nicholas scowled at Damien. He could still tell him now that Kate had turned him down, and yet ... If Damien was bent on seduction, he should say nothing. Uncertainty about Kate would keep Damien in line.

"You owe Kate an apology!"

"I know," Damien said equably. "I have already decided to apologize."

"Good." Sampling his drink, Nicholas leaned

205

against the winged back of his chair. "See that you do. You might also be less curt with her."

"I'll have you know that just before you barged in here, I decided to mend my ways. I'll be courteous, conciliatory, even deferential."

Nicholas made a choking sound. "Doesn't sound like you. I'll believe it when I see it. And if you're deferential, I fear Kate will rule the roost before long."

"Do I detect a note of disillusionment?"

Nicholas shook his head. "Only admiration."

To prevent further questioning about his feelings for Kate, he asked, "What about that crazy professor? Did he show up again to make you another offer on your ruin?"

Damien gave him a sharp look. A clear change in subject. Nicholas was quite obviously well on his way to regretting his proposal to Kate.

"Yes, indeed," he said. "And apparently Professor Crabb wants more than just my ruin. He came to tell me that Severeign offered him the hospitality of his house and board while they negotiate the sale of that wedge of land I've been trying to buy from Severeign for years."

"That narrow strip between your game preserve and the Bluebell Woods? What the deuce would the professor want with it?"

"It contains the ruin of a Norman chapel."

"No doubt that explains it to you, but I still don't understand why he'd want two ruins."

Damien raised a brow. "Are you implying I'm as crazy as he is? I assure you, my friend, it's not because of the chapel ruin that I want Severeign's land."

"I know," said Nicholas. "You want to remove a thorn from your side. But Crabb must be dicked in the nob to want to buy your ruin when he's been at loggerheads with you for years over your status in the Society of Antiquaries."

"I haven't the faintest notion what Crabb plans to do, and I daresay we shan't find out, for I'll sell him nothing. On the contrary, I'll do my best to outbid him with Sovereign."

"I thought you and the viscount were not on speaking terms."

"We're not. I've made my earlier offers through his solicitor. I shall do so again."

"If Crabb is staying with Sovereign, he might just steal a march on you."

For a moment or two, Damien swirled the remains of his cognac against the sides of the glass. "You're right," he said. "I'll make my offer to Sovereign directly. I'll send him a note in the morning."

"Good luck." Yawning, Nicholas rose. "I'm off to bed. Liza has asked me to practice the waltz with her, and Kate will be too busy to play the pianoforte for us, except right before breakfast."

"What on earth is she planning to do all day?"

"She said something about a calamity with the musicians who are supposed to fiddle at the ball, and flowers for the guest rooms and a million other details she must take care of."

"Then you'll have to play chaperon to Liza again?"

Nicholas regarded him steadily. "Yes, I'll play chaperon. And if you don't do anything stupid, my friend, you have nothing to fear regarding Liza and Dashwood. Good night."

Damien sent a pensive look after his friend. There was something to be said for keeping Kate occupied. Nicholas didn't seem to mind spending time with Liza. . . .

When he went downstairs the following morning, Damien found the breakfast parlor empty. "Where is everyone?" he asked when Boughey entered with a pot of coffee and fresh toast. "In the ballroom?"

"No, sir." The butler served Damien with kippered fillet of haddock and a poached egg. "Miss Liza and Lord Nicholas have ridden out. They'll be taking breakfast at Sir Shafto's."

"And Miss Elliott?"

"Miss Elliott is on the third floor, I believe."

"Flowers for the guest rooms," Damien muttered under his breath.

"I beg your pardon, sir?"

Damien pushed aside his plate. Mayhap an apology would come easier on an empty stomach, and besides, he really was not hungry.

He took a sealed letter from his coat pocket. "Have Ben take this to Lord Severeign's place. He can leave it with the butler. I don't expect an immediate reply."

With an expression of utter dumb-foundedness on his round face, Boughey stared after his master. *No* breakfast, and a note to Lord Severeign! Whatever was the world coming to? He turned the letter over in his pudgy fingers. *Edmund, Viscount Severeign.* Indeed!

Boughey started for the nether regions to send Ben on his way. He had almost reached the baize curtain when he experienced yet another shock. From the stairwell above, he heard his master's voice. Hesitant, almost humble. Boughey had never before heard Damien Ashcroft humble.

"Kate, I believed you on the third floor. At least, that's what Boughey told me."

"As you see, I am not," Miss Elliott replied tartly. "I finished in the guest rooms half an hour ago."

"In that case, could you spare me a few minutes of your time?"

"I am rather busy, Mr. Ashcroft. But perhaps after luncheon? I might be able to see you then."

"I— Couldn't I just accompany you now? Perhaps I can assist you with some of the last minute arrangements?"

A smile lit Boughey's face. The puzzle of no breakfast was explained. He could smell April and roses. Mr. Ashcroft sounded just like any bashful young swain, unsure of himself and uncertain of his acceptance. And it was high time, too, that he showed some interest in a really nice lady instead of some highflyer in Rome or Venice!

Boughey heard Miss Elliott's light tread and his master's heavier steps coming downstairs. He whisked through the curtain just as Miss Elliott inquired, with exaggerated concern, "Come with me to see the gardener? Mr. Ashcroft, are you feeling quite the thing today?"

"Kate, I want to—I must apologize for my conduct last night."

"You don't say!"

Boughey pricked his ears. Whatever could the master have done to make Miss Elliott all huffy with him?

He was not to find out, for Damien opened the front door, and Kate swept outside.

"Kate!" Damien felt the prickle of sweat beneath his collar. She was making it dashed difficult to apologize. "Can't you stand still for just a minute and allow me to do the thing properly?"

She stopped at the foot of the steps, where they widened into a semicircle. "Do what?"

Meeting her puzzled look, Damien realized with

a twinge of pique that she believed he was merely paying lip service with his apology. But he was not. Damn it! He had never been more serious in his life.

"Kate, I am truly sorry for what I said to you yesterday. I was a cad!"

She said nothing, only searched his face for a sign of sarcasm or insincerity. There was none.

"I threatened to whip Dashwood," he said, bitterness in his voice. "But if anyone deserves to be whipped, it is I."

"Well, I shan't deny it," she said slowly, still hardly daring to believe that he had actually apologized.

In her heart, she knew she would not find it hard to forgive him. He was a father driven by worry over his only child. She had been rather horrid herself, telling him he wasn't thinking of Liza at all, only of his thwarted plans. But she need not say that, did she? Not now, when, for the first time, he showed a crack in his armor of pride and self-confidence.

She gave him a reproachful look. "You did make some unforgivable accusations."

"Accusations I know to be unfounded," he admitted. "And I insulted you when I—"

Damien broke off, his composure deserting him completely. He had never been in a situation like this and, dammit, he didn't know how to handle it.

"When you told me that I'm an old maid?"

"Yes." He dashed a coat sleeve across his brow. "And I apologize for that as well."

"You need not," said Kate. "*I* shan't apologize for calling you pigheaded."

She turned away from the suddenly alert look in his eyes. "If you'll excuse me now. Your gardener is expecting me."

But Damien was not to be so easily deterred. He placed his hand under her chin and gently forced her to look at him again. "Please, Kate. Will you forgive me?"

Her pulse beat against his fingers. She feared that he, too, could feel the erratic flutter.

"I will try," she said, hardly daring to breathe. "For Liza's sake."

"Thank you," he replied gravely. Then he added, and she could have sworn the glint of deviltry was back in his eyes, "That must suffice—for now."

He dropped his hand, and Kate started walking toward the gardens. His thank you had once again been delivered in his old provoking style, but she had brushed through it all rather well, she thought. At least he could not boast that she was easily won over. He needed to be taken down a peg or two.

She realized that he was walking beside her. Astonished, she said, "Where are you going?"

"With you, to see the gardener. I want to atone for my boorishness yesterday by helping you. It seems there are still a million and one things to be done before the ball."

"But you don't help by following me around all day!" Kate stopped on the flagged walk. Arms akimbo, she gave him a challenging stare. "Do you really want to be of assistance?"

"Indeed, I do."

"Then see if you can find a violin."

Taken aback, he said, "I'll be glad to oblige. But must it be today?"

"I'm afraid so." He looked so aghast that she had difficulty suppressing a laugh. "It appears that one of the violinists who is to play tonight had an altercation with his wife. His instrument, unfortunately, took the brunt of their exchange, and he doesn't have the money to buy a new one."

"I may have to go all the way to Bath." That had not been his intention when he offered his help. He had rather anticipated spending several hours in her company to prove that he could be just as charming and attentive as Nicholas. "I might not be back before luncheon."

Her smile was wide and guileless. "I suggest you take your meal in Bath, then. You'll fare better than we shall at home. You see, I've told your chef to save his efforts for the dinner tonight. For luncheon we'll make do with some fruit, and bread and cheese."

Nineteen ladies and nineteen gentlemen, most of whom would spend the night at Dearworth, had been asked to dinner. In addition, invitations to the ball alone had been sent to and accepted by several respectable county families, so that all in all fifty-nine elegantly clad ladies and gentlemen trod the highly waxed and polished boards of the ballroom.

Granted, the number was not one a London hostess would boast of. Even by Bath standards it was a rather meager showing, but Kate had induced the head gardener to bid his minions carry every available tub and urn filled with greens or flowers into the ballroom. Thus, the long chamber furnished in white, crimson, and gilt gave at least the appearance of being comfortably crowded.

Kate stood at the refreshment table, where she intended to check on the amount of ice in the champagne punch that was to be served to the younger set, but her eyes were irresistibly drawn to the dance floor where Damien and Liza whirled to the strains of the opening waltz.

The waltz was unheard of during Kate's short season in Bath. A few years later, when the dance was performed in every London ballroom, the high sticklers of Bath society still condemned it as scandalous and immoral, and it had been as recently as two years ago that the waltz was finally included in the curriculum at Miss Venable's Seminary for Young Ladies. Kate had learned to play the lilting tunes on the pianoforte, but the only benefit she had derived from the dancing master's weekly visit was what little she gleaned by observation when it was her duty to provide the music and to chaperon the young ladies.

How different the picture of Damien and Liza circling the floor when compared to the spectacle of gawky damsels in the effort of shoving and dragging each other. It looked as though Liza's feet barely touched the floor as she dipped and swayed and whirled. And Damien . . .

Kate moved to one of the columns supporting the ornately carved and gilded ceiling. She tried to keep her eyes on the footmen Boughey had engaged to help Ben and Edward, she tried to concentrate on all the little things she ought to observe since she had been cast willy-nilly into the role of hostess, but again and again her gaze strayed to Damien. He was an accomplished dancer, and despite his height and muscular build, he was graceful.

He was a striking man at all times. When he was dressed for riding or driving, he caused a stir of admiration in her breast; when she saw him at the excavation site in breeches and shirtsleeves, he laid bare her most carefully guarded yearnings; but dressed in elegant, immaculately tailored evening clothes, he was breathtaking.

He was speaking to Liza while they danced, and the look and smile he bestowed on his daughter touched Kate's heart. He was so proud of Liza and loved her deeply. Pray God the girl would over-come her infatuation with Dashwood before she caused her father pain.

Kate shifted weight and tapped a foot in time to the music. This was the first ball she had attended in many a year. The scent of flowers, perfumes, and melting candles was heady, and the song of the violins stirred her blood. If she didn't hold on to something solid, she might float across the room to join the growing number of dancers.

With her hand pressed against the smooth plaster of the column, she continued to watch Damien and Liza. How she wished she were in the girl's place.

The music ceased, and the sensation of lightness left Kate abruptly as Mrs. Abbots's voice filled the ballroom instead.

"I tell you, my lady," Mrs. Abbots said shrilly, "she eloped with him! And now she's here as Liza's chaperon of all things."

Kate felt as though the walls of Damien's excava-tion had toppled and crushed her with tons of rock and limestone. She turned to face Mrs. Abbots, who sat with a bevy of matrons among the potted ferns and irises the gardeners had arranged along the walls, but Susannah's mother didn't look her way. She was busy listening to something a white-haired regal lady said to her in such low tones that Kate could not catch the words.

Mrs. Abbots's reply, delivered in the same stri-dent tones as earlier, was clearly audible. And not only to Kate. Several heads were turning in the direction of the ladies.

"But Lord Nicholas is staying at Dearworth as well!" Mrs. Abbots cried. "I tell you, my lady, it is a disgrace. And to think that she taught my Susannah at Miss Venable's. Innocent young girls supervised by a fallen woman!"

Chapter Sixteen

In the dead silence that followed Mrs. Abbots's words, Kate knew herself the cynosure of all eyes. And then the whispers started. Those hateful, sly whispers that had cut her to the quick eleven years ago and that would hurt her again. But not only her. Liza, who looked up to her and respected her, would hear the horrid innuendoes — Liza whose pleasure in her very first ball would be spoilt.

Above her mortification, Kate felt a rush of anger. If she must run the gauntlet of criticism and censure once again, she would do it. She was strong. But how dare Mrs. Abbots disrupt Liza's ball.

Kate squared her shoulders and held up her chin. She'd tell that prattlebox just what she thought of her.

It was not far to the circle of chairs where Mrs. Abbots sat surrounded by her friends and acquaintances, but for Kate the distance might have been that from Bath to London. Never had she felt such a coward and so alone.

She walked with deliberate slowness and pretended not to hear such carrying remarks as "she ruined herself," "cast her cap over the windmill," and "was caught in the most improper conduct."

When the music started up again, she breathed a sigh of relief, for the lively tune of a *contredanse* was well suited to drown out all but the most strident voices. Mrs. Abbots studiously avoided looking in Kate's direction, but the regal old lady seated beside Susannah's mother was watching her approach with keen light blue eyes.

Only a few more steps. She could do it. She must do it.

And then Kate was no longer alone. Damien walked beside her. His deep voice was calm and reassuring.

"Kate, take my arm. And for heaven's sake, smile a little."

She didn't think it would be possible to smile, but when she placed her hand in the crook of his arm, her apprehension and the cowardly wish to run shrank to manageable proportions. She relaxed, and the smile Damien had commanded was not at all difficult to produce.

Damien led her straight to the white-haired lady. Bowing, he said, "Lady Undersham, may I present Miss Kate Elliott, who took pity on Liza and me when the school closed so unexpectedly."

While Lady Undersham subjected her to a sharp scrutiny, Kate sank into a curtsey. So this was Lady Belinda's grandmother, who had in her salad days—if there was any truth to the tales her granddaughter had told at Miss Venable's—set the *ton,* and Bath society in particular, by the ears with her unpredictable and often hoydenish manner.

"It seems," the dowager countess said in the clear, soft tones of a young girl, "that you have landed yourself in something of a bumblebroth. What do you intend to do about it, miss?"

Another woman might have blushed and stammered when faced with such a personal question from a stranger. Kate, fortified by Damien's presence, said unhesitatingly, "I shall tell Mrs. Abbots that she is an interfering busybody who doesn't know what she is talking about."

She turned her head to face Mrs. Abbots directly. "You had plenty of time to spread your vicious gossip before the ball, ma'am. Waiting until now and spoiling Liza's pleasure is unforgivable. Just think if something like this had happened at your daughter's come-out ball."

Mrs. Abbots's long nose quivered with indignation, but under Lady Undersham's quelling stare she did not venture a reply.

In an undertone, Damien said, "Piqued, repiqued, and capotted. Congratulations, Kate." Then he addressed the dowager countess. "You may be acquainted with Miss Elliott's mother, ma'am. Lady Elliott has been a resident of Bath for several years."

Lady Undersham raised a white brow. "You are Alicia Elliott's daughter? Why, then, do you not reside with her?"

"I prefer my independence."

"Hmm." Lady Undersham gave Kate a shrewd look. "Met your brother once, and your sister-in-law. I daresay that explains your strange liking for independence."

The old lady lapsed into a pensive silence. When she spoke again, a twinkle lurked in her clear blue eyes. "Miss Elliott," she said succinctly, and no one around her could miss her words. "I admire a woman with spunk. I also like to act contrary to expectations. It would greatly please me if you'd call on me. Say Wednesday, the week after next?"

And thus, with the stamp of approval from the most powerful lady in the vicinity, Kate was dismissed.

For some time, she had been aware of movement

all around her, and when Damien led her away, she noticed that the Reverend and Mrs. Charteris, Sir Shafto and Lady Usborne, Dr. Bullen, the young physician who had treated Peter's ankle, and several others of Damien's closest neighbors had formed a silent, protective entourage behind her. Kate smiled a greeting and would have excused herself, but Damien forestalled her.

"Planning to run away?" he drawled.

"No, no," Sir Shafto said genially. "Miss Elliott would never turn tail. She just cleared her fences with inches to spare. She's not going to shy at a ditch."

"None of us who know you have paid the slightest heed to Mrs. Abbots," Phoebe Charteris said encouragingly. "And we shall circulate and do our best to quash any gossip while Damien introduces you to those families you have not yet met."

Kate slanted a look at Damien. "I have no intention of running. However, if my reputation should prove a stumbling block for Liza, I shall resign my post. I was assured by Mrs. Abbots on an earlier occasion that you, Mr. Ashcroft, are quite averse to any kind of scandal."

Damien's arm muscles tightened beneath her hand, and she saw Louisa Usborne and Phoebe Charteris exchange uneasy glances.

"Devil a bit!" said Damien. "It's the scandal created by Elizabeth, my . . . wife, that I don't want stirred up again for Liza's sake. I can deal with a bit of rumor about you."

"*Unfounded* rumor," Kate told him.

She would have liked to ask about Elizabeth, would have liked to know why Lady Usborne and Mrs. Charteris looked so upset at the mention of scandal caused by Elizabeth, but she could feel

Damien's anger and decided to be prudent for once and remain silent.

They strolled toward a group of matrons to whom Damien intended to introduce her. His eyes were on his daughter, surrounded by her young friends on the other side of the dance floor. The *contredanse* was over, and Liza was laughing and chatting. Yet her gaze was never long removed from Major Dashwood, who kept himself apart and stood with one shoulder propped against a flower-draped pillar.

Even across the distance, it was obvious that silent messages passed between Liza and the major, and Kate was not surprised to see Charles Dashwood push away from the pillar when the pianist and the four violinists played the opening bars of yet another waltz. But Charles was not quick enough. It was Nicholas, whose slender figure had been hidden from view by Hubert and Algernon, who swept Liza onto the dance floor.

Charles Dashwood stood irresolute, then, after scanning the ballroom repeatedly, started to wend his way toward Damien.

"By George!" said Damien. "I will not speak with the bounder."

He increased his pace, but instead of approaching the matrons, he veered toward the door. They were about twenty paces away from the double winged door when two newcomers made a belated entrance. Abruptly, Damien came to a stop.

Again Kate felt the tensing of his arm beneath her hand. She recognized Professor Crabb in an old-fashioned frock coat and creased pantaloons. The second gentleman, whom she judged to be little older than Damien, she did not know.

His thinning sandy hair was carefully brushed

and pomaded. His coat with wide lapels, a high collar, a wasp waist, and padded to enormous proportions at the shoulders was the dress of a dandy, as were the ruffles of lace at his throat and wrists and the great number of fobs and seals that dangled from a chain on his brocaded waistcoat.

He remained near the door, and when the professor would have stepped forward, he reached out with a bejeweled hand and tapped the thin little man on the shoulder. Instantly, Professor Crabb backtracked until he stood just behind his elegant companion.

"Severeign!" Damien muttered savagely and started to move again. "How dare he show his face."

Kate's stomach gave a lurch. Damien's tone of voice left no doubt about his feelings for the dandy.

"I sent him an invitation," she said breathlessly as she tried in vain to match her steps to Damien's long stride. "His name was on the list I found in the desk in the library."

Damien gave her a black look, but since they had reached Lord Severeign and Professor Crabb, he addressed himself to the viscount. "Severeign," he said, his voice tight with anger. "To what do I owe the honor?"

"Good evening, Ashcroft," Viscount Severeign said softly, his mouth curling in a smile that made Kate shiver. He inserted a hand into the pocket of his coat and withdrew a gilt-edged card, which she recognized as the invitation she herself had penned, and used it to fan himself.

"You sound put out," he said, again in that soft, insinuating tone of voice. "Was it not, then, in an effort to bury our . . . ah . . . little differences that you sent me the invitation?"

"Our differences will not be buried nor will they be forgotten until *you* are buried and forgotten. You know that. You must have known that the invitation was a mistake."

In reply, the viscount gave another of his sinister smiles.

"So what is it that you want?" Damien asked harshly.

The viscount dropped all pretense of politeness. Naked hatred blazed from his pale eyes that were neither gray nor green. Kate remembered Damien's words when he had ridden with Liza and her that first morning after the mares arrived. "Severeign would as soon pepper us with shot as allow us to view his Norman chapel," Damien had said, and she had wondered whether it was the viscount who had injured Damien's leg.

Then, she had dismissed her suspicion as absurd; now, witnessing the viscount's malevolence, she gave it full rein. There was something lethal about the look he bent on Damien.

Lord Severeign sneered. "You made me an offer this morning on that piece of land you've been wanting to buy. I thought I'd deliver my reply in person."

He stepped aside and with a sweep of his hand indicated Professor Crabb. "Meet the new owner, Ashcroft. Fergus Crabb will be your very close neighbor."

"Is that true?" Damien shot a look at the professor, but the untidy little man only shifted restlessly from one foot to the other, and it was Severeign who spoke again.

"Do you question my word, Ashcroft?" The viscount's hand touched his side as though he were

222

reaching for a sword.

Kate's mouth was dry. Behind her, laughter and music attested to the ball's success; yet here she was, embroiled in a nightmare where two men faced each other with hatred in their hearts and one, possibly both, hell-bent on issuing a challenge.

"Get out!" Damien did not raise his voice nor did he move, but there was menace in his soft-spokenness and the rigidity of his stance. Only Kate, whose hand still rested on Damien's arm, felt the tremor that ran through his body. Any moment, he might lose control over his tightly checked temper.

When someone cleared his throat behind her, Kate almost jumped out of her skin. She tightened her hold on Damien's arm. Surely he wouldn't do anything rash as long as he remembered that he was not alone. As much as she wished he'd slap the viscount's sneering face, she did not think this was the right time or place.

Slowly, she turned her head. Major Dashwood. Lud! Why did he have to show up now?

Oblivious to tension and the fact that he was quite obviously intruding, the major stepped around Kate, nodded to Viscount Severeign and the professor, then said peremptorily, "Ashcroft, I'd like a word with you, please. In private."

Professor Crabb dabbed his brow with a crumpled handkerchief and gave the major a nervous smile. Of the other two men, neither one paid the slightest heed to Charles Dashwood. Their eyes were locked in a battle of wills.

"You are *de trop*, major," Kate whispered furiously.

Dashwood's face darkened with anger. He

stepped back but did not remove himself from the vicinity.

"Get out, Sereign!" Damien repeated.

Kate held her breath, willing Lord Sovereign and the professor to leave.

"Or else?" the viscount asked softly. "Will you knock me down again, Ashcroft? Will you challenge me to a duel and kill me so I cannot tell your daughter the truth about Elizabeth?"

Damien jerked his arm free of Kate's restraining hand.

Professor Crabb started to retreat. "Come, my lord," he croaked. "Why stay if we're not wanted?"

Fists clenched at his sides, Damien advanced on Lord Sovereign.

Kate cried out. "Damien, no!"

The viscount merely laughed, then turned on his heel and strolled after the fast disappearing professor.

Kate looked at Damien. The veins on his neck and temples stood out like corded rope, the cloth of his coat was taut across his shoulders, and his stance was that of a panther ready to spring. When he started to walk from the ballroom, she followed him slowly.

Perhaps she was a silly fool, perhaps she was asking for trouble, but she could not leave him alone in the state he was in.

He followed the hallway to the west wing where his study was located. After a while, as though he were aware of Kate behind him, he stopped and waited until she had caught up.

He turned to face her, and the look he gave her was so bleak that she impulsively took his hand. "I am sorry! It was stupid and forward of me to send out invitations without checking with you first. I sincerely apologize."

He shook his head, whether in denial or merely as a gesture to clear his thoughts she did not know. But he did not administer the dressing-down she had expected and which, she admitted, she richly deserved.

"What is wrong, Damien? I'd like to help if I can."

He looked at her as though he realized only this instant who she was.

"You called me Damien," he said in astonishment. "The second time this evening."

Kate blinked. It was not a comment she had expected. Besides, in her mind she had called him Damien for such a long time that she was surprised it had not slipped out sooner.

"So I did," she said with as much aplomb as she could muster. "But I daresay I shan't have the opportunity much longer."

"Why?" Touching her elbow, he guided her to his study.

He was visibly relaxing, and Kate took care to keep her tone light. "Aren't you planning to dismiss me?"

Damien ushered her into the chamber, and when she was seated, he drew up a second chair opposite hers. His dark mood had lifted; there was actually a hint of a smile tugging at the corners of his mouth.

"By now you must have learned that my threats of dismissal are empty," he said. Then he turned serious, his dark eyes holding her captive. "I don't know what I want of you, Kate, but I shall not rest until I find out."

She swayed in her chair. The accursed lightheadedness was attacking her again.

"And do you expect me to submit to whatever it is you want of me?" she asked, despising the weakness of her voice. "I warn you, I am not at all docile."

His gaze softened. "That you're not. And I daresay you wouldn't be such a provocation if you were."

Kate sat up primly. For her own peace of mind, it was clearly time to change the subject. "You have obviously recovered from your black mood. I shall, therefore, leave you alone to smoke a cheroot or drink some brandy before you face your guests again. However, I do wish you'd explain Lord Severeign's threat to me."

Instantly, Damien's face assumed a closed, forbidding look. She thought he would not answer, but then he said, "I suppose I must. I wouldn't put it past the cad to approach Liza just to get even with me for throwing him out."

Damien rose and walked to the window. With his back toward Kate, he started to speak in a voice so devoid of expression that she found it hard to relate the ugly words to the woman who had been Damien's wife, Liza's mother.

"You see," Damien said, "Elizabeth was promiscuous. Sovereign was but one of her many lovers. He was one of the first, though, and she used to visit him at his house. At the time, I still believed I must fight for my wife's good name. I went to see Sovereign. Struck him down right there in front of Elizabeth and his foppish London friends."

A prickle of uneasiness made her shiver. "He'll never forget. He's the kind of man to carry a grudge into his grave."

"He took his shotgun and chased me from his house and off his property."

Kate saw Damien, a young man filled with love, jealousy, and pride. How the humiliation must have hurt him—twofold, because of Elizabeth and because of his defeat at the hands of his wife's lover.

"And that was when Liza saw you with blood streaming down your leg?" she asked huskily.

"Yes." Damien swung around to face her. "There is worse, Kate. But if you don't mind, I'd rather not talk about it yet."

Kate rose. "I understand. And I promise you I'll have Severeign's hide if he dares approach Liza."

She wanted to go to him, touch him, show him in some small way that she indeed understood, but cowardly, she walked to the door.

"Have you considered telling Liza the truth yourself?" she said over her shoulder.

"I shall give it some thought," he promised, following her to the door.

"There might be others not averse to a bit of scandalmongering."

"None of our friends here would breathe a word to Liza, and I—" He gave her a rueful look. "You see, long ago I made the decision to protect Liza at all cost—a mistaken decision, perhaps, but not an easy one to reverse."

"No, it will not be easy." Kate opened the door. "But," she said softly, "surely you have learned by now that women are not made of porcelain."

"Are they not?" he asked. "Are you made of sterner stuff than—" He broke off as he stepped out into the hall and saw Major Dashwood approaching. "Damn his impudence! If Dashwood is planning to ask for my consent, we'll find out very soon what Liza is made of. I'm afraid she will not be pleased with me at all."

227

"Stall him. Tell him Liza is too young. She must see a bit of the world before settling down in marriage."

There was no time to say more. Major Dashwood was upon them, a gleam of triumph in his eyes and a satisfied smile on his face.

"You shall not elude me again, Ashcroft," he said with false joviality. "I want a word with you. Now."

Damien measured him with a cold look, then turned to Kate. "For heaven's sake," he said for her ears alone. "Keep Liza away from here."

Chapter Seventeen

"I'll never forgive him. Never!" The skirt of her sprigged muslin gown caught up in one hand, hymn book and beaded reticule clutched in the other, Liza flounced down the stairs ahead of Kate.

"My dear," Kate said reprovingly. "If you hitch your skirts any higher, you will show more than just your ankles."

Liza paid no heed. "Papa is horrid and unkind!" she stormed. "He ruined my life! And you expect me to sit beside him in church as though *nothing* had happened."

"I expect you to behave like a lady. Pray remember that you have houseguests who will join us shortly. I certainly don't want to see a repeat of the tantrum you performed last night after the ball."

Liza swept into the foyer. Like a cat on a hot bake stone, she started to pace back and forth between the stairs and the front door, opened wide to admit the sun and the sweet perfume of a beautiful May morning.

"I thought *you* would understand," she flung at Kate. "You had your love torn from you by Nicholas's cruel father."

Kate feared that she was treading on very thin ice; nevertheless, she tried to convince the girl that their cases were not at all the same. "When I met Nicholas, my mother was not opposed to an engagement. It was after the elopement that she

229

changed her mind — mostly, I think, because she was awed by Lord Adair and his position in society. She feared that he could ruin us."

Liza came to a halt beside Kate. "And now that you have Nicholas back," she said accusingly, "you're so caught up in your plans that you don't see how miserable I feel."

"I do not have any plans regarding Nicholas."

On the point of delivering yet another shot, Liza gaped openmouthed. "No plans?" she stammered, temporarily diverted from her own woes. "Oh, Miss Elliott! Did Nicholas not come up to scratch?"

"We decided we would not suit."

"But you love each other!"

"Over the years, our feelings have changed. I love Nicholas as I would a brother." Kate remembered her lack of affection for Richard and corrected herself. "As I should love a brother. And Nicholas thinks of me as a very dear friend."

Liza gave Kate a look of disbelief. Tossing her head, she said, "You're saying that because you want me to think my feelings for Charles will change. But they won't."

"Then you have nothing to fear while you wait another year or two."

"But I don't want to wait." The mulish look returned to Liza's face. "I love Charles, and I want to marry him now."

Kate drew on her gloves. "Liza, you've just turned seventeen. *Yesterday.* You've just left the schoolroom. Your father said — "

"Oh!" cried Liza, clapping her hands to her ears. "I shan't listen to you. And I won't listen to Papa either. I won't! I won't!"

"Well," drawled Damien, descending the stairs with Nicholas. "I see we're still being treated to childish tantrums."

Liza stifled a sob. She turned to Nicholas with a plea in her big blue eyes. "If I were *your* daughter, would you forbid my marriage to the man I love?"

Nicholas looked as though Liza had slapped him. "If you—Dash it! You couldn't possibly be my daughter," he choked out. "I'm not old enough to be your father."

Kate said, "Liza, that was an unfair question. Your father did not forbid you to marry Charles Dashwood. He merely told the major that you are too young to make such an important and irrevocable decision."

Damien's expression caught her eye, and she wondered what she had said to make him look so cynical. He had assured her last night that he had been the epitome of diplomacy when he had talked with Major Dashwood; it could not, therefore, be the first part of her statement that had rubbed him the wrong way.

But, surely, he did not disagree with her that a commitment to marriage was irrevocable?

Nicholas had regained his composure and tried his best to calm Liza. "Your papa acted just as he ought. Major Dashwood will understand. It is only reasonable that your father asked him to wait a few years."

"That's not what Papa said to Charles!" Two angry spots of red appeared on Liza's cheeks. "Charles told me that Papa forbade him to ever see me again!"

Damien's jaw tightened. "Dashwood is a liar."

"No!" cried Liza. Tears welled up in her eyes and rolled down her suddenly pale cheeks. "You just want me to think ill of Charles. But you won't succeed, I promise you!"

231

"Hush! said Kate, whose keen ears had not missed the sound of commotion on the upper floors. "That must be Lady Undersham and her companions. Unfortunately, she witnessed your earlier tantrum. Surely you don't wish to subject her to such a spectacle again."

Needless to say, the drive to the old Monkton Combe church was not a very comfortable one. Liza's face closely resembled that of a tragedy queen, and she refused to be coaxed into a sunnier mood.

Liza might have gained a year in physical maturity, Kate reflected, but her emotional growth was sadly lagging behind. Perhaps because she had grown up motherless. On the other hand, if promiscuous Elizabeth were alive to take a hand in her daughter's development . . . No. It did not bear thinking of.

During the sermon, Liza gave every appearance of listening with rapt attention to Reverend Charteris, but Kate had to nudge her twice before the girl realized that the congregation was rising for the final hymn. After the service, she slipped away from Kate, who had stopped to speak to Phoebe Charteris and her daughters outside the church portals. When Kate looked around, Liza had joined Sir Shafto's party near the carriage drive and was whispering to Emily Usborne. Of Major Dashwood there was no sign.

Kate turned back to Phoebe Charteris. "I am sorry," she said. "I'm afraid I was not attending you."

"So I noticed." Phoebe's eyes held a twinkle. "But I think you need not worry about Liza. I saw

232

the major disappear through the lych-gate. I daresay he has taken the shortcut across the churchyard to fetch Sir Shafto's carriage from the inn."

Damien, followed by Lady Undersham's two tirewomen and her small black page, joined them with the dowager countess on his arm. Despite her slight stature, Lady Undersham looked imposing and regal in her black silks and laces. "I haven't visited here in years," she said to Phoebe. "I remember how during my girlhood we all scrambled for a patch of shade. Now, the elms have grown so tall and wide that nary a bit of sunshine penetrates. How much more comfortable this makes after-church visiting."

"Yes, indeed. And when we have summer picknicks and games for the children on quarter day, no one suffers from heat exhaustion." Phoebe Charteris became aware of a farm family in their Sunday best standing at a discreet distance. "Pray excuse me for a moment. The Vincents have a bedridden grandfather at home, and I promised them a recipe for a restorative."

While they waited for Phoebe, Kate looked about her. At the far end of the flagged forecourt, Liza and Emily Usborne were still whispering to each other. Near the church door, Nicholas stood deep in conversation with the vicar and Dr. Bullen, and all around, families were visiting. Kate recognized many faces from the ball. Most of the ladies smiled at her; very few pretended they had not seen her, and none returned her look with a high nosed stare or a rude sniff.

So much for Mrs. Abbots's gossip. It had not done half the damage it might have done.

"Lady Undersham," Damien said solicitously. "The carriages have arrived. I see no reason to

233

stand about if you're tired."

Like her voice, Lady Undersham's laugh was that of a young girl. It had a clear, bell-like sound. "I may be old," she said, "but I'm not too old to enjoy the ritual of visiting. I'd like a word with Louisa Usborne before we leave."

As they strolled across the flagstones toward the waiting carriages where Sir Shafto's party stood chatting with several of the neighboring yeoman farmers, Emily Usborne and Liza started to walk toward the lych-gate set in a hawthorn hedge.

That was where Phoebe Charteris had seen the major go. Murmuring an excuse, Kate would have followed the two young girls.

"No, Kate," said Damien. "No matter what Dashwood told Liza, I did not forbid them to see each other."

"Then you, too, suspect that he is there, behind the lych-gate?"

"I know he is." Damien gave her one of his quick heart-stirring smiles. "I am taller than you are. I can see his shako."

Lady Undersham rapped Damien's knuckles with the chicken bone fan she carried. "It is not right to make me eavesdrop on a private conversation. You should not have offered me your arm if you planned to discuss your daughter and her swain."

"My apologies, Lady Undersham. But I doubt you consider Liza's affairs as private as you'd like me to believe. You stopped on the half landing last night—to catch your breath, no doubt—when she flew at me for having turned down the major."

Without so much as a blush or a blink of an eye, the old lady admitted, "I had plenty of breath to take me out of earshot. I was curious. At my age, the affairs of others are the spice of life.

That's why I took an interest in Miss Elliott, and that's why I'm curious about your daughter. So she believes herself in love with that dashing major, does she?"

"Liza is in love with love," Damien said dismissively.

"A dangerous state to be in. You must keep her under close observation, Miss Elliott."

Kate looked toward the lych-gate. "Easier said than done, ma'am." Softly, so that only Damien could hear, she added, "When one must deal with a father who constantly interferes."

She hurried off, for Emily Usborne was returning—without Liza. Had the child no sense at all? Might as well tie her garter in public as tryst with the major in a churchyard of all places.

Kate skirted a knot of gossiping women and bored children. A young boy with slicked-down blond hair reached out and tugged at her arm. "Miss Elliott! Want ter know something?"

Kate stopped. For a moment, she looked blankly at the young face that had been scrubbed until it shone. She took in his immaculate coat and shirt, pantaloons without a hole at the knee, and a pair of highly glossed shoes.

"Walter! I hardly recognized you in all your finery."

"I'm here, too, Miss Elliott."

"How do you do, Peter? Please excuse me while I fetch Miss Liza. Then you can tell me all your news."

"Don't fash yerself, Miss Elliott." Walter gave her a knowing grin. "That bang-up-feller, that Lord Nicholas, already went and made sure Miss Liza ain't alone with the major."

And indeed, Nicholas had intercepted Emily and

235

was marching her back to the lych-gate. He looked into the churchyard and, apparently, asked the truants to come out of hiding, for Major Dashwood and Liza joined him and Emily shortly afterwards on the church side of the gate.

Reassured, Kate gave her full attention to the boys. "I did not expect to see you in Monkton Combe. Do you always attend church here?"

"Only while our vicar is away in Scotland," replied Peter. "Ma is awfully strong on attendin' church. She *makes* us come."

"Listen, Miss Elliott!" In his impatience to gain Kate's ear, Walter hopped from one foot to the other. "I'll wager ye don't know what's happenin' at Lord Severeign's ruin!"

"I know that he sold it."

Walter looked disappointed, but Peter chimed in, "To some crazy little man. A professor! An' he's goin' to rebuild the chapel. If that ain't a bedlamite notion!"

As farfetched as the notion seemed, Damien had suspected it. He had told Kate that he and Professor Crabb were engaged in constant dispute via the journal published by the Society of Antiquaries. A favorite bone of contention was the restoration of antiquities, with Damien contending that only materials found on site should be used, while the professor maintained that, in the case of a building, missing parts of a wall or pillar could be replaced by modern substitutions.

Unwittingly confirming Damien's suspicion, Walter said, "The professor went off yesterday to look at quarries. He's goin' to buy stone, 'cause so much of the walls is missin'."

"And how did you learn all this?"

The twins exchanged guilty looks.

"You were on Lord Severeign's property again," said Kate.

Walter raised his snub-nose defiantly. "It ain't the viscount's land anymore," he pointed out. "And we didn't climb the wall like Mr. Ashcroft told us. There's a fence on the village side."

"Aye," said Peter. "And it's as sturdy as can be."

"I don't think Professor Crabb will appreciate it if you keep pestering him."

"He were all right at first," said Peter. "Told us all we wanted to know. But then Lord Severeign showed up."

Walter nodded vigorously. "He told the crazy professor that we're destr—that we break things an' all."

"And that Mr. Ashcroft sent us to spy!" Peter spluttered indignantly.

A spark of defiance lit Walter's brown eyes. "Lord Severeign said the professor would shoot us if we ever showed up again."

Kate said warningly, "I know you don't believe that, Walter. But it would be foolhardy in the extreme to test Professor Crabb's patience. Best stay away from the Norman chapel and concentrate on Mr. Ashcroft's Roman villa."

The boys looked unconvinced.

"Promise?"

They nodded, but Kate did not miss that they took care to keep their hands behind their backs. She was quite familiar with the childish trick of crossing one's fingers when telling a lie. She did not challenge the boys but decided to leave it up to Damien to talk some sense into them.

"And pray don't call the professor crazy," she said sternly. "It is ill-mannered, and if it should come to his ears, you'll find yourselves in very hot water indeed."

Again, they nodded.

Their solemn faces did nothing to reassure Kate. She felt she had sadly failed in her duty to set them straight, but she said no more, for Rose Grimes, the boys' mother, left her friends and came bustling over.

"Walter! Peter!" she said breathlessly. "What can ye be thinking of, pestering Miss Elliott? As though the lady don't have nothing better to do than listen to yer jibber-jabber. Off with ye! Start walking home with the Gerwin boys. And mind yer clothes!" she called after her sons, who had directed sheepish grins at Kate and trotted off at the first onslaught of motherly reprimands.

Her color high, Mrs. Grimes would, no doubt, have apologized profoundly and at great length had Kate not forestalled her by saying, "They are an engaging pair, Mrs. Grimes. You must be very proud of them."

She stayed for a few moments, conversing with the seamstress, then, seeing that Damien was handing Lady Undersham and her attendants into the closed carriage and that Liza and Nicholas were already seated in the landaulet, Kate took her leave of Mrs. Grimes and wended her way toward the carriage drive.

Every now and again, she stopped to exchange a brief greeting with one or the other of the families who had attended the ball. Damien, looking for her, was struck by the picture of cool poise she presented as she listened to the apothecary's wife, then shook hands with the oldest farmer in the county, hundred-and-two-year-old Ned Bates who still milked a cow every morning and night.

Kate was a lady—to the manor born, as an old

saying went. She was as much at ease with the dowager Countess Undersham as she was with simple country folk.

But what if he succeeded and won her as his mistress? How would Kate feel among the demireps, the highflyers, the muslin company?

Everything in him rebelled at the thought of Kate as a social outcast. He would not be able to bring her to the two villages where she had made friends. Phoebe Charteris, even if she were willing, would not be able to receive Kate. Neither would the dowager countess renew her invitation for an afternoon visit.

In fact, he would not even have Kate's company at Dearworth. Lodging a mistress in one's home simply was not done.

Fleetingly, and very hastily suppressed, came the thought that there was another way.

No, he swore silently. *Never again.*

Not that he believed Kate would cuckold him the way Elizabeth had. But he had wanted Elizabeth, and fool that he was, he had married her to get her into his bed. Now he wanted Kate, but he was no longer a young, idealistic dreamer. No longer was he willing to commit himself into a bondage that was worse than slavery when the first passion had worn off.

He'd have Kate sooner or later. But not in marriage. What was it she had said to Liza earlier? To consent to marriage was an irrevocable decision. He had remembered Elizabeth and how she had fought and clawed her way out of their union. Elizabeth had not considered her decision irrevocable.

He watched Kate as she came toward him. When she left the shade of the elm trees, her dark brown hair under a flimsy confection of a hat caught the sunshine and glowed with deep chestnut highlights. The mouth that he had claimed twice and hungered to taste again was curved in a half smile, and her eyes . . .

Damien's throat felt dry as he encountered Kate's frank look. She cared for him. He'd wager his fortune, nay, his life on it.

But how would she feel about him when he made his offer?

His insides twisted sharply. Sudden nausea made him grip the side of the carriage. Then Kate stood before him. He assisted her onto the seat and climbed in beside her.

The faint scent of her perfume drifted into his nostrils, stiffening his resolve. He might feel disgust at himself for what he planned to do, but he'd still go ahead and proposition Kate when the right time came.

Chapter Eighteen

Damien was withdrawn and silent during the drive home. Every once in a while, he felt Kate's eyes resting on him, but he gave no sign of having noticed. Nicholas and Liza, apparently, saw nothing amiss. Liza had thrown off her sullenness and was chattering like a magpie; Nicholas, in turn, seemed more than happy to encourage her with leading questions and admiring interjections, making it easy for Damien to pursue his own thoughts.

However brief her *tête-à-tête* with Charles Dashwood, it had restored his daughter to good humor. Perhaps he had done the major an injustice. Perhaps Dashwood was more aware of the attendant complications of courting a very young lady than he had given him credit. Perhaps Major Dashwood had counseled Liza to be patient. Perhaps the major was a gentleman after all.

Damien's mouth twisted cynically at his own conjectures. *And, perhaps, the king was not mad?*

He'd give Dashwood the benefit of a doubt, but he would not wager so much as a groat on his integrity.

Kate, too, was quite pleased with Liza's changed attitude. If the girl maintained her bright smile and sparkling eyes, none of the houseguests still remaining at Dearworth—with the exception of

241

Lady Undersham, who could be trusted not to repeat her information — need be any wiser about the *contretemps* between father and daughter.

Kate did not, however, go so far as to give the major the benefit of a doubt. Far from crediting him even momentarily with wise counseling, she rather suspected that he had talked Liza into a secret meeting and she resolved to prevent such a tryst, even if it meant keeping watch all night long.

At luncheon, Liza played the role of seasoned hostess to perfection, and when the guests — again with the exception of Lady Undersham, who was a strict adherent to the old church law of no Sunday travel — called for their carriages, it was Liza who made their leave-taking a pleasant affair. Damien was still in an abstracted mood, and his good-byes were mechanical rather than cordial.

Soon afterward, Damien disappeared in his study. Liza and Nicholas spent the afternoon playing croquet, while Kate challenged Lady Undersham to a game of chess. Lulled by the pleasant, almost dull afternoon, Kate was on the point of dismissing her suspicions about Liza and the major as unfounded, when her charge suddenly pleaded a severe headache and asked to be excused right after dinner.

Lady Undersham's thoughts ran along the same lines as Kate's. When the drawing room door had closed behind Liza, she said, "What can she be up to now, the little Miss Hey-go-mad?"

"Planning and scheming, no doubt," Kate said ruefully.

"I shan't take it amiss if you wish to retire also, Miss Elliott. I take it, your bedchamber is close to Liza's and it would be no trouble for you to

242

check on her if her . . . ah . . . headache takes a turn for the worse?"

Kate met the dowager countess's meaningful look. "No trouble at all, ma'am. Only a small sitting room separates our chambers. But I do not like to desert you."

"Fustian! If you'll ring for a pot of tea now, I shall be ready to seek my own couch by the time Damien and Lord Nicholas have finished their port."

After a slight hesitation, Kate rose. "Thank you very much, Lady Undersham. You are very kind to Liza and me. I cannot tell you how much I appreciate your intervention with Mrs. Abbots."

"I have encountered my share of censure during my heydays. Someone, be it family or friend, always stood up for me. If you like, you may think of my assistance as the payment of an old debt. And besides, I beg leave to doubt that you are a fallen woman. Are you, Miss Elliott?"

"I am not."

The dowager countess nodded, satisfied. "I pride myself on being an excellent judge of character. If you have a fault, I'd say it is an overdeveloped sense of duty. I am fairly well acquainted with Damien and his vagaries. It cannot be easy for you to be a companion in his household."

A gleam lit Kate's eyes. "There were some initial misunderstandings," she said dryly. "But I have hopes that now we shall rub along fairly well."

"Hmm. Persistent, are you?"

"Stubborn and proud, Lady Undersham. And I generally achieve my aim."

"Good for you. Well, good night, Miss Elliott. It was a pleasure meeting you. And don't forget to come and see me."

"I shan't forget." Kate smiled at the dowager countess, then left the room, saying, "I'll tell Boughey to have your tea brought up immediately."

She went straight upstairs after giving her order to the butler. On the second-floor landing, she hesitated. Before she had time to make up her mind whether or not to check on Liza, the girl's bedroom door opened and Mary stepped out.

"Oh, Miss Elliott," the young maid said brightly. "I was just coming to look for you. Miss Liza has the headache so bad, she's asking for a drop of laudanum, poor thing."

Kate nodded. "You may go, Mary. I'll see to Miss Liza."

She waited until the maid had disappeared through the narrow door in the east wing that gave access to the back stairs, then knocked on Liza's door and entered.

The chamber was steeped in darkness except for a dim pool of light shed by a single candle atop a chest of drawers. The silk drapes were partially drawn around Liza's canopied four-poster bed, making it almost impossible to see the girl's blond head among the cushions.

"Liza? Mary said you wished to take a drop of laudanum."

Kate stepped around a chair whose bulky outline showed that the maid had not yet put away the garments Liza had removed before going to bed. Surely there had been ample time.

Picking up the candle, she marched to the bed.

"Oh, Miss Elliott, it's you," Liza said plaintively.

"Don't tell me you expected the Prince Regent, my dear."

"I believed it was Mary with the laudanum."

"There was hardly time, was there? I encountered her outside your door mere seconds ago."

Kate placed the candle on the nightstand, then pulled back the drapes so she could see Liza's face. Gently smoothing wisps of hair off the girl's forehead, she knew a moment of doubt. Could Liza indeed be ill? But, no. Despite a film of moisture, her skin felt cool. It was more likely that Liza was perspiring.

"You're hot," Kate said. "Allow me to remove some of your covers."

"I am cold." Liza clutched the sheet to her throat.

"It is a warm night. Are your windows open?"

"I asked Mary to close them. I feel quite chilled."

Kate raised a brow, but Liza avoided meeting her eyes and squirmed uncomfortably.

"If you won't allow me to make you more comfortable," said Kate, "I shall wish you a good night and retire. We'll have to be up early tomorrow. Lady Undersham requested breakfast at seven o'clock."

"She lives no more than two hours away," Liza said peevishly. "But she always leaves at an ungodly hour, as though she were starting on a daylong journey."

"The privilege of old age, my dear. Or the disadvantages, depending on your point of view. Lady Undersham told me that she doesn't travel well and therefore does not often venture abroad. When she is obliged to take her carriage out, she likes to make the most of it and stops every six or seven miles to visit those of her old friends she would not otherwise see."

Liza made no reply, and with a last glance at the girl's perspiring face, Kate turned to leave.

"Good night, Liza."

"What about the laudanum?"

"I recommend a glass of warm milk and honey. And rest."

As she closed Liza's door behind her, Kate started to tremble. Had she done right? Or should she have challenged the girl, asked her to get out of bed? Was the request for laudanum indeed a ruse, as she suspected, to make her believe Liza was ill?

She entered her sitting room, which nestled between her own and Liza's bedchambers. Leaving the door ajar, she felt her way in the dark to an armchair by the window. She eased the window open and sat quietly, breathing deeply of the scented night air until the tremors stopped.

She *had* acted correctly. Nothing would have been gained by forcing Liza out of bed and, perhaps, discovering that she was fully dressed beneath her night rail. She would have been forced to lock the girl in for the night—and then would have to sit up the next night, and the next.

Much better to catch her in the act of sneaking out, or, better yet, catching her with the major. She'd give *him* a piece of her mind. His ears would ring from the dressing-down she'd give him until he could think of nothing more tempting than fleeing to the opposite side of the country.

Kate rested her feet on a low padded stool. Snuggling deeper into the chair until she felt comfortable, she relaxed and even allowed her eyes to close. She was really wide awake, only needed to rest awhile.

She heard the younger footman's sprightly step

as he came upstairs to summon Lady Undersham's tirewomen to the drawing room. A short while later, the dowager countess was safely tucked away in her bedchamber.

The downstairs hall clock struck the hour of ten.

Kate concentrated on schemes for Liza's entertainment after the major had fled the field. The Bath season was in full swing. Liza must certainly attend the assemblies and the theater. And a pox on some old scandal about Elizabeth that might spoil Liza's pleasure!

Damien must be made to realize that Liza was entitled to know the truth about her mother. Gossip could hurt her only as long as she was ignorant of Elizabeth's peccadillos. Well, perhaps more than peccadillos, but Liza was of an enlightened generation that had been raised on the gossip about the Prince Regent's amours and his wife's scandalous conduct on the Continent. If she could not condone her mother's behavior, she'd at least bear it with grace.

Hearing a slight sound in the corridor, Kate sat up to listen. It must have been the opening and closing of the door to the back stairs she had heard, for soft footsteps approached from the east wing, whispered past the sitting room, then stopped. Kate heard the click of Liza's door and knew that Mary had entered Liza's bedchamber.

The downstairs clock struck eleven times.

About fifteen minutes later, Mary left Liza's room in the same quiet manner in which she had entered it.

Again Kate relaxed, then sat up like a shot. Had it been Mary or Liza who had left the chamber?

Kate knew no hesitation. If she made a fool of herself, so be it. Without ceremony, she entered Liza's bedroom and approached the four-poster, where the candle was still burning on the nightstand.

"Miss Elliott?" Liza blinked innocent blue eyes at her. "What is the matter? Aren't you asleep yet?"

"Not yet," Kate replied wryly. She suppressed the desire to apologize. Liza looked just a trifle *too* innocent. Well, two could play that game. "I thought I heard a noise in your room and became worried that you might be feeling worse."

"You probably heard Mary. Don't worry, Miss Elliott. I'm fine now. Only very sleepy." Liza stifled a yawn behind her hand. "I hope nothing else will disturb your rest."

"So do I." Kate imitated Liza's yawn. "I'll wish you a good night, then."

Back in her sitting room, Kate boxed a chair pillow in vexation. Like as not, she had now put Liza on her guard. The chit might postpone her assignation until some other night when she knew Kate well out of the way.

Her bed and sleep seemed suddenly most desirable. Should she give up her vigilance, snatch what rest she could, and then deal with Liza and the major in the morning? No doubt, she was on a wild-goose chase. Liza might be snickering into her pillows right this instant about her foolish companion.

She felt disloyal—but she could not believe in her charge's good sense and integrity. She still believed Liza was planning mischief.

The clock struck midnight, then one. Damien and Nicholas came upstairs. Kate heard their deep

248

voices and suppressed laughter. Undoubtedly, they had enjoyed more than one glass of port.

Nicholas passed her door on his way to his room in the east wing. Damien's footsteps receded in the opposite direction, where the master's suite was located.

Guiltily, Kate remembered that she had made no mention of her suspicions to Damien. It was undoubtedly her duty to alert him, but she could not burst into his bedchamber. She could well imagine what construction he would put on such impetuosity.

Kate fanned her heated face. It was now past one o'clock, and Liza had made no move to leave her room. It was probably just as well she had not alerted Damien. Unless Liza had purposely waited for her father to retire?

Kate decided to stay up just a little while longer. Again, she heard the clock strike.

And again.

She really should go to bed . . .

Liza came abruptly awake. The candle Miss Elliott had placed on the nightstand had burned down. It took her a few moments to find a fresh one in the drawer and light it.

She checked the time. Close to six o'clock. She was late! Charles might have given up in disgust. Oh, why had she fallen asleep on a night like this? Charles had promised her a most romantic adventure: a ride at sunrise, just the two of them.

With shaking fingers, she tore off the night-gown she wore over her riding habit, then fumbled under her bed for boots and gauntlets. Carrying these items, Liza fled the room.

She flew down the stairs into the basement. She must hurry, else she would be caught by the bootboy, whose duties also encompassed stoking the fire in cook's huge ovens.

The kitchen door was already unlocked; somewhere, the bootboy was up and around. Liza hesitated at the door, then, with a toss of her tousled curls, ran outside. Still in her stockinged feet, she ran until she reached the grassy slope that led to the Bluebell Woods.

In the fast increasing light, she saw a man step out of the woods. So much did the sight remind her of the nightmares she used to suffer that her heart skipped a beat. But, of course, it was Charles. He raised an arm in greeting, then came toward her, leading two horses.

Hastily, Liza pulled on her boots. As she ran to meet him, she could see his features more clearly. How handsome he was, how romantic he looked in his uniform. She wished she had known him when he was fighting Napoleon at Waterloo. She wished she could have greeted him in Brussels as he marched triumphantly into the city after the battle. She could have tossed him flowers as had so many English ladies who were fortunate enough to travel on the Continent at that time . . .

"Charles," she breathed when he reached her. "I am so glad you waited for me."

He tossed her unceremoniously into the saddle, then mounted his own horse. "We must hurry," he said curtly. "You're nearly an hour late."

A little daunted by this less-than-romantic reception, Liza allowed him to take her mount's bridle and lead the way along the edge of the woods.

"Where are we going?" she ventured to ask at last when the Bath road came in sight. "There's

250

always traffic on the highway. We might be seen."

"No one will notice us inside a closed carriage."

"Charles!"

Her sharp tug on the reins brought Charles Dashwood to his senses. He had been so absorbed in reaching the carriage as fast as possible that he had given no consideration to the quite natural surprise Liza must feel at mention of the vehicle.

He slowed the horses to a walk. Summoning the smile that had always paved his way with the ladies, be they old or young, he said caressingly, "My love, did you not, then, guess what was my intent when I asked you to meet me?"

Liza, no slowtop, stared at him with some trepidation. "Charles! Surely not — surely you cannot mean that we shall elope?" Her voice had risen until the final word came out as a birdlike screech.

Charles wanted to shake her, but he remembered his creditors who had followed him all the way to Somerset and would be back to dun him if his engagement or marriage to an acknowledged heiress was not made public within a sennight.

With a creditable show of affection and chagrin, he said, "You did not understand what I planned, did you, my love? And I believed your feelings for me as ardent as mine are for you."

"Oh, they are, Charles!" she assured him. "They are! But —"

"My darling, was I mistaken?" He gave her an anxious look. "You do *not* wish to marry me?"

"Of course I do. But elopement?" Liza asked doubtfully. "Charles, is there not another way?"

He shook his head. "Did you not see how quickly your father sent his friend to separate us at church? Even in public, we may not be to-

251

gether!"

Charles brought the horses to a complete halt. Looking deeply into Liza's eyes, he said, "No, my love. I am afraid we must marry secretly or resign ourselves to never see each other again."

Charles saw that Liza was about to raise more questions, and he shrewdly added, "You know I cannot stay with Cousin Louisa much longer. I must get back to London. There may be a command for me—but I must not speak of that. It must still be kept secret."

Liza's eyes widened. She saw herself, left at Dearworth with no hope of ever attending the Bath assemblies or having a season in London, while Charles was sent away, perhaps to South America or to India. She had read there was trouble brewing in several of the kingdom's domains.

No. It was not to be borne.

Elopement. Liza shivered. Whether from fright or excitement or a bit of each, she did not stop to consider. Romantic as it was, she would never have suggested a runaway marriage. Just look where it had gotten Miss Elliott! But she'd brave the scandal of an elopement rather than suffer the confinement of Dearworth—perhaps for years on end. Perhaps Papa planned to marry her off to Hubert or Algy once they had outgrown boyhood, but she'd much rather have Charles now.

Touching her heel to her horse's flank, she cried, "Hurry, Charles! Any moment Miss Elliott may discover that I'm gone. She was awfully suspicious last night."

Charles needed no more encouragement to urge the horses into a gallop. He did cast an occasional anxious glance at Liza, who was not noted for her riding skills, but she seemed safe enough and they covered the short stretch to the road without mishap.

A coach and two horses were waiting in the shelter of some ancient chestnut trees. Charles helped Liza down and into the carriage, while a surly, narrow-framed individual in a dun-colored friese coat stowed their saddles in the boot. With Charles's assistance, their horses were harnessed to the shaft in a trice, and they were off toward Bath.

Liza cast a surreptitious glance at Charles, who had flung himself onto the seat beside her. She felt shy and rather intimidated all of a sudden. The carriage seat was very narrow, and Charles was very broad. It did not help that he had drawn the curtains across the oval glass panes in the doors.

And he should be taking her hand, perhaps kissing it, and telling her how much he adored her. Instead, he sat in glum silence and scowled at the opposite seat.

"Charles?" she said timidly. "Are we getting married in the abbey?"

"The abbey in Bath?" He gave her such a scornful look that she shrank against the squabs. "Have you forgotten that you're a minor?"

"I thought—" Liza swallowed. Why did Charles not smile? He frightened her when he looked at her as though she had angered him. "I thought that, perhaps, you had procured a special license."

Charles noted that she was shrinking even farther away from him and called himself sharply to order. Despite the ease with which he had captured her heart, he had not been certain that she would go with him if he asked her to elope. Ever cautious, he had resorted to subterfuge, inviting her to ride with him at sunrise. If she proved unwilling, he could easily have overpowered her. But she had gone with him voluntarily, even eagerly.

He must not antagonize her now. Because of her tardiness, they had lost a precious hour. However, she would hardly be missed before nine o'clock, perhaps later. Liza might fret about a suspicious Miss Elliott; he did not. None of the ladies of his acquaintance ever rose before nine or ten. By then they would have left Bath far behind, should even be past Bristol and well on their way to Gloucester. In strange surroundings, should she change her mind, Liza would think twice before crying for help when he claimed his husbandly rights. And seduce her or take her by force he would. Then let Ashcroft catch up with them!

"Charles?"

He took in the anxiously widened eyes, the trembling mouth, and quickly placed an arm around her shoulders. "Why do you trouble your pretty head about things like licenses and such? Don't you trust me, my love?"

For a moment, she sat stiff and unresponsive. Then, with a sigh, she rested her head against him. "Yes, of course I trust you. I daresay I'm asking a lot of silly questions, but—"

She turned up her face to look at him. "Charles, are we going to Gretna Green?"

"We must, sweetheart. Even if I had a special license in my pocket, we should not be able to wed in England. There's no getting around the fact that you are underage."

That was true, but . . . "Charles, I am not equipped for a long journey."

"I'll buy you everything you need." How? he wondered. His pockets contained barely enough money to cover the hire of horses.

Liza was satisfied with his explanations. She prattled happily about London and where they would take a house should he not be immediately posted abroad. She wondered whether she would like India and whether the older officers' wives would be cattish or willing to take a very young, inexperienced bride under their wings.

Charles wanted to shout at her to stop, that there would be no command for him in India or anywhere else. That, until her father settled money on her, they'd be forced to live on credit. But he gritted his teeth and bore his future wife's silliness for as long as he could endure. Exasperated, he finally suggested that she should try to sleep, since the journey would be a long and arduous one.

Liza obediently closed her eyes and did, indeed, fall asleep. She slept through two changes of horses and only woke up when, well past the halfway point between Bristol and Gloucester, the condition of the road took a turn for the worse, jolting and shaking the carriage until she thought her head would burst.

"Charles, what time is it?"

"Close to ten o'clock."

"When do we stop? I am hungry and thirsty." She also needed to retire to assuage a need of a more intimate nature, but that she could not say to him.

"Here, my love." Charles, who had been passing the time by consuming the better part of two flasks he had thoughtfully stowed away in the pockets of his greatcoat, generously offered her one of the leather-encased bottles. "This'll have to do until we reach Cheltenham."

Liza gave him a startled look. His voice sounded strange—thick and slurred. And with the sun shining through the flimsy curtains on the carriage door, she could not fail to notice that his eyes were bloodshot.

"Charles!" Alarmed, she pushed away from him. "Are you feeling quite the thing?"

"Never felt better, my sweet little honeybee. Do you want a drink, or don't you?"

"You are foxed!"

Charles smiled, but this time his smile failed to reassure her. There was something predatory about his full red mouth and his gleaming teeth.

Several particularly nasty jolts made it easy for Liza to edge away from him until the armrest of the seat prevented further retreat. Heart pounding, she watched him down the last of whatever liquor the flask held. A trickle of amber dripped down his chin, but he did not notice.

Liza shuddered and turned her back on him. Suddenly, Charles did not look romantic at all. And neither was an elopement romantic. Had Miss Elliott experienced the discomforts and misery that plagued Liza? She could not imagine Nicholas getting bosky in the presence of a young lady, or dribbling drink down his chin, or being insensitive to his beloved's needs. Still, Miss Elliott might have been assailed by doubt, as was Liza now. Perhaps she had been secretly pleased when Nicholas's father caught up with them and put a stop to their elopement.

Liza felt the prickle of tears under her eyelids. By now, Miss Elliott must have discovered her flight. Surely Papa was on his way. If only he would catch up with her and Charles, she'd gladly promise to wait another year or two before thinking of marriage again.

Then she remembered that her maid had been waiting at the edge of the Bluebell Woods. She had asked Mary to meet her at seven, so she would not miss the dowager countess's departure and might pretend they had been out for a walk. Liza smiled tremulously. Lady Undersham's early traveling habits might yet prove a blessing in disguise. It was quite possible that Papa was closer than she thought.

Having momentarily forgotten Charles's presence, Liza was totally unprepared when two arms snaked around her waist and dragged her backward until she rested on a hard lap. She screamed in fright, then, seeing Charles's leering face so close to hers, tried to slap him.

He caught her hand, forcing it down. "Vixen! I meant to be gentle with you, introduce you gradually to the pleasures of love. But it seems I must teach you your lesson in one fell swoop."

Covering Liza's face and neck with moist, greedy kisses, he jerked up the skirt of her riding habit and started to fondle her thighs. His common sense would never have permitted him to make such bald mistake, but his mind was clouded with brandy fumes, and determination alone drove him. He must show her who was master. Must show her now.

Liza screamed again. The most ardent token of manly passion bestowed on her had been a chaste kiss on her cheek when she had sneaked away from school to meet Lady Belinda's brother in the Sydney Gardens. It had not prepared her for the fumbling and slobbering of Charles Dashwood.

Fear and growing fury lent her strength and courage. She clawed and scratched his face and neck until he snatched his roaming hand from her thigh.

But now he had two hands free to pin her arms to her sides, rendering her helpless.

With growing horror, Liza stared at his wet mouth as it came closer and closer to hers. Just when she thought he would kiss her again, the carriage gave a jolt that threw them off the seat. A sickening lurch and the crack of splintering wood told its own horrible tale: They had lost a wheel, perhaps broken an axle.

Charles let off a string of oaths that would have made Liza blush had she been listening. But Liza had only one thought after she recovered from the stun of being knocked to the floor with Charles atop her: *Now Papa can catch up with us!*

As though he read her mind, Charles Dashwood pulled himself upright in the awkwardly tilting vehicle. "A pox on Cousin Louisa's ancient carriage! No doubt, your father will drive his racing curricle."

Gingerly, he touched his forehead where a lumpy bruise was beginning to form. He swore again, tore open the door closest to the ground, and jumped down.

"You imbecile! Cow-handed oaf!" Liza heard him shout at the driver. "Not only did you break the wheel, you cracked the axle as well."

The carriage trembled as Charles kicked it angrily. Then everything was quiet.

Cautiously, Liza slid toward the open door and peeked outside. If she expected a farmstead or an inn nearby, she was sadly disappointed. North and south, as far as she could see, stretched miles of empty road with fields and meadows to either side.

Still, while Charles was kept busy repairing the carriage, she might have a chance to run away or to stop some passing vehicle.

But before she could alight, Charles Dashwood stepped around the chaise from the back. Grinning, he held out his hand to her.

"Come, my love," he said thickly. "We may not have a carriage, but we have horses and we have saddles to carry us to the next posting house. I dare anyone to catch up with us before I make you mine!"

Chapter Nineteen

Kate awoke with a stiff neck and aching back. Slowly, she sat up and stared at the sitting room furnishings with disbelieving eyes. All night long, she had sat in the chair. No wonder her back felt as though it had snapped.

And Liza had not stirred.

But Lady Undersham was leaving! Wincing, Kate rose and went into her bedroom. The small ormolu clock on her mantel shelf showed six-thirty. Only half an hour until breakfast would be served.

She took her seat at the table just as Boughey carried in coffee and tea. If Lady Undersham suspected that Kate had sat up all night, she made no mention of it, and neither did she comment on Liza's conspicuously empty chair.

Nicholas greeted Kate with a friendly smile, but Damien gave her a sharp look. Had he noticed the dark smudges beneath her eyes? Surely he could not guess from her immaculately coiffed hair or the pristine condition of her gown that she had washed and changed with unseemly haste.

Kate's eyes strayed to Liza's chair. The girl knew that Lady Undersham would depart shortly. Why had she not come down?

She was about to rise and fetch Liza when Damien addressed the footman, who entered with a platter of freshly baked scones. "Edward, please send Mary upstairs to remind Miss Liza of her duties as hostess."

Then he turned to Kate. "It seems," he drawled, "that neither Liza nor you derived any benefit from going to bed early. You look as though you'd been carousing all night, and my daughter doesn't rise at all."

Stung, she retorted, "It seems to me that you and Nicholas did the carousing. You were noisy enough when you came upstairs at one o'clock."

Damien's brows knitted. "Were we noisy, Nicholas?"

"I don't think so."

"You cannot remember," said Kate. "That is proof enough for me that you were in your cups."

Nicholas considered the matter, then shook his head. "No," he said decisively. "I wasn't drunk, not even a trifle above par."

"My late husband," said Lady Undersham, "always started to sing when he was in his altitudes. Poor man. He was tone-deaf."

Nicholas grinned. "I assure you, ma'am, I am not tone-deaf. Neither was I noisy. I only get boisterous when I'm foxed, which I wasn't. And Damien was sober as a judge. He was miffed, you know," he said with a wink at Kate, "because you ladies deserted us."

Damien looked as though he took exception to Nicholas's observation, but Edward returned just then to report that neither Liza nor her maid were in the house.

The slice of toast Kate had eaten turned into a lump of lead—or so, at least, it seemed to her stomach.

Lady Undersham said calmly, "I daresay Liza has gone for a walk. It is such a lovely morning."

"Yes, of course. That's what she must have

done." Kate breathed easier. No matter where Liza had gone, Mary was with her. "But it is very thoughtless of her when she knows that you're eager to get an early start."

"Well, I shan't wait for her. Bring her with you when you visit me. She may apologize to me then."

Both Damien and Nicholas jumped to Lady Undersham's assistance when she pushed back her chair, and they helped her to rise. The dowager countess's abigail and dresser were waiting in the foyer with wraps and her ladyship's jewelry case. There was a brief delay while a footman was dispatched to search for and fetch Lady Undersham's small page, who had developed the habit of disappearing at the most inopportune moments. Finally, however, the countess and her cortege were safely deposited in her old-fashioned traveling chaise.

Damien, Nicholas, and Kate stood patiently in the courtyard while Lady Undersham let down her window to once more adjure her coachman to drive slowly and mind the ruts and bumps in the road. When the carriage at last started to roll down the drive, Kate let out a small sigh of relief. Rather hastily, she went up the front steps and was about to rush inside to change her shoes so that she might go after Liza, when Damien called out to her. She stopped under the portico, giving him an impatient look.

"And now, Miss Elliott," Damien said softly. "Will you kindly explain why you turned the color of green cheese when you heard that Liza is not in her room?"

Lack of sleep and worry about Liza had sapped Kate's diplomatic skills. "Because, Mr. Ashcroft," she said tartly, "I believe that she has gone out to meet Charles Dashwood."

Damien's face darkened, and she hastened to add, "Since Mary is with her, I don't think there is cause for alarm."

"There's the maid now, said Nicholas, whose attention had been caught by a slight figure racing across the lawn from the direction of the woods. "But Liza is not with her."

Kate picked up her skirts and started to run toward the maid, Damien at her side and Nicholas not far behind them.

"Oh, Miss Elliott!" Mary wailed when she saw Kate. She stopped and broke into ~~hear~~ heartrending sobs.

"What happened, Mary?" Kate came to a breathless halt before the distraught maid. "Where is Miss Liza?"

"I—Oh, miss! I dunno what to do!" Mary snatched up her apron and buried her face in it.

"Mary!" Damien shook her shoulders. "Stop sniveling and tell us where Miss Liza is."

The maid only cried harder, and Damien gave up in disgust. "Females!" he said scathingly. "I knew I'd rue the day I consented to hire female staff."

"Nonsense. You just don't know how to handle her." Kate stepped past him and administered one sharp stinging slap to the girl's face.

"Ho! So it's brutishness you want me to apply. Dash it, Kate!" Damien scowled but said no more, for Mary had stopped crying.

Nicholas, looking rather pale, awkwardly patted the maid's shoulder. "There's a good girl. Now tell us what happened, Mary, so that we may help your mistress."

"I was supposed to meet Miss Liza at seven," Mary said in a low voice, and only occasionally interrupted by a sob or a sniff. "At the edge of the

263

Bluebell Woods. You see, she went for a ride with the major. They was planning to watch the sunrise. But I waited and waited, and Miss Liza didn't come back! And I don't know what to do!"

"To watch the sunrise," said Kate, stunned as though she had just received a slap much more forceful than the one she had administered to Mary. "And I believed she planned to meet him late last night."

She looked at Damien. He was pale beneath his tan, and in his eyes she saw anxiety and burgeoning anger.

"Tell me!" he demanded, glaring from Mary to Kate. "When did Liza go out, and how the devil could she do so unobserved?"

Mary shrank away, looking as though she wished to hide behind her apron once again.

Kate was made of sterner stuff. "I am to blame. But if you believe I will stand here while you rake me over the coals, you are very much mistaken. I shall change and ride out after her. If Liza has not come back by now, I very much fear that she has taken a toss."

"You are right."

Shouting for his groom, Damien strode off toward the stables. His limp, Kate noticed, was more noticeable than she had seen it in quite some time. Nicholas, setting out after him, had no trouble catching up.

Kate hesitated, torn between desire to change into her riding habit and fear that Damien and Nicholas would ride off without her if she left the yard.

"Come, Mary," she said. "Perhaps Hinkson or Henry will know something."

When Hinkson came running into the stable

yard, Damien ordered Worcester and Satan, the two fastest horses, saddled, then addressed the undergroom. "Henry, you and the lads prepare a stretcher. Miss Liza may have taken a tumble. She didn't return from her ride."

Henry touched his forelock. "Beggin' yer pardon, Mr. Ashcroft. But Miss Liza didn't take out her mare this mornin'."

Kate stepped closer. "Perhaps she took my mount."

"No, miss. I just curried Lady."

"Then, please, have her saddled as well, Henry."

Damien slapped a fist against his open palm. "The maid!" he said. "Where the devil is that dratted girl?"

"Here, sir." Mary pushed away from the mounting block. Trembling, she approached her irate master.

"Are you certain Miss Liza went riding, not driving?"

"Aye, sir. She told me so, and she changed into her riding habit afore she went to bed and wore her nightgown over it so's"—Mary swallowed tearfully,—"so's she could hoax Miss Elliott if she came checking."

No wonder Liza had been perspiring under the covers. Kate gave the maid a stern look, then turned to Damien. "Perhaps someone should ride over to Sir Shafto."

Damien nodded. "Nicholas, would you—"

"Of course." Nicholas took Worcester's bridle from Hinkson, who was just leading the two geldings into the yard. "What if Dashwood did not take the horses from the squire's stable?"

"Then find out where their precious cousin is. If he isn't there—"

265

In her mind, Kate finished Damien's thought. *If he isn't there, we must assume that he hired a carriage and eloped with Liza.*

With the clatter of Worcester's hooves ringing in her ears, Kate walked toward the house. There was nothing she could do until Nicholas returned, except to change and fight her growing fears.

If only she had stayed awake. If only she had paid attention when Liza told her she wished to be married to Dashwood *now*. If only . . .

The full skirt of her black riding habit caught up in one hand, Kate descended to the foyer a scant ten minutes later. It was far too early for news from Nicholas, but she'd rather confront Damien and his uncertain temper than spend the time in her room with only her guilty conscience for company. There was nothing Damien could say to her that she had not already told herself, no accusation he could level at her that she had not already faced.

Yet when she opened the front door and found him standing there, on the point of entering, she took an involuntary step backward. His expression was grimmer than she had ever seen it before, and she had seen him harsh on several occasions.

He checked when he saw her, then stepped inside.

"I've sent three of the grooms to the timber hill with a stretcher." He spoke curtly, as though he were unwilling to admit what he had done. "It's worth a try. The sunrise is best observed from up there."

Following him as he strode off toward the library, Kate said, as much to calm herself as to comfort Damien, "I'm glad you started a search. There's no telling where they are. They might have

266

decided to walk so as not to arouse suspicion by taking out Liza's mare."

"Don't!" Damien slammed the library door closed behind Kate. "You know it is only to avoid doing *nothing* while we wait that I sent out the grooms." And because he could not afford to rush off himself to search for his daughter without a definite lead to follow. What a time for his blasted leg to act up. Already his boot fitted much too tight.

Torn by fear for his daughter's safety and frustrated by his physical handicap, he said bitingly, "You know as well as I do that she has run off with Dashwood. *You* probably knew it all along."

No sooner did he hurl one of the accusations Kate had made against herself than she turned on him in affront. "And just what do you mean by that? Are you implying that I helped her elope?"

He flung himself into a chair. In a gesture of utter weariness, he leaned his head against the upholstered back. Before his accusation, Kate would not have fought the temptation to go to him and offer what comfort she could. Now, she steeled herself against the urge to soothe his brow. And it was just as well she did, for Damien straightened his back almost immediately.

"Sit down," he said curtly. "I have no wish to be accused of rudeness toward a lady."

Kate sat primly on the edge of a chair opposite him. "*You* are accusing *me* of something," she pointed out.

"No, I am not." He sounded angry. "I don't repeat mistakes. But when Mary told us of Liza's sunrise tryst, you said that you had expected her to meet the major late last night."

Kate nodded.

"Why the devil didn't you tell me?" he shouted. "Do you think I have no interest in my daughter's life? Perhaps you believe that I don't care? Or that a mere father has no right to know when his daughter is about to do something that could endanger her?"

Kate clenched her hands in her lap to prevent their shaking. She knew she had been remiss, but at the time it had not occurred to her that Damien should be notified until she heard him go to his room. She had believed herself quite capable of dealing with Liza—and the major—once she caught them at the secret meeting place.

But she had not caught them.

"What is this?" Damien asked mockingly. "The tongue-valiant Miss Elliott has no pat answer? No counter question?"

"Yes, I have," Kate said bitingly. "Why do you waste time skirmishing with me when you could be studying a map to see which route they would most likely have taken? I shan't run away, I promise you."

"No. You will come with me to fetch Liza back."

It was exactly what Kate planned to do, but from his mouth it sounded like a threat.

"And I need no map," he went on, "to show me that the only fast roads away from here originate in Bath. They may have gone east to London, south to Bournemouth, or they followed the road to Bristol, thence north—the same road you traveled eleven years ago."

Kate remembered herself and Nicholas within the confines of a traveling chaise. How kind Nicholas had been, how thoughtful of her every comfort. And in contrast, Kate saw the major's dissipated

268

face, his full, sensuous mouth, the calculating green eyes.

She jumped up. "For pity's sake," she cried. "Let us be gone!"

"Why the hurry?" Rising, Damien watched her with narrowed eyes and wondered if she indeed knew more than she told.

"If they left at five," he said, "which I assume they did if all the talk of sunrise had any foundation at all, we are only"—he glanced at the tall clock standing near the desk—"three and a half hours behind. Dashwood is familiar with Liza's poor horsemanship; hence, he must have hired a carriage. On horseback and riding cross-country, we should be able to catch them somewhere near Cheltenham."

Kate shook her head. "That's all very well. You're thinking, no doubt, that I came to no harm. But you forget, Damien. *I* was with a gentleman. Liza is at the mercy of a shameless cad!"

There was a strange light in Damien's eyes, but it died quickly, to be replaced by bitter frustration.

"Lady and Satan are saddled and waiting at the front door, but there's nothing we can do until Nicholas—" He cocked his head, listening, then tore from the room with Kate close behind him.

When Damien flung open the front door, Nicholas was dismounting from his foam-flecked gelding. He threw the reins to the lad holding Lady and Satan, then turned to enter the house just as Damien and Kate hurried down the steps to meet him.

"Dashwood took Sir Shafto's chaise and four of his horses," Nicholas reported, breathless. "We know he went to Bristol, then north, for he told Sir Shafto's groom he could fetch the horses at a posting inn about five miles out of Bristol."

"Thank you, my friend!" Gripping Kate around the waist, Damien tossed her up into the saddle, then mounted Satan, and off they went.

"Wait!" shouted Nicholas. "I'll go with you. All I need is a fresh mount."

But no one heard him. Damien and Kate galloped across the yard, past the stables in a northwesterly direction that would take them through the valley just north of the Bluebell Woods, then allow them to ride cross-country in a more or less straight line north until they met up with the Bristol-Gloucester road about ten miles south of Gloucester.

Kate's mare was not as fast as Damien's gelding, and more often than not, she found herself following the cloud of dust Satan left in his wake. But Lady had stamina and more than her share of obstinacy, and eventually, as the gelding ran off some of his ardor, Lady caught up to Satan and tenaciously clung to her position at his side.

If Kate had not been so worried about Liza, she might have enjoyed the chase wholeheartedly. The terrain was as varied as any lover of the steeplechase would like, the sky was clear, and the air was mild with just a hint of summer's warmth. Every now and again, despite her worry over Liza, Kate's heart soared at a jump well done, and she could not help but feel exhilarated by the breakneck speed that took them closer and closer to their goal.

About a mile off the point where they would join the Bristol-Gloucester road, they rounded a bend leading them past a tree-studded copse. Suddenly, a brick wall loomed ahead. Kate judged it to be at least six feet high. She saw Damien glance at her in concern and nodded to him. She well remembered her father's warning never to take an unfamiliar brick wall without being prepared to land in a ditch on the far side.

Ready to kick free of the stirrup should the need arise, Kate leaned low over Lady's neck. She felt her mare's powerful muscles bunch. They soared over the obstacle, Lady's hooves clearing the top easily, and landed on the other side. Only a few drops of water splattered Kate as Lady's hind feet touched the edge of a shallow body of water.

Satan came down smoothly beside Lady, and Damien saluted Kate with his riding crop. Her mouth stretched in a smile. She was proud to know that in all those years when she had been deprived of a horse, she had lost none of her skills.

It was almost anticlimactic when, after a two-hour chase, they joined the post road and within five minutes came upon a wrecked chaise bearing Sir Shafto's coat of arms. Of Liza and Dashwood there was no sign, but a short distance later, they caught up with a wiry, narrow-framed individual leading two horses along the verge of the road.

Some prodding and gold pieces liberally applied soon had Damien in possession of pertinent facts: that the horses were indeed two of the team that had pulled Sir Shafto's chaise; that the individual was in Major Dashwood's employ and none too pleased with being left to walk the two horses, which had proven too recalcitrant to carry a rider, be it with saddle or without; and, most important of all, that the major and his female companion had set out for Gloucester on the other two horses only about ten minutes ago.

"Took the major a full half hour to get missy atop her mount," the surly man reported with obvious satisfaction. "A'kickin' and a'screamin' she was, and when he finally had her in the saddle, she refused to go faster 'n a walk."

There was a dangerous glint in Damien's dark eyes. "He forced her, the cad! When I'm through with him, he'll wish he had never come to Somerset."

"What I don't understand," said Kate with a glance at the watch pinned to a lapel of her riding jacket, "is why we are catching up with them almost a full hour sooner than we calculated. Surely Dashwood was not fool enough to dawdle or stop to see the sights."

"No, ma'am." The major's coachman scratched the grizzled hair showing beneath his beaver hat. "That'd be on account of the young lady bein' an hour tardy. Major Dashwood, he were plannin' to leave at five, but missy didn't show up until almost six o'clock."

Exchanging a brief look, Kate and Damien set out at a steady canter. They kept to the stretch of grass running alongside the road to muffle the sound of their approach and rode for what seemed to Kate twice ten minutes without encountering the runaways. The only traffic they met was a dray pulled by six plodding horses, going in the opposite direction.

Kate was just beginning to believe that Dashwood's servant had duped them, when Damien reined in. He put up a gloved hand to shade his eyes as he stared at some point ahead of them. Kate could distinguish nothing in the distance, but Damien nodded, apparently satisfied with what he saw.

He reached into his coat pocket and pulled out a small silver-mounted pistol. Handing it to Kate, he asked, "Do you know how to handle this little

272

gun?"

"Very well. But—My God, Damien! What are you planning to do? Will you fight him?"

Damien's jaw tightened. "Of course I will fight him. But not with pistol or sword. I'll beat him to a pulp, the mangy cur!"

Expertly, she weighed the balance of the little gun in her hand. "Then why do I need a pistol?"

His eyes bored into hers. "I want you to stay with Liza. No matter what happens. The pistol has three shots. You are to use them only if Dashwood comes after you or Liza. For no other purpose. Do you understand, Kate?"

She did not understand at all. Damien, she felt sure, was well able to defeat the major at fisticuffs and defend her and Liza as well. But he looked so anxious that she nodded, to set his mind at ease, and tucked the pistol into the pocket of her skirt.

Damien directed Satan into the middle of the road and urged him to a full gallop. Dismissing a strange sense of foreboding as silly, Kate followed his lead, and very soon she recognized Liza's blue riding habit, then Liza herself when she turned back and raised a hand as though to beckon them on.

It was only when Kate passed Satan and galloped toward their quarry that she remembered Damien's leg. After a two-hour neck-or-nothing race, his leg would be a considerable handicap in a fist fight. He must fear that Dashwood might get the upper hand.

And he had forbidden her to use the pistol for any purpose but Liza's or her own defense, the proud, foolish man.

Well, once he was engaged with the major, *she* would make the decisions. Afterward, Damien might have the satisfaction of raking her down in his thundering style. She would not grudge him that—if she could prevent his getting hurt.

They were close enough now that Kate could hear Liza calling out to them, although she could not make out the words. To Kate it looked as though Liza were trying to rein in. She saw Charles Dashwood raise his crop and hit Liza's mount.

The horse reared, then surged forward in a bucking motion. Under Kate's horrified gaze, Liza's slight body was tossed into the air, then crashed to the hard ground.

Chapter Twenty

"Liza!"

Kate was not aware that she had screamed nor that she was pressing Lady to the limits of her strength. She was conscious only of Liza's inert body lying in the road, Liza's horse running off, and, after a moment of hesitation, Charles Dashwood whipping his mount and taking off as well.

Satan leaped ahead, past Lady. Kate had a blurred impression of Damien, his face pressed against the side of Satan's neck. Then he was gone, closing in on Major Dashwood.

And Kate had reached Liza, who lay like a crushed blue flower in the dusty road. She reined in and jumped off Lady's back before the mare had slowed to a walk. Her legs buckled under her, but her heavy gauntlets and the folds of her skirt cushioned the impact as she hit the ground on hands and knees beside Liza.

The girl was lying on her side, her legs curled, one arm flung above her bare head, the other caught beneath her. Apparently, she had had the presence of mind to try to break her fall. She was deathly pale and her eyes were closed, but Kate saw the rise and fall of her chest.

Kate spared a glance for Damien, side by side with the major, about fifty or sixty yards away, approaching a shrub-lined bend in the road. Her breath caught as she saw Damien lunge off his speeding horse and catch Dashwood around the waist.

For Kate, time hung suspended while Damien clung to the major, his feet dragging on the road, and Dashwood hitting him on the neck and shoulders with his riding crop. It seemed like hours while she prayed for Damien's strength to sustain him, but it was, in fact, mere seconds before Dashwood's horse reared and threw them both.

Rolling over and over, the men came to a halt at the verge of the road while their horses thundered off and disappeared around the bend. When she saw Damien rise, Kate tore her gaze away.

Pulling off her gloves, she opened the top buttons of Liza's blouse and jacket, then felt for her pulse and heartbeat. Both were strong but erratic.

"Liza! she said, rubbing the girl's temples. Look at me!"

But she did not open her eyes. Not daring to move her until she knew whether Liza had broken any bones, Kate chafed the girl's hands and berated herself for not having had the forethought to carry a flask of watered brandy or smelling salts. After a moment, she took off her jacket and carefully slipped it under Liza's head, then positioned herself so that her body would shade the girl's face.

Kate darted another look at the spot where she had last seen the two men. She blinked in disbelief. They were both up, had stripped to their shirts, and were circling and testing each other in the middle of the road like pugilists in the ring during a prize fight.

Without the major's scarlet coat, it would have been difficult to distinguish one man from the other had Kate not been familiar with Damien in his shirtsleeves. There was a certain set to his shoulders, a certain tilt to his neck and head that made it impossible to mistake him for another.

Damien pounded the major's chin and midsection with a rapid assault of his fists, driving him backward until Dashwood stumbled and went down.

Kate glanced at Liza. The girl had not stirred, and Kate's anxiety grew. She might be suffering from a concussion or broken ribs. She needed help, but her father was too busy proving his mettle to spare a thought for his only child.

The watch on Kate's lapel showed a quarter till eleven. It had been ten-thirty when they had stopped Dashwood's servant, and during those fifteen minutes she had seen only that one dray going toward Bristol. Apparently, she could not count on assistance from passing travelers.

Her gaze returned to the men. Dashwood was up again. Damien still delivered his hits hard and fast, but he was taking more blows as well. His body movements were jerkier than they had been earlier; he favored his left leg noticeably.

Kate watched with impatience. If he must engage in fisticuffs with the major, he should knock him out. Quickly! He could then ride into Gloucester and fetch a carriage and a physician. Together, they could also shift Liza out of the road and into the shade beneath the lone, scraggly pine where Lady had taken refuge to cool her heaving sides.

But Damien was at a definite disadvantage now. No longer was he moving his feet to add momentum to an attack but stood, swaying a little and warding off Dashwood's erratic blows as best he could.

Despite the sunshine, Kate felt a cold prickle on her skin. Damien was now taking the brunt of the blows, and it was obvious that he could not last. Not if he had lost the use of his leg.

Torn between her anxiety for Liza and growing concern for Damien, Kate felt trapped. She wanted to give aid and support to both, and could help neither. It seemed to her that she had been sitting in the dusty road beside Liza for a long time, and no one to whom she might apply for assistance had come next or nigh. Not even Dashwood's surly servant with his horses. Surely, on a late Monday morning it was not unreasonable to expect a fair amount of traffic.

She checked her watch again, but the minute hand had moved only a tiny fraction. Kate shifted her legs. As she straightened her skirt, something hard knocked against her thigh.

The pistol. A shot, well placed, would put a speedy end to the fight.

Dare she leave Liza? A little color had returned to the girl's face; she looked as though she were peacefully asleep.

After spreading a handkerchief over Liza's face to protect it from the sun, Kate rose. Carefully, she checked the chambers of the small silver-mounted gun, cocked it, then hurried toward the men.

To Kate it looked as though Damien held Charles Dashwood locked in a macabre embrace. The major's arms were pinned to his sides by Damien's stranglehold around his chest, but he tried to break the hold by kicking against Damien's legs.

As she came closer, Kate heard their grunts of

strain and the awful sound of their breathing—like someone dying from one of the dreaded lung diseases.

She heard another sound in the distance. The thud of horses' hooves.

The heel of Dashwood's boot hit Damien's left leg just above the ankle. Both men went crashing to the ground. The fall broke Damien's grip, and Dashwood rolled free.

Damien lay sprawled on his back. He did not move.

Hitching up her skirts, Kate ran faster. She saw the major scramble to the side of the road and snatch up his coat. So he would flee, the lily-livered knave!

"Stop!" she shouted. Still running, she aimed her pistol even though she reckoned she was too far away to hit him. But she would try, by God!

The hoofbeat was stronger but still too far distant to bring instant help. Two or three riders, she judged. Carriage horses would hardly be driven at a gallop on this beastly road.

Kate kept running. Just a little closer . . .

Dashwood dropped his coat. In his hand he held a pistol much larger and heavier than her own. And Dashwood was only a few feet from Damien—not too far to hit a vital spot.

Kate wanted to cry out to distract Dashwood, but she could not make a sound.

At that moment, when she must be cool and calm and, above all, must have a steady hand to save Damien, a snippet of truth that she had long denied knocked the breath out of her and made her shake so much that she was in the greatest danger of dropping her gun.

She loved Damien.

If Damien were to die, some vital part of her would also die.

The major leveled his pistol and took careful aim at his enemy's heart.

Damien, fighting dizziness and nausea caused by the pain in his leg, stared at the firearm in Dashwood's hand. Wrath and frustration, bitter as gall, rose in him. He was defeated, betrayed by a blasted leg. A cripple, who couldn't even stand. Not man enough to avenge his daughter.

But he would not squirm under Dashwood's gun.

Two shots rent the air, one just a hairsbreadth before the other. Clods of dirt peppered Damien as one of the balls dug into the road near him. He wiped the cold sweat off his forehead, then sat up.

He heard horses galloping, and he saw Dashwood staring in stupefaction at a red streak on the back of his gun hand.

Damien looked for the approaching riders — and saw Kate standing not ten paces away, right arm extended, the small silver-mounted pistol still trained on the major. Her hand was steady and her face held a look of grim determination.

He wanted to call out to her, to, thank her for deflecting the shot that would have killed him, but the thunder of hooves behind her was too noisy — Nicholas arriving like a *deus ex machina*. He took a flying leap off his lathered mount, knocking the major down.

Dashwood dropped his gun. He tried to fend Nicholas off, but despite his slight frame, Nicholas was a man of muscle and wiry strength. And Nicholas was very angry. With a well-aimed blow to Dashwood's liver, followed by as neat an uppercut as Damien had seen in a long while, he felled his much larger opponent.

"Nicholas, well done!" Damien struggled to get to his feet, but the fierce pain in his leg forced him down again.

When Nicholas would have helped him, he shook his head. "No point in getting me up until you've found a horse for me, or a carriage. Did you see Liza? How is she?"

"She is hurt?" Nicholas asked quickly, anxiously.

"Took a tumble off her horse."

"I heard the shots and did not stop, but ordered Hinkson to stay with her. She seemed all right, sitting at the side of the road and waving to us." Nicholas looked back where he had seen the young girl. "Oh, good man! Hinkson is settling her beneath a tree."

A corner of Damien's mouth curved upward. "It's not the first time that my groom took care of her after a toss."

Nicholas shifted restlessly. "Damien, if you don't need me? . . ."

"No. But if you're planning to go to Liza, you had better hand me Dashwood's pistol before he comes to."

Nicholas brought the gun and three cartridges he found in Dashwood's coat.

"And *you* had better do something about Kate, my friend. It seems the shock of hitting Dashwood was too much for her," he said, then, leading his horse, hurried off toward Liza and Hinkson.

A frown crept into Damien's eyes as he looked at Kate, who still stood where she had fired the little pistol. Indeed, the gun still dangled from her hand, its stubby nose pointing to the ground. The

281

look of determination on her face was gone, however. Kate seemed stunned. She was looking at him, but Damien doubted she saw him.

It was quite unlike the Kate he knew to turn squeamish at the sight of a graze on Dashwood's hand. He'd wager a pony that she had aimed for the hand and would have been as surprised as he if she had missed her target. The way Kate had handled the gun when he gave it to her had shown him that she was not unfamiliar with firearms.

Neither could he believe that her conscience smote her because she had blatantly disregarded his order to use the pistol only in defense of herself or Liza.

Still, shooting a man was not the same as shooting at wafers.

"Kate," he said gently. "You only grazed him. Don't take it so hard."

She said nothing.

"Thank heaven you're such a good shot!" He wished she would come closer. He was beginning to feel extremely awkward lounging on the ground while she stood. Surely she knew he could not get up.

Or could he? Using only his right leg and arm, he managed, after some struggle, to stand up. He felt as wobbly as a toddler, but as long as he need not use his left leg for balance, he was all right.

His painful efforts seemed to bring Kate to her senses. Thrusting the pistol into the pocket of her skirt, she came running. "Here, let me help you."

"Dammit, Kate," he said as his left foot came in contact with the ground. "Don't touch me, or I'll topple." He looked at her, half shamefaced, half defiant. "I must indeed have been a pitiful sight if my squirming jolted you out of your shock."

"Shock! How can you know?" Her eyes widened. She blinked, focusing on his face. "Damien, you're bleeding! And your eye—does it hurt?"

"It's nothing. No! Don't touch."

Kate stepped back. *Don't touch.* He was right. The more distance she put between herself and Damien, the better.

For a moment, while she had aimed her pistol at Dashwood's hand, she had been able to block her mind to everything but the target. Then Damien had sat up, and together with relief, her new knowledge had flooded back.

Could he see it in her face, read it in her eyes, that his daughter's foolish companion had fallen in love with him? More horrible still, her love might have been there all along for him to see, undisguised, because she had not been aware of her feelings.

Again she felt the tremors that had assailed her when Dashwood pulled out his gun. Starting in her legs, they traveled the length of her body until even her teeth chattered. How mortifying.

"I am sorry," she stammered.

"Kate, I understand, believe me." Damien cursed his leg that kept him from going to her and taking her into his arms to comfort and soothe. "You didn't expect to hit your man. And when you did, you were horrified."

She made an effort to stop her trembling. A glint of steel appeared in her eyes. "I would have killed him and not be horrified. But you," she said, recalling her grievance against him. "How could you engage in a bout of fisticuffs when you knew I needed your help with Liza?"

He raised a brow. "Reprimands from you, who left her when I had expressly forbidden it? But we

283

shall discuss that some other time. Now I want to know what stunned you if it was not the shock of hitting Dashwood." He hesitated, frowning. "Not Nicholas, rushing off to Liza?"

She was about to reply, then clamped her mouth shut.

"No," he said, speaking very slowly. "You were looking at me, weren't you?"

She blanched. Whatever he had seen, she must take care not to admit her foolishness.

He gave her a hard look. "I was on the ground. Helpless. *That* shocked you."

"Damien, you are wrong! Let it rest. Don't pester me with questions when we should be sending for a physician or finding a carriage or doing anything to get away from this awful place."

His face grim, he persisted. "It was I who gave you a shock, wasn't it, Kate?"

"Yes!" she cried. "It was you!"

Shaken, Kate spun and turned her back on him. She saw Charles Dashwood stir, but she no longer cared whether he fled or stayed. She stormed off, her only concern getting away from Damien, who saw too much and asked too many questions. Until she gained her composure, she'd be safe with Nicholas. He saw only Liza and would ask no awkward questions.

But when she reached the scraggly pine where Nicholas sat with Liza cradled in his arms and with Hinkson, Lady, and the men's mounts hovering at his side, the question he posed proved no less awkward than Damien's.

"Kate! Why the devil did you leave Damien? Dashwood won't be out forever. What if the cad jumps him?"

"Do you think Damien would appreciate it if I

tussled Dashwood in his stead?" she shot back.

Ignoring the strange look Nicholas gave her, she dropped to her knees beside him. Anxiously searching Liza's face, she asked, "How are you feeling, my dear? You gave me quite a scare when I could not rouse you."

"I have a headache and Hinkson says I sprained my wrist."

Kate breathed a sigh of relief. She had feared to see Liza in tears because Dashwood had forced himself on her in the privacy of the carriage—an injury that would have been far more difficult to heal than bruises and a sprained wrist.

"Nicholas removed his neckcloth to make me a sling," said Liza.

"So I perceive." Kate glanced from Liza's left wrist, wrapped in Nicholas's handkerchief and resting in the sling fashioned from the snowy muslin of his cravat, to Nicholas's bare neck, which gave him a slightly rakish air. "Can you stand up, or are you still feeling faint?"

"I hurt all over, Miss Elliott. But I daresay I shan't swoon again." She raised her eyes to Nicholas's face. "Nicholas knocked the major out. Did you see that, Miss Elliott?"

"I did. Well," Kate said, rising to her feet. "I am grateful to see you recovered. I never had much use for smelling salts, but when I saw you unconscious, I wished very much I carried some on me."

Liza said mischievously, "Fie, Miss Elliott! Hinkson came better prepared than you. He made me drink some vile stuff."

The groom gave a discreet cough. "Only a drop of watered brandy Mrs. Boughey sent along."

Kate grimaced wryly. Trust the competent housekeeper to remember what she had forgotten.

"Mayhap I'd better join the master," said Hinkson. "I see Major Dashwood pickin' hisself up."

"We'll all go." Despite his fair burden, Nicholas rose smoothly and set out toward Damien. "By George!" he said suddenly. "He's letting Dashwood go!"

"He can hardly drag him to a magistrate and lodge a complaint," Kate pointed out as she watched the major stride hurriedly in the direction of Gloucester. "It'll be a good five-mile walk to the Cambridge Inn where he might find a horse," she said with some satisfaction. "A long enough walk to make him rue this day."

Nicholas scowled and muttered something under his breath.

Liza said with a shudder, "Please don't fetch him back, Nicholas. I am very glad I need not speak to Charles again."

"Oh, in that case!" Nicholas's face cleared. "Are you comfortable?" he asked solicitously. "I am not jolting you too much?"

To Kate's critical eyes, Liza looked as comfortable as a kitten in a basket and appeared to be quite amazingly recovered from her fall. She was still pale, and Kate could see a bruise forming on her right temple, but her eyes were full of spark and vivacity.

Nestling her head against Nicholas's chest, Liza gave him a smile that showed off her dimples. "Very comfortable," she murmured. "And I haven't thanked you yet for coming to my rescue."

Nicholas grinned down at her. " 'Twas nothing, my dear. Just a bit of exercise to banish the tedium of a Monday morning. Besides, your father and Miss Elliott did most of the work before I ever got here."

Liza had the grace to blush. "Thank you, Miss Elliott," she murmured politely, then looked at Nicholas again. "When I saw you gallop past me," she said in an awed little voice, "I was reminded of those knights of old, who were forever dashing off to rescue young ladies."

Kate, walking beside them, felt a rush of annoyance. The minx was barely saved from Major Dashwood, and already she was flirting again. Even if Dashwood had not taken advantage of her, she should be subdued, frightened. But she sounded as though she were enjoying herself. A damsel in distress. Drat the girl and her hankering for romantic adventure!

"Let us hope," Kate said repressively, "that our knight has thought of a solution to get us home. You have no horse, Liza, and Satan ran off as well. And in any case, I doubt you or your father should ride."

"The carriage, my lady, will arrive shortly," Nicholas told her airily.

Liza asked, "What is the matter with Papa?"

"He injured his weak leg when he fought with Charles Dashwood," said Kate.

"Oh." Liza turned a shade paler.

Nicholas instantly assured her that everything would be all right and that she had no need to worry. He gave Kate a look asking her support, but Kate said nothing.

It was time Liza faced certain facts. One of them was that her father was hurt because of her escapade. Dashwood might have had to use force to get Liza to elope; the fact remained that she had sneaked out to meet Dashwood in the first place. Kate had no intention of scolding the girl now, but she hoped Liza would face her father with a certain degree of humility. Damien had been hurt enough without having to watch Liza in the role of heroine she seemed to have assumed when she regained consciousness.

Damien, his anxious gaze trained on his daughter, stood rigidly in the same spot where Kate had left him. A pang of guilt assailed her when she saw the darkening bruises and lines of pain etched in his lean face. She should have stayed with him no matter how upset and shaken she was.

"Nicholas, please set me down," said Liza. "I feel quite stout now."

Damien allowed himself to relax a little when he saw that his daughter was indeed quite capable of standing and walking. But she had been in Dashwood's company, in a closed carriage, for nigh on three hours. "Liza," he said hoarsely. "Are you all right, child?"

She hung her head. "Yes, indeed. Oh, Papa, I am so very sorry! Will you ever forgive me?"

"Forgive you, Princess, yes." Damien wanted to crush her to his breast but feared to make that violent a move. A pat on her tousled locks must suffice.

"But don't think you've heard the last of this," he warned. "We must have a talk. Soon. First we must get you home, though. You and your — what is it? A broken arm?"

"I sprained my wrist, Papa."

The blast of a horn announced the approach of a stagecoach from Gloucester.

"Damn!" said Damien. "I hoped to be gone from here without getting gawked at by bored travelers."

288

Kate checked her watch. It was just a little past eleven-fifteen. "Shall we stop the coach?" she asked. "You and Liza may ride in comfort to Bath. By the time you arrive at the White Hart, Nicholas and I will have sent the carriage for you and alerted Dr. Bullen."

"I'll be damned if I—"

"There's no need to go by stage," Nicholas interrupted. He pointed in the direction of Bristol. "Our own carriage is being delivered."

Nicholas's carriage turned out to be a dilapidated traveling coach driven by Dashwood's servant. Nicholas, too, had met and talked with the surly man and had sent him off with his two horses to hire what transportation he could at the nearest farm on one of the intersecting roads.

After some argument all around, it was decided that Dashwood's servant would be paid off, Hinkson should take their tired mounts to the nearest posting inn for a day's rest while he searched for Satan, and Nicholas would drive the coach with Liza, Kate, and Damien inside.

When Damien had been helped into the carriage by Nicholas and Hinkson, Kate climbed in, wrinkling her nose at the musty smell.

"Tell me," she said. "Shall we see the major again?"

Damien shrugged. "I doubt it. When he recovered from Nicholas's blow, he recalled that he had urgent business abroad. It appears that some of the principalities in Germany are in desperate need of soldiers. He did not take the time to give me particulars. He was in quite a hurry to be gone."

"I am sure he was," Kate said dryly. "And I wager it was you who helped him remember the Continental opportunities, and the sight of his pistol in your hand that sped him on his way."

Damien's mouth curled in a bitter smile. "Yes," he said harshly. "With a pistol in his hand, even a cripple can inspire fear."

Before Kate had fully comprehended the significance of his words and could formulate a blistering reply, Damien addressed his daughter still standing in the road beside Nicholas.

"Dashwood begs your pardon, Liza. He fears that his commitments won't allow him to return to England for quite some time."

Liza blushed and gave her father an uncertain look. "Papa, believe me, I really do not like Charles any longer. He is not a gentleman."

Turning to Nicholas, who was patiently waiting to hand her into the coach, she said, "Miss Elliott can count herself lucky that she eloped with you. I wager you'd never behave dishonorably."

Chapter Twenty-one

"What!" shouted Damien. "Liza, you assured me you were all right!"

Nicholas's face took on a darker hue. Eyes blazing, he looked into the carriage. "And *you* let the cad go," he said to Damien. "If I must pursue him to the other side of the globe, I swear I'll find him. I'll make him pay for—"

"Nicholas, take a damper." Kate frowned at him. "You totally misunderstood Liza."

There was a moment of silence while both men directed a look of painful intensity at Kate. Then, leaning out of the carriage, Damien asked, "Is that true, Liza? Did we misunderstand?"

Her face scarlet, the girl whispered, "Yes, indeed. I only wanted to make Nicholas a compliment. I am sorry if I led you to believe that he . . . that Charles . . ." She looked helplessly at Kate.

"That Charles Dashwood ravished you," Kate said crisply. "I daresay the gentlemen cannot help but jump to that conclusion."

Again she felt Damien's eyes on her and braced herself for a scathing remark. Just let him say something! Angered by his earlier reference to himself as a cripple, she'd be more than happy to deliver a set-down he would not soon forget.

But Damien, for once, had nothing more to say. Liza, with a timid glance at her father, joined them in the coach. Nicholas shut the door, then climbed onto the coachman's box and set the carriage in motion.

After assuring herself that Liza was as comfortable as was possible in a coach of such ancient and neglected state, Kate subjected Damien to a covert study. He sat opposite her, his back and head resting against the splintering side paneling of the coach, his injured leg stretched out across the seat and his right leg braced against the floorboards. Each time the wheels hit a rut, he gritted his teeth. A film of moisture glistened on his forehead, and he clutched the leather strap set in the roof of the carriage in such a tight grip that his knuckles showed white.

Kate leaned back in her corner and closed her eyes. He might be infuriating, but it was more than she could bear to watch him suffer and not be able to help.

By coach, the journey to Dearworth would take three and a half hours, possibly longer since they'd have to make do with two horses until they reached the nearest posting house. Three and a half hours of agony.

Kate looked again at Damien. He was paler than before. His boot cut deeply into the swollen flesh of his leg, and a dark stain spread where his breeches met the top of his boot. Blood.

"Damien," she said impulsively. "Let me take off your boot. I daresay you'll be more comfortable."

He shook his head. "Too late. Needs cutting off."

"Well?" She challenged him with a look. "Don't you carry a knife? Or is it that you will not entrust the task to me?"

A gleam entered his eyes, making him look

292

more like the Damien she knew. "The intrepid Miss Elliott. Is there nothing you would not dare?"

"Nonsense. The leather is soft, and unless your knife is as dull as a gardener's hoe, I shall have that boot off in a trice."

But when she knelt on the dusty carriage floor and he handed her a razor-sharp clasp knife from his pocket, her confidence fled. She had thought only of easing his discomfort, had given no consideration to the bouncing and jolting of the coach.

Liza, who had sat staring out the grimy window, turned suddenly and said, "Pray put away that knife, Miss Elliott. You will hurt Papa."

"I fear you may be right." Kate's voice held a slight tremor, but a glance at Damien's leg stiffened her resolve. "If the boot is not removed immediately, however, a surgeon may have to cut it out of his flesh. The leg is still swelling."

Stretching a little, Kate could just reach the small communications panel to the coachman's box and opened it. "Nicholas, how far to the next coaching inn?"

"All of five miles, but with the abominable condition of the road and the sluggishness of the two steeds I've been trying to urge into at least a dog trot, I daresay it will take us forty, mayhap forty-five minutes."

Her face set in lines of grim resolution, Kate said, "Stop the coach, Nicholas, and come help me."

Nicholas complied instantly, and a very short moment later, he opened the door. "What is it? Is Liza—"

"No, it's Damien," said Kate. We must cut his

293

boot. Just look at that leg! I dare not wait until we reach an inn."

"A lady of courage," muttered Damien. "Undeterred by my cowardly fear of seeing the deadly knife in her tender hands."

Kate's eyes flew to his face, but his smile, though strained, was free of cynicism.

"It would be preferable, I admit, if we could have the benefit of brandy or whisky to dull the pain," she said. "Do you want to wait until we reach an inn?"

He shook his head.

Liza said, "I have Hinkson's watered brandy. Would that help?"

"Indeed." Kate passed the flask to Damien, who kept following her every movement with dark, glittering eyes.

That glitter, Kate thought worriedly, might well be a sign of fever and not, as she had first believed, a return of his pugnacious mood.

She watched him drink most of the watered brandy. "That is enough," she said firmly when only a finger's width was left in the flask. She poured it onto her handkerchief and wiped the thin, pointed blade of the knife.

"What a waste," said Damien. "You should have drunk it yourself to steady your hand."

Nicholas squeezed past Kate. Holding Damien's booted foot in a firm grip, he knelt beside her. "I'd offer to do the cutting," he said, turning a trifle pale around the mouth, "but I fear my fingers are too thick to get a hold of the boot."

Kate merely nodded. Even her slender fingers seemed the size of pigs' knuckles when she tried to insert them beneath the boot top. But she could not cut without leverage.

Through the thickness of his stockings and breeches, she felt the heat and tautness of Damien's leg and the stickiness of blood. Clenching her teeth, she started to cut.

She heard Liza moan, but not a sound came from Damien. She gave him a quick look. He had not, as she feared, fainted dead away but was watching her hands.

"I think I'll go and check on the horses," Liza murmured.

The skirt of Liza's riding habit brushed Kate's back as the girl left her seat. Kate saw Nicholas's anxious look follow Liza, but he remained on his post. Resolutely, she resumed her task. She had cut the boot about halfway when she felt a change in Damien. Again she looked up.

Damien had squeezed his eyes shut. His face was ashen, and he held himself so rigidly that she became alarmed.

"Go on, Kate," Nicholas said in an urgent undertone. "It always hurts the most just after the constricted flesh is freed. Cut as quickly as you can."

She did, wondering all the while why Damien's leg should be covered in blood. As far as she knew, he had not been touched by Charles Dashwood's shot.

"There!" With a grunt of relief, Nicholas tugged on the boot and pulled it off almost before Kate had removed her knife from the instep section.

She cut the leg of Damien's breeches to above his knee, then peeled off the stocking, which again necessitated the occasional use of her knife. When his leg was bared, she could not suppress a gasp. Not only was it swollen to almost twice its size, but it was riddled with old scars and punctuated

295

with tiny bleeding craters.

Kate rose and stood for a moment, trembling.

"Damien, you fool," she heard Nicholas say. "You should have seen a doctor weeks ago. If I don't miss my mark, more of the old lead worked its way to the surface. You must have known that."

"Of course I knew. Had the devil of a time getting into my boots this past week or longer. But what did you expect me to do?"

Kate wiped her perspiring brow. "Do you mean this"—her hand swept over Damien's bleeding leg—"is still the result of your old shotgun injury?"

He gave her a sardonic look. "I daresay today you won't insist that my limp is so negligible as to be almost nonexistent," he said, echoing the words she had uttered during one of their early confrontations.

"But how?" Bewildered, Kate looked at Nicholas, for Damien had closed his eyes as if to stress that he did not wish to further discuss his injury.

"At the time, the doctor could not find all the lead," Nicholas said absently. "Every now and again more pieces work their way to the surface. Kate, we must bind his leg. What do you say? Will Damien's neckcloth do?"

She shook her head. Turning her back on the two men, she raised the front of her skirt, and without ado slipped off her linen petticoat. She ripped the first flounce, but it was too dusty to be of use. Tearing off the next layer, she handed the garment to Nicholas. "Use the knife. Cut strips about the width of your hand."

While Nicholas was thus employed, Kate wrapped the flounce around Damien's leg.

"A shocking sight, isn't it?" Damien said in a low voice. "Elizabeth found the scars nauseating."

Anger swelled in Kate. Anger at the woman who had caused scars that went much deeper than those on Damien's leg. But Elizabeth was dead, and Damien was no longer a confused young man to be pitied.

Rather sharply, she said, "Well, I am *not* Elizabeth."

"No." He gave a weak chuckle. "Thank God."

She glanced at him, wondering what he meant. He did not elaborate, and she refused to ask for clarification. Deftly, she finished her task and, as soon as the last knot was tied in the bandage, called to Liza to resume her seat and admonished Nicholas to avoid ruts and potholes whenever possible.

Damien seemed a little more comfortable now that the boot was off, but while the carriage rattled and jolted over the worst stretch of road it had been her misfortune to travel, Kate kept a close watch on his bandaged leg and his face, where several bruises showed up starkly against the sallowness of his skin.

Don't touch! The warning he had uttered earlier was fresh in her mind, but how she was to refrain from wiping his brow or soothing the deep lines of pain etched beside his mouth she did not know.

She did not suggest that they stop at the inn and send for a physician. Now that he knew Liza was not seriously injured, he'd never consent to a delay in getting her home. It would be of no use pointing out that they could easily fabricate a story to satisfy the landlord's and the physician's curiosity. He would pay no more heed than he had to her advice to tell Liza the truth about her mother.

Her eyes met Damien's, and she became aware that he was watching her as closely as she was watching him. Warmth stole into her face, as though she had been caught in an improper act.

"You are scowling," he said. "No doubt you're thinking that I botched this affair."

"I am thinking," Kate said with asperity, "that you should see a physician immediately but are far too stubborn to admit it."

"You are quite correct." There was a smile in his voice. "But you're mellowing, Kate. Or growing forgetful. You did not mention that I am also arrogant and overbearing."

Against her will, her mouth curved in an answering smile. "And odious and aggravating. Will you at least allow me to procure a glass of brandy for you while we change horses?"

He grimaced as a jolt of the chaise knocked his head against the paneling. "As long as you're charitably inclined, you may also get me a pillow."

"If I sat beside you," Kate said diffidently, "you could rest your head upon my shoulder."

She half expected a brusque refusal, but he said with exaggerated meekness, "How very kind of you, Miss Elliott."

Again, she noticed the glitter of his dark eyes. A glitter that might be the sign of a fever—or his deviltry asserting itself.

She glanced at Liza, but, as she had done earlier, the girl was staring out the chaise window. An unusual pose for a volatile miss, and her prolonged silence was disquieting. Liza must have been more affected by her adventure with Major Dashwood than Kate had suspected. A few hours of sober reflection, however, would do the girl no

298

harm.

Refusing to worry about Liza at this point, Kate rose and waited for Damien to make room for her on the seat. And a very narrow space it was. Kate sat wedged between the armrest and Damien's hip, then found that seated as he was, sideways, with his injured leg taking up most of the bench, his head kept sliding off her shoulder.

"Perhaps," said Damien, "if you were to turn just a little?"

She adjusted her position, her back against the side of the carriage as Damien's had been earlier, and with a sigh of content, he leaned against her. For a moment, she was undecided what to do with her hands, then clasped them around his chest.

The weight of his head was warm against her breasts. It was a strange feeling. Unsettling and disturbing, yet, at the same time, his closeness provided a certain measure of peacefulness. For a short while, holding him in her arms, she could allow herself to think about her feelings for Damien.

Before she had ever met him, she had judged him to be a most uncaring and selfish father, a harsh man, opinionated and interested only in getting his own way. A totally unlovable man. Their initial confrontations had done nothing to change her opinion of him, but gradually, as she watched him with Liza, with his neighbors, and with those who worked for him, she had seen him with different eyes. He was still arrogant and overbearing, still apt to browbeat rather than persuade, but she had realized that it was a strong sense of responsibility and a deep love for his daughter that drove him.

When he had taken her into his arms in the

squire's study, she had been shaken, but the incident had not changed their relationship — or so she had told herself at the time. Then he had kissed her again, and no longer had she been able to deny a fatal attraction. But physical desire was not the same as love, and Kate did not make the assumption that it was during their passionate embrace at the excavation site that she had fallen in love with Damien.

But when? And why? They were forever at loggerheads. Except on the day of the ball when Damien had apologized, he had made no effort to be conciliatory or to please her. How on earth had it happened that she had fallen in love — and not even been aware of it?

Holding him in her arms, it would be easy to make believe that he might return her feelings. But Kate had outgrown the age of daydreaming. She understood that his experience with Elizabeth had turned Damien into a cynic. She remembered Phoebe Charteris's warning that Damien would never marry again, and her mother's outraged cry that he had not only consorted with opera dancers in Italy but had taken a mistress as well.

This had neither surprised nor shocked Kate. She labored under no misapprehension. Be it in England, Italy, or Egypt, Damien would not suffer from a lack of female companionship. Should he find himself attracted to a not-so-young, impoverished companion of questionable reputation, he would have no need to request her hand in marriage. He could ask her to be his mistress and, should she refuse, smile and turn away, secure in the knowledge that the next lady would be more compliant.

So absorbed was Kate in her reflections that she

hardly noticed when the jolting of the carriage eased and Nicholas pulled into the noisy, bustling yard of a coaching inn to exchange the pair of sluggards for a team of first-rate post horses. And when Nicholas opened the door and thrust a bottle of finest French cognac and a glass at her, it totally slipped her mind to procure pillows or cushions to take her place as Damien's backrest.

It was only after they rolled to a halt in the courtyard of Dearworth and Marston, Damien's valet, had climbed into the chaise and freed his master from her tight clutch that Kate felt the armrest digging into her back and pricks of discomfort in her thighs where circulation had been impeded by Damien's weight.

"Ben! Edward! Stir yourselves," shouted Marston and, in the same breath, said to Damien, "Dr. Bullen is in the library, sir. I knew just how it'd be with your leg after you went off in that neck-or-nothing fashion and took the liberty of sending for him an hour ago."

Damien grunted something unintelligible as Marston and Edward helped him off the seat, but as soon as he had been lifted out of the chaise, said, "Set me down, dammit! If one of you will give me your shoulder, I can manage quite well."

The valet and the footman exchanged looks, then, retaining a firm grip on his arms, carefully set Damien down. With a sinking feeling, Kate watched as he gritted his teeth and started to hobble toward the front steps with Edward's and Marston's able assistance.

"I suppose," he said testily to his valet, "that you expect to be thanked for calling in Dr. Bullen. Well, you may take him to see Miss Liza just as soon as she is settled in her chamber. She took a toss off her horse, and I'm afraid she has several bruises and a sprained wrist."

Quite unmoved, the valet replied, "I'm certain Dr. Bullen will be happy to take a look at Miss Liza's wrist — after he has seen to your leg."

Damien gave a wry laugh that was abruptly cut off when he set his left foot on a step. "Damn your impudence, Marston! I should—"

The rest of his angry muttering was lost to Kate as Damien entered the foyer. She became aware of the second footman, who had helped Liza out of the chaise, deposited her in Mrs. Boughey's capable hands, and now stood patiently waiting for her to descend. She gave him an apologetic smile and hurried into the house.

She saw Edward and Marston assist Damien up the wide oaken stairway. The trio was followed by Mrs. Boughey, Liza, and Dr. Bullen, who must have heard the commotion of their arrival and had come from the library to see to his patients. Boughey stood in the middle of the wide entrance hall and looked as though he had just discovered that someone had stolen the silverware.

"Cheer up, Boughey. There is no need to worry," Kate said quietly but firmly. "You may tell the staff that Miss Liza is unharmed save for a bruise or two. I need not remind you, I trust, that there must be no gossip about her. But you will know best how to handle it."

The butler drew himself up. "Miss Liza took a toss as she's done many a time before," he said with dignity. "And there's no one here at Dearworth as would say otherwise."

"What about Sir Shafto's people? Lord Nicholas may have aroused some speculation when he rode over this morning."

"No need to fret, Miss Elliott. First order the master gave when he entered the house was to send over to the court and ask the squire to call at his earliest convenience."

Kate turned to go upstairs. "I suppose," she said over her shoulder, "Dr. Bullen will see Mr. Ashcroft before he takes a look at Miss Liza?"

"That he will." Boughey permitted himself a grim smile. "But whether the master will allow him to look at his leg is another question. Mr. Ashcroft, if you'll pardon my saying so, can be a very stubborn man."

"You may say so with my goodwill," said Kate, mounting the first step.

"Yes, miss." Boughey shuffled closer. "But I think you ought to know, Miss Elliott, that old Dr. Manswick, when the accident happened, overlooked most of the shot. And then, about ten years ago if I recollect rightly, some of the bits had moved and were giving Mr. Ashcroft a good deal of trouble. The master almost lost his leg that time because of the old doddering fool of a doctor."

"Yes, I see. Thank you for telling me, Boughey. But, thank goodness, we do not have to deal with Dr. Manswick any longer."

"No, miss." A hint of Boughey's cheerful smile returned to his cherubic countenance. "Old Manswick's been dead and buried these past seven years."

Kate hurried upstairs. As she approached Liza's door, she could hear Mrs. Boughey's astringent voice urging Mary to hurry up with Miss Liza's bath. After a perfunctory knock, Kate entered. Mary, her face flushed, was busy pouring hot water into a round copper tub set on old sheets in

303

front of the fireplace. Liza sat on the edge of her bed, while Mrs. Boughey pulled off the second riding boot and placed it neatly beside its mate at the foot of the four-poster.

Liza hardly glanced at Kate when she approached her. She looked tired and listless, but Mrs. Boughey, as thin and angular as her husband was round, turned to Kate with brisk efficiency.

"Ah, Miss Elliott! I daresay you'll be wantin' your own bath. I've sent one of the maids to your chamber. And after your bath, you'll be wantin' a bite of luncheon and a nice pot of tea."

Startled, Kate looked at the clock on Liza's dresser. But, indeed, it was only going on three o'clock. So much had happened since she had taken breakfast with Lady Undersham that she had expected the time to be much closer to dinner than to luncheon.

Misunderstanding Kate's silence, Mrs. Boughey said, "I'll take good care of Miss Liza. Many a time have I given her a rubdown and watched over her after she tumbled off her horse. Isn't that so, Miss Liza?"

Liza only nodded.

"Well," said Kate. "If you're sure you won't need me, Liza?"

"Thank you, Miss Elliott." A wan smile flitted across Liza's face. "I have everything I require."

Mrs. Boughey started to undo the frogging and lacing of Liza's riding jacket. "Just get yourself a good rest," the housekeeper advised briskly. "You look all done in, miss."

Kate hesitated no longer. Liza was in no shape for the talk Kate had planned to have with her, and any assistance she might require would undoubtedly be rendered by the efficient Mrs.

Boughey and by Mary. Besides, Kate was indeed very tired and hungry.

In her own chamber, she found the promised tub of steaming water. She had barely finished her bath and slipped into a robe of soft white cotton when a maid carried in a tray loaded with covered dishes and a pot of tea.

There was rice and a mild, tangy curry, a rich, creamy vegetable soup, a salad, and a plate of apricot tarts. Kate had taken only a few bites of the curry when the exertions of the day overpowered her. She was too tired to eat and only drank a cup of tea while she brushed her hair before tumbling onto her bed and falling instantly asleep.

A loud knocking on her door and Marston's persistent voice roused her. She could not have slept long. Although there was no sign of sunshine, it was still light outside. Rather groggily, Kate sat up and bade the valet enter.

"I'm sorry to disturb you, Miss Elliott." The elderly man, who usually presented a self-assured, even masterful front, twisted his hands nervously. "But I'm at the end of my tether, and Mr. Boughey . . . well, he suggested that you might be able to help."

Kate's sleep-drugged mind was working very slowly, but it finally conveyed to her that something must be truly amiss if Damien's valet had come to *her* for help.

"What is the matter?" she asked sharply. "Mr. Ashcroft's leg, it is not worse, is it?"

"Not yet," Marston said gloomily. "But there's no telling what'll happen."

He then informed Kate that Dr. Bullen had prevailed upon Damien to show him his leg. The young physician had removed eleven pieces of shot that had either pierced the skin or were about to do so. He had bandaged the leg and ordered Damien to stay in bed for the next two or three days and to abstain from the consumption of wines and brandy until he could be certain that no fever would develop.

Resignedly, Kate shook her head. "Dr. Bullen has much to learn yet. If bed rest was his order, he should also have prescribed a gaoler, for, naturally, Mr. Ashcroft would not follow his advice. Where is he, Marston?"

"In his study, miss. And he's already emptied the brandy bottle halfway."

A martial gleam lit Kate's eyes. She tucked a strand of hair behind her ear and slipped off the bed. "We shall see about that."

"I should, perhaps, warn you, Miss Elliott, that Mr. Ashcroft is not in one of his better moods."

Kate gave the valet a knowing look. "Testy, is he?"

"He threw a book at me when I suggested that he should retire. And Mrs. Boughey received a tongue-lashing that made her take to her couch with a bottle of smelling salts."

Kate compressed her lips. Head high, she sailed from the room, descended to the first floor, and marched purposefully toward the study. Without knocking, she swept inside and closed the door behind her.

She had several pungent remarks in mind that she wished to address to the aggravating man. None of them were uttered as she checked in the middle of the room and stared at Damien sitting in front of the wide open window, glass and decanter on a small table at his elbow, a book in his hands, and his leg, wrapped in a more professional bandage than her petticoat had provided, propped on a cushioned footstool.

But it was not the sight of Damien that rendered her speechless. While she had rested, the weather had changed. A blustery wind had come up, and the breeze blowing through the open window played with her unpinned hair. Worse, it tugged at the folds of her thin cotton robe, alerting her that, shockingly, she had not dressed before storming off to see Damien.

Chapter Twenty-two

Damien raised his eyes from the heavy tome he was perusing. He closed the book with a snap and set it on the floor beside his chair.

"Ah, the intrepid Kate," he drawled. "I rather expected that you would come. What I did not dream was that you'd try to charm me with your hair down and gowned in the most delectable state of *déshabillé* it has been my privilege to behold."

A lady of sensibility would surely have swooned under his dark gaze that raked her from her disheveled hair to her bare toes. Kate had too much sense to engage in such a ploy. Damien's leg would prevent him from catching her as she fell, and besides, knowing Damien, he would not believe that she had been overcome by mortification and would tease her unmercifully.

Marveling at her own daring, Kate stepped closer. Propriety and decorum, after all, held no significance when pitched against the necessity of making Damien mind the physician's orders.

"I don't know why you should have expected me," she said coolly. "I was fast asleep until Marston woke me to complain about your recalcitrance."

His eyes narrowed. "Marston came to you?" he asked incredulously. "I thought Nicholas . . . well, it makes no odds, I suppose."

"Nicholas? No, why should he? Or did you throw a book at him as well?" Kate swept the decanter and glass off the table and placed them well out of Damien's reach on one of the bookshelves. "Actually, it was Boughey who told Marston that I might be able to make you mind Dr. Bullen's orders."

"Kate." His voice, dangerously soft, raised goose bumps on her arms and neck. "How dare you meddle? And bring back the brandy. If I want to take a glass or two, I'll damn well do as I please."

She drew up a chair next to his footstool. "There is no need to swear," she said severely. "Now, about the brandy. Aren't you just a bit too old for childish defiance? Or," she added with a challenging look, "are you so sunk in self-pity that you must seek oblivion?"

He stiffened. "I advise you, madam, to guard your tongue. I have never indulged in self-pity and never shall."

"Why, then, the brandy?"

He gave her a look of resentment. "It should be obvious even to a female that my pride suffered a blow today. I am furious with myself. First vanquished by Dashwood and saved by you. Then Nicholas fells the cad with two blows. Two hits, Kate, that *I* should have easily dealt. Gad! How I loathe this leg!"

Kate steeled herself against the pain in his eyes. "Loathing, anger, self-pity," she said. "It seems to me there's not much to choose between the three. And speaking of hits and blows, why the dickens

309

did you start that boxing match while Liza was lying unconscious in the road?"

He leaned toward her. "You're in no position to reprimand me. *You* left Liza when I specifically ordered you to stay with her. What if the mail or a stagecoach had passed? Or, heaven forbid, some mad whipster racing his curricle? They don't expect anyone lying in the road. Liza might have been maimed for life."

"You exaggerate. It was a straight stretch of road. The nearest bend was fifty or sixty yards away. Even the most reckless driver must have noticed Liza's blue riding habit. It was you and Dashwood, who chose to prove your mettle within a short distance of a hedge-bordered curve."

"That still does not change the fact that you disobeyed a direct order."

"I told you once before that I'd be the first to honor a *reasonable* request or order. But you, Damien, are not only arrogant and aggravating, you're *un*reasonable!"

There was an arrested look in his eyes. "Since you were close enough to take careful aim at Dashwood's hand, I assume you started for us quite a while earlier, when we were still wrestling each other. Did you mind so much that he was besting me?"

Kate's heart beat faster. She must take care how she replied. Damien might be unreasonable, but he was by no means a dullard.

"You and the major wasted precious time," she said tartly. "I was becoming quite impatient, let me tell you! And had I foreseen how very odious you'd be afterward, I would have gladly assisted Dashwood in wringing your neck instead of shooting him."

"Odious!" he said, stung. "I thanked the heavens that you are such a good shot."

"You also accused me of feeling revulsion for your helplessness!"

"Oh, that," he said gruffly. "I realized very soon that I had done you an injustice. If it still rankles, I must beg your pardon."

"Yes, you must. But I daresay I'll never get to hear your apology. You're a great one for voicing your intent and not following up."

The corners of his mouth twitched, and it seemed as though he would actually smile. Kate's next words, however, brought on a most forbidding frown.

"And now," she said, "I'll ring for Marston so that he may help you to your bed."

"The devil you will! I shall go to bed when I please, and I shall also go out to the site in the morning, no matter what that fool Bullen says."

"It takes a fool to recognize one," Kate snapped. She got up and started pacing between his desk and the window. "You are the most obstinate, pigheaded man I have ever encountered. And I am all out of patience with you!"

Her anger seemed to calm him, for he spoke quite reasonably. "Kate, I must go to the site. If I'm not there to set them to work, there's no telling what those pesky twins will do."

"They are sensible boys," Kate said with more conviction than she felt. "They'll understand."

"No, they won't. And the worst part is that I have only myself to blame. I have told them so much about ancient history that now they are well and truly caught by excavating fever. Do you know that they started pestering Professor Crabb?"

311

"Yes, and I warned them to stay away from him. Especially after they told me that Lord Severeign believes they are spying for you."

"Damn! I don't like it that he's still around. Never before has he stayed away so long from the gaming tables."

"He may be here on a repairing lease," she suggested, wishing she could erase the deep crease etched into his forehead.

"With the money from the sale of his land burning a hole in his pocket?"

Her perambulations had brought Kate once again to the window. Coming to a halt beside his chair, she said, "Never mind the viscount. If you're worried about Walter-Peter, Nicholas and I can go out to the site and put them to work. You only have to tell us what you want done."

"Ah, yes." Damien's hand shot out, gripping her wrist so that it was impossible for her to start pacing again without engaging in a tug-of-war. "Let us talk about you and Nicholas for a moment."

"There is nothing to discuss," Kate said, stiffening.

"Not even that you are losing him to Liza? Or has it escaped your attention that he is practically living in her pocket?"

She forced herself to meet his intent gaze. "Nicholas is at liberty to form an attachment wherever he pleases. He and I agreed some time ago that we will not suit."

"I *knew* it." His grip on her wrist tightened. "But you tried to deceive me, did you not, Kate? I wonder why?"

"You knew that Nicholas had made me an offer. Do you think I'd boast of turning him

312

down?" His watchfulness flustered her, and she added sharply, "It was up to him to tell you. *I* wonder why he chose not to."

"Yes, that is rather strange. I believe Nicholas knows me better than I do myself."

She ignored the cryptic utterance and gave a tug on her wrist. "Will you kindly let go of me?"

"One moment, Kate. Dash it! I don't like craning my neck to look up at you, but if I let go, you'll no doubt rush off."

"Why? Are you planning to say something outrageous?"

He met her challenging look with perfect sincerity. "Yes. And you had better sit on my knees while I do so."

She gave a little jump, and so, unfortunately, did her voice. "*What?*"

"Sit down, Kate."

There was no opposing him. His leg might give him a momentary handicap, but the arm that wound around her hips like a steel band inexorably pulled and lifted her onto his knees.

She sat as stiff as a puppet, her shoulder squeezed against his chest. She dared not relax, for he kept one arm around her waist, holding her firmly in place, and already the dizzying effect of his closeness was making itself felt. His hand warmed her waist and abdomen through the thin cotton of her robe, and it would take very little imagination to make believe that he was touching her skin. It took a great deal of resolution not to turn and fling her arms around his neck and press against that solid chest.

"Now, if only you would look at me," he said in a cajoling tone—almost as though he knew what she'd been thinking.

Close to panic, Kate held on to her dignity and refused to budge. And if it worried her that her weight on his knees was injurious to his leg, she gave no outward sign of her concern. Let him suffer the consequences of his folly.

"Kate, have you given any consideration to your future?"

Now she did look at him, her eyes wide and questioning.

"About what you'll do once Liza is settled?" Damien said. The breeze stirred her long hair, and a delicate herbal scent drifted into his nose.

"I shall find another teaching post. Damien, pray let me get up. Suppose someone saw us!"

"No one but you dares enter my study without waiting to be asked." Absently, he stroked his thumb over the material of her robe. "There must be something more pleasant, more enjoyable than teaching that you could do."

She moved restlessly. If he had not already been fully aware of Kate and her state of undress, her shifting would have banished all doubt that bare skin was—unsuccessfully—hidden beneath the robe.

"The window," Kate murmured, more than half convinced that this moment was fated. She had acknowledged her love for Damien. What could be more natural than to receive his kiss once more? "Damien, someone might pass in the garden and look up."

Deftly, he switched arms, so that now his left arm was keeping her imprisoned, his hand pressing against her back instead of her abdomen. With his free hand, he unhooked the cords that kept the heavy velvet drapes tied back. Instantly, the room was plunged into an intimate twilight.

She saw his features, but the sharpness was gone. More than ever was she aware of his presence, of his strength and, above all, of his powerful magnetism.

"I am a fool," she said, knowing that he would kiss her and she would not tell him nay.

"No, Kate." His voice was a warm caress. "Never foolish. You're honest and courageous. You do not deny what we feel for each other."

We . . . for each other?

Almost, she could allow herself to believe in a miracle.

"Magic is at work between us," Damien said huskily. "Even when your willfulness exasperates me, even when I am most aggravated by your demands, I am still drawn to you. No woman has ever affected me the way you do. Kate, I do not want to lose you."

A miracle.

He put both arms around her, pulling her closer. Hardly daring to breathe, Kate offered no resistance.

"I'll buy you a house in London, Kate. Or you may live in Paris or Rome. Wherever you wish. Only say you'll be mine."

Kate was aware of a hollow feeling inside her. Her mind accepted what her heart as yet refused to believe. He would not offer her Paris and Rome if he planned to make her his wife.

Placing her palms against his chest, she pushed away. "Damien, let us please not mince words. Are you—are you propositioning me to be your mistress?"

"Kate, I am inviting you to share—"

"Are you?"

"Yes."

Quick and sharp as the sting of a wasp, the flat of her hand connected with his cheek. He was so surprised, he did not try to stop her when she flung off his arms and left his knees.

"How dare you!" Angrily, she brushed her hands over the rumpled skirt of her robe. She had known that an indecent proposal was all she could possibly expect, yet actually receiving it was a painful blow. "If you were not tied to that chair, I swear I'd box your ears until they ring!"

"And what would you call that slap you gave me?" he asked, rubbing his cheek. "Kate, what the devil is the matter with you? One moment you're as cuddly as a kitten, the next you turn into a tigress."

Kate gave him a cold look. She stepped over to the window, flung back the drapes, and tied them with a vicious twist of the cords. "I tell you what is the matter. I am furious! Furious with myself for having wanted you to kiss me, and furious with you for insulting me."

"I meant no insult," he said quietly. "Kate, you are no green miss. You know of the desires that flare between a man and a woman. I believed you felt the same as I."

If she knew of desire, it was *he* who had taught her.

"What if I do?" Her eyes were veiled by long lashes, but her mouth curled in a mocking smile. "I may be a girl no longer, I may be reduced to earn a living, but unfortunately, I am still a lady."

Turning on her bare heel, Kate left the room the way she had entered it — with her head held high and seething with indignation and other emotions that she could not or would not identify.

Kate whisked up to her room and slammed the door, grateful that she had encountered no one who might have stopped her to inquire if Mr. Ashcroft was now willing to listen to the doctor's orders. Damien might sit in his study and pickle himself in brandy for all she cared.

She tore open her wardrobe, dragged out her cloakbags, and started to pull her gowns off the hangers. When she had collected an armful of dresses, she tossed them onto the bed, continuing the procedure until every garment was removed.

"There!" she said with satisfaction. "You may address your precious proposition to some other companion, Mr. Ashcroft. May she be a wrinkled, toothless, squint-eyed old hag!"

Furiously, Kate brushed at the tears she hadn't noticed running down her face until they dropped onto the blue silk dinner gown she still held in her arms. The gown she had worn when Damien had kissed her the first time.

"The devil take you, Damien Ashcroft!" She flung the frock atop the untidy pile on the coverlet. "And me, too, if I don't stop sniveling!"

Exhausted, Kate sat down on the daybed beneath the window and blew her nose. Naturally, she'd take none of the gowns Damien had supplied. Tearing them from the wardrobe had been a gesture only, one that had provided immeasurable relief for her lacerated feelings.

Eyeing the few garments she had brought with her, she gave an involuntary shudder. How she hated gray! But, perhaps, if she had dressed according to her station, Damien would not have noticed her. He would never have kissed her. Never made her an indecent proposal.

Somehow, the thought failed to comfort. And

317

in all fairness to Damien, she had to admit that the sequence of events had been inevitable. Damien was not a man to judge a woman by her plumage. He was attracted to her—perhaps even liked and admired her. He would have kissed her had she been gowned in sackcloth.

Only if she had told him nay, would he . . .

Kate rose. Picking out her oldest gray cotton, she dressed and pinned up her hair, but her mind was not on the task. Frowning, she pondered what might have happened if she had not allowed Damien to kiss her. The more she thought about it, the less likely it seemed to her that he would have meekly submitted.

All sorts of tantalizing possibilities flitted through her mind, but a knock on her sitting room door interrupted her musings.

"Come in, please!"

Kate glanced at her reflection in the mirror to assure herself that no trace of tears would betray the turmoil in her heart. Giving her cheeks a quick pinch, she stepped through the connecting door just as Phoebe Charteris entered the sitting room from the hallway. Her plump figure set off to advantage in a walking dress of striped poplin, Phoebe rushed toward Kate.

"My dear Miss Elliott! I was visiting one of Godfrey's parishioners nearby and only stopped to see if you and Liza had recovered from the ball and Lady Undersham's visit, but Mrs. Boughey waylaid me and—" She broke off to draw breath and raise a trembling hand to her forehead. "Dear Lord, how Liza must have hurt Damien!"

Liza! Kate thought guiltily. *What am I to do?* Aloud, she said, "Please, ma'am, won't you have a seat? Have you heard, then, of Liza's ignominious tumble?"

Disregarding Kate's offer of a chair, Phoebe said, "Miss Elliott, you have no need to be careful with me. Mrs. Boughey told me *all!* You see, I have forever been her confidante in times of stress, and you need not fear that Damien will mind. Sooner or later he would have told me himself."

"Yes, I see." What Kate did, in fact, see very clearly was that in her obsession with Damien and his most improper offer, she had spared no thought for the girl who had brought her to Dearworth in the first place.

"Mrs. Boughey assures me that Liza is unharmed," said Phoebe. "A sprained wrist." She shrugged dismissively. "What does it signify when her fate could have been much worse?"

"Yes, she escaped ravishment." Kate forced her mind to concentrate on Liza's problems—no easy task when every thought in her head wanted to dwell on Damien and his nefarious scheme for her future. "But I believe Dashwood may have frightened her. Liza was unusually quiet during the ride home."

"Surely that does not worry you? It would not have surprised me to hear that she was in tears."

"I, too, expected tears. Earlier, though, just after she regained consciousness, Liza played the heroine to the hilt. She called Nicholas a *knight* because he knocked Dashwood out and fashioned a sling for her arm."

As Kate had done earlier in the study, Phoebe started to pace. "That is Liza all over. Romantic to a fault. However, I do not think she'll come to any harm by adoring Lord Nicholas for a while."

"No," Kate said dryly. "Nicholas is a gentleman." *He* would never insult a lady with such a slight as Damien had offered her.

Over her shoulder, Phoebe gave Kate an arch look. "Since you're not interested in Lord Nicholas, perhaps he and Liza will make a match of it. He seems quite taken with her."

"Nothing could please Liza's father more." *Or me, for then I need not feel guilty about leaving her. If only I had not promised to stay until Liza is settled.*

Kate moved to the small writing table set in the corner between the bedroom and the hall doors. A letter addressed in Lady Elliott's spidery hand caught her eye. It must have been delivered in the mail that day, for Kate had not seen it before. Praying that her mama was not suffering from one of her bad spells that would make it impossible for her to offer hospitality to her daughter, Kate broke the seal.

Phoebe came to a stop at the window where Kate had spent the previous night listening for Liza. "It is time, however, that Liza learned to use her common sense."

"Yes, indeed," Kate said absently, her attention on the crossed and double crossed lines of her letter, which told her, as far as she could make out, that her brother and his family had unexpectedly descended upon the dowager. From some undisclosed source, Sir Richard had learned that Kate was employed by Damien Ashcroft, and he was making his mama's life miserable with a constant assault of unanswerable questions. Could Kate, *please,* come to Queen's Square to soothe his ruffled feathers? Richard was, after all, the head of the family, etcetera, etcetera.

"Miss Elliott? Are you all right? You have not

heard a word I said."

"I beg your pardon." Kate folded the letter and replaced it on the desk. A pox on Richard! He couldn't have chosen a better time to make trouble for her.

Calling a smile to her lips, Kate turned her attention to Phoebe. "You said, I believe, that Liza must learn to use her common sense."

Phoebe left the window. "I did say that—some time ago. But you look pale, my dear. Sit down. I shall ring for some tea or a glass of wine."

She reached for the bell pull next to the open bedroom door. Before she could give the tasseled cord a tug, her eyes fell on the two cloakbags and the untidy heap of clothing on Kate's bed.

In openmouthed astonishment, she looked at Kate. "You're packing!"

Relieved to have it out in the open, Kate nodded. If she could persuade Mrs. Charteris to take Liza under her wing, perhaps invite the girl to live at the vicarage for a while, she could leave Dearworth with a clear conscience.

"But why?" asked Phoebe, still incredulous.

"A family matter." Kate waved her hand vaguely toward the desk. She did not mean to imply that the letter was in any way responsible for her sudden decision, but Phoebe Charteris interpreted the gesture as such.

She narrowed her eyes. "You only just read the letter. I saw you break the seal. No, no, Miss Elliott! I wasn't born yesterday. This is Damien's doing, confess!"

Kate's face stung. "Yes, but my folly as well."

Phoebe placed her fists on her plump hips. "Well! I never would have believed it possible. If it isn't just like Damien to blame you for Liza's escapade! No doubt he insisted that you had planted the notion of an elopement in her silly head?"

"No." Shaken, Kate sank down on the nearest chair. "If it were only that, I could deal with it. In fact, I expected something like it, and he never said a word. Only reproached me for not warning him of my suspicions."

"Godfrey does not like for me to meddle, but"—Phoebe gave Kate a shrewd look—"if ever a situation cried for some friendly interference, it is this one."

"There's nothing you can do or say to change my mind."

Phoebe drew up a chair and sat down. "My dear Miss Elliott, I totally agree. There's nothing I can do until you tell me exactly what happened."

Her warm brown eyes twinkled at Kate with more understanding than she had ever been offered by her own mother. And Kate, sensible, independent Kate, did exactly as Phoebe Charteris suggested. She laid before the vicar's good-natured wife all that had happened, from the moment she realized Liza had slipped off despite her vigilance until Marston came to request her help with Damien.

The latter brought a satisfied smile to Phoebe's face. "And no doubt Damien was surprised that Boughey had sent his valet to you. What a numbskull Damien is. But then," she said cheerfully, "he is but a man."

Kate regarded her confidante with a fascinated eye. "And *you* are not surprised?"

"Lud, no!" Phoebe's smile deepened. "Servants—I daresay because of their utter dependency

322

on their employers — have learned to read their master's mind before he is aware of his own feelings. Boughey has made it quite clear to me that he regards you as the new mistress of Dearworth."

Chapter Twenty-three

Bereft of words, Kate stared at Phoebe Charteris. "Boughey is correct," she said finally, fighting a hysterical laugh. "At least in part. You see, it's not a mistress for Dearworth that Damien wants but . . . a mistress for himself."

Again, Phoebe's eyes narrowed. "Does he now?" she said slowly. "By George, that isn't too bad for a start."

"Mrs. Charteris." Kate shot to her feet to embark on an agitated turn about the small room. "Surely you are jesting. How could I possibly consider Damien's absurd offer? Why, if I had a mind to be a kept woman, I could have become my brother's pensioner years ago."

Phoebe chuckled. "It's hardly the same, my dear."

"No, but much as I—" Warmth rushed to Kate's face as she realized how close she had come to betraying her feelings. More temperate, she tried again. "I am sure I'm no different from any other woman in that I wish for a man's affection and companionship. However, pride and an obligation to family and society will not permit me—"

"Stuff and nonsense!" Phoebe interrupted. "You're in love with Damien, and you're hurt and angry that he has offered you a slip on the shoulder."

"Indeed," Kate said stiffly. "Are you suggesting I should feel honored and, perhaps, accept his offer of a house in Paris or Rome?"

"Paris or Rome? You may want to remind him of that later on. Paris is nothing to be sneezed at. I'd be one of your regular visitors."

Kate could only shake her head. Resuming her seat, she said, "Now I know you're jesting. Your husband would never permit you to visit me. Oh, I think I shall miss you dreadfully, ma'am!"

Phoebe laughed. "If you're still laboring under the notion that you will live in Paris as Damien's mistress, then you are perfectly correct. Godfrey would be aghast if I suggested a visit. But only think, my dear! Would Damien have lost his head and made you this most improper offer *while you're living under his roof* if his affections were not engaged?"

Feeling rather breathless, Kate said, "He might have been in his cups."

"Nonsense. Damien is head over heels in love with you."

Phoebe Charteris and the chair she occupied started to wobble and seesaw in front of Kate's eyes. She blinked. For one crazy moment, she had believed that Phoebe assured her Damien was head over heels. He was no such thing, of course. It was Kate who was tails over tops, seeing everything in a blur. Just went to show, didn't it, what wishful thinking could do for one?

"I have suspected it for some time," Phoebe said, preening herself a little. "He has a certain way of looking at you that is quite unmistakable. And how he jumped to your defense when that Abbots woman tried to blacken your character!"

325

Kate's focus was clear again. "No father would like to see his daughter's companion exposed as a female with a questionable reputation," she said dismissively.

"Don't talk fustian, Miss Elliott. Damien went far beyond an employer's duty. Why, he made certain Lady Undersham would invite you. If that isn't inconsistent with making you an improper proposal."

Kate could not deny that it was highly inconsistent, but perversely, she said, "Lady Undersham does not live in Paris."

Mrs. Charteris dealt with that argument in the manner it deserved. She brushed it aside with a wave of her plump hand. "I can see only one reason for his behavior," she said, frowning. "He made up his mind all those years ago, after Elizabeth, never to marry again, and he simply has not realized that he has changed his mind."

The furnishings did not dance this time, but Kate could not deny that wishful thinking had taken a strong hold again.

"Damien told me a few things about Elizabeth that fairly made my blood boil. And yet, if he loved me—" Kate shook her head. "No, Mrs. Charteris. I *cannot* believe he does. But if he did, I am convinced that his experiences with Elizabeth would not deter him from offering me marriage."

"Of course it would not stop him. He's not such a looby as that! But has he recognized yet that he loves you? He's proud and cynical. He must first admit that not all women are like Elizabeth."

Kate thought that he had, but she did not say so. Phoebe would only find other reasons why Damien had not acknowledged his love, and it was already hard enough to squash the bright flame of hope flaring in her breast.

"What few things did he tell you?" asked Phoebe.

"Oh, about Elizabeth's affairs and her refusal to give him another child. And that it was Lord Severeign who shot him in the leg."

"That is all?"

Kate raised a brow. "Is there more?"

"Yes. And I do not doubt that Damien, since he told you as much as he did, will eventually tell you the rest."

"I shan't be here to listen."

Phoebe got to her feet. Briskly, she shook out the folds of her green and white striped gown.

"You will be here," she said calmly as she started for the door leading into the hallway. "You are a woman of sense and courage. I cannot believe that you will pack up and leave because of a few thoughtless words."

At the door, Phoebe turned, giving Kate a frank stare. "If you love Damien, you will not put up with his nonsense. You will show him how wrong he is."

Kate stared at the door closing softly behind the older woman. A tiny frown marred Kate's forehead and a pensive look darkened her eyes to charcoal. Gradually, her features relaxed as she recalled snippets of a conversation with Lady Undersham.

The dowager countess had ventured to say that it could not be easy to be a companion in Damien's household. An understatement! But Kate also recalled that she had assured Lady Undersham she was stubborn and proud and generally achieved her aim.

Well, she would *not* leave, would *not* break her promise. After all, it was Damien who had misbehaved, and she was not afraid of facing him. She had only one apprehension. She feared that Phoebe's assurances had taken a rather firmer hold in her mind than was desirable.

But if Damien wanted her, he'd have to make the effort of courting her. She would settle for nothing less than being his wife.

Leaning her head against the back of her chair, Kate contemplated the scrolled and painted ceiling of her sitting room. But it wasn't the plasterwork she saw that made her jawline tighten with determination.

Liza, who came charging into the room a little later, checked her impetuous step when she caught sight of Kate's face.

"Oh, I am sorry," she stammered. "I came at a bad moment, didn't I? But, Miss Elliott, if I do not speak with you now, I may never find the courage again."

Kate gave a start, but nothing in her voice or manner toward Liza betrayed that she had just been torn from a stormy—if imaginary—confrontation with the girl's father.

"As a matter of fact," she said calmly, "I was hoping you wouldn't be too exhausted to have a talk today. Come and sit down, dear. Does your wrist still pain you?"

"A little." Eschewing the chair Kate patted invitingly, Liza pulled up a low footstool. Carefully arranging her bandaged wrist in her lap, she said, "My head hurts, too, but Dr. Bullen says I do not have a concussion."

Liza kept to herself that the young physician had callously diagnosed her headache as mainly caused by lack of sleep the night before and too much excitement and had, therefore, lowered himself several degrees in her esteem.

"I suppose, Kate said mildly, "we may look upon your discomfort as punishment for your thoughtless behavior."

She felt she was being very forebearing and was surprised to see a look of hurt in Liza's eyes. "Child, you may count yourself lucky if a sprained wrist and a headache is all you will suffer from your escapade. If you will remember, I lost my reputation and was banished from the social scene."

"Oh, I know, Miss Elliott." Liza blinked away the tears welling in her eyes. "I know how reprehensible my behavior has been. And you need not tell me that I am wicked and stupid and quite sunk beneath reproach!"

She sounded so despairing that Kate reached out to touch the girl's cheek. "Not wicked, only thoughtless. If you had not gone to meet Charles Dashwood in such a clandestine manner, he would not have found an opportunity to force you into his carriage."

The tears would no longer be blinked away but spilled over and ran down Liza's cheeks in an endless stream. "I *have* been wicked!" She buried her face in Kate's skirts. "So very, very wicked, and it was only because I realized Charles was not at all romantic or kind that I changed my mind about the elopement."

"You did plan it," Kate said with dismay. "Oh, Liza! It needs only that you tell me my elopement with Nicholas put the notion into your head, and I shall be ready to sink."

Liza shook her head. Muffled by the folds of

Kate's gray cotton gown, the details of her reckless decision and Charles Dashwood's iniquity tumbled from Liza's lips. Kate did not interrupt. Mechanically, she stroked the girl's locks. She was hard put not to scold, but Liza was already blaming herself enough to make any reprimand superfluous.

"I'll never, never trust a man again!" cried Liza, still sobbing.

Kate looked down at the blond head half buried in her skirts. She could not quite suppress a little smile, for she knew better than to believe Liza's anguished words. But neither could she deny a feeling of kinship with the young girl. She, too, had felt betrayed when Damien made his proposal. But that Liza must never know.

"What?" she asked in a cajoling tone. "Won't you even trust your papa?"

Kate did not doubt that Liza would. It was Damien's trust in his daughter that might be destroyed when he learned the truth. He might, with just cause, feel that Liza had deceived him—as had her mother before her.

"Papa says—" Liza sat up and gratefully accepted the handkerchief Kate offered. "Papa says that every young woman is entitled to a mistake. As long as she learns her lesson."

"Is she now?" said Kate, fascinated. If so, Damien had even less of an excuse for asking her to join the muslin company. "And when did you see your papa?"

After a last dab at her tear-stained face, Liza tucked the sodden handkerchief into her sling. "Just now. I did not speak to him for very long just long—enough to explain. Marston kept popping his head into the sitting room. I daresay he

330

wanted to get Papa settled in bed before he changed his mind again."

Kate feared she had not heard right. "Damien was *in his rooms?*"

"Yes." Some of the old liveliness returned to Liza's eyes. "He said he could do no less after the dreadful scold you read him."

"Well!"

"And then Marston peeked in again and said that he had yet to meet a more sensible lady than you and that Papa had the choice of staying abed five days to get well quickly, or be stubborn and foolhardy and make a nuisance of himself for several weeks, with the whole household in an uproar because he would be in a foul temper and unable to do anything."

"And what did your papa say to that?" Kate asked in a hollow voice.

Liza frowned, trying to recall the exact words. "Thank you very much, Marston," she said in an imitation of her father's most cutting tone. "I was already informed by the *sensible* Miss Elliott that I am obstinate and pigheaded. So you need not waste your breath."

She gave Kate a look of awe. "Did you really say that? I would not have dared."

"And so I should hope," Kate said at her most dampening.

She rose and busied herself lighting one of the lamps, for dusk was coming on rapidly. "Well, if your papa has forgiven you, I see no reason for me to make a great ado about your escapade."

"Oh, but, Miss Elliott," said Liza in a small voice. "Papa also said since you raked *him* over the coals, he thought it only fair to bid me present my head for washing as well."

331

If Kate had performed the office recommended by Damien, the result could not have been more obvious, for Liza was on her best, her most ladylike behavior during the following days. Since she had *not* scolded the girl, Kate found that Liza's subdued demeanor and docility added one more worry to the lot she carried.

It was useless to deny that Kate did not look with trepidation to the day when Damien would emerge from his rooms. She still maintained stoutly that she was not afraid to face him, and yet, a certain awkwardness, some measure of embarrassment, must be expected during their next meeting.

And after that first moment, what then? If Phoebe Charteris were wrong . . .

For the present, Kate succeeded quite well in evading these fears by keeping herself occupied with more mundane but nevertheless pressing matters. She penned a soothing letter to her mama and one to her brother Richard that told him in no uncertain terms to return to Elliott Chase and mind his own business. She accompanied Nicholas to the excavation site and, together with the twins, helped restore the mosaic floor of a twenty-foot chamber that had been uncovered.

Any tendency to fret about Damien's leg she suppressed ruthlessly. She asked Marston every morning about the invalid's progress but, unlike Nicholas and Liza, made no visits to the sickroom. After hearing Dr. Bullen's assurance that Damien's leg was healing well and quickly, Kate concentrated her fretting on Liza's unnatural behavior.

When Emily Usborne invited her to ride, Liza would order one of the grooms to follow behind if Hubert and Algy accompanied their sister. When Nicholas asked her to take a turn about the garden with him, she'd say, "With pleasure, sir," and ring for her maid.

At mealtime—when Damien's empty chair at the head of the table already cast a pall on Kate's spirits—Liza was so subdued and polite that Kate was tempted to excuse herself and request a tray in her room. Only Nicholas's bewildered look and his valiant attempts to draw the girl out kept her from following such cowardly impulse.

When the ladies left the dining table, and Nicholas, for the fifth night, joined Damien in his bedroom to drink a glass of port and smoke a cigar, Kate could not forbear questioning Liza.

"My dear, what has come over you?" she asked as she and Liza entered the morning room, where they had formed the habit of reading or stitching needlepoint chair covers until it was time for the tea tray. "Surely you'll do yourself an injury if you persist in being so restrained, so lifeless."

Liza blushed. She bent her head low over her embroidery frame. "I thought it was what you would wish."

Kate gave her a sharp look. "Did you, dear? I wonder what could have given you such a notion."

Liza said nothing.

Kate pulled a lamp closer and started to ply her needle. "Even Nicholas is shocked at the change in you. You must have seen his look of dismay when he asked whether you planned to accompany us to the site tomorrow and you replied, 'If you like, sir.'"

The rather dim light of the oil lamps did not hide the deepening color in Liza's cheeks.

"And when you said 'No, thank you, sir' to an

333

offer of a visit to the lending library in Bath," Kate said musingly, "I truly believed Nicholas would spill his wine."

For a moment or two longer, Liza kept her head bent over the embroidery frame. Then she looked up. "But don't you see, Miss Elliott? Nicholas is only testing me!"

Kate's eyes widened. "Testing you? In what way? I should rather say he's being very kind."

"Oh, he's all that's kind and obliging, but I *know* he was disgusted with me after I made that terrible gaffe about your being lucky you eloped with him instead of the major. Now I must show Nicholas that I can behave like a lady."

"What nonsense, Liza. A man who graciously overlooks that you sneaked out of the house for a clandestine meeting will not poker up at a few ill-chosen words. And you cannot deny that Nicholas never uttered one word of reproach when he helped rescue you."

"No. Nicholas is a true gentleman, is he not?" A soft, dreamy smile curved Liza's mouth, but not for long. With a sigh, she said, "But after I mentioned your elopement with him, he was different. And when you cut Papa's boot and I left the carriage because I was feeling faint, why, Nicholas did not even worry about me."

Kate could have reassured her on that head, for she had seen Nicholas's anxious look following the girl. If it had been any other than Damien requiring his help, Kate felt certain Nicholas would have rushed after Liza. Suspecting that Liza had more to say, Kate said nothing, merely raised an inquiring brow.

She was not disappointed, for Liza said, with a valiant attempt at diffidence, "I wish I had known before I went off with Charles that Nicholas's companionship means so much to me. Nicholas used to spend quite a bit of time with me. Now he is mostly with Papa, playing chess or whist, or accompanying you to that dumb Roman ruin."

"My dear child! Surely you do not grudge your papa the solace of Nicholas's company. How else do you suppose a man of your father's caliber would tolerate his enforced inactivity? I assure you, a pack of cards can be an excellent distraction."

"Yes, I suppose."

Kate snipped off a thread of royal-blue floss. Taking her time selecting one out of several green shades, she said, "I do not think you have reason to lose any sleep over Nicholas's temporary defection. Marston tells me that Dr. Bullen has given permission for your papa to be up and about for a few hours tomorrow. I wager Nicholas would be more than pleased to take your groom's place if you should wish to ride."

"Do you, Miss Elliott?" Liza's eyes shone. "Do you think so, indeed?"

Closing the doors of the French armoire, Marston cast a wary look at his master's back sharply outlined against the bright light streaming through the bedroom window. If he'd had his way, Mr. Ashcroft would have dressed in nothing more formal than his dressing robe worn with pantaloons and a pair of bedroom slippers.

But, no, his nibs must insist on breeches and riding coat. As if Marston hadn't known how it would be! No sooner had he tried to ease the bandaged leg into a boot than Mr. Ashcroft damned his impudence and ordered him to bring pantaloons and a pair of Hessians. It was still not what Marston considered the dress of an invalid, but at least he could be fairly certain that his reckless master would not order a horse saddled — not if it meant riding in pantaloons and soft calf-length boots.

Marston cleared his throat. "Will there be anything else, sir?"

Damien swung away from the window and the view it offered of the stable yard, where Kate, Nicholas, and Liza had mounted their horses and were disappearing in the direction of the excavation site.

"Damn you, Marston," he said, but a rueful smile robbed the words of their sting. "I wager you applied an extra amount of bandage just to keep me in the house."

Marston saw the smile, but since Damien's words contained a grain of truth, he couldn't help being just a trifle nettled. "And next you'll be accusing me of having shrunk your boots!"

Damien grinned and said no more. Knowing the watchful eye of his valet would follow him, he strode briskly from the room.

As soon as the door had closed behind him, Damien allowed himself to favor his left leg. The pain was minimal compared to the agony he had suffered the first few days, but even soft Hessians managed to rub annoyingly against the tender flesh. What the hell! As long as no one saw him, he'd limp as much as he pleased.

In his study, he tried to concentrate on the notes he had made on his excavation, but to his annoyance, the scene he had witnessed in the stable yard kept superimposing itself on the scrawled notations.

He had seen Nicholas and Liza trot off in the direction of the excavation site. There was nothing disturbing about that. Nicholas had earlier that morning assured him that he would put Walter and Peter to work scraping the contours of two stumps of pillars Damien had unearthed the previous week. When they finished, Nicholas would send the twins up to the house to try their hands at piecing together shards of pottery that rested cleaned and labeled on the shelves in one of the stillrooms.

"Kate, no doubt, will wish to return to the house with the boys," Nicholas had said, giving Damien a wide grin. "After all, she knows you'll be up and around, and she'll want to make certain you don't overdo."

Damien ignored the provocation. "And you, my friend? What are *your* plans?"

"If it's all the same to you," Nicholas replied loftily, "I shall try to bring Liza out of the doldrums. Poor child, she's been moping around the house long enough. It's time she enjoyed herself again."

Damien raised a brow. "Any particular notion how you'll bring it about?"

"Just a short ride today. I know an inn on the road to Wells that serves the best cider and a fine luncheon." Nicholas took a turn about Damien's room, came to a halt, and bent a steely gaze upon his friend. "But starting tomorrow, I shall take Liza to Bath."

He cocked his head, as though waiting for objections. When none were forthcoming, he said, "We'll take a walk in the Sydney Gardens, visit the library, take tea in the Assembly Rooms—you know the kind of stuff I'm talking about. It's just what she needs to get her mind off the ugly experience with Dashwood."

Damien leaned back against the pillows. "Are you," he drawled, "asking my permission to court my daughter?"

A twinkle lit Nicholas's blue eyes. "Isn't that why you were so dashed persistent when you asked me to come here? At the beginning of the season, too!"

"What about Kate?"

"Devil a bit!" Nicholas raked his fingers through his carefully brushed hair. "Do you take me for a commoner? If you think I would pay my addresses to Liza while still hankering after Kate . . . well, then all I can say is that you're a dashed loose-screw."

"But you never gave me reason to believe that you and Kate had decided against marriage," Damien reminded him.

Nicholas colored, but there was no apology in his words or in his tone of voice. "The reason for that, my friend, is of your own making. If you will persist in dangling after Kate—dash it, Damien! It's more than flesh and blood can stand."

Damien had not told Nicholas that his protective measure had availed him nothing. He had merely nodded and started to talk about the remains of the Roman villa that were slowly unearthed in his woods.

When Nicholas left the room, a satisfied grin had spread over Damien's face. Liza and Nicholas. Just the way he'd planned it.

And even now, sitting in his study with his bandaged leg resting on a cushioned stool as though he were a gout-ridden octogenarian, he could not help but smile. No, indeed. There was nothing disturbing in seeing Liza and Nicholas ride off together.

Kate had been the disturbing factor in that scene in the stable yard.

Kate, who always drew a response from him. She might provoke him, aggravate him, or she might arouse warm, tender feelings, even passion, but she never left him indifferent.

When he had come into the study, he had purposely chosen a chair far removed from the window where she had perched on his knees. Even so, he knew he had but to close his eyes to feel the softness of her slender body beneath the thin robe, to smell the scent of her long hair.

He had not seen her since she had stormed out of the study, but for five days, her reply when he had demanded to know whether she did not feel the desire flaring between them had disturbed his waking and even his sleeping moments.

"*What if I do?*" Proudly and unafraid, she had flung the words at him. "*I may be a girl no longer, I may be reduced to earn a living, but unfortunately, I am still a lady.*"

A lady. He should not have asked a lady to be his lover.

Elizabeth had been a lady, a married one to boot, yet she had thrived on taking lovers.

But Kate was not Elizabeth.

Damien shook his head and tried once again to concentrate on his notes. Kate, however, was not easily banished from his mind. Again, as though he were standing at his bedroom window, he saw her in the stable yard atop her mare. She had looked across the yard right at his window. He did not think she could have seen him, for the glare of the sun had been full upon the glass, but she had raised her crop, greeting him as though she knew he would be watching, before following Nicholas and Liza.

And now he was waiting for the moment of her return. He did not know what he would say to her, but speak with Kate he must.

Chapter Twenty-four

Returning from the excavation site, Kate dismounted at the edge of the woods. She waited for the two boisterous youngsters, charging like overgrown puppies around her and Lady, to calm down, then offered them a ride. Instantly, a noisy squabble broke out as to who would sit in the *lady's* saddle and who would manfully ride pillion, but Kate put an effective stop to the bickering when she grasped Lady's bridle and walked off.

"Miss Elliott, wait up!" Walter came to a breathless halt beside her. "I'll let Peter ride pillion if he'll let me hold the reins."

Peter was agreeable, and soon the twins trotted across the grassy slope leading to the stable yard.

Kate followed slowly. Ever since she had learned that Nicholas and Liza would not be returning to the house with her, a quite uncharacteristic lassitude had seized her. The closer to the yard and house she got, the more languid became her steps. One might almost think she was reluctant to enter the house.

What nonsense! Forcing herself to a briskness she did not feel, Kate marched through the rose garden and caught up with Walter and Peter, who had dutifully taken Lady to the stables and were chasing each other to the side door that opened into the kitchens from the herb garden.

Again, Kate's steps slowed as she followed the

boys through the tiled passage and into the stillroom. In little over an hour, luncheon would be served and she must face Damien alone, without Nicholas and Liza to lend, albeit unwittingly, their support. It was one thing to decide on a bold plan of action while Phoebe Charteris's heartening words still rang in her ears, but quite another when doubts had time to undermine her confidence.

Of course, she might take luncheon in her room — except that Kate Elliott had never been one to shy at her fences.

Stripping off her gloves, Kate took several shards of pottery off one of the stillroom shelves and placed them on the scrubbed table. "You are to do no more than sort the pieces that may fit together. Watch for the color and thickness of the ceramic, the molded patterns, and—"

She glanced searchingly about. "Lord Nicholas said — ah, yes. Here they are." Kate removed three sheets of paper from a shelf and showed them to the boys. "Mr. Ashcroft made drawings of several styles of vases and bowls that might have been in use at the time the villa was occupied. If you find parts of an inscription or of a potter's stamp like this" — she pointed to the drawings — "keep the pieces separate from the others. Also painted shards or those that have relief decorations. They are very rare."

She remained a while longer in the stillroom, watching the boys and patiently answering their questions. She found it a source of never-ending wonder that, the moment they were involved in their work, they were transformed from rambunctious brats into studious, nimble-fingered young antiquarians. There was no risk at all in leaving them with Damien's precious shards.

She turned and started to walk off, then lingered in the doorway. "Mind you wash your hands when Mrs. Boughey calls you to take your dinner in the servants' hall. And close the stillroom door firmly. It sticks a little, and once the cat squeezed in and inspected the ceramics."

Walter nodded absently, but Peter raised his head and said, with an air of grave reproach, "Don't ye worry none, Miss Elliott. Walter an' me will take good care of everything. An' iffen we don't wash our hands, Mrs. Boughey's like to do it for us. *An'* wash our faces as well."

Bereft of all further excuses to linger, Kate trod purposefully up the steep basement stairs. At the top, parting the baize curtains from the foyer, the younger of the two footmen gave her a bashful smile.

"Pardon me, Miss Elliott. The master is askin' to have a word with you. In his study."

"Thank you, Ben." Not a trace of reluctance remained under the rush of anticipation that flooded Kate. "Tell Mr. Ashcroft that I will see him as soon as I have changed."

She did not hurry, but neither did she dawdle. After a quick wash, she donned a gown of sprigged muslin tied with blue ribbon. She brushed her hair, pinning it loosely, and fastened a matching blue ribbon among the dark brown tresses, with the bow sitting saucily above her left ear.

Swiftly, she descended to the first floor. It did not perturb her that Damien had summoned her to the very same room where he had made his improper offer, but as she knocked on the panel of the study door, it occurred to her that he could not know this.

If he had any sensibility at all, she thought indignantly, any consideration for her feelings, he would have chosen the library or one of the drawing rooms for this interview.

She entered hard upon his invitation to do so. He was seated behind his desk, a book and several pages scrawled with notations in his forceful hand spread before him. She could not help a quick, anxious search of his face. His bruises had faded and no sign of pain was visible—nor was there a trace of embarrassment.

"Ah, Kate." In a glance, Damien took in her becomingly flushed cheeks, the glint in her eyes, and the determined jut of her chin. "Thank you for being so prompt. Please, sit down."

Her heart pounded. "I am happy to see you looking well," she replied, equally polite but distant.

Seating herself on one of the straight-backed chairs in front of his desk, her stiffness suffered a slight setback. "Shouldn't you keep your leg elevated, Damien?" she burst out. "I feel certain Dr. Bullen would advise it."

"There is a footstool under my desk." To conceal his satisfaction at her concern, he started to stack the sheets of paper in a neat pile.

Unhesitatingly, he dismissed the carefully rehearsed apology and all the other namby-pamby stuff he had planned to say to her. Only the truth would do. And if it shocked her, so be it. He could still count on her staying at Dearworth—at least until Liza and Nicholas were wed. She had promised that much, and Kate would never go back on her word.

Much could happen in the span of several months or a year.

344

"Elizabeth is not dead," he said, looking up.

"Not—"

For a moment, Kate was numb. His words went around and around in her mind, whirling like leaves before the wind. Elusive, evading her grasp.

Then, as she started to realize what Elizabeth alive and well meant to her and any relationship she might expect from Damien, the blood drained from her face. Never before had she come so close to fainting. As from a far distance, she heard Damien speak.

"Elizabeth has remarried. She is now the Baroness Graaznach and lives in Vienna."

Her eyes flew to his face. "Remarried? But that means—"

"That we're divorced," Damien said, tight-lipped.

Kate was filled with an overwhelming sense of relief, but hard on its heels followed anger such as she had never known before.

How dare he! He made her almost swoon with despair, and the next moment made her feel the greatest fool on earth.

She rose, thrusting back her chair so violently that its legs scraped the floorboards with a protesting screech.

"Elizabeth remarried." She did not recognize her own voice. It was thin and sharp, like the blade of the clasp knife that had cut his boot. "You should be telling this to your daughter, not to me."

He came around the desk in rather more of a hurry than was prudent for his leg. "Kate, pray don't run off. Hear me out."

"Have I ever run from you?"

"Elizabeth divorced *me*."

Startled, Kate sank back on the chair. "How is that possible? It was Elizabeth who—"

"Who committed adultery?" he finished for her. "Exactly so."

He perched on the edge of the desk, his eyes as cold and cynical as she had seen them at the start of their acquaintance. "And she wanted a divorce," he said, bitingly. "Elizabeth cared nothing for the fact that it was *my* name that would be dragged through two courts and bandied about in Parliament. I refused her."

Kate could only stare at him, and after a moment Damien said in a calmer voice, "What would you know of divorce, my innocent, puritanical Kate? Do you realize that before I can be granted a decree of absolute divorce, I must be granted divorce *a mensa et thoro*—from bed and board, my dear—in one of the ecclesiastical courts? Then I must bring an action in a court of common law, and if that is successful, I may apply to Parliament."

Still, Kate said nothing. Her mind was in such a whirl that even had she wished to make some appropriate comment, she might not have found a word to say save "oh."

"I was prepared to go as far as a divorce *a mensa et thoro*, but then neither of us would have been free to remarry. That did not suit Elizabeth at all. She had by then met the Baron Graaznach and planned to be a baroness."

"But how did she obtain a divorce?" Slowly, Kate's brain started to function. She had noted his words, "*neither of us* would have been free to remarry," and stored them away. "Did she have reason to sue you for adultery?"

She saw a hint of his devilish smile, gone as fast as it had appeared. "A lady wishful of divorcing her husband would have a hard time proving adul-

346

tery. But there are two other grounds for an absolute divorce: desertion and cruelty."

Cruelty? . . . She knew very well that he would not have deserted Elizabeth or Liza.

Damien slid off the desk to take a turn about the room. It did not do his leg any good, but only vigorous motion could ease the pain of his memories.

"Sovereign was quite glad by then that Elizabeth was showing an interest in someone else," he said harshly. "She was rather expensive, you see, and the sooner she could marry Graaznach, the better for Sovereign. He thought of a wonderful scheme. Under the guise of taking Liza for a pleasure ride, Elizabeth would kidnap the child until I agreed to divorce her."

All other feelings forgotten, Kate cried in horror, "I cannot believe it! No woman could be so cruel."

"Elizabeth could."

Damien came to a halt at the window. His back toward her, he said, in a voice drained of all emotion, "The nurse, fortunately, was suspicious, for Elizabeth had never before taken the child for a drive. With the excuse of having to change the child's clothes, she brought Liza to me and asked for guidance."

He whipped around. "The rest, my dear Kate, is simple. I struck Elizabeth. She fell against one of the carved posts of her bed, bruising her face, neck, and shoulder, and ran off to Sovereign. He immediately advised her to divorce me on the grounds of cruelty. The way she looked at the time . . . well, you can imagine."

"But she tried your patience to the limit," Kate protested. "I do not wonder that you struck her.

347

Did you not explain?"

He shrugged. "Ordinarily, she would not have succeeded with her petition. The law states clearly that the person complaining of cruelty must not be the author of his or her own wrong."

Slowly, he returned to the desk and resumed his perch. "Believe me, Kate," he said with feeling. "By that time, I had no desire to prove her culpability. All I wanted was to be rid of her. The proceedings she had put in motion, even though they branded me a cruel blackguard, were the fastest way."

Kate sat in stunned silence as she tried to picture how Liza would take the awful truth. Divorce was one of those unmentionable words only whispered behind a concealing hand. Perhaps Damien had been right not to tell his daughter. But now she was a young woman and, if Kate read the signs correctly, about to receive a proposal of marriage.

"Liza must be told," she said, more to herself than to Damien. "And Nicholas. If anyone can assure that she won't take it too hard, it is he."

Looking up, she found Damien's dark gaze fixed on her. "I told him some years ago," he said, "when we were invited to Vienna by the Count and Countess von Oberndorf. There was some slight chance that we might run into Elizabeth, for Graaznach and the count are related on the distaff side." His look turned quizzical. "But it was not to start you fretting about Liza that I brought up the divorce."

"No," Kate said much more calmly than she felt. "You believe it will help me understand why you offered me *carte blanche*."

"And it does not?" he asked softly.

348

"No, Damien."

She did not lower her gaze as any demure young lady would have done; instead, she met his intent look unflinchingly. For the better part of five days, she had wrangled with the problem of how to convince Damien that he really would rather have her for a wife than a mistress. Five days, she had kept up her spirits and her determination by repeating Phoebe Charteris's words to herself.

Well, Kate thought, at least Phoebe was correct when she said that Damien would eventually tell her the worst about Elizabeth. As to the rest of Phoebe's assumptions, they were as flawed as a cheap length of muslin.

Damien sighed. "It was too soon, I think, to speak of it again. But as you know, patience is not one of my virtues."

"And you need not learn it on my account," she countered. "No matter how long you wait before you ask me again, I will never be your mistress."

In the foyer below, a gong sounded to announce luncheon. Kate rose. "Shall we go down?"

"Kate!" Sliding off the desk, he placed a hand on her shoulder, the other beneath her chin so that she could not help but look at him again. "Perhaps I have taken too much for granted. I believed you knew how I feel about you, but perhaps you don't. I have never told you, have I?"

It took all of Kate's willpower not to succumb instantly to the familiar weakness evoked by his touch and the hope awakened by his words. But she called on her resolve and merely raised a questioning brow.

He saw her struggle and, despite his elation, knew a moment of guilt. He had planned to make a little speech assuring her of his regard, to briefly touch on their mutual desire, and to promise that she would never have to know financial difficulties again. The words that tumbled from his mouth were unrehearsed and filled with such ardor that he shocked himself.

"I want you, Kate, as I have never wanted another woman. I admire you. You're stubborn, proud, independent, and irrepressible—traits I believed I disliked the most in a lady. *You* have taught me to delight in them and to delight in pitting my wits against you. Kate, I don't want to live without you."

"Damien, stop!" She pulled away from him sharply. This was the kind of courting that could lead only to disaster and shame.

The luncheon gong sounded again, but neither paid it the slightest attention.

"Why?" he asked harshly. "Are you afraid of your own desires? I dare you to tell me that you do not feel the same as I."

He looked baffled, but Kate also saw a hint of the old arrogance in his raised brows and the set of his mouth.

"Oh!" she said, overcome by a rush of anger very like the one that had assaulted her earlier when she had learned that Elizabeth was remarried. "You would dare me, would you? Well, let me tell you, sir, that what I feel for you is quite different from what you feel for me."

He took a step closer. "How?"

"Your feelings for me are lust." Her heart pounded in her throat, but no force on earth could stop her now. "Mine for you are love."

If a cannonball had shattered right beside him, the effect of Kate's words on Damien could not have been more devastating. He loved his daughter,

350

had loved his mother. But love between man and woman had held no meaning for him since he had recognized that his passion for Elizabeth had been nothing but a youthful infatuation that did not survive the third month of their marriage.

He stared at Kate, understanding her words but refusing to believe their meaning. Love was something unreal, something poets tried to capture in words. Love was in the marriage vows: " 'till death do us part."

Kate saw the rebuff on his face, indeed, in the rigid stance of his whole body. She clenched her hands until her nails cut into her palms, but the pain was as nothing to the pain tearing at her heart.

"I am sorry," she said tonelessly. "I can no more help the way I feel than you can change your feelings."

She turned away and started to walk to the door. Without looking back, she added, "If I did as you ask, I would soon despise myself. And then, I fear, my love for you would turn into hate."

Blindly, she fumbled for the doorknob, wrenched the door open, and hurried away. She ran the length of the corridor, then slowed her steps to descend the stairs at a more decorous speed.

Had she been asked, she would have been unable to give a reason for fleeing downstairs rather than to the sanctity of her own room on the floor above. Perhaps it was merely a streak of stubbornness that drove her toward that region of the house where the presence of a footman ringing the gong and a butler coming to answer the imperative summons of the door knocker must force her to behave as though nothing untoward had happened. Perhaps it was a premonition that yet more disaster must be met head-on.

Kate reached the foot of the staircase just in time to have a perfect view of the front door as Boughey swung it open, and of the portly, florid-faced gentleman standing outside with his hand half raised to give another sharp rap with the knocker.

"Sir?" Boughey said politely.

The gentleman unceremoniously pushed past the old retainer. "About time someone answered the door," he said irritably as he stopped near the polished oak table, which, on this day, supported a tall crystal vase filled with red and white peonies.

Tugging off his driving gloves, he ordered, "Fetch Miss Elliott. Tell her—"

"Richard!" cried Kate. "What the devil do *you* want?"

Chapter Twenty-five

The capes of his driving coat flared, then settled back against his thickset frame as Sir Richard Elliott spun to face the stairway. His eyes, blue-gray like Kate's but smaller and placed rather close together, narrowed to angry slits.

"Your manners are deplorable as ever," he said coldly. "How dare you use that tone and language with me."

"Today, brother, I dare anything."

Kate crossed the foyer swiftly. "No, Boughey! There's no need to take Sir Richard's hat and gloves. He will not stay above a moment."

Sir Richard slapped the articles on the table. A shower of peony petals rained onto the glossy surface and into the salver holding visiting cards, burying them beneath their red and white fragrance.

"You're right, Kate," he bit out. "I shan't stay—only long enough for you to pack and get your bags into the phaeton."

Kate gave an angry little laugh. "You don't change, do you, Richard? When you last honored me with a visit—at Miss Venable's seven years ago, wasn't it?—you stalked in and ordered me to pack. I snapped my fingers at you then. What the deuce makes you think I'd obey you today, when I am well and truly within my right to order my own life?"

"A great deal of good your obstinacy has done you so far!" Richard exclaimed bitterly. "You're still unwed, and what's worse—"

He caught sight of the butler and footman hovering just beyond the great oaken stairway. His choler rose. That Kate would brangle in front of gaping servants did not surprise him. She had always flaunted the conventions. But that *he* had allowed himself to be carried away. Damn the girl! It was all her fault.

Curtly, he ordered the men to leave. Edward looked as though for two pins he would have hared off, but Boughey assumed his most haughty expression. He knew where his duty lay.

Ignoring the irate baronet, he addressed himself with fatherly and, at the same time, respectful solicitude to Kate. "Do you wish the gentleman to leave, Miss Elliott? I shall be more than happy to escort him to the door."

Sir Richard spluttered indignantly, while Kate looked at the butler in some astonishment. Boughey was no lightweight, but he was old and rather feeble. How he intended to *escort* Richard, who must weigh at least sixteen stone, was beyond her powers of imagination.

"Thank you, Boughey. How kind of you," she said gravely. "But there's no need to fret, you know. I am quite capable of dealing with my brother."

Richard squared his jaw, which gave him the look of an incensed, rather vicious hound. "You!" He pointed a blunt finger at Edward. "Go and fetch Mr. Ashcroft. Immediately!"

"That won't be necessary," Damien said from the stairs. "I am quite at your disposal, sir."

At the sound of the deep voice, Kate spun around. How long he had stood there, she did not know, but she wished with all her heart that he would return to the study. She could not possibly face him now—especially with Richard looking on.

Her wish was not granted, for Damien descended the last few steps in a leisurely manner and walked toward Richard.

She tried to intercept him. "Damien, this is none of your concern. I regret if Richard and I disturbed you. Unfortunately, it seems, we can never converse without shouting."

Save for giving her a rather distracted nod, Damien paid her no heed. He stepped around her and shook hands with the grim-faced Richard, saying, "You're Kate's brother if I understood correctly. Won't you step into the library? I can offer you a glass of very tolerable Madeira."

To Boughey, he said sharply, "Take Sir Richard's coat and see that his cattle is stabled."

Preserving a wooden countenance, Boughey received the caped driving coat from Sir Richard and, with nothing more than a nod to the front door, sent Edward scurrying to carry the master's orders to the stables.

Since Richard, still with that look of grim determination on his face, was already following Damien into the library, Kate could only trail after them. Nothing would induce her to leave the two gentlemen alone. Each had, in his own opinion, a perfectly logical reason to want to settle her fate. Each was wrong. What she did or did not do with her life was *her* business alone.

She shut the library door. "Richard, I warned you not to meddle in my affairs. How dare you come here and kick up a dust!"

"I am the head of the family! It is my duty to preserve the honor of our good name!"

Damien had poured two glasses of wine. He

turned, his dark eyes raking brother and sister as they stood facing each other like two mettlesome fighting cocks. "Kate? Would you care for a glass of Madeira?"

She was about to decline when she saw Richard's shocked expression. "Thank you, Damien. I should love to take a glass of wine."

Damien's mouth twitched as he poured out a third glass, but Richard's face turned a mottled red. "Kate!" he roared. "Is there no end to your depravity? Taking wine with gentlemen! Calling your employer by his given name, and he not even what he claims he is. He's not a widower. Mama finally remembered all about it. Dash it, Kate! He's—"

"—divorced. I know that, Richard."

Having thus had the wind taken out of his sails, Sir Richard accepted the glass Damien handed him. He could read nothing in Damien's face. The amusement had gone, but save for a rather harsh look in his dark eyes, he showed no emotion and seemed quite content to withdraw to the fireplace, where he propped a shoulder against the mantel and sipped his wine.

Richard fortified himself from his own glass, then turned his attention to his sister, who had flung herself into a chair—rather too close to the fireplace and to Damien Ashcroft for his liking.

"Now listen to me, Kate," he said ponderously. "If you knew that Mr. Ashcroft is neither a widower nor a respectably married man, you should not have stayed here."

"Stuff and nonsense!"

Whatever Damien lacked in emotion was more than compensated by Kate's stormy countenance. Richard knew well the portent of blue sparks in his sister's eyes, but even more so he knew himself to be in the right, and he was not one to shirk his duty.

"You should have gone to Queen's Square or come to Margaret and me," he continued doggedly. "I could never like it when you insisted to teach at that school, but it was preferable to hiring out as a governess or a companion. And you an Elliott of Elliott Chase!"

Kate sat stiffly on the very edge of her chair. "Finish your wine, Richard," she said, holding onto her temper with great difficulty. "You don't want to keep Margaret waiting. You know how impatient she becomes if you don't return when she expects you."

This, unfortunately, recalled to Richard's mind the purpose of his visit. "Pack your bags. I'm ready to leave whenever you are."

Kate glanced at Damien's expressionless face. She could not tell what he was thinking, but his presence alone sufficed to strengthen her resolve not to give in to Richard's demands.

"I am not going anywhere with you."

"Dammit, Kate! Margaret is right. You are a shameless, brazen hussy!"

Richard tossed off his wine and, ignoring Damien's suddenly threatening stance, approached Kate—to drag her off the chair if necessary. "Your reputation, my girl, is such that you cannot afford another scandal. You'll come with me, or I'll know why!"

"Elliott, you go too far!" Damien set his glass down upon the mantel shelf with such violence that it cracked and the dregs of his wine dripped down the white marble.

He pushed away from the mantel, but Kate jumped to her feet and met her brother with such fury blazing from her eyes that he held back, not quite certain which of the siblings he might be called upon to protect. Most likely, it would be Sir Richard who'd need saving.

"My reputation!" Kate said scathingly. "You're a fine one to talk, Richard. It was *you* who set the rumors going. *You* who cannot hold your wine and starts to blab when in your cups."

Damien strolled closer for a better view of her magnificent rage.

His Kate.

His intrepid, adorable Kate.

Richard's ruddy countenance had turned a pasty color. He knew that Kate was right, but he would never own his mistake. "Upon my word! Next you'll be saying that I counseled you to elope with Nicholas Adair."

"Would you do so?" asked Kate in ominously dulcet tones. "He stays here, you know. At Dearworth. And he is quite as charming as ever."

"A flush hit," murmured Damien under his breath. "A leveler if ever I heard one."

"Why, you little—" In vain, Richard searched for a word to describe his sister.

"Don't fret, brother dear. I am no longer contemplating running off with Nicholas. You see, Damien has done me the honor of asking me to be his *mistress*. That, you will agree, is much more in my style!"

Turning a brilliant smile on Damien, she said, in a voice that might have been pronouncing Richard's death sentence, "I shall be pleased to accept your offer. Whenever you wish, I'll go with you to Paris or to Rome—or even to Egypt!"

Hiding his astonishment with considerable aplomb, Damien stepped past Sir Richard, who looked as though he were about to explode or to expire.

"My beautiful, outrageous Kate," he murmured, raising her hand to his lips. "So you want to be off to Paris? How can I respond to that? Only, 'First kiss me, Kate, and then we will.' "

His mouth brushed over hers, and before she could collect her wits, he spun her around and marched her to the door. Without ceremony, he pushed her out into the hallway and closed the door in her face.

Kate heard the key grate in the lock, then silence. She considered hammering on the door and demanding admittance, but somewhere between her angry tirade at Richard and her promise to Damien, her rage had spent itself.

Her promise to Damien!

Kate's stomach performed an agonizing flip, and the paneled walls of the hallway tilted and spun as though they were about to crash on her.

Lud! Whatever had come over her to say that she'd become his mistress?

With legs that threatened to give with each step, she dragged herself through the foyer and out the front door. Once outside, she felt a little better but inclined to hide herself away from prying eyes. The clop-clop of horses' hooves in the lane beyond the gate reminded her that Nicholas and Liza might be returning. She hurried to the side of the house, where she would neither be seen from the front door or the stables, nor from the back of the house where the library opened onto the terrace.

She sank down on a bench half hidden by a large rhododendron and buried her face in her hands.

Her wretched tongue! Her wicked temper! This time, she had really and truly landed herself in the basket.

Dropping her hands into her lap, she stared blindly at a bed of budding lilies. For an instant, she contemplated explaining to Damien that she had not meant what she said, had, in fact, not *known* what she was saying in her rage. But her pride would not allow such cowardly retreat. She was committed to a life of sin. Never would she know true happiness.

Her eyes misted. She blinked, but one lone tear refused to be banished. It clung to her lashes, then fell and coursed down her cheek, her neck, until it disappeared with hardly a trace in the muslin of her gown. Surely one puny tear for a way of life forever barred to her could not be called self-pity.

Lost in thought, Kate paid no attention to her surroundings, but the approach of the twins was not to be ignored. Their penetrating voices and much scuffling and kicking on the graveled path must alert the most inattentive. Kate slid to the corner of the bench that was screened by the rhododendron. Perhaps they'd pass without seeing her.

They almost did. Then Peter stubbed his toe. Grimacing wildly, he danced around on one foot — and caught sight of Kate.

Toe forgotten, he came running. "Miss Elliott, they be lookin' for you inside!"

"They?" she asked cautiously.

"Well, Miss Liza is," he amended. "An' Lord Nicholas is with her."

She did not know whether to be relieved or annoyed that it was not Damien and Richard who were looking for her. "I shall go in directly," she said. "And where are you off to? Home already?"

"*Already?*" mimicked Walter, who had joined his brother. "It be past four o'clock, Miss Elliott. Ma would have our hides iffen we didn't get home before dark."

"That late!" Kate rose in a hurry. She had been in the garden close to two hours. Surely Richard must have left by now.

She sped the boys on their way and hurried to the house. This time she did not avoid the terrace outside the morning room and library. Passing through the lilac arbor, she ran up the wide, shallow steps to the terrace and entered the house through the library.

No one was in the room. Even the glasses had been removed and all trace of the spilled wine on the marble fireplace had been wiped off. It was as though Richard had never been here. But if he had not, then she would not have lost her temper and committed the most foolish act of her life.

Slowly, she went through to the foyer where Boughey was supervising Ben in the cleaning of the oil lamps. Through the open door of the morning room, she heard Liza's voice and Nicholas's deep chuckle, but not a sound that indicated Damien was with them.

"Boughey, has Mr. Ashcroft retired?"

"No, Miss Elliott," the butler said gloomily. "Although, if you ask me, that's what he should have done on his first day out of bed."

"Where is he?"

"Drove off to Bath with your brother, miss."

"*What?*"

Poking his head around the morning room door, Nicholas said, "I gather from that cry of outrage that you've heard of Damien's folly. Come and join us, Kate. Liza and I are following the wonderful English custom of maudling our insides with tea."

Kate accepted a cup of tea, but despite a missed luncheon she could not bring herself to partake of the cakes and biscuits cook had sent up. Liza, she

361

noted, was her cheerful old self again and had reverted to her free and natural manner toward Nicholas.

Barely had Kate reassured herself on that point when her thoughts began to drift to the girl's father. Only five days ago, Dr. Bullen had removed several pieces of shot. Granted, Damien had received permission to get out of bed, but for a few hours only and certainly not to go careening about the countryside. It would serve him right if his leg started to swell again and he found himself laid up for weeks.

Why had he driven to Bath with Richard? He must know that she would worry about her future. He must know that she needed to talk to him.

"Kate, is it concern about Damien's leg that has you looking as queer as Dick's hatband?" asked Nicholas. "You're about to spill your tea, you know."

With a start, Kate set down her cup. Damien's leg was the least of her concerns at the moment, but she could hardly tell Nicholas and Liza that she was ill with trepidation about her commitment to a life of sin.

"I apologize. I fear I'm not good company today."

"We know," said Liza. "Your brother called and caused a stir about Papa not being a widower."

"You *know?*"

"Papa had a talk with me before he left with your brother, and Nicholas—" Liza reached for his hand. Hers was warmly received in his large one, and she said, with a shy little smile at him, "Nicholas has been answering more of my questions."

"Are you—does it worry you?" asked Kate, grateful to be able to give her thoughts a different turn.

Liza shook her head decisively. "No. Whether my mother is dead or married to that baron in Austria, it makes no difference to me. I have no memories of her, and from what Papa and Nicholas—mostly Nicholas—told me, I'd really rather not remember anything."

She rose. "Please, Miss Elliott, will you help me choose a gown for dinner? I'd like it to be something special to cheer Papa. *He* is the one who is a bit upset."

"Not upset. Distracted," said Nicholas.

Kate was more concerned about the time of his return than his feelings at his departure. "You are expecting him back in time for dinner, then?"

"Well," said Liza. "He did say not to wait for him, but even if he does not come back until later, I still want to look my best for him."

The two ladies withdrew to discuss the rival merits of primrose silk, pink muslin, and white batiste in Liza's chamber, but Kate was so obviously distracted that Liza said, after a moment, "I fear I'm giving you a headache with my prattling. You are very pale, Miss Elliott. Why don't you lie down and rest?"

Kate's head was indeed throbbing, and Liza's thoughtfulness drove foolish moisture to her eyes. But she did not wish to be alone. She did not want to think about Damien, about her future.

"I shall rest in a little while, Liza. Let us look at your white silk gown. The ribbon knots match your eyes exactly, and I believe it is one of your papa's favorites."

Liza gave Kate a searching glance. She was about to demur, but caught a fleeting look of anguish in Kate's eyes and changed her mind. She turned to the wardrobe and pulled out the white silk gown.

The hall clock struck six when Kate excused herself. As she was about to enter her own chamber, Edward came up the stairs with more haste than dignity.

"Miss Elliott!" he said, panting a little from his efforts. "Mrs. Boughey's askin' the privilege of a word with you."

Another reprieve. "Is anything amiss?"

"Well"—the footman stepped aside to let her precede him down the stairs—"as to that, we can't be sure yet. But it looks as if those pesky boys got in some kind of mischief betwixt here and Monkton Combe."

Reserving further questions for Mrs. Boughey, Kate hurried to the housekeeper's sitting room. There she found not only Mrs. Boughey and her husband, but also Mrs. Grimes, who had set out from her house shortly before five o'clock to meet her sons on their way back from Dearworth.

"It being such a lovely evening an' all," said Rose Grimes, dabbing at her eyes with a much-used handkerchief, "I thought I'd surprise Walter and Peter. They used to like it when I had the time to go walking with them, but I saw neither hair nor hide of 'em!"

Kate laid a comforting hand on the woman's shoulder. "I don't think there's cause for alarm, Mrs. Grimes. They may have stopped at the excavation site."

Rose Grimes shook her head. "I met Mr. Ramsden. He'd just checked on Mr. Ashcroft's ruin. There was no one there. An' here's Mrs. Boughey, telling me they left just after dinner. Oh, I can't help but worry that Peter sprained his ankle again, or worse, that he broke it!"

Dinner was served in the servants' hall at three

o'clock. Kate had seen the twins in the garden shortly after four, and they had assured her that they were going home. After considering the possibilities, Kate said, "I think you should return to your home in case the boys arrived during your absence. Henry can drive you in the gig."

She looked at the butler. "We'll send out men with lanterns. It'll be dusk in a little while, and if some mishap occurred, the sooner we start a search the better."

Boughey nodded and left to get a search party together.

"Take my word for it, Rose," said Mrs. Boughey, pouring out a small measure of cordial for her distressed friend. "They went off birdnestin' after they left here, and when you get home, they'll be waitin' and wonderin' what has become of you."

"Well, I don't say they wouldn't have. In fact, 'twas the first thing that came to me head, but then I remembered that they told me most of the birds have hatched already."

"Whatever they did," Kate said reassuringly, "we'll find them."

A short while later, Ben, Edward, two of the stable lads, and Nicholas, who had no sooner learned of the boys' possible disappearance than he offered his assistance, set off for the woods. Mrs. Grimes, seated beside Henry in the gig and fortified as much by Kate's assurances as by Mrs. Boughey's cordial, drove off in style.

If truth be told, Kate expected Henry to return with the tidings that the twins had been at home all the time while their mother was out walking, but when he came to make his report, his face was so grave that she had no need to ask him what he had found at the Grimes house.

"Think I'll take me a lantern and join t' others."

Henry shook his head. "Y'never know what these young 'uns be up to."

Deeply worried now, Kate only gave him an abstracted nod. Where on earth could the twins be? If some accident had befallen the boys anywhere near Dearworth, surely Nicholas and the men would have found them by now.

And then Kate remembered Professor Crabb's ruin. The old Norman chapel on Lord Severeign's former property.

Chapter Twenty-six

Kate did not stop to change into her riding habit. Gripping Lady's bridle in one hand and a lantern in the other, for darkness had fallen while Henry had taken Rose Grimes home, she perched on her mare's bare back, galloping toward the woods.

She planned to do no more than find the search party and direct them to Professor Crabb's ruin, but when she reached the spot where Liza had wanted to jump the wall to the viscount's property—how long ago it seemed, that ride when Damien's refusal had first aroused her suspicions that all was not well between him and Viscount Severeign—Kate heard not a sound that indicated Nicholas and his men were anywhere nearby.

Pulling Lady to a stop, she wondered whether the silence meant that the boys had been found or whether the searchers had moved farther afield. Still undecided, she opened the shutters of her lantern and studied the wall. Lady should be able to jump the five feet or so. But the wall *was* crumbling, no doubt about it. The top was jagged where several of the soft sandstone bricks had fallen.

No, she wouldn't risk Lady's legs jumping her in the dark, but over the wall she'd go.

Kate slid off the mare's back—and the devil of a time she'd have getting back up in her narrow skirts and without a mounting block. She draped the bridle over some shrubbery on the Dearworth side of the path, tightened her grip on the lantern, and approached the wall. Surely, if Walter-Peter could climb it, then so could she.

Setting the lantern atop the wall, she groped for what she prayed were secure handholds and footholds. Scaling would be quite easy, if only she weren't wearing skirts. Just as she brought one knee up on the top of the wall, a ripping sound confirmed that she had lost at least a part of a flounce. Moments later, another rip split the side of her skirt, giving her more freedom of movement but also arousing a strong desire to box the twins' ears.

She sat for a moment atop the wall, rubbing her sore hands and what she feared would turn into a nasty bruise on her right shin. She did not know exactly where the Norman chapel was located, but it could not be far away. She remembered that Damien had described Lord Severeign's property as a wedge-shaped piece of land dividing the game preserve and the Bluebell Woods, and the area she was facing was the narrow part of the wedge.

Somewhere, an owl hooted. It was a lonely, eerie sound and made her shiver. Kate wondered if Damien had returned from Bath. If so, he might be on his way to join the search party. He might see Lady.

Drawing comfort from that thought, Kate jumped down. Armed with her lantern, she started forward, periodically calling the boys' names.

She had walked for what she judged to be about two hundred yards when she heard sounds startlingly different from the tiny rustling night noises that dogged her steps. She stopped. Holding her breath, she listened. And there it was again. A chinking, clinking sound — like stone hitting against metal.

"Walter! Peter!"

The only answer, if answer it were, was the pounding stone.

Kate started to run, imagining the twins trapped beneath the crumbling walls of the old chapel. The lantern bobbed in her hand and the circle of light was never where she needed it. More than once she stumbled over an exposed tree root or some small shrub, but she hurried on until dark shapes — definitely not trees — loomed before her. The Norman chapel.

Again she called the boys' names, and this time she was rewarded by muffled cries that seemed to come from underground.

Holding the lantern above her head, she tried to get a better view of the ruin. She had expected some overgrown scraps of wall, perhaps the remains of a pillar or two, but amazingly, at least two complete Norman arches had survived, and the remains of the walls were fairly high. It would not surprise her if, in daylight, the cruciform plan of the chapel were clearly discernible.

"Walter! Peter! Where are you?"

"Miss Elliott!" She recognized Peter's voice. "We're in the cellar."

"We're locked in!" shouted Walter.

Following the sound of their voices, Kate arrived at a wooden trapdoor set in the ground near the wall facing her. Definitely not a door of Norman construction. It was made of sturdy new boards, reinforced by iron.

Usually, a trapdoor was supplied with a metal noose or some kind of handhold to pull it open.

This one had only a very small iron ring, just large enough to insert a finger — or a rope, thought Kate, for try as she might, she could not lift the trap with one finger.

Sitting back on her heels, she said, "I cannot raise the door. Why did you shut it when you went down?"

"*We* didn't!" shouted Walter. " 'Twas that bedlamite professor!"

Kate caught her breath. The man *was* crazy.

"We didn't destroy nothin', Miss Elliott." Peter sounded close to tears. "We was only lookin', but he said he'd teach us a lesson for spyin' and destroyin' his ruin."

"Men!" said Kate, exasperated. "Can they do nothing but create havoc? Well, I shall have to go and fetch help."

"Are ye leavin' us, Miss Elliott?" This time, it was Walter who sounded panicked.

Kate could picture them in that dark, probably damp cellar, huddled together and shivering with cold and fright. "I must, Walter. I have nothing that I could use to pry the trap open."

"Don't go! Please, Miss Elliott, don't leave us!" the boys cried in chorus, and Peter added, "There's rats down here."

Kate sighed. "All right. I'll stay." After all, they were only eleven years old.

She settled herself on the ground next to the trapdoor and rather gingerly leaned her back against the chapel wall. If it had not crumbled under the stress of half a dozen centuries, surely it would take her weight until the search party stumbled upon Lady and came looking for her.

Perhaps Damien would come for her.

While she talked with the boys to keep their

minds off rats and other horrors of a damp cellar, one part of her mind stayed occupied with thoughts of Damien. He had turned on her brother when Richard had abused her. With the least bit of encouragement, he would have knocked Richard down.

So chivalrous one minute, and the next he kissed her to seal the bargain she struck with him in a moment of ungoverned rage. A bargain she was determined to keep. It was important that Damien knew she was a woman of principle.

And yet . . .

While assuring Walter-Peter that they had been very clever indeed to pound a large stone against the metal of the trapdoor—they had taken turns standing upon each other's shoulders—Kate prayed that Damien would refuse her. She knew herself well enough to know that she had spoken the truth when she assured him that her love would change to hate were she to become his mistress.

First she would hate herself; then she would hate Damien.

The knowledge filled her with such pain that she doubled over, burying her face on her knees.

"Miss Elliott!" Peter's voice was high with fear. "Where are you?"

She sat up. Her face felt icy-cold and damp, but she was too weak and shaken to even raise a hand and wipe her brow. She must stop thinking about Damien and herself.

Her heart was thumping madly, and it took her a moment to distinguish a different kind of thudding above her heartbeat. But there was no mistake. A rider was approaching fast.

"Miss Elliott!"

"I'm here, Peter." Her voice shook a little,

whether from relief that rescue was near or from the effects of her sudden weakness, she did not know. "And help is on the way."

She rose. Her knees would barely hold her, but she picked up the lamp and swung it in an arch above her head. "Damien! Over here!"

It must be Damien. Nicholas and the men had left on foot. It had to be Damien coming to the rescue.

The hoofbeat was louder. The shadow of a horse and rider leaped through the darkness and came to a halt not ten paces from her.

A black horse. Satan? But the man who dismounted was slighter than Damien.

With quick strides he reached her side, and she found herself staring at the pale, dissipated face of Viscount Severeign.

His thin lips stretched into a sneer. "And what do we have here? Well, well. If it isn't the young lady from Dearworth."

Kate sensed danger in the softly spoken words but did not give in to cowardly instinct that bade her run.

"Sir," she said imperiously. "By some mischance, Professor Crabb closed the trapdoor while two young boys from Monkton Combe were still below. Pray take your horse's bridle and help me open the trap."

His laugh was as low and sinister as his voice. "I know the little devils are caught inside. I took great care to make our dear professor suspicious of them, and it was I who suggested to him but yesterday that they would greatly benefit from a night spent in the chapel cellar."

A shiver ran down her spine. "But why?"

"I knew the alarm would be raised at

372

Dearworth." His eyes narrowed. "I thought I knew Ashcroft well enough to count on his going out himself to search for the boys. Why did he send *you*?"

Kate did not answer. Indeed, she did not know what to say. If she understood him correctly, he had meant to *lure* Damien out here.

His gaze raked her up and down, missing neither her pallor nor the tear in her skirt. "You don't look it right now," he drawled. "But there's talk you'll be the new mistress of Dearworth. What a comedown after Elizabeth."

The cad! How dare he talk to her of Elizabeth. She raised her chin. "If it is Damien you wish to see, you will have to go into Bath. Help me release the boys, and you may be on your way."

Again he laughed. "Think on it, my dear! The professor complained many a time about the boys, but I did not suggest their incarceration until I heard that Ashcroft would leave his sickbed today. He might go out to search for the boys, but even *he* would not be fool enough to drive into Bath with his leg."

The twins, who had not uttered a sound from the moment they heard the viscount's voice, now started to clamor and shout. Kate could not make out a word until Peter ceased his shouting and only Walter's strong voice rang out.

"Run, Miss Elliott! He's a bad 'un! Don't let him catch ye!"

The viscount's hand shot out and grabbed her wrist. "You won't listen to them, will you?" he asked softly. "Your presence here will serve my purpose better than a dozen scruffy boys could. Coward though he may be, Ashcroft would not leave his bride-to-be at the mercy of his wife's

373

lover."

"You are mad!"

She fought against him, but to no avail. The hand on her wrist was like a band of iron. With the other, he dealt her a blow to the head that made her ears ring.

Kate dropped the lantern. The light flickered, then went out.

Sovereign jerked her against his chest. "That was foolish, my dear. Let us hope I carry a tinderbox in my saddlebags."

He stooped to pick up the lantern, then dragged her willy-nilly to his horse. There he stood, at a loss, for he needed his hands to light the lamp.

"I'll not leave the boys, if that's what you fear," Kate said contemptuously. "But I don't want you to touch me."

He seemed to consider her words. His grip slackened, and she twisted her arm free. She heard flint strike against steel. A light flickered, then burned in a bright flame as Sovereign held the tinder against the wick of the lantern.

She heard another rider and, above the horse's hooves, Damien's voice calling her name, but before she could respond, Sovereign's arm clamped around her waist and the nuzzle of a pistol pressed against her ribs.

"I did not misjudge," Sovereign said triumphantly. "Now call him."

"Damien, turn back! He means to shoot you."

She might have saved her breath. The hoofbeat came closer. Damien atop Satan burst through the trees at a reckless clip.

Relief, joy, and fear warred in Kate's breast as he pulled his mount to a halt beside her. "Release her, Sovereign," he said harshly. "She has nothing to do with the score you and I must settle."

Severeign laughed. It was a sound that made Kate's hair curl. "Happy to oblige, Ashcroft. *After* you've dismounted."

"Damien," she said urgently. "He—"

"Hush, Kate." He searched her face, quickly, anxiously, then dismounted and gave her the reins to hold. "This was inevitable. Severeign and I should have met years ago."

Severeign stepped away from Kate. "That's right," he said almost pleasantly. "And if I hadn't lost my head and peppered you with shot after you knocked me down, the challenge would have been mine."

Damien paid no heed to him. "Kate, can you handle Satan?"

Her heart raced. "What are you planning to do?"

Again, Severeign laughed. "You were a coward then, Ashcroft, and you still are. You'd rather choke on the insults offered you at your ball than issue a challenge. That's why I resorted to a little trickery."

Save for a tightening of his mouth, Damien gave no sign of having heard the viscount's taunts. "Kate, I want you to leave."

She dropped the bridle. "No!"

A plaintive cry came from the chapel. "Miss Elliott? Are ye still here?"

Her eyes did not leave Damien as she responded. "Yes, Peter! And you'll be out of that cellar in no time at all."

Sick with fear for Damien's safety, his very life, she turned from him and walked back to the trapdoor. He could not make her leave him now.

"Mr. Ashcroft is here," she called to the boys.

"Everything will be all right."

If only she could believe in her own words.

The viscount handed her the lantern. "Most improper to have a female second," he said with a sneer. "But I daresay you'll want to know if you will be a widow before you ever were a bride."

A bride? No. But perhaps she would have no chance to be a mistress, either.

As though spellbound in the horror of a nightmare, she saw Damien examine a brace of dueling pistols the viscount held out to him. Choosing one, he looked at her as though he wished to tell her something, then turned back to back with Sovereign.

She heard Damien count aloud as the two men paced away from each other, saw the viscount spin and fire at the count of ten — just a fraction before Damien leveled his pistol and pulled the trigger.

She screamed — or thought she did — but the sound of her scream existed only in her mind, swelling to unbearable pitch until her head threatened to explode with pain.

Someone took the lantern from her hand and enfolded her in a warm embrace.

"You may open your eyes now, my love," Damien murmured into her ear.

Until that moment, she had not realized that her eyes were squeezed shut. And then it did not matter, for Damien claimed her mouth in a ruthless, possessive kiss that erased pain, doubts, and all thought of the danger he'd been in.

She knew only that she loved him and could not live without him. If the only way to assure a place at his side was to be his mistress, then so be it.

When Damien would have let her go, she made some small protesting sound and tightened her hold on him, for somehow, sometime during the kiss, her arms had wound around his waist.

He laughed softly. "My love, do but consider our audience."

At that, she looked about her and saw that Nicholas had arrived with the stable lads. Walter and Peter danced around like a double version of Pan, and Dr. Bullen was kneeling beside the prone figure of Viscount Severeign.

The physician looked at Damien. "A good thing that Lord Nicholas sent for me. Not that those two little rascals need me, but you shattered Lord Severeign's knee," he said reproachfully.

Damien nodded. "I know. I aimed for the knee. Do for him what you can, will you, Bullen? It's time I took Kate home."

Nicholas, with a boy hanging onto each of his coat sleeves, said with a grin, "I'll see Walter-Peter home. Give Liza my love—if you get back before I do."

The next thing Kate knew was that she sat before Damien on Satan's back and that they were riding off—alone. Warm and strong and reassuring, his body pressed against hers as he urged Satan into a canter. They jumped the wall at a point where it was no more than two or three feet high, but instead of turning to his left, toward Dearworth, Damien guided the horse in the opposite direction. He turned into the path leading to the excavation site. To the beech tree where she had kissed him with abandon.

Where she would become his mistress.

Panic welled, then subsided. It would be easy to discard the shackles of propriety and convention. It would be pure pleasure to submit to Damien's demands.

377

He helped her dismount and settled her beneath the tree with all the concern and tenderness of a lover. She had no trouble reading his face, for here in the clearing the moonlight was as bright as any lamp in Dearworth's lofty rooms. She saw love and, difficult as it was to believe of Damien, embarrassment.

Kate had not realized how tense she was until, at the sight of his discomfiture, her body relaxed muscle by muscle, limb by limb. It was reassuring to know that Damien was not the hardened rake who felt nothing but triumph at her surrender.

Lounging beside her, he took her hand in his. "We must have a talk, my love."

"Can it not wait? Damien, I must confess I am not at all certain I shall be able to go through with it if we wait," she said, studying the buttons on his coat with great interest. "I keep telling myself that I shall like it very much to submit to you, but I think you had best prove it to me quickly."

"Submit?" He sounded puzzled. "My poor Kate, you'd find that impossible."

She looked up and encountered such a gleam of devilment in his eyes that it took her breath away.

"Kate, the last thing on earth I want is—" His voice shook. He took a deep breath.

"Don't you dare laugh at me, Damien Ashcroft!" She tried to free her hand but instead found her other hand captured as well.

His look challenged and caressed. "The last thing on earth I want," he repeated, "is a meek, submissive wife."

The moonlit clearing spun around her. "Damien, if this is a proposal of marriage—"

"Miss Elliott!" he interrupted with mock severity.

"If you did not understand why I quoted a line from Shakespeare's most delightful comedy, you had best say yes and be quick about it, for no one in his right mind will offer you another teaching post."

"Well, it's what Petruchio said to Kate, but—"

"It's what Petruchio said to his *wife!*"

"Oh."

He drew her closer until she nestled within the shelter of his arm. "Kate, I love you. Will you marry me?"

"Yes." With unladylike ardor, she flung her arms around his neck, then drew back a little. "But are you sure? After all, you first asked me to be your—"

He sealed her mouth with a kiss, and by the time he allowed her to take a breath, she had forgotten what she meant to say.

Not so Damien. With his most devilish smile, he said, "How could I allow you to make such a sacrifice? I was well aware that you only wished to serve Richard his comeuppance."

She tried, not very successfully, to scowl at him. "Are you telling me that your offer of marriage was made out of chivalry?"

His smile faded. "I swear I love you, Kate! If I had not been such a block-headed fool, I would have realized it even before you shamed me by confessing your love for me. I came downstairs to tell you, but Richard was very much in the way."

"He always is," she said with feeling. "But why the dickens did you go to Bath with him?"

His arm tightened around her waist. "I am an impatient man," he said huskily. "And you, my delightful Kate, have no notion how to properly rebuff an ardent lover. I went to procure a special license."

"But the bishop resides in Wells."

"The bishop is visiting Bath."

With a sigh, she leaned against him. "I wish that once, just once, you would let me have the last word."

LOVE'S BRIGHTEST STARS SHINE
WITH ZEBRA BOOKS!

CATALINA'S CARESS (2202, $3.95)
by Sylvie F. Sommerfield
Catalina Carrington was determined to buy her riverboat back from the handsome gambler who'd beaten her brother at cards. But when dashing Marc Copeland named his price—three days as his mistress—Catalina swore she'd never meet his terms . . . even as she imagined the rapture a night in his arms would bring!

BELOVED EMBRACE (2135, $3.95)
by Cassie Edwards
Leana Rutherford was terrified when the ship carrying her family from New York to Texas was attacked by savage pirates. But when she gazed upon the bold sea-bandit Brandon Seton, Leana longed to share the ecstasy she was sure sure his passionate caress would ignite!

ELUSIVE SWAN (2061, $3.95)
by Sylvie F. Sommerfield
Just one glance from the handsome stranger in the dockside tavern in boisterous St. Augustine made Arianne tremble with excitement. But the innocent young woman was already running from one man . . . and no matter how fiercely the flames of desire burned within her, Arianne dared not submit to another!

SAVAGE PARADISE (1985, $3.95)
by Cassie Edwards
Marianna Fowler detested the desolate wilderness of the unsettled Montana Territory. But once the hot-blooded Chippewa brave Lone Hawk saved her life, the spirited young beauty wished never to leave, longing to experience the fire of the handsome warrior's passionate embrace!

MOONLIT MAGIC (1941, $3.95)
by Sylvie F. Sommerfield
When she found the slick railroad negotiator Trace Cord trespassing on her property and bathing in her river, innocent Jenny Graham could barely contain her rage. But when she saw how the setting sun gilded Trace's magnificent physique, Jenny's seething fury was transformed into burning desire!

Available wherever paperbacks are sold, or order direct from the Publisher. Send cover price plus 50¢ per copy for mailing and handling to Zebra Books, Dept. 2691, 475 Park Avenue South, New York, N.Y. 10016. Residents of New York, New Jersey and Pennsylvania must include sales tax. DO NOT SEND CASH.

ROMANTIC GEMS
BY F. ROSANNE BITTNER

HEART'S SURRENDER (2253, $3.95)

Beautiful Andrea Sanders was frightened to be living so close to the Cherokee—and terrified by turbulent passions the handsome Indian warrior, Adam, aroused within her!

PRAIRIE EMBRACE (2035, $3.95)

Katie Russell kept reminding herself that her savage Indian captor was beneath her contempt—but deep inside she longed to yield to his passionate caress!

SAVAGE DESTINY
A REMARKABLE SAGA OF BREATHLESS, BOLD LOVE IN A WILD AND SAVAGE LAND!

SAVAGE DESTINY #1:
SWEET PRAIRIE PASSION (2635, $3.95)

A spirited White woman and a handsome Cheyenne brave—a forbidden love blossoms into a courageous vision. Together they set out to forge a destiny of their own on the brutal, untamed frontier!

SAVAGE DESTINY #2:
RIDE THE FREE WIND (2636, $3.95)

Abigail Trent and Lone Eagle had chosen passionate love over loyalty to their own people. Now they could never return to their separate lives—even if it meant warfare and death!

SAVAGE DESTINY #3:
RIVER OF LOVE (1373, $3.50)

Though encroaching civilization is setting White man against Red, Abigail's and Lone Eagle's passion remains undiminished. Together they fight the onrush of fate to build their own empire of love in the wilderness!

SAVAGE DESTINY #6:
MEET THE NEW DAWN (1811, $3.95)

Frontier progress threatens all Abigail and Lone Eagle have struggled for. Forced to part to hold together what they cherish most, they wonder if their loving lips will ever meet again!

Available wherever paperbacks are sold, or order direct from the Publisher. Send cover price plus 50¢ per copy for mailing and handling to Zebra Books, Dept. 2691, 475 Park Avenue South, New York, N.Y. 10016. Residents of New York, New Jersey and Pennsylvania must include sales tax. DO NOT SEND CASH.